www.penguin.co.uk

www.kateatkinson.co.uk

Kate Atkinson

Doubleday

LONDON · TORONTO · SYDNEY · AUCKLAND · JOHANNESBURG

TRANSWORLD PUBLISHERS
61–63 Uxbridge Road, London W5 5SA
www.penguin.co.uk

Transworld is part of the Penguin Random House group of companies
whose addresses can be found at global.penguinrandomhouse.com

Penguin
Random House
UK

First published in Great Britain in 2018 by Doubleday
an imprint of Transworld Publishers

A CIP catalogue record for this book
is available from the British Library.

ISBNs 9780857525888 (hb)
9780857525895 (tpb)

Typeset in 11.75/15.25pt Goudy by Jouve (UK), Milton Keynes
Printed and bound in Great Britain by Clays Ltd, Elcograf S.p.A.

Penguin Random House is committed to a sustainable
future for our business, our readers and our planet. This book
is made from Forest Stewardship Council® certified paper.

MIX
Paper from
responsible sources
FSC® C018179

1 3 5 7 9 10 8 6 4 2

For Marianne Velmans

'In wartime, truth is so precious that she should always be attended by a bodyguard of lies.'

Winston Churchill

This Temple of the Arts and Muses is dedicated to Almighty God by the first Governors of Broadcasting in the year 1931, Sir John Reith being Director General. It is their prayer that good seed sown may bring forth a good harvest, that all things hostile to peace or purity may be banished from this house, and that the people, inclining their ear to whatsoever things are beautiful and honest and of good report, may tread the path of wisdom and uprightness.

Translation of Latin inscription in the foyer of British Broadcasting House

Z   Stands for 'Zero', the hour still abed
      When a new England rises and the old one is dead.

From the Right Club's 'War Alphabet'

1981

The Children's Hour

'MISS ARMSTRONG? MISS Armstrong, can you hear me?'

She could, although she didn't seem able to respond. She was badly damaged. Broken. She had been hit by a car. It might have been her own fault, she had been distracted – she had lived for so long abroad that she had probably looked the wrong way when she was crossing Wigmore Street in the midsummer twilight. *Between the darkness and the daylight.*

'Miss Armstrong?'

A policeman? Or a paramedic. Someone official, someone who must have looked in her bag and found something with her name on it. She had been at a concert – Shostakovich. The string quartets, all fifteen parsed out in servings of three a day at the Wigmore Hall. It was Wednesday – the Seventh, Eighth and Ninth. She supposed she would miss the rest of them now.

'Miss Armstrong?'

In the June of 1942 she had been in the Royal Albert Hall for the concert premiere of the Seventh Symphony, the 'Leningrad'. A man she knew had finessed a ticket for her. The hall had been packed to the rafters and the atmosphere had been electrifying, magnificent – it had felt as though they were at one with the occupants of the siege. And with Shostakovich, too. A collective swelling of the heart. So long ago. So meaningless now.

3

The Russians had been their enemies and then they were their allies, and then they were enemies again. The Germans the same – the great enemy, the worst of all of them, and now they were our friends, one of the mainstays of Europe. It was all such a waste of breath. War and peace. Peace and war. It would go on for ever without end.

'Miss Armstrong, I'm just going to put this neck collar on you.'

She found herself thinking about her son. Matteo. He was twenty-six years old, the result of a brief liaison with an Italian musician – she had lived in Italy for many years. Juliet's love for Matteo had been one of the overwhelming wonders of her life. She was worried for him – he was living in Milan with a girl who made him unhappy and she was fretting over this when the car hit her.

Lying on the pavement of Wigmore Street with concerned bystanders all around, she knew there was no way out from this. She was just sixty years old, although it had probably been a long enough life. Yet suddenly it all seemed like an illusion, a dream that had happened to someone else. What an odd thing existence was.

There was to be a royal wedding. Even now, as she lay on this London pavement with these kind strangers around her, a sacrificial virgin was being prepared somewhere up the road, to satisfy the need for pomp and circumstance. Union Jacks draped everywhere. There was no mistaking that she was home. At last.

'This England,' she murmured.

1950

Mr Toby! Mr Toby!

JULIET CAME UP from the Underground and made her way along Great Portland Street. Checking her watch, she saw that she was surprisingly late for work. She had overslept, a result of a late evening in the Belle Meunière in Charlotte Street with a man who had proved less and less interesting as the night had worn on. Inertia – or ennui, perhaps – had kept her at the table, although the house specialities of *Viande de boeuf Diane* and *Crêpes Suzette* had helped.

Her somewhat lacklustre dinner companion was an architect who said he was 'rebuilding post-war London'. 'All on your own?' she had asked, rather unkindly. She allowed him a – brief – kiss as he handed her into a taxi at the end of the night. From politeness rather than desire. He had paid for the dinner, after all, and she had been unnecessarily mean to him although he hadn't seemed to notice. The whole evening had left her feeling rather sour. I am a disappointment to myself, she thought as Broadcasting House hove into view.

Juliet was a producer in Schools, and as she approached Portland Place she found her spirits drooping at the prospect of the tedious day ahead – a departmental meeting with Prendergast, followed by a recording of *Past Lives*, a series she was looking after for Joan Timpson, who was having an operation. ('Just a small one, dear.')

Schools had recently had to move from the basement of Film House in Wardour Street and Juliet missed the dilapidated

7

raffishness of Soho. The BBC didn't have room for them in Broadcasting House so they had been parked across the road in No. 1 and gazed, not without envy, at their mother-ship, the great, many-decked ocean liner of Broadcasting House, scrubbed clean now of its wartime camouflage and thrusting its prow into a new decade and an unknown future.

Unlike the non-stop to-and-fro across the road, the Schools building was quiet when Juliet entered. The carafe of red wine that she had shared with the architect had left her with a very dull head and it was a relief not to have to partake of the usual exchange of morning greetings. The girl on reception looked rather pointedly at the clock when she saw Juliet coming through the door. The girl was having an affair with a producer in the World Service and seemed to think it gave her licence to be brazen. The girls on Schools reception came and went with astonishing rapidity. Juliet liked to imagine they were being eaten by something monstrous – a Minotaur, perhaps, in the mazy bowels of the building – although actually they were simply transferring to more glamorous departments across the road in Broadcasting House.

'The Circle line was running late,' Juliet said, although she hardly felt she needed to give the girl an explanation, true or otherwise.

'Again?'

'Yes, it's a very poor service on that route.'

'Apparently so.' (The cheek of the girl!) 'Mr Prendergast's meeting is on the first floor,' the girl said. 'I expect it's already begun.'

'I expect it has.'

'A day in the working life,' Prendergast said earnestly to the rump assembled around the table. Several people, Juliet noticed, had absented themselves. Prendergast's meetings required a certain kind of stamina.

'Ah, Miss Armstrong, here you are,' Prendergast said when he caught sight of her. 'I was beginning to think that you were lost.'

'But now I am found,' Juliet said.

'I'm garnering new ideas for programmes. A visit to the blacksmith in his smithy, for example. The kind of subject that children are interested in.'

Juliet couldn't ever recall being interested in a smithy as a child. Or indeed now.

'Out and about with a shepherd,' Prendergast persevered. 'At lambing time, perhaps. All children like lambs.'

'Don't we get enough of farming in *For Rural Schools*?' Charles Lofthouse asked. Charles had 'trod the boards' until his leg was blown off in the Café de Paris bomb in '41 and he could tread no more. Now he had an artificial leg that you could never mistake for a real one. It made people kind to him, although there was no real reason why they should be as he was the waspish sort and it was doubtful that losing a leg had improved him. He was the producer in charge of the *Explorers' Club* series. Juliet could think of no one less suitable.

'But lambs are attractive to everyone, not just country children,' Prendergast protested. He was a General Programmes Manager and as such they were all his flock, one way or another, Juliet supposed. He peered vaguely at the top of Daisy Gibbs's neatly shorn head as he spoke. He had a problem with his sight – he had been gassed during the First World War – and rarely managed to look anyone in the eye. A staunch Methodist, he was a lay preacher and had a pastoral 'calling', something he had confided to Juliet over a distressingly weak pot of tea in the cafeteria six months ago when she returned to London from *Children's Hour* in Manchester and started in Schools. 'You, I expect, understand the concept of vocation, Miss Armstrong.'

'Yes, Mr Prendergast,' Juliet had said, because it seemed a much simpler answer than 'no'. She had learnt from experience.

She tried to think what dog it was that he reminded her of. A Boxer, perhaps. Or an English Bulldog. Rumpled and rather mournful. How old was Prendergast, Juliet wondered? He had been with the BBC since time began, having joined the Corporation in its pioneering infancy under Reith, when it was located at Savoy Hill. Schools was sacrosanct to Prendergast – children, lambs and so on.

'Of course the problem with Reith,' he said, 'was that he didn't really want people to *enjoy* the radio. He was terribly puritanical. People should enjoy themselves, don't you think? We should all live joyfully.'

Prendergast seemed lost in thought – about joy, or more likely the lack of it, Juliet supposed – but then after a few seconds he seemed to pull himself together with a little shake. A Bulldog, not a Boxer, she decided. Did he live alone, she wondered? Prendergast's marital status was unclear and no one seemed interested enough to question him on the subject.

'Joy is an admirable goal,' Juliet said. 'Completely unobtainable, of course.'

'Oh dear. Such cynicism in one so young.'

Juliet was fond of him, but she was perhaps the only one. Older men of a certain type were drawn to her. They seemed to want to improve her in some way. Juliet was almost thirty and didn't feel she needed much more improvement. The war had seen to that.

'At sea with the trawlermen,' someone – Lester Pelling – suggested. He reminded Juliet of one of Lewis Carroll's unfortunate young oysters, *all eager for the treat*. He was a Junior Programme Engineer, only seventeen, his voice barely broken. Why was he in this meeting?

'Quite.' Prendergast nodded benignly.

'My father was—' Lester Pelling began but was cut off by another genial 'Quite' from Prendergast, who raised his hand in a gesture more papal than Wesleyan. Juliet wondered if they would ever know what Lester Pelling's father was. A trawlerman, a war hero, a lunatic? Rich man, poor man, beggar man, thief?

'Everyday stories of country folk, that kind of thing,' Prendergast said. Did he know that Beasley in the BBC's Midland Region was working on a concept for a series that styled itself like that? Some kind of agricultural information programme disguised as fiction, a 'farming Dick Barton' she had heard it described as. (Who on earth would want to listen to that?) Juliet felt a mild curiosity. Was Prendergast stealing other people's ideas?

'Working in a cotton mill,' Daisy Gibbs offered. She glanced at Juliet and smiled. She was the new Junior Programme Assistant, fresh from Cambridge and more capable than was strictly necessary. There was something cryptical about her that Juliet had yet to fathom. Like Juliet, Daisy had no teaching qualifications. ('Not a drawback,' Prendergast had said, 'not at all. Possibly quite the opposite.')

'Oh, no, Miss Gibbs,' Prendergast said. 'The North would be possessive of industry, would it not, Miss Armstrong?' Juliet was regarded as their expert in all things northern, having come to them from Manchester.

When the war was over and her country, in the form of the Security Service, said that it no longer needed her, Juliet had moved to the other great national monolith and started a career in broadcasting, although even now, five years later, she failed to think of it as a career, it was simply something that she happened to be doing.

The BBC studios in Manchester were above a bank in Piccadilly. Juliet had been employed as an Announcer. It had a capital letter. ('A woman!' everyone said, as if they'd never heard a woman speak before.) She still had nightmares about Continuity – the fear of silence or of speaking over the pips, or of simply running out of words. It was not a job for the faint-hearted. She was acting as Duty Officer one night when an SOS notice from the police came in – from time to time someone would be dangerously ill and they would need to find a relative urgently. On this occasion they were looking for someone's son 'believed to be in the Windermere area' when a cat suddenly appeared in the continuity suite (formerly a broom cupboard). The cat, a ginger one – they were the worst type of cat, in Juliet's opinion – had jumped up on the desk and bitten her – quite sharply, so that she couldn't help but give a little yelp of pain. It then proceeded to roll around on the desk before rubbing its face on the microphone and purring so loudly that anyone listening must have thought there was a panther loose in the studio, one that was very pleased with itself for having killed a woman.

Eventually someone grabbed the darn thing by the scruff and yanked it away. Juliet sneezed her way through the rest of the announcement and then cued up Schubert's 'Trout' wrongly.

'Perseverance' was the watchword of the Corporation. Juliet had introduced the Hallé once – Barbirolli conducting Tchaikovsky's 'Pathétique' – and had succumbed to a terrific nosebleed just as she began with 'This is the Northern Home Service.' She had drawn courage from the memory of listening to the *Nine o'Clock News* in 1940 and hearing a bomb exploding on air. (Oh, for heaven's sake, she had thought, not the BBC.) The newsreader, Bruce Belfrage, had paused – there was the usual terrible racket a bomb makes – and then a faint voice could be just made out, saying, 'It's all right,' and Belfrage had continued as if nothing had happened. As did Juliet, even though her desk was splattered with blood (her own – generally more alarming than someone else's). Someone had stuck a bunch of cold keys down her back, a cure that had never been known to work.

It hadn't been all right at the BBC, of course, for seven members of staff were dead on the floors above, but Belfrage couldn't have known that, and even if he had he would still have carried on.

At the time Juliet had been so attuned to listening to Godfrey Toby's indistinct conversations in Dolphin Square that she wondered if she alone had heard that faint voice of reassurance. Perhaps it was why she was drawn to work for the BBC after the war. *It's all right.*

It was almost lunchtime when Prendergast's meeting stuttered to an inconclusive halt.

'Lunch in our cafeteria, perhaps, Miss Armstrong?' he asked before she could make good her escape. They had their own cafeteria at No. 1, a poor shade of the one in the basement of their flagship across the road, and Juliet tried to avoid its smoky, rather foetid atmosphere.

'I've got sandwiches, I'm afraid, Mr Prendergast,' she said, with a regretful air. A little bit of acting went a long way with Prendergast. 'Why don't you ask Fräulein Rosenfeld?' Fräulein Rosenfeld, an Austrian although everyone insisted on referring to her as German ('Same thing,' Charles Lofthouse said), was their German-language advisor. In her sixties, 'the Fräulein', as she was often referred to, was stout and very badly dressed and forlornly earnest about even the most trivial things. She had come over in '37 to attend a conference on ethics and had made the wise choice not to go back. And then, of course, after the war there was no one to go back to. She had shown Juliet a photograph: five pretty girls enjoying a picnic long ago. White dresses, big white ribbons in their long dark hair. 'My sisters,' Fräulein Rosenfeld said. 'I'm in the middle – there.' She pointed shyly to the least pretty of the five. 'I was the eldest.'

Juliet liked Fräulein Rosenfeld, she was so intensely European and everyone else around Juliet was so intensely English. Before the war, Fräulein Rosenfeld had been a different person – a lecturer in philosophy at the University of Vienna – and Juliet supposed that any one of those things – the war, philosophy, Vienna – was capable of making you both forlorn and earnest, and perhaps badly dressed too. It would be a challenge for Prendergast to introduce joy into their lunch.

*

Actually it happened to be true, Juliet did have sandwiches – salad cream and an egg boiled hastily while she yawned her way round the kitchen this morning. It was still only early March but there had been a bright pinch of spring in the air and she had thought it would make a change to eat al fresco.

In Cavendish Square Gardens an unoccupied bench was easy to find, as clearly no one else was foolish enough to consider it warm enough to eat their packed lunch outside. There was a blush of crocuses on the grass and daffodils were bravely spearing their way out of the earth, but there was no warmth in the anaemic sun and Juliet soon began to grow numb with cold.

The sandwich was no comfort, it was a pale, limp thing, a long way from the *déjeuner sur l'herbe* of her imagination that morning; nonetheless she ate it dutifully. Recently she had bought a new book, by Elizabeth David – *A Book of Mediterranean Food*. A hopeful purchase. The only olive oil she could find was sold in her local chemist in a small bottle. 'For softening earwax?' he asked when she handed over her money. There was a better life somewhere, Juliet supposed, if only she could be bothered to find it.

When she had finished her sandwich, she stood to shake the crumbs off her coat, causing alarm to an attentive retinue of sparrows which rose as one and fluttered away on dusty London wings, ready to return to their scraps as soon as she was gone.

Juliet set off for Charlotte Street again, not to last night's restaurant but to Moretti's, a café near the Scala theatre that she frequented occasionally.

It was just as she was passing the top of Berners Street that she saw him.

'Mr Toby! Mr Toby!' Juliet picked up her pace and reached him as he was about to round the corner into Cleveland Street. She plucked at his coat sleeve. It seemed a bold move. She had once startled him by doing the same when she had handed him back a glove he had dropped. She remembered thinking, isn't this how a woman signals her intention to a man, by letting fall the coy handkerchief, the flirtatious glove? 'Why, thank you, Miss Armstrong,' he had said at the time. 'I would have been perplexed as to its whereabouts.' Flirting had been on neither of their minds.

She had succeeded now in halting him in his progress. He turned round, seemingly unsurprised, so she was sure that he must have heard her shouting his name. He looked steadily at her, waiting for more.

'Mr Toby? It's Juliet, remember me?' (How could he not!) Pedestrians flowed awkwardly around them. We are a little island, she thought, the two of us. 'Juliet Armstrong.'

He tipped his hat – a grey trilby that she thought she recognized. He offered a faint smile and said, 'I'm sorry, Miss . . . Armstrong? I think you have confused me with someone else. Good day to you.' He turned on his heel and began to walk away.

It *was* him, she knew it was him. The same (somewhat portly) figure, the bland, owlish face, the tortoiseshell spectacles, the old trilby. And, finally, the irrefutable – and rather unnerving – evidence of the silver-topped cane.

She said his real name. 'John Hazeldine.' She had never once called him that. It sounded like an accusation to her ears.

He paused in his stride, his back to her. There was the lightest talcum of dandruff on the shoulders of his greasy gabardine trench. It looked the same as the one that he had worn throughout the war. Did he never buy new clothes? She waited for him to turn round and deny himself again, but after a beat he simply walked on, the cane *tap-tap-tapping* on the grey London pavement. She had been discarded. Like a glove, she thought.

I think you have confused me with someone else. How strange to hear his voice again. It *was* him, why would he pretend otherwise, Juliet puzzled as she settled at a table in Moretti's and ordered a coffee from the surly waiter.

She used to come to this café before the war. The name remained, although the ownership was different. The café itself was small and rather scruffy, the red-and-white-checked tablecloths never entirely clean. The staff seemed to change all the time and no one ever acknowledged Juliet or appeared to recognize her, which was in itself not an unwelcome thing. It was a terrible place really but she was predisposed towards it. It was a thread in the labyrinth, one that she could follow back to the world before the war, to her self before the war. Innocence and experience butting up against each other in the greasy fug of Moretti's. It had been rather a relief to find it was still here when she returned to London. So much else had gone. She lit a cigarette and waited for her coffee.

The café was largely frequented by foreigners of one kind or another and Juliet liked to sit and simply listen, trying to decipher where their accents might have originated. When she first started coming here, the café was run by Mr Moretti himself. He was always attentive to her, calling her 'Signorina' and asking after her mother. ('How's your *mamma?*') Not that Mr Moretti had ever met her mother, but that was Italians, Juliet supposed. Keener on mothers than the British were.

She always replied, 'Very well, thank you, Mr Moretti,' never bold enough to say 'Signor' instead of 'Mr' – that seemed a presumptuous step to take into someone else's linguistic territory. The nameless man currently behind the counter at Moretti's claimed to be Armenian and never asked Juliet about anything, least of all her mother.

It had been a lie, of course. Her mother hadn't been well, not at all, in fact she had been dying, in the Middlesex, just up the road from Moretti's, but Juliet had preferred the subterfuge of her mother's health.

Before she grew too ill to work, her mother had been a dressmaker and Juliet had been accustomed to hearing her mother's 'ladies' complaining their way up the three flights of stairs to their small flat in Kentish Town in order to stand stiffly to attention in their corsets and ample bras while they were pinned into garments. Sometimes Juliet would hold on to them reassuringly while they balanced precariously on a little three-legged stool while her mother shuffled around on her knees, pinning up their hems. Then her mother grew too sick to sew even the simplest seam and the ladies no longer came. Juliet had missed them – they patted her hand and gave her boiled sweets and took an interest in how well she did at school. (*What a clever daughter you have, Mrs Armstrong.*)

Her mother had scrimped and saved and worked endless hours in order to burnish Juliet, polishing her up for a bright future, paying for ballet classes and piano lessons, even elocution with a woman in Kensington. She had been a scholarship girl in a fee-paying school, a school populated by determined girls and even more determined female staff. Her headmistress had suggested she study Modern Languages or Law at university. Or perhaps she should take the Oxbridge entrance? 'They're looking for girls like you,' her headmistress said, but didn't elaborate as to what kind of girl that might be.

Juliet had stopped going to that school, stopped preparing for that bright future, so that she could care for her mother – there had always been only the two of them – and had not returned after her mother's death. It seemed impossible somehow. That eager-to-please, academic sixth-former, who played on the left wing in hockey, who was the leading light of the drama club and practised piano almost every day at school (because there was no room for a piano at home), that girl who was a keen Girl Guide and who loved drama and music and art, that girl, transmuted by bereavement, had gone. And, as far as Juliet could tell, she had never really come back.

Juliet had got into the habit of coming to Moretti's whenever her mother had hospital treatment, and this was where she was when her mother died. It was only 'a matter of days', according to the doctor who had admitted her mother on to a ward in the Middlesex that morning. 'It's time,' he said to Juliet. Did she understand what that meant? Yes, she did, Juliet said. It meant that she was about to lose the only person who loved her. She was seventeen and her grief for herself was almost as great as her grief for her mother.

Never having known him, Juliet felt nothing for her father. Her mother had been somewhat ambivalent on the subject and Juliet appeared to be the only evidence that he had ever existed. He had been a seaman in the Merchant Navy, killed in an accident and buried at sea before Juliet was born, and although she sometimes might indulge in conjuring his pearlish eyes and coralline bones she remained dispassionate about the man himself.

Her mother's death, on the other hand, demanded poeticism. As the first clod of earth hit her mother's coffin, Juliet could barely catch a breath. Her mother would suffocate beneath all that earth, she thought, but Juliet was suffocating too. An image came to her mind – the martyrs who were pressed to death by stones piled on top of them. That is me, she thought, I am crushed by loss. 'Don't seek out elaborate metaphors,' her English teacher had said of her school essays, but her mother's death had revealed that there was no metaphor too ostentatious for grief. It was a terrible thing and demanded embellishment.

It had been foul weather, wet and windy, the day that her mother died. Juliet had lingered in the warm sanctuary of Moretti's for as long as possible. She had eaten cheese on toast for lunch – the cheese on toast that Mr Moretti made was infinitely superior to anything they made at home ('Italian cheese,' he explained. 'And Italian bread'), and then had fought her umbrella all the way along Charlotte Street back to the Middlesex. When she arrived at the ward she discovered that it wasn't safe to believe anything that anyone told you. It turned out that her mother had not had 'a matter of days' but only a handful of hours, and she had died while Juliet was enjoying her lunch. When she kissed her mother's forehead it was still warm and the faint scent of her perfume – lily of the valley – could be caught beneath the awful hospital smells.

'You just missed it,' the nurse said, as though her mother's death was a bus or the opening of a play, when really it was the denouement of her drama.

And that was that. *Finito*.

The end, too, for the staff of Moretti's, for when war was declared they were all interned and none of them ever came back. Juliet heard that Mr Moretti went down on the *Arandora Star* in the summer of 1940, along with hundreds of his imprisoned countrymen. Many of them, like Mr Moretti, had been in the catering trade.

'It's a bloody nuisance,' Hartley said. 'You can't get decent service in the Dorchester any more.' But that was Hartley for you.

It made Juliet melancholic to come back to Moretti's, and yet she did. The lowering of her spirits at the memory of her mother provided a kind of ballast, a counterbalance to what was (in Juliet's opinion) her own shallow, rather careless character. Her mother had represented a form of truth for her, something that Juliet knew she had moved away from in the decade since her death.

She fingered the strand of pearls at her neck. Inside each pearl there was a little piece of grit. That was the true self of the pearl, wasn't it? The beauty of the pearl was just the poor oyster trying to protect itself. From the grit. From the truth.

Oysters made her think of Lester Pelling, the Junior Programme Engineer, and Lester made her think of Cyril, with whom she had worked during the war. Cyril and Lester had much in common. This thread of thought led to many others until eventually she arrived back at Godfrey Toby. Everything was interconnected, a great web that stretched across time and history. Forster might have said *Only connect* but Juliet thought there was something to be said for cutting all those threads and disconnecting oneself.

The pearls at her neck were not Juliet's, she had taken them from the body of a dead woman. Death was a truth too, of course, because it was an absolute. *Rather heavier than she looks, I'm afraid. Lift on my three – one – two – three!* Juliet shuddered at the memory. Best not to think about that. Best not to think at all, probably. Thinking had always been her downfall. Juliet drained her cup and lit another cigarette.

Mr Moretti used to make her a lovely coffee – 'Viennese' – with whipped cream and cinnamon. The war did for that too, of course, and the beverage on offer in Moretti's nowadays was Turkish and more or less undrinkable. It was served in a thick thimble of a cup and was bitter and grainy, made palatable only by the addition of several spoonfuls of sugar. Europe and the Ottoman Empire in the history of a cup. Juliet was in charge of a series for the Juniors called *Looking At Things*. She knew a lot about cups. She had Looked At them.

She ordered another awful coffee and, for fear of encouraging him in some way, tried not to look in the direction of the funny little man who was sitting at a corner table. He had been staring at her on and off since she first sat down, in a way that was extremely disconcerting. Like many in Moretti's, he had the shabby air of the post-war European diaspora. There was a trollish look to him too, as if he had been put together from leftovers. He could have been sent from Booking to play one of the dispossessed. A hunched shoulder, eyes like pebbles – slightly uneven, as if one had slipped a little – and pockmarked skin that looked as if it had been peppered with shot. (Perhaps it had been.) The wounds of war, Juliet thought, rather pleased with the way the words sounded in her head. It could be the title of a novel. Perhaps she should write one. But wasn't artistic endeavour the final refuge of the uncommitted?

Juliet was contemplating confronting the odd little man in the polite way of an English woman – *Excuse me, do I know you?* – although she was fairly certain that she would have remembered someone so odd, but before she could get as far as addressing him, he stood up abruptly.

She felt sure he was going to come over and speak to her and readied herself for some kind of conflict, but instead he shambled towards the door – he had a limp, she noticed, and in lieu of a walking-stick he was supporting himself with a large furled umbrella. He disappeared into the street. He hadn't paid, but the Armenian behind the counter merely glanced up at him as he left and remained uncharacteristically unperturbed.

When her coffee arrived, Juliet swallowed it down like medicine, hoping it would perk her up for the afternoon's onslaught, and then gazed like a clairvoyant at the coffee grounds that were left at the bottom of the small cup. Why would Godfrey Toby refuse to acknowledge her?

He had been coming out of a bank. That used to be his cover – bank clerk. It was clever really, no one wanted to engage a bank clerk in conversation about his job. Juliet used to think that someone who seemed as ordinary as Godfrey Toby must be harbouring a secret – a thrilling past, a dreadful tragedy – but as time had gone by she'd realized that being ordinary *was* his secret. It was the best disguise of all really, wasn't it?

Juliet never thought of him as 'John Hazeldine' for he had inhabited the rather dull-seeming domain of Godfrey Toby so thoroughly, so magnificently.

To his face he had been 'Mr Toby', but really 'Godfrey' was how everyone used to refer to him. It indicated neither familiarity nor intimacy, it was simply a habit that had formed. They had called their operation 'the Godfrey case' and there were a number of files in the Registry that had been headed simply 'Godfrey', and not all of them were successfully cross-referenced. That was the kind of thing that used to send the Registry queens into a tizzy, of course.

There had been talk of moving him abroad after the war ended. New Zealand. Somewhere like that anyway. South Africa, perhaps. To protect him, in case of reprisals. But wasn't retribution – one way or another – something they were all at risk of?

And his informants, the fifth columnists – what of them? There had been a plan to monitor them in peacetime, but Juliet wasn't sure if it had ever been implemented. She did know that the decision had been made to leave them in ignorance after the war. No one had told them about MI5's duplicity. They never knew that they had been recorded by microphones embedded in the plaster of the walls of the flat in Dolphin Square to which they came so eagerly every week. Nor did they have any idea that Godfrey Toby worked for MI5 and was not the Gestapo agent to whom they thought they were bringing traitorous information. And they would have been very surprised to know that the following day a girl sat at a big Imperial typewriter in the flat next door and transcribed those traitorous conversations, one top copy and two carbons at a time. And that girl, for her sins, had been Juliet.

When the operation was wound up at the end of '44 they were told that Godfrey had been stood down and 'evacuated' to Portugal, although in reality he had been sent to Paris to interview captured German officers.

Where had he been since the end of the war? Why had he returned? And, most puzzling of all, why would he pretend not to recognize her?

I *know* him, Juliet thought. They had worked together throughout the war. She had been in his home, for heaven's sake – in Finchley – where he had lived in a house with a solid oak front door and a robust brass door-knocker in the shape of a lion's head. A house with leaded lights and parquet flooring. She had sat on the cut moquette of his solid sofa. (*Can I get you a cup of tea, Miss Armstrong? Would that help? We've had rather a shock.*) She had washed her hands with the freesia-scented soap in his bathroom, seen the array of coats and shoes in his hall cupboard. Why, she had even glimpsed the pink satin eiderdown beneath which he and Mrs Toby (if there ever really had been such a person) slept.

And together they had committed a hideous act, the kind of thing that binds you to someone for ever, whether you like it or not. Was that why he had denied her now? (*Two sugars, that's right, isn't it, Miss Armstrong?*) Or was that why he had come back?

I should have followed him, she thought. But he would have lost her. He had been rather good at evasion.

1940

One of Us

'GODFREY TOBY IS his name,' Peregrine Gibbons said. 'He poses as an agent of the German government, but of course he is one of us.'

It was the first time Juliet had heard the name Godfrey Toby and she said, 'He's not actually German then?'

'Goodness, no. There is no one more English than Godfrey.' But surely, Juliet thought, Peregrine Gibbons – the name alone – was the apotheosis of an Englishman. 'No one more trustworthy either,' he said. 'Godfrey's been in "deep cover" for a long time, attending Fascist meetings and so on throughout the Thirties. He had contacts with workers at Siemens before the war – their factories in England have always been hotbeds for German intelligence. He is well known to the fifth column, they feel quite safe with him. I presume you are familiar with the ins and outs of the fifth column, Miss Armstrong?'

'Fascist sympathizers, supporters of the enemy, sir?'

'Exactly. Subversives. The Nordic League, the Link, the Right Club, the Imperial Fascist League, and a hundred smaller factions. The people who meet with Godfrey are mostly old British Union of Fascists members – Mosley's lot. Our own home-grown evil, I'm sorry to say. And instead of rooting them out, the plan is to let them flourish – but within a walled garden from which they cannot escape and spread their evil seed.'

A girl could die of old age following a metaphor like this, Juliet thought. 'Very nicely put, sir,' she said.

Juliet had been working in the Registry for a tedious two months when yesterday Peregrine Gibbons had approached her in the canteen and said, 'I need a girl.'

And, lo and behold, today she was here. His girl.

'I'm setting up a special operation,' he told her. 'A kind of deception game. You will be an important part of it.' Was she to be an agent then? (A spy!) No, it seemed she was to remain shackled to a typewriter. 'We cannot choose our weapons in a time of war, Miss Armstrong,' he said. I don't see why not, Juliet thought. What would she choose, she wondered? A sharp sabre? A bow of flaming gold? Perhaps arrows of desire.

Nonetheless, she had been singled out – chosen. 'The work we're doing requires a special kind of person, Miss Armstrong,' he told her. Peregrine Gibbons ('Do call me Perry') had a way of speaking to you that made you feel you must be a cut above everyone else – the elite of the herd. He was attractive, perhaps not leading-man material, more of a character actor, she thought. He was tall, and rather natty with his bow-tie and top-to-toe herringbone tweed – a double-breasted three-piece, beneath a large overcoat (yes, tweed), all worn with a rather careless panache. Amongst other things, she learnt later, he had studied mesmerism when he was younger, and Juliet wondered if he used it on people without them knowing. Was she to be the Trilby to his Svengali? (She always thought of the hat. It seemed absurd.)

And now here they were in Pimlico, in Dolphin Square, so that he could show her the 'set-up'. He had taken two flats next door to each other – 'Isolation is the best form of secrecy,' he said. 'Mosley has a flat here. He'll be one of our neighbours.' This seemed to amuse him. 'Cheek by jowl with the enemy.'

Dolphin Square was built a few years ago, close to the Thames, and until now Juliet had only seen it from the outside. Entering through the large arch on the river side it presented quite a daunting sight – ten blocks of flats, each ten storeys high, built around a kind of garden quadrangle with trees and flower beds and a winter-dry fountain. 'Quite Soviet in its conception and execution, don't you think?' Perry said.

'I suppose,' Juliet said, although she didn't think the Russians would have named their housing towers after legendary British admirals and sea-captains – Beatty, Collingwood, Drake, and so on. They were to be in Nelson House, Perry said. He would live and work in one flat – Juliet would work there too – while in the next-door flat an MI5 officer – Godfrey Toby – would masquerade as a Nazi agent and encourage people with pro-Fascist sympathies to report to him. 'If they're telling Godfrey their secrets,' Perry said, 'then they are not telling the Germans. Godfrey will be a conduit to divert their treachery into our own reservoir.' Metaphor really wasn't his forte.

'And one will lead us to another, and so on,' he continued. 'The beauty of it is that they are doing the rounding-up themselves.'

Perry was already lodged in the flat – Juliet caught a glimpse of his shaving-kit on a shelf above the sink in the tiny bathroom and through a half-open bedroom door she could see a white shirt on a hanger on the wardrobe door – a good heavy twill, she noticed. Her mother would have approved of the quality. The rest of the room, however, appeared so austere that it might have been a monk's cell. 'I have a flat elsewhere, of course,' he said. 'In Petty France. But this arrangement is practical for Godfrey's operation. And everything we need is here – a restaurant, a shopping arcade, a swimming pool, even our own taxi service.'

The living room of the Dolphin Square flat had been turned into an office, although, Juliet was pleased to note, it retained the comfort of a small sofa. Peregrine Gibbons's desk was a beast of a roll-top, a manifold affair composed of little pull-out shelves and tiny cupboards and endless drawers containing bulldog clips, rubber bands, drawing-pins and so on, all punctiliously arranged (and rearranged) by Perry himself. He was the orderly sort, she noted. And I am disorderly, she thought regretfully. It was bound to annoy.

The only adornment to his desk was a small, heavy bust of Beethoven, who glared furiously at Juliet when she sat at her own desk – a piece of furniture that in comparison to Perry's was little more than a rather dejected-looking table.

'Do you like Beethoven, sir?' she asked.

'Not particularly,' he said, seemingly puzzled by the question. 'He makes for a good paperweight though.'

'I'm sure he would be pleased to know that, sir.' She noticed his brow furrow slightly and thought, I must restrain my inclination to levity. It seemed to confuse him.

'And,' Perry continued, pausing for a beat, as if he were waiting to see if she had anything more of inconsequence to add, 'of course, as well as our special little operation' (*Ours*, she thought, pleased by the possessive) 'you will carry out general secretarial duties for me, and so on. I am running other operations as well as this one, but don't worry, I shan't burden you with too much.' (Not true!) 'I like to type my own reports.' (He didn't!) 'The fewer people who see things, the better. Isolation is the best form of secrecy.' You said that already, she thought. He must be keen on it.

It had seemed like an attractive prospect. She had been working in a prison for the last couple of months – MI5 had relocated to Wormwood Scrubs so as best to accommodate their burgeoning ranks, necessitated by war. It was an unpleasant place to work. All day long, people clattered up and down the open metal staircases. The female staff had even been given special dispensation to wear trousers because the men could see up their skirts when they were going up the stairs. And the Ladies were not ladies' toilets at all but horrid things designed for prisoners, with stable-type doors that left you completely visible from the bust upwards and the knees downward. The cells functioned as their offices and people were forever getting locked in by accident.

Pimlico had seemed an attractive proposition in comparison. And yet. All this talk of isolation and secrecy – was she to be locked away here too?

It seemed peculiar that she was to spend her working days in such proximity to Perry Gibbons's domestic arrangements – within breathing distance of where he slept, not to mention the even more intimate proceedings of daily life. What if she were to come across his 'smalls' drying in the bathroom, or smell his Finnan haddock from the previous night? Or – worse – if she were to hear him using the bathroom (or – horrors – vice versa!)? It would be too much to bear. But, of course, his laundry was sent out and he never cooked for himself. And as for the bathroom, he seemed oblivious to bodily functions, his own and hers.

She wondered if she might not have been better off staying in the Registry, after all. Not that she had been given much choice in the matter. Choice, it seemed, was one of the first casualties of war.

Juliet hadn't applied to the Security Service; she had wanted to join one of the women's armed forces, not particularly from patriotism but because she was worn out with fending for herself in the months after her mother's death. But then after war was declared she had been summoned to an interview, and the summons was on government notepaper so she supposed she would have to obey it.

She had been flustered when she arrived because her bus had broken down, right on Piccadilly Circus, and she'd had to run all the way to an obscure office in an even more obscure building on Pall

Mall. You had to go through the building in front of it to discover the entrance. She wondered if it was some kind of test. 'Passport Office', it said on a small brass plaque on the door, but there was no sign of anyone wanting a passport or of anyone issuing one.

Juliet hadn't really caught the name of the man (Morton?) who was interviewing her. He was leaning back in his chair rather non-chalantly, as if he was waiting to be entertained by her. He didn't usually conduct the interviews, he said, but Miss Dicker was indisposed. Juliet had no idea who Miss Dicker was.

'Juliet?' the man said contemplatively. 'As in *Romeo and Juliet*? Very romantic.' He laughed as if this was some kind of private joke.

'I believe it was actually a tragedy, sir.'

'Is there a difference?'

He wasn't old, but he didn't look young either and perhaps never had. He had the air of an aesthete and was thin, elongated almost – a heron or a stork. He seemed amused by everything she said – everything he said himself, too. He reached for a pipe that was sitting on his desk and proceeded to light it, taking his time, puffing and tamping and sucking and all the other strange rituals pipe smokers seemed to find it necessary to go through, before saying, 'Tell me about your father.'

'My father?'

'Your father.'

'He's dead.' There was a silence that she supposed she was meant to fill. 'He was buried at sea,' she offered.

'Really? Royal Navy?'

'No, Merchant,' she said.

'Ah.' His eyebrow lifted slightly.

She didn't like that supercilious eyebrow and so she gave her unfathomable father a promotion. 'An officer.'

'Of course,' he said. 'And your mother? How is she?'

'She's very well, thank you,' Juliet answered automatically. She was beginning to get a headache. Her mother used to say that she thought too much. Juliet thought that possibly she didn't think enough. The mention of her mother laid another stone on her heart. Her mother was still more of a presence than an absence in her life. Juliet supposed that one day in the future it would be the other way round, but she doubted that would be an improvement.

'I see you went to quite a good school,' the man (Marsden?) said. 'Quite expensive too, I expect – for your mother. She takes in sewing, doesn't she? A seamstress.'

'A dressmaker. It's different.'

'Is it? I wouldn't know about these things.' (She felt rather sure he would.) 'You must have wondered how she managed to afford the fees.'

'I was on a scholarship.'

'How did that make you feel?'

'Feel?'

'Inferior?'

'Inferior? Of course not.'

'Do you like art?' he asked abruptly, taking her off her guard.

'Art?' What did he mean by that? She had come under the wing of an enthusiastic art teacher at school, Miss Gillies. ('You have an eye,' Miss Gillies told her. I have two, she thought.) She used to visit the National Gallery before her mother died. She disliked Fragonard and Watteau and all that pretty French stuff that would make any self-respecting *sans-culottes* want to chop someone's head off. Similarly Gainsborough and his affluent aristocrats posing smugly with their grand perspectives. And Rembrandt, for whom she had a particular disregard. What was so wonderful about an ugly old man who kept painting himself all the time?

Perhaps she didn't like art, in fact she felt quite opinionated about it. 'Of course I like art,' she said. 'Doesn't everyone?'

'You'd be surprised. Anyone in particular?'

'Rembrandt,' she said, placing her hand on her heart in a gesture of devotion. She liked Vermeer, but she wasn't going to share that with a stranger. 'I revere Vermeer,' she had once told Miss Gillies. It seemed a lifetime ago now.

'What about languages?' he asked.

'Do I *like* them?'

'Do you *have* them?' He clamped his teeth on the stem of his pipe as if it were a baby's teething-ring.

Oh, for heaven's sake, she thought. She was surprised by how antagonistic she was feeling towards this man. Later she learnt that this was his forte. He was one of their interrogation specialists, although it seemed to be sheer chance that he had volunteered to sit in for Miss Dicker this afternoon.

'Not really,' she said.

'Really? No languages? Not French, or perhaps a smattering of German?'

'Barely.'

'What about a musical instrument. Do you play?'

'No.'

'Not even a little piano?'

Before she could deny further, there was a knock at the door and a woman put her head round it and said, 'Mr Merton,' (Merton!) 'Colonel Lightwater was wondering if he could have a word when you're free?'

'Tell him I'll be along in ten minutes.'

Crikey, ten more minutes of this cross-examination, Juliet thought.

'So . . .' he said – a small word that seemed freighted with significance. More business with his pipe only added weight to the load. Had the War Office begun to ration words, she wondered? 'You're eighteen?' He made it sound like an accusation.

'I am.'

'Quite advanced for your age, aren't you?'

Was he insulting her? 'No, not at all,' she answered robustly. 'I am completely average for my age.'

He laughed, a genuine bark of mirth, and glanced at some papers on his desk, then stared at her and said, 'St James's Secretarial College?'

St James's was where well-bred girls went. Juliet had spent the time since her mother's death attending night classes in a ramshackle college in Paddington while she worked as a chambermaid during the day in an equally ramshackle hotel in Fitzrovia. She had stepped through the doors of St James's to enquire about fees and so felt justified in saying now, 'Yes. I started there, but I finished somewhere else.'

'And are you?'

'Am I what?'

'Finished?'

'Quite. Thank you.'

'Good speeds?'

'I'm sorry?' Juliet was puzzled; it sounded as if he were sending her on her way. (God speed?) Because he didn't think she was finished. She wasn't. She was extremely unfinished, in her own opinion.

'Speeds – typing and so on,' he said, waving his pipe around in the air. He was clueless, Juliet thought.

'Oh, *speeds*,' she said. 'Yes. They're good. I have certificates.' She didn't elaborate – he made her feel mulishly uncooperative. Not the best attitude in a candidate in an interview, she supposed. But she hadn't wanted a clerical job.

'Anything else you want to tell me about yourself?'

'No. Not really. Sir.'

He looked disappointed.

And then, in an offhand manner – he may as well have been asking her if she preferred bread to potatoes, or red rather than green – he said, 'If you had to choose, which would you be – a Communist or a Fascist?'

'It's not much of a choice, is it, sir?'

'You have to choose. There's a gun to your head.'

'I could choose to be shot.' (Who was holding the gun, she wondered?)

'No, you couldn't. You have to choose one or the other.'

Communism, it seemed to Juliet, was a kinder doctrine. 'Fascism,' she bluffed. He laughed.

He was trying to extract something from her but she wasn't sure what. She might pop into a Lyons for lunch, she thought. Treat herself. No one else would.

Merton took her by surprise, standing up suddenly and walking round his desk towards her. Juliet stood up too, rather defensively. He moved closer and Juliet felt oddly unsure about what he intended to do. For a wild moment she thought he was going to try to kiss her. What would she do if he did? She had received plenty of unwanted attention in the hotel in Fitzrovia, many of the guests were travelling salesmen away from their wives and she could usually fend them off with a sharp kick to the shin. But Merton worked for the government. There might be penalties attached to kicking him. It might even be treason.

He put out his hand and she realized that he was waiting for her to shake it. 'I'm sure Miss Dicker will run her eye over your *bona fides* and so on and get you all signed up to the Official Secrets Act.'

Did she have the job then? Was that it?

'Of course,' he said. 'You had the job before you walked in the door, Miss Armstrong. I just needed to ask the right questions. To be reassured that you are honourable and upright. And so on.'

But I don't want the job, she thought. 'I was thinking of joining the ATS,' she said boldly.

He laughed, the way you might laugh at a child, and said, 'You will do more good for the war working with us, Miss Armstrong.'

Later she learnt that Miles Merton (for that was his entire name) knew everything about her – more than she knew herself – including every lie and half-truth she told him at the interview. It didn't seem to matter. In fact, she suspected that it helped in some way.

Afterwards she had gone to the Lyons Corner House on Lower Regent Street and ordered a ham salad with boiled potatoes. They still had good ham. It couldn't last, she supposed. The salad seemed a meagre choice if they were all soon to starve in the war, so she added tea and two iced buns to her order. The Corner House's orchestra, she noticed, was already depleted by the war.

After her meal she walked over to the National Gallery. Having been reminded of Vermeer, she had intended to look at the two of his works that were housed there, but discovered that all the paintings had been evacuated.

The following morning she received a telegram with confirmation of 'the post' – the wording still mysteriously vague – and instructions to wait at the bus stop opposite the Natural History Museum at 9.00 a.m. the following day. The telegram was signed 'Room 055'.

After twenty minutes of waiting as instructed – in an unforgiving wind – a Bedford bus pulled up in front of Juliet. It was a single-decker and on its side it announced 'Highland Tours' and Juliet thought, crumbs – were they going to Scotland and shouldn't someone have told her so she could have packed a suitcase?

The driver opened the door and shouted over to her, 'MI5, love? Hop in.' So much for secrecy, she thought.

The bus proceeded to stop several times to pick up more people: a couple of youngish men in bowler hats, but mostly girls – girls who looked as though they had just stepped out of a charm school, or indeed St James's Secretarial College.

'Debs – rotten, the lot of them,' the girl in the seat next to her said, rather loudly. She was a swan, pale and elegant. 'Do you want a fag?' she said. She spoke with a debutante drawl herself – a laryngitic, smoke-infused one, it was true, but nonetheless it betrayed the unmistakeable timbre of the upper echelons. She held out a cigarette packet to Juliet, who shook her head and said, 'No, thanks, I don't smoke.'

'You will eventually,' the girl said. 'You may as well start now and get it over with.' There was a gold crest on the cigarette packet, and, more extraordinarily still, a tiny gold crest embossed on the cigarette itself. 'Morland's,' the girl said, lighting the cigarette and sucking hard on it. 'Pa's a duke. They make them specially for him.'

'Goodness,' Juliet said. 'I didn't know they did that.'

'I know. Mad, isn't it? My name's Clarissa, by the way.'

'Juliet.'

'Oh, bad luck. I bet everyone's always asking you where Romeo is. I myself was named for a bloody awful novel.'

'And do you have a sister called Pamela?' Juliet asked curiously.

'I do!' Clarissa roared with laughter. She had a filthy laugh, despite her blue blood. 'How on earth did you know that? You must be one of the clever ones. Books are such a waste of time,' she added. 'I have no idea why people go on and on about them.' She tilted her head back and blew smoke out of her mouth in an admirably long, thin stream in a way that made smoking look suddenly inviting. 'They're all inbred,' she added, indicating a red-haired girl swaying her precarious way down the aisle – the driver seemed to think he was at Brooklands.

The red-haired girl was wearing a nice twin-set in a pale apple-green that had clearly come from an expensive shop rather than being made by hand. Juliet's sweater – cherry-red moss stitch – had been knitted by her mother and she felt almost embarrassingly homespun compared to the other girls. The pale-green-twin-set girl wore pearls, too. Of course. A quick inventory of the coach led

Juliet to the conclusion that she might be the only girl without them.

'Her mother's a lady-in-waiting to the Queen,' Clarissa murmured, indicating the pale-green-twin-set girl with her cigarette. She shifted closer to Juliet and whispered in her ear, 'Rumour has it that—' but at that moment the vehicle lurched around a corner and the girls all squealed in delighted fear. 'A bus!' someone exclaimed. 'What a hoot!'

The girl in the apple-green twin-set had been flung on to someone's lap by the sudden movement of the bus and along with all those around her was screaming with laughter.

'A curse on all their houses,' Clarissa muttered.

'But you're one yourself,' Juliet ventured.

Clarissa shrugged. 'Fourth daughter of a duke – it hardly counts.' She caught Juliet's eye and laughed. 'I know, I sound like a spoiled brat.'

'Are you?'

'Oh, completely. Do have a fag, I know we're going to be great friends.'

Juliet took a cigarette from the heraldic packet and Clarissa lit it for her with her lighter – gold, of course. 'There,' she laughed. 'You're on your way.'

'That's it, ladies and gents!' the bus driver yelled. 'The charabanc holiday's over, your sentence starts here – everybody off!'

The coach disgorged the rather bewildered group outside the main gates of a prison. The driver banged on a small studded wooden door to the side of the gates. 'Another lot for you!' he yelled, and the door was opened by an invisible gatekeeper.

'Wormwood Scrubs?' Juliet puzzled to Clarissa. 'We're to *work* here?' Not much fear that the subject of Art would raise its ugly head here, she thought.

Clarissa ground out her cigarette beneath her expensive-looking shoes ('Ferragamo – would you like them? You can have them') and said, 'Well, Pa always said I'd end up behind bars.'

And that was how Juliet's career in espionage began.

The Scrubs, as everyone called it, was chaotic, full of people totally unsuited to the job in hand. MI5 were recruiting an enormous number of new people, girls mostly, into 'A' Division, which was administrative. The debs in particular were useless. A few of them brought picnic hampers and ate lunch on the grass as if they were at Henley Regatta. There were still prisoners in some of the blocks, waiting to be moved elsewhere. If they were unlucky enough to catch sight of the new arrivals, Juliet wondered what they would make of all these lovely girls nibbling on chicken drumsticks. There would be some winnowing soon, Juliet expected. It would be menials who would win this war, she thought, not girls in pearls.

She was siphoned off into the Registry – a place seething with discontent – and her days consisted mainly of moving buff folders from one filing-cabinet drawer to another, or shuffling the endless index cards around according to some impenetrably arcane system.

And yet there was much fun to be had once they escaped from jail every evening. Clarissa was a real friend (perhaps her first), gold crests notwithstanding. They went out together almost every night, bumping their way through the streets in the blackout – Juliet was black and blue from nightly encounters with post boxes and lamp posts. The Four Hundred, the Embassy, the Berkeley, the Milroy, the Astoria ballroom – there was no end to the entertainment to be had during a war. They were pushed around overcrowded dance floors in a blur by a succession of men in different uniforms, temporary swains who seemed like mayflies, their faces hardly worth committing to memory.

There was a late-night coffee stall on Park Lane that they would stop at on the way home in the small hours, or sometimes they wouldn't go to bed at all but would get breakfast in a Lyons – porridge, bacon and fried bread, toast and marmalade and a pot of tea, all for 1s 6d – and then come straight to the Scrubs and start all over again.

Nonetheless, it had been something of a relief when Perry Gibbons approached her yesterday while she was eating lunch in the canteen with Clarissa. The canteen was the same one that had previously catered for the prison population, and Juliet suspected that the unpalatable food was also unchanged. They were dining on some kind of gamey hash when she suddenly found him smiling down at her. 'Miss Armstrong, don't get up. My name's Perry Gibbons. I need a girl, I'm afraid.'

'Well,' Juliet said, adopting a note of caution, 'I *am* a girl, I suppose.'

'Good! Then can you come to my office after lunch? Do you know where it is?'

Juliet had no idea, but he had a firm voice, a nice low register that spoke of both kindness and unassailable authority, which seemed the perfect combination in a man – in the romance novels her mother had been fond of, anyway – so she promptly said, 'Yes, sir.'

'Excellent. I'll see you shortly. Don't rush, enjoy your lunch.' He tipped his head in Clarissa's direction.

'Who *was* that?' Juliet asked.

'The famous Peregrine Gibbons. He's running B5b – or is it Bc1? It's hard to keep track – "counter-subversion".' Clarissa laughed. 'I think you've been plucked.'

'That sounds unpleasant.'

'Like a rose,' Clarissa assuaged. 'A lovely innocent rose.'

Juliet didn't think a rose could be innocent. Or indeed guilty.

'And here is the hidden magic,' Perry Gibbons said now, opening a door in the Dolphin Square flat to reveal not enchantment but another, smaller bedroom, containing an array of recording equipment and two men who were currently clambering over each other in the confined space in order to install it. To be more accurate, a man and a boy. The man – Reginald Applethwaite ('Bit of a mouthful, just call me Reg, love') – was from the GPO Research Station at Dollis Hill. The boy, Cyril Forbes, was a junior engineer who worked there too. It was Cyril (rhymes with squirrel, Juliet thought) who would be operating the equipment whenever a meeting of the fifth column was held next door.

'RCA Victor, model MI-12700,' Reg said proudly, displaying the recording equipment with the enthusiasm of a showman.

'It's American kit,' Cyril added shyly.

'As used at Trent Park,' Perry Gibbons added. 'The interrogation centre,' he said, when Juliet looked blank. 'Merton works there sometimes, I think. He recruited you, didn't he?'

'Mr Merton? Yes, he did.' She hadn't seen Miles Merton since he had interviewed her. (*I just needed to ask the right questions.*)

Both Reginald and Cyril were eager to show off their technical skills and bombarded her with information about the recording equipment – *cutter-head float stabilizer . . . styrol diaphragm . . . moving coil element . . . pressure operated . . . steel and sapphire recording styli* – until Perry laughed in a rather strained way (laughter didn't seem to come naturally to him) and said, 'Enough now, gentlemen. We don't want to overwhelm Miss Armstrong. She is here to be a typist, not an engineer.'

The walls were soundproofed, he explained as he led her next door, Reginald and Cyril on their heels, still chattering cheerfully about *instantaneous recording discs* and 88A *microphones.*

It was the mirror-image of the flat they had just left, as if they had gone through the looking-glass. The autumn-leaves carpet, the unremarkable Harlequin wallpaper – which Juliet recognized immediately as the same rose-and-trellis pattern that her mother had chosen for the walls of their living room in Kentish Town. The unexpected sight of it was a kick to her heart.

'Bugged!' Cyril said.

'The microphones are in the walls,' Reg explained.

'In the walls?' Juliet said. 'Really?'

'Can't tell there's anything in there, can you?' Reg said, tapping the wall.

'Gosh, no,' Juliet said, genuinely impressed.

'Good, eh, miss?' Cyril said, grinning at her. He looked incredibly young, as if he still belonged in infant school. Juliet could imagine him in the school playground, dirty knees, wrinkled grey socks falling around his ankles, conker ready to fly.

Reg laughed and said, 'He's a little charmer, that one, isn't he?'

Cyril's face was engulfed by blushes and he said, 'Don't listen to him, miss.'

'Lock up your daughters, eh, Mr Gibbons?' Reg said.

'I don't have any, I'm afraid,' Perry Gibbons laughed, again rather stiffly. (Would he lock them up if he did, Juliet wondered?) He smiled at Juliet, as if apologizing for something – his awkwardness, perhaps. He had a lovely smile. He should smile more often, Juliet thought.

'He's considered a bit of a renegade within the Service,' Clarissa told her that evening over drinks at the Four Hundred Club. 'I've been mugging up on Perry Gibbons on your behalf.' His wealth of talents apparently included very clever card tricks – he was a member of the Magic Circle – and he spoke Swahili (What was the point of that, Juliet wondered? Unless you were a Swahili, of course) and used to play badminton 'almost' at a professional level. 'Also a keen naturalist and he read Classics at Cambridge.'

'Who didn't?' Hartley grunted.

'Do shut up, Hartley,' Clarissa said. Hartley – his first name was Rupert but Juliet never once heard him called that – had barged his way into their company. 'Oh, not Hartley,' Clarissa had sighed when she caught sight of him bulldozing his way through the crowds towards their table. 'He's such a boor.' He had sat down and promptly ordered two rounds of cocktails for them, to be delivered ten minutes apart. Hartley was a drinker – it was what defined him really. He was remarkably unattractive, with brushy dark red hair and freckles splotching his face and hands (and presumably the rest of him, although that didn't really bear thinking about), giving the illusion that somewhere in the ancestral line a giraffe had been introduced.

'He likes to play the buffoon,' Clarissa had said, 'but he's acute really. He has an entrée into society, of course – his father's in the Cabinet.' Oh, *that* Hartley, Juliet thought. He had come to MI5 via Eton, Cambridge and the BBC – a well-trodden path.

'Well, chin-chin,' Hartley said, downing his drink in one. 'Gibbons is a queer fish. Everyone goes on about him being a polymath, but you can sometimes know *too* much. It makes him very dry. I wouldn't be at all surprised to find a hair shirt beneath all that tweed.'

'Well, good luck with him, anyway,' Clarissa said to Juliet. 'The girls in the Scrubs think he has SA.'

'SA?'

'Sex appeal!' Hartley snorted. (He had been denied it at birth by some malign spell.)

Sex was a subject that was still largely a mystery to Juliet. Her *éducation sexuelle* (it was easier to think of it as something French) was woefully riddled with lacunae. They had drawn diagrams to show the domestic plumbing system at school in Housecraft. It was a pointless subject – how to lay a tea tray, what to feed an invalid, what to look for when buying meat (beef should be 'marbled with fat'). How much more useful if they had taught you about sex.

And her mother's romantic novels were no help either, containing as they did an endless parade of sheikhs and oil barons in whose arms women routinely swooned. These same women also had a tendency to melt at crucial moments, but that only made Juliet think of the witch in *The Wizard of Oz*, and that could hardly be what was intended.

'And Gibbons has got no small talk whatsoever,' Hartley said. 'It makes people suspicious of him. The Service runs on small talk. No wonder he's isolated himself in Dolphin Square.'

'Is your agent going to live here then?' Juliet asked, absently tracing the rose-and-trellis with her finger.

'Godfrey? Good Lord, no,' Perry said. 'Godfrey lives in Finchley. Up until now, our "spies" have had ad hoc meetings – pubs, restaurants and so on. They believe that this flat has been secretly paid for by the German government, specifically to serve as a meeting place for them and their "Gestapo agent". A place of safety.'

There was a desk and a telephone and four comfortable chairs arranged around a coffee table in front of the fireplace. Ashtrays were plentiful. There was a portrait of the King on the wall.

'Will the informants not think that odd?' Juliet asked.

'There is a certain irony, is there not? But they will believe it's all part of the disguise.'

He checked his watch and said, 'Godfrey will be here in a minute, he's coming to inspect the set-up. The whole operation hinges on him, you know.'

They returned to 'their' flat next door and Perry said, 'Why don't you make us all a cup of tea, Miss Armstrong?' Juliet sighed. At least in the Scrubs she had been no one's skivvy.

There was a modest knock at the door and Perry Gibbons said, 'Ah, there he is – right on time. You can set your watch by Godfrey.'

Juliet was expecting someone strapping, a kind of Bulldog Drummond, so she was rather disappointed that in the flesh he cut an unassuming, Pooterish figure. With his bashed trilby and old trench coat, Godfrey Toby had a slightly used air about him. He was carrying a cane – walnut, topped with a silver knob – an accoutrement that in the hand of another man might have looked rather affected, but he made it seem quite natural. It gave him a somewhat jaunty, almost Chaplinesque air – which was perhaps not his character. ('But you would think he'd be better off with an umbrella,' the ever-practical Cyril said to her later. 'He doesn't need a stick, there's nothing wrong with his legs, is there? And a cane's not much good if it rains, is it, miss?')

Godfrey was introduced to Reg and Cyril, and Juliet last of all, as she was struggling in the kitchen with the tea tray (milk jug to the top right, sugar bowl to the bottom left, according to those Housecraft lessons).

The set-up was gone through again and this time Cyril was told to go next door so that Reg could demonstrate the recording process. Cyril – not as bashful as he looked, apparently – launched into a rendition of the 'Beer Barrel Polka' with some gusto and at some length, until Juliet was dispatched to tell him to stop.

'We could send him in instead of tanks,' Reg said. 'That'd put the wind up Hitler.'

Juliet's part in the proceedings was then explored. Godfrey Toby listened in on the headphones as the recording of Cyril singing was played back ('The gang's all here!' he concluded in a rousing *fortissimo*). 'And then Miss Armstrong types what she hears,' Peregrine Gibbons said – Juliet obligingly hit a few keys on the Imperial to demonstrate – 'and thus we have a transcription of everything that is said next door.'

'Yes, yes, I see,' Godfrey said. He stood beside Juliet and read the words she'd typed. '"The gang's all here",' he said. 'Very apt, I'm sure.'

'And now we simply have to wait for our guests,' Peregrine Gibbons said. 'And then the real work will begin.'

Perry, Godfrey, Cyril, Juliet. *The gang's all here*, she thought.

*

'So you're working with old Toby Jug, are you?' Hartley said. They had encountered him again in the Café de Paris. He was proving relentlessly unavoidable.

'Who?' Clarissa asked.

'Godfrey Toby,' Juliet said. 'Do you know him?' Clarissa seemed to know everyone.

'No, I don't think so. My mother always said not to trust a man with two Christian names.'

It seemed an arbitrary rule of thumb, although Juliet's own mother had been dismissive of men with blue eyes, perhaps forgetting that she had once told Juliet that her father, the drowned sailor, had eyes 'as blue as the sea' into which he had eventually sunk.

'And what is it exactly,' Hartley said, 'that the old Toby Jug is doing?'

'I'm not supposed to talk about the operation,' Juliet said primly.

'Oh, we're all friends here, aren't we?'

'Are we?' Clarissa murmured.

'He's a mystery, your Toby Jug,' Hartley said. 'No one knows what he's been doing all these years. "The Great Enigma". That's what he's called behind his back.'

'The Great Enigma?' Juliet mused. It made Godfrey sound like a stage act.

'Godfrey Toby is a master of obfuscation,' Hartley said. 'It's easy to get lost in his fog. Shall we order another round? Yours is a gimlet, isn't it?'

Here's Dolly

J.A.

22.03.40

RECORD 1.

18.00 Arrival. GODFREY, TRUDE and BETTY present.

Social chat and commenting on the weather.

GODFREY commented on BETTY'S cold (resulting in an unfortunate loss of her voice).

There was some talk about a friend of BETTY'S called PATRICIA (or LETITIA?) who lives near the docks in Portsmouth and how that could be useful.

TRUDE. A friend to us?
BETTY. Very much to our way of thinking. I said she should get a job in a pub. She used to work in one, she got experience when she was in Guildford.
TRUDE. The pubs in Portsmouth are full of sailors.
GODFREY. Yes, yes.
TRUDE. And dockworkers. A couple of drinks and they'll tell you anything probably.

BETTY. Movement of the fleet (?) and so on.

The doorbell rings. GODFREY leaves the room to answer it. A lot of commotion in the hall.

BETTY. (whispering, partly inaudible) How much do you think this place costs the Gestapo?
TRUDE. At least three guineas a week, I imagine. I've seen them advertised. (four or five words inaudible due to BETTY'S coughing)

GODFREY returns with DOLLY.

GODFREY. Here's Dolly.

Some conversation about the weather. Some abusive chat about the portrait of the King on the wall.

GODFREY. How's NORMA? (NORMAN?)
DOLLY. The same. Not much help to us I don't think. She's being married at Easter. To CAPTAIN BARKER.
GODFREY. And he's against . . . ?
DOLLY. Yes. At Virginia Water. You look peaky (?)
BETTY. It's all the coughing (??) and strain (??)

Or perhaps Betty was thinking of taking a train. Or cleaning the drains. Oh, do speak clearly, Juliet thought crossly. They were such a bunch of mumblers and Betty's dratted cold made understanding them even more difficult. Half the time, of course, they didn't even make sense and they were always talking over each other (infuriating!). Juliet had been relieved to discover that, unlike his tamed band of fifth columnists, Godfrey articulated clearly. He was nicely spoken, a tenor rather than a baritone, with just a hint of something other – Scottish, perhaps, even Canadian might have been hazarded, although he was actually from Bexhill. He possessed a soft, rather mellifluous voice, and if she had never met him Juliet might have imagined him to look rather like Robert Donat.

Juliet pressed the lever that lifted the stylus off the record and then removed her earphones, yawned and stretched her arms above her head. The effort of concentrating had made her feel slightly sick. It was still an hour to lunchtime if she didn't die of starvation in the meantime. She had a Ryvita cracker somewhere in her hand-bag. Should she eat it or save it? Save it, she decided, feeling rather superior to her usual self, which was shamefully inclined to intemperance.

She sighed, replaced her earphones and pressed down the lever on the playback equipment. The stylus dropped scratchily on to the record and Dolly began to say something, but Betty chose that moment to sneeze (in an unnecessarily dramatic way, in Juliet's opinion). Oh, Lord, Juliet thought, her fingers poised above the Imperial's solid keys. Here we go again.

She decided to eat the Ryvita after all.

'Our neighbours' was what Cyril called the informants, and soon the name stuck; even Perry had been heard to employ the term. It was a handy shorthand for the cavalcade of people who had been coming for nearly a month now to the Dolphin Square flat with their talk of potential sympathizers, of RAF camps being built, of the location of Army recruitment centres – not to mention the end-less reports on the low morale and general unwillingness to commit to war amongst the populace. A fountain of bitterness tapped by Godfrey Toby.

Chatter and gossip, a lot of it, yet somehow more alarming because of that. The willingness of seemingly ordinary people to bring any scrap of information if they thought it would help the enemy's cause. The main characters in this cast of perfidy were Dolly, Betty, Victor, Walter, Trude and Edith. Each reported on a myriad others, filaments in an evangelistic web of treachery that stretched across the country.

There was a timetable, drawn up by Godfrey himself, that charted all the prospective to-ings and fro-ings of the neighbours. It was mostly for Cyril's benefit, so he knew when to pitch up in Dolphin Square, but it helped all of them to keep out of the way at the designated times. 'We don't want them to get to know our faces,' Perry said. 'We must remain anonymous. It is *we* who are the neighbours, as far as they are concerned.'

Godfrey's informants were given expenses for transport and phone calls and treated to meals and drinks by him. Trude, however, was paid. She was a rather peevish and controlling Norwegian, naturalized here for many years now, and was particularly busy recruiting and truffling out Nazi sympathizers. She seemed to have contacts all over Britain and thought nothing of going to Dover or Manchester or Liverpool to sound out potential allies to their cause. Her mother had been half-German and Trude had spent many holidays in Bavaria. She had worked at Siemens, which was where Godfrey had first met her ('Some kind of social club,' Perry said), and in many ways she was the originator of the entire Godfrey operation. Like the first person to be a victim of the Black Death, Juliet thought. 'Or Eve,' Perry said, 'and original sin.'

'A bit unfair on Eve, sir.'

'The blame generally has to fall somewhere, Miss Armstrong. Women and the Jews tend to be first in line, unfortunately.'

Edith was in her fifties and worked in a dress shop in Brighton, patrolling the English Channel during her daily clifftop walks. Walter was a naturalized German who worked in the offices of the Great Western Railway and knew a great deal about tracks and trains and timetables. Victor was a machinist in an aircraft factory. Perry worried about these last two the most, as they had access to blueprints 'and so on' – 'Sabotage is one of our greatest fears,' he said.

Betty and Dolly, old comrades from the British Union of Fascists, behaved like mother hens around Godfrey, clucking about the state of his health and the strain of the incessant demands made on him by the Third Reich. Betty was in her thirties, married to a man called Grieve whom she appeared to dislike with a passion. Dolly, at forty-five, was an unwilling spinster who worked in a large laundry in Peckham, dealing with military uniforms. She believed that from the arrival and departure of these uniforms she was able to deduce the deployment of troops across the south-east of England. ('The woman's a fool,' Perry said.)

Dolly often brought her dog to these meetings, a yappy thing that had the knack of barking at crucial moments, making the inform-ants' conversations even more inaudible. The dog was called Dib. Betty, Dolly and Dib, like a music-hall act, Juliet thought. A par-ticularly poor one.

Juliet knew them by their voices, not their faces. Trude's sing-song Scandinavian, Victor's thick Geordie lilt, Betty's Essex-housewife whine. Godfrey was always careful to introduce each person as they made their entrance into the flat, a master of ceremonies announ-cing his acts on stage. 'Hello, Dolly – how are you tonight?' or 'Ah, here's Victor.' But he didn't really need to as Juliet soon learnt to recognize them.

'You have a good ear,' Perry complimented her.

'I have two, sir.' I am too frivolous for him, Juliet thought. It put more of a responsibility on her than him. Being flippant was harder work than being earnest. Perhaps Perry was beginning to get the true measure of her character and was finding her wanting.

He had been rather irritable recently, constantly in and out of Dolphin Square, off to Whitehall, St James's, the Scrubs. He some-times took Juliet with him, introducing her as his 'right-hand woman' (although he was left-handed, she noted). She was also his 'Girl Friday' and occasionally his 'indispensable aide-de-camp, Miss

Armstrong'. He seemed to regard her as a rather precocious child (or a particularly clever dog), although more often than not she was just a girl, and an invisible one at that.

He had invited her to accompany him to a drinks party at the Admiralty. 'Colleagues,' he said, 'but women will be there, wives mostly.' It proved to be quite a sedate affair and Juliet had the impression that she was being exhibited, like an accessory, or perhaps a curiosity. 'You're a sly old dog,' she heard a man murmur in Perry's ear. 'You have a bit of fluff, after all, Gibbons. Who would have thought it?'

Perry seemed intent on her learning who everyone was. 'That's Alleyne over there by the window.'

'Alleyne?' she queried. She had heard the name. He had the air of a man who knew he was attractive.

'Oliver Alleyne,' Perry said. 'He's one of us. He's rather ambitious.' He said this last regretfully – Perry was not someone who lauded ambition. Or admired good looks. 'His wife's on the stage.' He made it sound disreputable. He's old-fashioned, Juliet thought. Tremendously upright. She would, undoubtedly, fail to come up to his standards. 'And that's Liddell, of course,' he continued. 'Huddled with your friend Merton.'

'Hardly *my* friend,' Juliet protested. 'More like my Spanish Inquisitor.' (*You have to choose. There's a gun to your head.*) Miles Merton was staring at her in an unnerving manner, but didn't acknowledge her and she turned away from his gaze.

'A somewhat Machiavellian character,' Perry murmured. 'I wouldn't trust him, if I were you.'

'I am too lowly for him to notice.'

'The lowlier the better for Merton.'

When she looked again, Merton had disappeared.

'That's Hore-Belisha over there,' Perry continued, 'talking to Hankey – the Minister without Portfolio.' ('Hanky-panky,' Hartley referred to him as. Of course. Hartley was irredeemably juvenile.) What a silly title, Juliet thought, as if he's left his portfolio on the Tube somewhere. She supposed these men didn't travel by Tube, they all had cars and drivers, organized by Hartley's poor overworked secretary – Hartley was in charge of Transport, based on his passion for cars rather than any proficiency in the role.

'And that's Halifax, of course, Secretary of State for Foreign Affairs,' Perry continued (rather relentlessly), 'and over by the door . . . that's . . .' He was an educator, Juliet thought (and she was currently his pupil). That was his character. It seemed a waste of an attractive man.

Or a cultivator, perhaps, and she was his field, waiting to be ploughed and sown. A rather risqué sort of thought that made her blush. He was immensely grown up (thirty-eight) and necessarily more sophisticated than the untried airmen and soldiers who were her usual beaux. Juliet was waiting to be seduced by him. By anyone really, but preferably him. It was turning into a rather long wait.

'Are you all right, Miss Armstrong? You look a little flushed.'

'It's quite hot in here, sir.'

'So many of those men have no morals,' he told her as they were retrieving their coats at the end of the night. 'They're with their wives and yet half of them will have a mistress tucked away somewhere.' Was that the function she was fulfilling for him, Juliet wondered? 'Tucked away' in Dolphin Square as she was. But which was it – wife or mistress?

Certainly quite a lot of people had drawn the conclusion that because of their seclusion in Nelson House there must be something 'going on' between them, whereas the truth was that he was bewilderingly reticent with her. He was the perfect gentleman and, unlike the salesmen in the Fitzrovia hotel, there were no attempts at fumbling – in fact they often performed an awkward little dance around their small office to avoid touching at all, as if Juliet were a desk or a chair, not a girl in her prime. It seemed that she had acquired all the drawbacks of being a mistress and none of the advantages – like sex. (She was becoming bolder with the word, if not the act.) For Perry, it seemed to be the other way round – he had all the advantages of having a mistress and none of the drawbacks. Like sex.

As well as transcribing his conversations with the 'neighbours', Juliet also typed up Godfrey's own records of the meetings, which were rather masterly precis. Sometimes he referred to her transcripts to 'jog his memory', although Godfrey seemed to have a remarkably good memory, keeping constant track of his informants' comings and goings. ('And how is that naval engineer you met, Betty – Hodges, wasn't it?' or 'How is your wife's mother, Walter, Mrs Popper?')

And, of course, Juliet was at Perry's beck and call for a miscellany of his own dictation and note-taking. She also spent many a dreary hour typing up 'spy fever' reports from agents all around the country, who had interviewed people anxious to let the government know that they thought they had seen a contingent of Hitler Youth cycling across the South Downs, or that their next-door neighbour – a 'Germanic-looking woman' – was hanging out her nappies on the line in a way that 'suggested semaphore', as well as all the usual complaints about people who owned German Shepherds.

Juliet also typed up Perry's diary – nothing personal, just a record of meetings and events. Did he keep a personal diary? And if so, what would he write in it? (*Miss Armstrong becomes more attractive to me every day, but I must resist the temptation!*)

He had been at a succession of meetings in Whitehall recently (without her), none of which seemed to have gone his way, and now, as well as Godfrey's transcripts, she was spending her time typing an endless series of memos and letters and diary entries documenting his frustration – *Why does AC still not see that ALL alien residents MUST be interned?! We must work on the basis of guilty until proved innocent.* (Rather harsh, Juliet thought, thinking of the staff in Moretti's.) *There is an old-fashioned liberalism which seems to proliferate within the Cabinet – this will become lethal! . . . The DG is anxious that COMPLETE censorship be imposed on Eire . . . met with Rothschild at the Athenaeum . . . GD was believed to be recruited by the Abwehr in '38 yet he is still in place! . . . leakages all over the place . . . bureaucratic ineptitude . . . the prostitute LK is known to be having an affair with Wilson in the Foreign Office and yet . . . complacency . . . muddle-headedness . . .* And so on. And on.

And on.

And on.

Godfrey's conversations next door – for the most part numbingly mundane – were really quite a relief.

-20-

GODFREY. And that man - BENSON (HENSON?)
BETTY. He said he doesn't like MOSLEY very much, he
   seemed to be talking mostly from a B.U. angle
   (four words inaudible)
GODFREY. Yes, I see.

(Biscuit interval.)

GODFREY leaves the room. Some inaudible whispering
between BETTY and TRUDE. GODFREY returns.

RECORD 13

BETTY. Apparently Chelmsford has become a hot-bed
   of Communism. MRS HENDRY (HENRY?) -
GODFREY. The Scots woman?

BETTY. Yes, works in a pub there, the Red Lion, or
   the Three Lions, and says that the man who owns
   it - BROWN, I think - says he was rooked for
   whisky at £2.15s.6d a bottle from the Premier
   Guaranteed Trust - a Jewish company.

Conversation only partly heard due to their whispering. Something about people who were strongly Jewish,
something about the British Israel Foundation.

BETTY. And it's difficult to retaliate when people
   say it was the Germans who started it, because
   then you'll just draw attention to yourself.
TRUDE. I say - quite casually - 'I do wish it hadn't
   been us that started the war.' That usually stops
   them in their tracks.
GODFREY. Have any of the gun positions been altered
   along the front at Broadstairs? (Apparently TRUDE
   has recently visited the coast.)
TRUDE. No. They're manned by crews of three or maybe
   five. (four or five words inaudible) Troops from
   the Staffords, I think.
GODFREY. Yes, yes, I see.

The informants rambled on tirelessly with their fragmentary
thoughts and ideas and Godfrey absorbed it all like a patient
sponge. They incriminated themselves at every turn, while he said
almost nothing. He had a wonderful way of drawing them out
with his placid responses (Hm? and Yes, yes and I see), not so much
an agent provocateur as an agent passif, if such a thing could be
said to exist. ('Sometimes,' Perry said, 'saying nothing can be your
strongest weapon.') Juliet, and perhaps Juliet alone, had begun
to sense Godfrey's impatience. She had learnt to read between the
lines. But wasn't that where the most important things were said?

-21-

BETTY. I don't know when I can come. Tuesday or
    Friday.
GODFREY. You can telephone here.
TRUDE. Can you bring the invisible ink? Would you
    mind?
BETTY. Yes, I meant to bring the other bottle back.

GODFREY said it was rather scarce and then gave DOLLY
some instructions how to use the ink.
Some inaudible conversation due to paper rustling.

(Cigarettes)

GODFREY. Will I see you next week?
TRUDE. Not for two weeks. I'm going to Bristol. I'll
    call in on that farmer (three words inaudible).
    He had a lot to say about Kitzbuhl (??)

(Laughter all together)

There was some discussion about the different routes
home they were going to take. Godfrey said it was a
good idea to vary the routes.

GODFREY. Thank you for a very fruitful evening.

They all leave together.

End of RECORD 21. <u>19.45</u>

Invisible ink, Juliet snorted to herself. Perry and Godfrey, together
with MI5's department of tricks, were always coming up with little
gifts and gimmicks to keep the neighbours fooled. The invisible
ink ('Hard to get, use sparingly,' Godfrey advised them), or rice
paper that could be eaten ('If necessary,' he said solemnly). Stamps
and envelopes, too, for all their endless communications with

other people. Money for telephone calls. Godfrey's flat had a telephone – VICtoria 3011 – so they could contact him when he was there. Apparently GPO engineers had spent some time trying to devise a remote answering machine before giving it up as a thankless task.

Godfrey's informants were suitably impressed by how much value the Third Reich placed on them. They were hopelessly gullible. 'We believe what we want to believe,' Perry said.

Occasionally someone from MI5 would phone Juliet and ask her to take a message for Godfrey. She would write it down and then nip next door and leave it on the little hall table for him.

'While you're in there, Miss Armstrong,' Perry said, 'perhaps you could whisk around with a duster, empty ashtrays and so on. Better you do it than have some charwoman snooping around.'

By the time she had formulated a response to this (*But surely, sir, I wasn't recruited by MI5 to whisk dusters around?*) he was out of the door. A moment later he was back and, giving her the encouragement of his really rather lovely smile, said, 'There's a carpet sweeper somewhere, I believe.'

Cyril arrived, eager as ever. 'Evening, miss.'

'Evening, Cyril.'

'Do you fancy a cuppa, miss?'

'No, thanks, I'm almost finished.'

'Well, I'll get on then, the equipment needs a bit of tinkering with.' The equipment was sacred to Cyril, he tended it constantly. He was a listener, too, an amateur radio enthusiast who had been 'volunteered' by MI18 to spend his spare time intercepting German broadcasts, scanning shortwave bands and transcribing Morse code. Juliet wondered when he ever got time to sleep.

Juliet hammered her way to the end of the final record. She rubbed her temples – she had been getting more headaches than usual because she had to concentrate so hard to understand what the informants were saying. Quite a bit of it was guesswork. Sometimes she wondered if she wasn't just making things up, filling in the gaps to make sense of it. Not that anyone would notice. And if she didn't, she would look like an idiot and Perry might go looking for another girl – although whoever he found would need to have the hearing of a bat.

Juliet had been off for a couple of days with a cold and another girl – Stella Chalmers – had been drafted in to take her place. 'I don't know why Miss Chalmers bothered,' Perry said, showing Juliet the transcriptions, which were as full of holes as a fishing-net. 'It's hardly worth you going to the bother of filing this nonsense. Apparently Cyril found her weeping over the typewriter.'

'It is rather frustrating work, sir,' Juliet said, secretly pleased with how inadequate poor Stella had been. She obviously hadn't learnt how to fill in the gaps.

'It's work that needs a good ear,' Perry said. 'Or two,' he amended and laughed self-consciously – in an attempt to please her, she supposed. 'I hope your cold is better. You were missed.' (Oh, be still, my beating heart, she thought.) 'No one makes as good a pot of tea as you do, Miss Armstrong.'

Juliet rolled the last sheet of paper and the carbons out of the Imperial. Her fingers, as usual, were smudged with purple from the carbon. She put the dustcover on the typewriter and placed the top copy of the transcription on Perry's desk for him to read later. One carbon was filed and another was placed in an out-tray for a messenger boy to pick up eventually and take somewhere else. Juliet imagined that it lingered unread in yet another filing cabinet, in a Ministry somewhere, or back at the Scrubs. There was going to be an awful lot of paper left at the end of the war.

Juliet was surprised to find that she missed the Scrubs, even the worst bits – the debs, the awful metal staircases, even the horrible lavatories inspired a kind of nostalgia. She still saw Clarissa all the time though, pulled into her hectic social orbit three or four evenings a week – in fact she was meeting her tonight.

'Mr Gibbons here?' Cyril asked.

'No, I haven't seen him since first thing,' she said, shrugging her coat on.

She had no idea where Perry was. She saw much less of him than she had originally envisaged. Sometimes when she came into work in the mornings the flat didn't seem to have been occupied all night and she presumed he had stayed at his 'other place' in Petty France. Although it wasn't easy to tell as Perry had the frugal presence of an ascetic, strangely at odds with both his exemplary taste in restaurants (l'Escargot, l'Etoile, the Café Royal) and his rather flashy style. The Oxford bags, the rakish fedora, the bow-tie all seemed to indicate a different Perry.

She was certainly finding him quite mercurial. There was the charm – for he really could be extraordinarily charming – and then the darker side when he seemed moody, almost fierce. A man of contradictions. Or thesis and antithesis. She had read Hegel for the Oxbridge entrance she had never taken. Perhaps there was a synthesis to be had, a Perry who was on an even keel every day, helped by the devoted girl who was his helpmeet. (*I would be nothing without you, Miss Armstrong.*)

On leaving the flat, Juliet came across Godfrey Toby standing indecisively in the corridor. The key to 'his' flat was in his hand but he was gazing absently at the front door as if lost in thought.

'Good evening, Mr Toby.'

'Ah, Miss Armstrong. Good evening.' He tipped his hat and with a faint smile said, 'I'm early. You and I seem destined to be ships that always pass in the night.'

'Or the couple in the weather house.'

'Weather house?' he puzzled pleasantly.

'You know, the woman comes out when it's sunny, the man when it rains. German, usually,' she added, feeling suddenly and rather ridiculously unpatriotic to have mentioned it.

'Yes.'

'I meant – we're hardly ever in the same place at the same time, as if . . . as if . . .' She was twisting herself into knots trying to explain something she didn't understand. 'As if it were impossible for us both to exist at the same time.'

'A transgression of the natural laws.'

'Yes. Exactly!'

'And yet patently we can both exist at the same time as we are both standing here together, Miss Armstrong.' After a rather awkward pause he said, 'It is interesting, don't you think, that the man represents the rain while the woman is the sunshine? Are you leaving? Shall I walk you to the lift?'

'That's really not necessary, Mr Toby.' Too late – he was already steering her down the corridor.

Was there a Mrs Toby at home in Finchley, Juliet wondered? Or a Mrs Hazeldine, she supposed, for it seemed unlikely that an English housewife would be part of MI5's charade. She was not supposed to know his real name but Clarissa had investigated the esoteric depths of the Registry for her.

He seemed the type of man who grew potatoes and roses and kept a neatly trimmed lawn. The type who sat by the wireless in the evening, reading his newspaper, and attended church on a Sunday. What Godfrey Toby did not seem, even in Juliet's wildest imagination, was the type to have been working for years as a spy.

He pressed the button to summon the lift. 'Do you have plans for this evening, Miss Armstrong?'

'I'm going to the Royal Opera House. We always go on a Thursday.'

'Ah, some culture to light the way in these dark days. I am fond of a little Verdi myself.'

'Nothing so highbrow as Verdi, I'm afraid, Mr Toby. The Royal Opera House is a Mecca ballroom now. I'm going dancing with a friend.'

Godfrey removed his tortoiseshell spectacles and began polishing them with a handkerchief that he pulled with a conjuror's flourish from his coat pocket.

'You are young,' he said, smiling wanly at her. 'You will not feel it as much. As you grow older – I am fifty – you begin to despair of the wicked foolishness of the world. It is a bottomless pit, I fear.'

Juliet wasn't sure what this had to do with dancing or Verdi – neither struck her as particularly wicked. She supposed it must be quite a strain for Godfrey to sit for hours on end with the 'neighbours', pretending to be something he was not.

'But you seem to get on quite well with them,' she ventured. 'The informants.'

'Ah, yes. Of course.' He gave a little chuckle. 'I sometimes forget that you hear everything.'

'Well, not everything, unfortunately,' Juliet said, thinking of the endless 'inaudible' gaps that peppered the transcriptions.

'If you met them without knowing,' Godfrey said, 'you would think they were quite ordinary people. They *are* ordinary people, but very wrong-headed, unfortunately.'

Juliet felt rather ashamed, as her mind had been on what dress to wear this evening rather than bottomless pits of evil. The war still seemed like a matter of inconvenience rather than a threat. The Finns had just capitulated to the Soviets, and Hitler and Mussolini had recently met at the Brenner Pass to discuss their 'friendship', but real war, the one where you might be killed, still seemed a long way away. Juliet was currently more concerned with the introduction of meat rationing.

'Yes, my wife and I shall miss our Sunday roast,' Godfrey said. So there *was* a Mrs Toby. (Or he said there was one, which was different. *Never take anything at face value*, Perry had told her.) 'Where *is* that lift?' (Yes, where is it, she wondered? She was going to be late.) Godfrey banged his silver-topped cane on the floor as if that would help to bring the lift. Juliet had seen a stage magician do the same thing when making something appear from behind a curtain. (Or had it been a rabbit in a hat? And perhaps it had been disappearing, not appearing.) 'They'll be here soon,' Godfrey said. He gave a little chuckle. 'The neighbours, as you call them.'

The small lift announced its imminence with a cheerful little *ding*. 'Ah, here comes your *deus ex machina*, Miss Armstrong.'

The lift doors opened, revealing a woman and a dog. The woman looked alarmed at the sight of Juliet and the dog lifted its lip in a rather half-hearted snarl. The woman's eyes roamed nervously from Juliet to Godfrey, as if trying to work out what they were doing in each other's company. The dog started to bark, a sound that Juliet knew only too well. Dib, she thought. Dib and Dolly. It was the first time that Juliet had put a face to any of them, including Dib, who, it turned out, was a poodle, rather moth-eaten.

Dolly glared distrustfully at Juliet. She gave off a sour, dissatisfied aura, but Godfrey said, 'Dolly!' as if she were a long-awaited guest at a party. 'You're early, come along. I was just saying to this young lady that this lift has a mind of its own.' (He was good, Juliet thought.) Dolly stepped out of the lift, giving Juliet a dirty look. Juliet replaced her in the lift. 'Miss . . . ?' Godfrey said, tipping his hat again.

'Armstrong,' Juliet supplied helpfully.

'Miss Armstrong. Have a pleasant evening.'

Before the lift doors closed she heard Dolly say suspiciously to Godfrey, 'Who was that?' and Godfrey's offhand reply, 'Oh, just one of the neighbours. No one to worry about.'

Looking At Otters

J.A.

RECORD 1.

17.20

GODFREY, EDITH and DOLLY. Some chat about the weather and EDITH'S health.

DOLLY. Yes, he was with a young lady. (laughter)
EDITH. A young lady? That's (inaudible, due to Dib)
GODFREY. Yes, yes.
DOLLY. Very friendly! (laughter from all) I thought -
    a new friend.
EDITH. He likes young ladies.
GODFREY. One of the neighbours.
EDITH. Do you know them then?
GODFREY. Ships that pass in the night.
DOLLY. They've no idea?
GODFREY. No idea?
DOLLY. What we're up to!

Giggles.

Some chat about finding some 'nice blond SS men' for
DOLLY and EDITH 'after the invasion'.

GODFREY. Will you have another cigarette?
DOLLY. Don't mind if I do.
GODFREY. I've got to see someone at a quarter past
    6. I'm wondering the best way to arrange things.
    Perhaps -

Behind her, Peregrine Gibbons cleared his throat as if about to make an announcement, but really he was just trying not to startle her with his entry into the room. He had a way of moving very quietly, prowling almost. Juliet supposed he had learnt that from his nature studies. She imagined him creeping up on some poor unsuspecting hedgehog and giving it the fright of its life.

He read over her shoulder; he was very close, she could hear him breathing. 'Who is this "young lady" they're talking about, do you suppose?' he asked.

'Me, sir! I encountered Dolly coming out of the lift yesterday evening. Godfrey – Mr Toby – pretended not to know me. He was very good.'

'Excellent.' He cleared his throat again. 'Sorry to interrupt, Miss Armstrong.'

'That's all right, sir. Did you want something?'

'Today is Friday, Miss Armstrong.'

'All day, sir.'

'And tomorrow is Saturday.'

'It is,' she agreed. Was he going to name all the days of the week, she wondered?

'I was . . . thinking.'

'Sir?'

'Would you like to come on a little expedition with me?'

'An expedition, sir?' The word made her think of Scott and

Shackleton, but it seemed unlikely that he was planning on taking her to the South Pole.

'Yes. I've been thinking about you.'

'Me?' She felt herself growing rather hot.

'About how perhaps your duties here might be imposing a limit on your talents.'

What did that mean? Sometimes he had such a roundabout manner of speaking that his intentions got lost along the way.

'I thought perhaps we should become better acquainted.'

To assess her suitability for practising the dark arts of counter-espionage? An induction? Or – blimey – a seduction?

A car and a driver had been requisitioned (from Hartley, presumably) for the 'expedition', for which Juliet had to rise from her bed several hours earlier than she had planned. She yawned her way through the first hour of the journey, and then for the second hour she could think of nothing but the breakfast she hadn't eaten.

A mist had only just begun to clear as they drove past Windsor, the round tower of the castle rising white and ghostly from the brume. 'This England,' Perry said. Juliet thought he was about to quote Shakespeare (*this sceptr'd isle*), but instead he said, '*This* England' (as if there were another one somewhere). 'Or perhaps I should say, *that* England.' He nodded in the direction of Windsor in the distance. 'Is it worth fighting for, do you think?'

She wasn't sure if he was asking the question of her or himself, but she said, 'Yes.' What other answer was there, really?

They drove to the Hambledon Valley, where they swapped the comforting warmth of the car's interior for a chilly riverbank. It's still only April, for heaven's sake, she thought, but Perry seemed insensible to weather, although his layers of tweed must be keeping him warmer than her own ensemble – a rather light coat, thin sweater and her best skirt. Not to mention her good pair of stockings and smart shoes, for she had been expecting to be viewing the landscape from the windows of the car, not to find herself standing in the middle of it. 'Countryside' was more of a concept for Juliet than a reality.

'Otters,' he whispered, spreading a tarpaulin sheet on the riverbank.

'Sir?' Had he said *otters*? Not seduction then.

Time rolled by, very slowly. Very damply. Very coldly. Juliet wondered if waiting for the otters was perhaps part of her training in some way – surveillance, perhaps. Or patience. She did need training in patience, she knew that. And it did feel strangely like an undercover mission as they sat, breathlessly still, on the riverbank, waiting for a little family of otters to show themselves.

He glanced at her when the first otter appeared and flashed her a delighted smile. He really did have a nice smile, his whole face changed, and he became a man who looked capable of happiness – which was not the impression he normally gave. The otters, she realized, were an offering to her in some way.

'Neither fish nor flesh,' she murmured, and then felt embarrassed because she recalled there was something bawdy about Falstaff's description of an otter, although she wasn't quite sure what. The quotation, vulgar or otherwise, was wasted on Perry, who said, 'Well, certainly not a fish. The European otter – *Lutra lutra* – is from the family *Mustelidae*, which includes badgers and weasels.'

'Of course,' she said.

Juliet had never seen otters before and the kits (and she knew that was the term for them because he told her) were charming – sleek and playful. But really they were just *otters*, and if he was going to give her anything she would rather it was the picnic that she had expected him to bring. She had to hide her disappointment when she caught a glance of the empty boot of the car. Perhaps they would have a pub lunch later – she imagined a half of shandy and a beef and ale pie, and the idea lifted her spirits.

The otters, however, so slow to make an appearance, now seemed intent on putting on an all-day show, and Juliet was relieved when her fit of coughing startled them and they slipped under the water and disappeared. Perry frowned, but she wasn't sure if he was disappointed in her or the otters.

'Sorry, sir,' she said. 'I get hay fever.' She didn't; she was, regrettably, in excellent health. It must be lunchtime by now, surely? But no, instead they returned to the car and Perry said, 'Drive in the direction of Christmas Common,' and rather than stopping at the wayside inn of her imagination they parked on a track next to a field. Her heart sank when he said to the driver, 'We're going for a ramble, we'll be a while.'

'Righty-ho,' the driver said, taking out a greaseproof packet of sandwiches from his pocket. 'I'll have my lunch then.'

'Come on, then, Miss Armstrong,' Perry said to her. 'Follow me.'

He had binoculars with him and she wondered if he was looking for anything in particular.

'Kites,' he said. 'They're long gone from this part of the world and I don't suppose we'll see them again, but you can live in hope.' Kites? Did he mean birds? First kits, now kites. Her mind ran on to Kit Kats, a thought that made her immeasurably sad as she knew there were going to be none.

He cupped his ear and said, 'Can you hear that woodpecker?'

'That' (annoying) 'knocking sound?'

Juliet knew nothing about birds. She could manage the common ones – pigeons, sparrows, and so on – but her ornithology didn't extend beyond the streets of London. She was a complete philistine where wildlife was concerned. Perry, on the other hand, was a nature enthusiast. He didn't find kites, but he spotted and named an awful lot of other birds. An awful lot.

'You need a good memory in our line of work,' he said. But she wasn't going to be identifying birds, was she? (*Was* she?) 'Look,' he whispered, crouching and pulling her down with him. 'Hares – boxing. It's the female who throws the punches. Wonderful!'

Any romantic notions she may have been fostering had been entirely numbed by cold and hunger. He was currently expounding on the regurgitating habits of owls. 'Fur and bone of voles and mice,' he said, and she thought of the witches in *Macbeth* and she laughed and responded with, 'Eye of newt and toe of frog.'

'Well, yes,' he said, perplexed by the allusion. 'Frogs – and rats – are occasionally found in their pellets. Shrews are common. You can identify the different species by their jawbones.' He had no Shakespeare, she realized.

He strode ahead of her and she had to go almost at a trot to keep up with him, trailing on his heels like a dutiful retriever. A nippy breeze had got up now and started to carry away his words and she missed a lot of information about the breeding habits of roe deer and the architecture of rabbit warrens. She thought longingly of the driver's neat white sandwich triangles.

The brooding landscape they were currently traversing, the lowering sky above their heads and the rugged terrain beneath their feet, were all conspiring to make her feel like an unfortunate Brontë sister, traipsing endlessly across the moors after unobtainable fulfilment. Perry himself was not entirely without Heathcliffian qualities – the absence of levity, the ruthless disregard for a girl's comfort, the way he had of scrutinizing you as if you were a puzzle to be solved. *Would* he solve her? Perhaps she wasn't complicated enough for him. (On the other hand, perhaps she was too complicated.)

He turned suddenly on his heel and she almost bumped into him. 'Are you all right, Miss Armstrong? How's your hay fever?'

'Gone, sir, thank you.'

'Good!'

And so they carried on, tramping across fields, over streams, up hills that were still slippery with the morning's rain. Her shoes were being slowly ruined with every step (and they were going to have to do all this in reverse on the way back!).

Thankfully, he finally came to a halt and said, 'Shall we have a rest?' He laid the tarpaulin sheet down again in the inadequate shelter of a bare hawthorn hedge. She only knew it was hawthorn because he told her so. Juliet shivered. It really wasn't the weather for this kind of thing.

'Do you smoke?' he asked, taking out a heavy lighter from somewhere in his tweeds.

'Yes, sir.'

'I don't, I'm afraid,' he said, and so she had to fumble in her handbag for her own pack. He lit her cigarette after several attempts as the wind was intent on extinguishing the little flame. No handy flask of tea, of course, and she was just bemoaning its absence to herself when he knelt down next to her and placed his hand on her thigh and began, rather absent-mindedly, to stroke the fabric of her coat as if it were an animal skin (and she was the animal).

Oh, my giddy aunt, Juliet thought, was this – finally – what she thought it was? Was there protocol for this? Was it another test? She felt that some kind of protest was possibly required (*It's the female who throws the punches. Wonderful!*) and said, 'Sir? Mr Gibbons?'

'Call me Perry, do, please.'

For a moment she thought he was going to open her coat. To unwrap her like a gift. (I *am* a gift, she thought), but he contented himself with fiddling with one of the buttons. He took his fedora off

71

and placed it on the ground next to them. The wind was bound to blow it away, didn't he realize that?

He took her cigarette from her and stubbed it out on the ground and Juliet thought, Oh, here we go. An induction *and* a seduction.

'I studied to be a priest, you know,' he said. The balance tilted away from seduction. There certainly was a kind of Jesuitical cast to him; she could imagine him sombre in a black cassock. 'Unfortunately I lost my faith,' he said, and added ruefully, 'Not so much lost as misplaced.'

Were they going to discuss theology? He leant in closer as if to inspect her and she caught his tweedy tobacco scent. The balance tipped towards seduction again. He frowned at her. The balance wavered uncertainly.

'Are you . . . intact, Miss Armstrong?'

'Intact?' She had to think for a moment what he meant by that. (She thought of the Latin. *Untouched*.) 'Oh,' she said eventually. The balance lurched towards seduction. 'Yes, sir.' She blushed all over again, dreadfully hot suddenly, despite the weather. It wasn't a question you asked if you weren't intending to do something about it, was it? Although in her imagination this act had involved dim lighting, satin sheets, perhaps flutes of champagne and a discreet veil drawn over the crude mechanics of the act, mainly because she still had little idea of what they were.

Also, on a practical level she had imagined a bed, not a hillocky field beneath a thundery sky that was the colour of putty. An uncomfortable tussock was sticking into her left buttock. She could see dark clouds moving in from the west and thought, We're going to get rained on. Out of the corner of her eye she saw his hat blow away. 'Oh,' Juliet said again.

He leant closer. Very close. He did not look as attractive from this distance, in fact he looked not a little unlike an otter. She closed her eyes.

Nothing happened, so she opened them again and found him gazing steadily at her. She remembered he had learnt mesmerism when he was younger and she thought, Good Lord – was he hypnotizing her? She felt quite woozy all of a sudden, although she supposed she was now officially starving so it was no wonder. And then he was on his feet, pointing at the sky and saying, 'Look, a sparrowhawk!'

Was that it then?

Juliet struggled to her feet and craned her neck obediently. The first fat wet drops of rain fell on her face. 'It's raining, sir,' she said to him. He was heedless, lost in tracing the bird with his binoculars. After a while he handed them to her and she put them to her eyes, but she could see nothing but the dismal sky.

'Did you see it?' he asked when she lowered the binoculars.

'Yes,' she said. 'Wonderful.'

'It doesn't know there's a war on,' he said. The bird seemed to have brought on a fit of melancholy.

'No, I don't suppose it does, sir.'

'Perry,' he reminded her.

They spent the next twenty minutes looking for his hat before giving up and returning to the car.

The driver got out of the car when he saw them approaching. Juliet could see him smirking at Perry's hatless head and the rather mucky knees of his trousers where the tarpaulin had failed to protect him.

'Good walk, sir?' the driver asked.

'Excellent,' Perry said. 'We saw a sparrowhawk.'

'Did you enjoy yourself today, Miss Armstrong?'

'Yes,' she said. 'It was very nice. Thank you.' To be honest, not one jot, she thought.

She sat in the back of the car on the way home while Perry sat up at the front with the driver.

'Miss Armstrong – all right in the back there?'

'Yes, sir. Perry.'

'Why don't you take a nap?'

So she did, while Perry and the driver talked about Association Football, on which subject they both appeared to be experts, although only the driver had ever kicked a round ball.

When they arrived back in London he took her to the Bon Viveur in Shepherd Market for dinner and she forgave him for the day-long famine he had subjected her to. She had to change first, of course, her shoes and coat were caked in mud and her stockings laddered beyond repair. Even a good dinner was hard-pressed to make up for that.

It was a very good dinner, though. 'Eat up,' he said. 'You're probably still growing. You look as though you need fattening up.' (Like a veal calf?) There was chicken in a white sauce and some kind of marmalade pudding, and they drank 'an excellent Pouilly' that the sommelier said he'd been saving for Perry. 'Becoming rather scarce now, sir,' he murmured.

She had never had an 'excellent' wine before, never been to dinner with a man, never been to an expensive restaurant, one with linen napkins and little red-shaded lamps on the table and waiters who called her 'madam'.

Perry raised his glass and, smiling, said, 'To victory.' She had passed the test, apparently, although she couldn't quite quash the suspicion that she had been 'put under'. What if he had planted a suggestion in her mind? She had seen hypnotists on stage and worried that she would suddenly start quacking like a duck in the canteen or think she was a cat when she was on the Tube. (Or worse.)

He unexpectedly reached for her hand across the table and, holding it a little too firmly for comfort, he gazed intently into her eyes and said, 'We understand each other, don't we, Miss Armstrong?'

'Yes,' she said, although she didn't understand him in the slightest. She had been plucked. More pigeon perhaps than rose.

Have You Met a Spy?

<u>RECORD 10 (contd.)</u>

(Sound of a map being unfolded.)

GODFREY. What are the landmarks like?
WALTER. A gas works.

Some conversation, mostly inaudible due to the map,
about a gasometer. WALTER says something about 'a
small road' or load(?)

(Two minutes lost through technical hitch. Record
very indistinct afterwards.)

WALTER. It is difficult, you see, here is ... (ab.
    6 words) exactly how to cross (?)
GODFREY. Cross here?
WALTER. The main point is this, you see. But you
    know I expect they will (inaudible)
GODFREY. Yes, yes.
WALTER. But they will (inaudible but the word 'aero-
    drome' heard)
GODFREY. (Sound of the map) Is that the (?) building
    here?
WALTER. What do you want to know?

```
GODFREY. You're going to Hertford? (Or Hatford?)
WALTER. This factory here is near Abbot's Langley.
    Near the river. This is the canal.
GODFREY. I see.
WALTER. Near the railway line. This is a pill box,
    then this barbed wire fence. Then the railway
    cutting. Ammunition or gunpowder, I think. They've
    put up a notice - 'No Smoking within 100 yards',
    you see.
GODFREY. Yes. Have you put a cross against it?
WALTER. Not this one. It's just by Abbot's Langley.
    You can probably (inaudible).

(Drinks. Some social chat.)

GODFREY. How is your wife doing?
WALTER. Why do you ask?
GODFREY. We take an interest in our agents' domes-
    tic affairs.
```

If only Perry would take an interest in my 'domestic affairs', Juliet thought. (*Is there a man in your life, Juliet – may I call you Juliet? I would be honoured to be that man and—*)

'Do you have a minute, Miss Armstrong?'

'Yes, of course, sir.'

'I have been mulling it over,' Perry said, 'and I've come to the conclusion that perhaps you are ready.'

Blimey – for what? Not more otter expeditions, she hoped.

She was to be a spy. At last. Her *nom de guerre* was to be 'Iris Carter-Jenkins'. At least it was devoid of Shakespearian connotations. No more people quoting '*Romeo, Romeo, wherefore art thou Romeo?*' at her.

'I've bumped you up a bit,' Perry said. 'Got you out of Kentish Town, as it were. Iris grew up in Hampstead, father was a consultant at St Thomas's. Orthopaedics – bones and so on.'

'Was?' she queried.

'Dead. Your mother too. I thought that it would be more authentic, easier for you to "play".'

Must she always be an orphan, even in her fictional life?

Her main task, he explained, was to try to infiltrate the Right Club. 'These people are a cut above our Bettys and Dollys,' he said. 'The Right Club is drawn from the Establishment – a membership peppered with the names of the great and the good. Brocklehurst, Redesdale, the Duke of Wellington. There's a book, supposedly – the Red Book – that lists them all. We would very much like to get our hands on it. A lot of its members have been swept up by Defence Regulation 18b, of course, but there are still many left – too many.

'As an extra lure for them, you – in the shape of Iris Carter-Jenkins – work in the War Office, something clerical, you know the kind of thing.' (I do, for my sins, she thought.) 'You have a fiancé in the Navy, a lieutenant, Scottish. "Ian" – he's on HMS *Hood*, a battlecruiser. I've given your mother some rather tenuous connections to the Royal household – you'll be their kind of people, or at least you'll appear to be.'

'So I'm to find out what they're up to?'

'In a nutshell. I already have agents in place, but I particularly want you to get close to a Mrs Scaife, she's near the top of the heap. Iris has been "designed" to appeal to her. We think she'll respond well to her.'

'To me, you mean.'

'No, I mean to her, Iris. Don't let your imagination run away with you, Miss Armstrong. You have an unfortunate tendency to do so. Iris isn't real, don't forget that.' (But how can she not be? Juliet thought.

She's me and I'm real.) 'And don't get the two confused – that way madness lies, believe me.' (Had he ever been mad then, she wondered?) He'd been rather crabby of late, glowering darkly at the bust on his roll-top desk as if Beethoven were personally responsible for the frustrations of war.

He'd torn in to Dolphin Square before lunch this morning, tweeds flying, speaking to her before he'd even got through the door. 'The climate in the Home Office is *staggeringly* lax. I had a meeting this morning at nine a.m. and Rothschild and I waited for nearly *two hours*. The only other person there was the charwoman! Do they *know* there's a war on?' He took on a different character when he was angry – really quite handsome.

She persuaded him to go downstairs with her to the Dolphin Square restaurant for tea and cakes (a 'staggeringly lax' thing to do, probably). 'Sorry, Miss Armstrong,' he said, over a coffee jap, 'I'm a bit of a bear at the moment.' Of course, Perry knew things that other people didn't, it was bound to have an effect. A man of secrets – both his own and other people's.

His list of (somewhat relentless) character notes continued once they were back in the office, the cake not having mollified him to any noticeable degree. 'You will have an official existence – identity card, ration book and so on, all in Iris's name. If anyone were to, say, rifle through your handbag, they would have no idea you were not her. It's best to have a separate handbag when you are Iris, in case anyone is suspicious of you and they take a look. Stick close to the truth, if you can,' he said. 'It means you're less likely to slip up. You are, for example, perfectly free to like shepherd's pie and the colour blue and lily of the valley and Shostakovich – though God knows why.' He laughed good-naturedly.

What a lot he knew about her! She wasn't even sure how. When had she ever talked about shepherd's pie to anyone? Or Shostakovich, for that matter. What other things about her did he know?

'Actually, on reflection,' Perry said, 'I can't imagine Iris liking Shostakovich – a little too outré for her. Stick to the lighter stuff, if you have to talk about music. You know, *The Merry Widow*, something of that ilk. It's in the details, Miss Armstrong – never forget that. You can, essentially, be *you* – the essence of you, as it were – you just can't be Juliet Armstrong who works for MI5. Try not to *act*,' he added, 'try just to *be*. And remember, if you're going to tell a lie, tell a good one.'

He scrutinized her. 'It can be a difficult concept, fabricating a life – the falsehoods and so on. Some people find it challenging to dissemble in this way.'

Not me, Juliet thought. 'I'll give it a go,' she said, adopting a spirited tone. She had already decided that Iris Carter-Jenkins was a gutsy kind of girl. Plucky, even.

'Good girl. It'll be a bit of an adventure for you, I expect. I'm going to start by sending you to the Russian Tea Room in Kensington. A rehearsal, if you like. It's not far from where you live. Do you know it?'

No, she thought. 'Yes,' she said.

'It's a hotbed of Nazi sentiment – the Right Club holds its meetings there. It's run by a woman called Anna Wolkoff, she's the daughter of the Tsar's naval attaché. The family's been marooned here since the Revolution. All these White Russian émigrés see Hitler as a means to reclaiming their country. Utterly deluded, of course, he'll turn on them eventually.'

Juliet was well acquainted with Russian émigrés as there had been a family of very disgruntled ones next door to her and her mother in Kentish Town. They seemed to live on boiled cabbage and pigs' trotters and their savage arguments could be clearly heard but not understood. Her mother had been sympathetic but exasperated.

Juliet felt a spasm of pain as she remembered the little moue of vexation her mother made when she heard the Russians start up, usually just after (or perhaps as a consequence of) their cabbage supper.

'Do you follow, Miss Armstrong? Juliet?' Perry amended, softening his tone. He had admitted yesterday that he perhaps castigated her too much – her unpunctuality, her daydreaming and lack of attention, 'and so on'. 'It is not my job to reform your character,' he said. (That didn't seem to stop him trying.) She was still waiting to be seduced. It had been over a month since the otter expedition. A less resilient girl might have given up hope by now.

'Yes, sorry, I am listening.'

'Drop in and have a cup of tea in the tea room. Show your face. I've set up a little test for you – for you to rehearse your character, as it were.'

'A test?' She supposed that's what war was – one test after another. Sooner or later, she was bound to fail.

He opened a drawer in his desk and took out a gun. So it was not just paper clips and rubber bands in the big roll-top desk. The gun was a little pocket one. 'A Mauser 6.35mm,' he said. For a dizzying moment Juliet wondered if he was going to shoot her, but he said, 'Here. Keep it in your handbag. Only use it as a last resort, of course.'

'A gun?' she said.

'Just a small one.'

It was a tea room, for heaven's sake, not a Wild West saloon. Still, she rather liked the way the little gun nestled so comfortably in her hand.

'I can give you a lesson in how to use it, if you like.'

That sounded as if it might involve more tramping through hostile landscape, but he laughed and said, 'We have a shooting range we use. You will still be doing all this work as well, of course,' he said, indicating the Imperial. 'It may involve longer hours. Don't let me keep you. I have an engagement elsewhere.'

She had been rather hoping he would take her to dinner to discuss her new role more, but apparently he had other plans. He had changed his tie and was sporting one far too flamboyant for Whitehall or one of his (several) clubs. He must have brought it with him from his 'other place' in Petty France, as his Dolphin Square wardrobe (she had thoroughly investigated his room) contained no brash neckwear. She was curious to know what his other mysterious quarters were like. Were they quite different from here? Was *he* quite different when he was there? Like Jekyll and Hyde.

She was half expecting to walk in on a nest of spies, people of doubtful demeanour hiding furtively in dark corners, but it really *was* just a tea room. An open fireplace, quite dingy, and not much room between the oil-clothed tables. There were bentwood chairs and a scattering of quite ordinary people sitting on them, none of whom looked like Fascist sympathizers, but then how could you tell what anyone was in their heart? Really?

She conducted a covert study of the customers. A couple of matronly Englishwomen chatting *sotto voce* and an older woman on her own – wearing a peculiar maroon hat that looked hand-made and sporting thick, lumpy, mushroom-coloured stockings. There was also a man in a worn suit and with a large briefcase at his feet. A salesman, Juliet thought. She knew them.

You may be approached by someone, Perry had said. He already had people 'on the inside'. He – or she – would speak a sentence that contained the question 'Can I tempt you?' and that was how Juliet would recognize them as a fellow agent. She was to reply, 'That's very kind of you. I think I will.' It seemed a bit of a Faustian cypher to Juliet and the whole thing a rather silly charade.

She read the menu. It was blotched with stains and contained mysterious items – *pierogi, blini, stroganoff.* Apparently they also served vodka. It wasn't on the menu, however. 'Just tea, thank you,' she said, rather stiffly, when a waiter came to take her order.

A man came in, not a bad-looking one and lacking a salesman's downtrodden air. He sat at a table near the window, caught her eye and smiled at her. Juliet smiled back. In return the man gave her a conspiratorial little nod. Perry's agent, she thought. She smiled at him again and he grinned and got up from the table. Oh, here we go, Juliet thought. He walked over to her and produced a pack of cigarettes.

'Can I tempt you?' he said.

'That's very kind of you,' Juliet said. 'I think I will.' She took a cigarette and he sat down on the chair next to her and leant in to light it with a match.

'Dennis,' he said.

'Iris Carter-Jenkins,' she responded. It was the first time she had said her code name to anyone other than her reflection in the mirror. She could almost feel Iris inflating, taking on life like a butterfly newly emerged from its chrysalis.

'So, what's a good-looking girl like you doing in a crummy joint like this?' 'Dennis' asked. Was he basing his own character on someone in a film? A gangster, by the sound of it. Juliet had no script beyond the initial temptation. This was all part of the test, wasn't it – to play it by ear?

'Well . . .' she said, 'I live quite close by.'

'Do you now?' He had remained uncomfortably close after lighting her cigarette and she was taken aback when he put his hand on top of hers and said, 'Close by, eh? That's handy. Shall we get out of this dump?' He took his wallet out and said, 'What's the damage?' Juliet was confused. Was he asking her to guess the bill? Or to contribute to it? Out of the corner of her eye she saw the maroon-hatted woman get up from her table and advance towards them.

Arriving at the table, she grabbed Juliet's other hand and said,

'Iris, isn't it? You're a friend of my niece – Marjorie.' She smiled at Dennis and said, 'So sorry, but Iris and I have such a lot to catch up on.'

''Fraid we were just going,' Dennis said, standing up. 'Weren't we, Iris? Coming?' He pulled her to her feet, but the maroon-hatted woman still held on (rather tightly) to her other hand. Ignoring Dennis, she said to Juliet, 'Did you know that Marjorie's living in Harpenden now?'

'Why, no,' Juliet said, deciding to take her cue from the woman (*Don't act, just be*). 'I thought Marjorie was in Berkhamsted.' (Wouldn't this have been a better coded exchange? Less liable to misinterpretation?) The woman and Dennis began to conduct a tug-of-war, with Juliet as the prize in the middle, and she wondered if they would only be satisfied when they had succeeded in pulling her apart. Luckily, Dennis, sensing a tenacious opponent, let go of the trophy and retreated to his table, muttering what may well have been obscenities.

The victoress sat down without being invited and said to Juliet, 'Can I tempt you to the *verushka*?' Juliet was puzzled, it sounded as though she was being offered a verruca. (Luckily, it turned out to be some kind of cake.) 'It's the speciality here,' the woman elucidated, 'and it's really rather good.'

'That's very kind of you,' Juliet said. 'I will.'

'You will, or you think you will?'

Oh, for heaven's sake, Juliet thought, how ridiculous. 'I *think* I will.'

'Good. I'm Mrs Ambrose, by the way,' Mrs Ambrose said.

'You see, Iris dear,' Mrs Scaife said, 'the power behind world revolution is international Jewry. Jews have instigated widespread social upheaval since the Middle Ages, haven't they, Mrs Ambrose?'

'They have,' Mrs Ambrose agreed complacently. Mrs Ambrose's

real name was Florence Eckersley. Perry had been running her for years.

Mrs Scaife bit into a maid of honour. It was a delicate act for a woman of her size. She seemed fond of lace, it decorated her substantial hull in many manifestations. Dabbing her mouth neatly with a napkin, Mrs Scaife continued, 'The Russian Revolution and the Spanish Civil War are just the most recent examples. Will you have more tea?'

'Thank you,' Juliet said. 'Shall I pour? Mrs Ambrose – another cup for you?' Mrs Ambrose mumbled assent; she had not been quite as refined as Mrs Scaife in her eager engagement with the little cakes.

It was a Saturday afternoon and here they were, Juliet thought, Englishwomen doing what Englishwomen did best wherever they were in the world – taking tea and having cosy chats, albeit the topic of conversation on this occasion was treason, not to mention the destruction of civilization and the British way of life, although no doubt Mrs Scaife would have claimed to be a vigorous defender of both.

Mrs Scaife's husband was Ellory Scaife, a retired Rear Admiral who was an MP for an obscure Northamptonshire constituency as well as a leading light of the Right Club. He was currently languishing in prison along with his Nazi-sympathizing cohorts under Regulation 18b. Mrs Scaife ('as good as a widow') had taken over her husband's interests. 'Become a young friend to her,' Perry had said. 'See what you can find out about her activities. We think she's rather important. And it's rumoured that she's in possession of a copy of the Red Book. Sniff around, see what you can find.'

As far as Mrs Scaife knew, Iris was a friend of Mrs Ambrose's niece – the aforesaid Marjorie from Harpenden – and was 'having doubts' about 'our attitude' towards Germany. She was 'firmly in favour of appeasement' and she didn't like the way that people who disagreed with the war were made to feel so wrong-headed. ('Just come out with some naïve illiberal sentiments,' Perry advised. 'But never overplay your hand.')

'It's all part and parcel of one and the same plan,' Mrs Scaife explained assiduously to Juliet. 'The plan is secretly operated and controlled by world Jewry, exactly on the lines laid down by the *Protocols of the Elders of Zion*. Do you have a copy, dear?'

'I don't,' Juliet said, although she did. Perry had lent her his own copy so that she could 'get the measure of what these people believe'.

'Let me find you one,' Mrs Scaife said, ringing a little bell on the tea tray. 'So good of Mrs Ambrose to bring you today. She's such a good friend to us.' The maid who had brought them their tea hurried back in.

'Dodds, fetch Miss Carter-Jenkins a copy of the book – you know the one.' Dodds did, apparently, and squeaked her assent before scurrying away on her errand.

The sun was flooding into the upstairs drawing room in Pelham Place although the weather remained chill. In the street below, the trees were beginning to display their fresh young leaves. It was such a hopeful time of year and yet Denmark had just surrendered and the Germans had taken Oslo and set up a government under Quisling. Poland, Norway, Denmark – Hitler was collecting countries like stamps. How long before he had the full set?

The future was coming nearer, one relentless goose-step after the next. Juliet could still remember when Hitler had seemed like a harmless clown. No one was amused now. ('The clowns are the dangerous ones,' Perry said.)

The house in Pelham Place seemed an odd locus for a cloak-and-dagger operation. The Scaifes' drawing room was rather lovely, with Persian carpets and a pair of sofas covered in a sea of salmon-pink damask silk. A Chinese vase filled with narcissi sat on a side table and a fire burned brightly in the grate. The windows too were enormous, each one swathed in enough material for a proscenium arch. There was a grand piano – did someone play? Mrs Scaife didn't look the type to place much value on a nocturne. Juliet felt her fingers spreading and curling with desire for the keys. She wondered what it would have been like to have been a child in a house like this. If she had, would her beliefs have been the same as Mrs Scaife's?

Mrs Scaife had two grown-up children – Minerva and Ivo. What bizarre names to be saddled with, Juliet thought. Minerva 'hunted' (as if that were a profession) and ran a livery stable deep in the countryside somewhere – Cornwall or Dorset, places beyond Juliet's imagination. Ivo was not mentioned. ('He's rather left-leaning,' Mrs Ambrose explained.) For all her faults, there was a certain motherliness about Mrs Scaife that Juliet tried hard not to find attractive. If it weren't for her rabid anti-Semitism or her worship of Hitler, they might have got on. (Quite big 'ifs', Perry pointed out.)

Mrs Scaife had already lost her 'manservant' to the war and her German maid had been interned, so now she was reduced to a cook, poor little Dodds and an all-purpose factotum called Wiggins, who lumbered around Pelham Place, filling coal scuttles and pulling weeds from the flower beds.

'I wish to save Britain,' Mrs Scaife declared, adopting a rather heroic pose over the teacups.

'Like Boadicea,' Mrs Ambrose suggested.

'But not from the Romans,' Mrs Scaife said. 'From the Jews and the Communists and the Masons. The scum of the earth,' she added pleasantly. 'Judaeo-Bolshevism – *that* is the enemy, and if Britain is to be great again then the foe must be eradicated from these shores.' ('Do not equate nationalism with patriotism,' Perry warned Juliet. 'Nationalism is the first step on the road to Fascism.')

Mrs Ambrose had begun to nod off, and if she wasn't careful, Juliet thought, she would too. Mrs Scaife droned on, her proselytism soporific. Jews here, Jews there, Jews everywhere. It sounded quite absurd in its wrong-headedness, like a mad nursery rhyme. It must be awfully handy to have a scapegoat for the world's ills. (*Women and the Jews tend to be first in line, unfortunately.*)

It seemed unlikely to Juliet that the Jews were brewing 'world revolution'. Although really, why wouldn't you? It seemed like an excellent idea from where Juliet was, drowning amongst the salmon damask cushions.

She replaced her cup carefully in her saucer, attentive to her movements, as if she might betray herself through clumsiness. It was a small triumph to have achieved an invitation to the inner sanctum of Pelham Place, but it remained a somewhat nerve-wracking audition.

The maid returned, clutching the *Protocols of the Elders of Zion* before handing it mutely to Juliet with a little bobbed curtsey. She scampered away to whatever mousehole she lived in before Juliet had time to thank her.

'Dodds is an utterly hopeless girl,' Mrs Scaife sighed. (Mrs Scaife possessed a large vocabulary of sighs.) 'She's so reluctant to dirty her hands with housework that you would think she was a Brahmin. Of course, the girl came straight from an orphanage. They have a scheme where they train them to be domestics. All I can say is that they don't train them very well. We had a very good German maid but, of course, they interned her. She's on the Isle of Man. She *was* Category A, but after all the fuss about Norway and now Denmark that has been changed to Category B. She's a *maid*, for goodness' sake, how can she be a threat to anyone?'

'Have you visited her on the Isle of Man?' Mrs Ambrose asked, perking up suddenly. Perry was always interested in any communication with internees.

'On the Isle of Man?' Mrs Scaife asked incredulously. Mrs Ambrose might as well have asked if she'd visited someone on the moon.

'No, of course not,' Mrs Ambrose said with an inoffensive little laugh. 'Silly me. Whatever was I thinking?' In an effort to lighten the mood, she said, 'Iris is an orphan too.' She made it sound like an accomplishment.

Mrs Ambrose retrieved her knitting from her bag. She was always accompanied by her knitting, although it seemed to Juliet that she was forever working on the same thing – it never appeared to grow or take on any particular shape. 'Iris has some . . . questions,' she said. 'Doubts. Criticisms even. Of the war and our part in it.'

Juliet was able to parrot quite a lot of what Godfrey's informants said. 'Yes, it's difficult to retaliate when people say it was the Germans who started it, because then you'll just draw attention to yourself.'

'How true,' Mrs Scaife said.

'Well, I say, "I do wish it hadn't been us that started the war." That usually stops them in their tracks.'

'Iris works in the War Office, you know,' Mrs Ambrose said.

'Oh?' Mrs Scaife said.

'Frightfully dull stuff,' Juliet said. 'Filing, mainly.' Mrs Scaife looked disappointed and Mrs Ambrose's needles paused warningly mid-stitch. 'But that's how wars are won and lost, isn't it?' Juliet added hurriedly.

'Yes. I suppose it is,' Mrs Scaife said thoughtfully. 'I expect you see all kinds of things.'

Mrs Ambrose resumed the relentless clack-clacking of her needles. 'And Iris's fiancé is in the Navy,' she murmured. 'I expect he sees all kinds of things too.'

'Oh, yes, Ian,' Juliet said helpfully. 'He's on HMS *Hood*. Oh, no, I shouldn't have said that! It's probably a secret!' I am the picture of innocence, she thought.

'I shan't tell anyone,' Mrs Scaife said soothingly. She was also rather good at feigning innocence.

Juliet pretended to examine the horrid little book. 'Thank you for this, Mrs Scaife, I look forward to reading it.'

'Oh, call me Rosamund, dear,' Mrs Scaife said and Juliet sensed a little flutter of gratification on the part of Mrs Ambrose, like a director observing an actress succeed in a part.

The telephone rang, an intrusive sound in this genteel atmosphere. The device stood on a little Louis Quinze commode by the window and Mrs Scaife launched herself off the salmon damask to answer it.

Juliet leafed through the pages of the *Protocols*, feigning interest in its fraudulent contents while eavesdropping on Mrs Scaife. The Scaifes' phone was tapped but so far the tapes had yielded little of interest.

The telephone conversation seemed – disappointingly – to concern the subject of pork chops and was being conducted, presumably, with Mrs Scaife's butcher, unless 'pork chops' was some kind of code. A butcher in the East End had recently displayed a sign that said 'If you eat pork you're welcome here', an anti-Semitic message that proved too subtle for most of his customers. Special Branch arrested him, but Juliet supposed he was back plying his trade by now.

Surely the Scaifes' cook would be the one who dealt with the butcher? Mrs Scaife didn't seem the kind of person to bother herself with the domestic hum-drum. Juliet glanced at Mrs Ambrose to see if the same thought might have crossed her mind, but she continued to knit and purl placidly. It was her very passivity, Perry said, that made her so good – everyone thought she was a harmless old lady, albeit one with extreme Christian views and a violent loathing for Communists. 'She came to us via the Militant Christian Patriots,' he explained.

'They sound rather frightening.'

'They are a bit,' he admitted and smiled. It had been a relief to see him shaking off his recent despondency. If he kissed her (the gift right under his nose, the apple on the tree, the pearl in the oyster) he might smile more, she thought, despite the war.

Click, click, click, click went Mrs Ambrose's needles. If you could hear but not see her you might think her to be a giant demented insect, although perhaps it was easier to imagine Mrs Ambrose as one of the *tricoteuses* at the guillotine, knitting serenely as heads rolled bloodily at her feet.

Mrs Scaife's return to the sofa involved a voyage around the room, during the course of which she pointed out her 'better pieces'. 'Sèvres,' she said, indicating a cabinet full of heartbreakingly pretty china – yellow and gold painted with pastoral scenes. She took out a little coffee cup and saucer for Juliet to admire. The cup was adorned with cherubs who were playing with a pretty goat. Frolicking, Juliet thought.

On the matching saucer, more cherubs were garlanding a lamb with flowers. Juliet felt quite covetous, not so much of the porcelain as of the Arcadian lives that were being led on it.

Mrs Scaife continued the review of her goods and chattels, stroking a large inlaid escritoire fondly ('Sheraton'), wafting a possessive hand at a variety of ancestral portraits, before pausing in front of one of the large windows. 'I am under threat,' she said casually. 'I am being watched by the government, of course.' She indicated the street below with a dismissive flick of her hand. Was she? Perry hadn't mentioned any Watchers, but Juliet supposed it made sense. 'But I have my own "guards", as it were. People who are protecting me.'

The voyage resumed. Mrs Scaife paused in her passage again, this time at a silver-framed photograph of the Duke and Duchess of Windsor that had pride of place on a little ('Hepplethwaite') side table. 'Ah, the Duchess,' Mrs Scaife said, picking up the photograph and gazing admiringly at the Duchess's thin arrogance. 'She was very *comme il faut*. One of us, of course. They will be restored, you know – once Fascism triumphs here.'

'Queen Wallis?' Juliet queried. It hardly sounded regal.

'Why not?' Mrs Scaife said, navigating her way back to the sofa and dropping anchor (*'Ouf'*) on the salmon damask.

'Shall I read the tea leaves?' Mrs Ambrose asked.

Mrs Ambrose was, by her own admission, 'something of a clairvoyant'. She claimed it was a God-given skill so it was quite compatible with her Christian beliefs. It seemed unlikely to Juliet, but apparently Mrs Scaife was attracted by all things occult and she had spent long hours closeted with Mrs Ambrose, staring into pieces of crystal and bowls of water, waiting for signs and portents. 'The Führer believes that our fate is in the stars, of course,' Mrs Ambrose said. Juliet wondered if Mrs Ambrose knew that MI5 had employed an astrologer to try to mirror what Hitler's own astrologer was advising him so they would know what moves he might be planning. ('Hints at desperation,' Perry said.)

'Oh, read Iris's!' Mrs Scaife exclaimed.

Juliet passed her cup over, rather unwillingly, and Mrs Ambrose squinted at the dregs. 'There are difficulties ahead, but you will weather them,' she intoned. (Was the Sybil at Delphi this insipid, Juliet wondered?) 'You have already met someone who will change your life.'

'For the better, I hope,' Mrs Scaife laughed.

Oh, what fairground nonsense, Juliet thought.

Juliet was heartily glad when Mrs Ambrose said, 'We should get going, Iris.'

'Thank you so much, Mrs Scaife,' Juliet said, tucking the *Protocols* into her handbag. 'It was so kind of you to invite me. And so interesting. I would love to talk more.'

'It's been a pleasure, Iris, dear. You must come again.'

Dodds, the timorous maid, saw them out, bobbing another

curtsey after she had opened the door for them. Juliet slipped her a sympathetic sixpence, which the girl swiftly pocketed with another little dip of her knee.

'Well, it seems you passed,' Mrs Ambrose whispered delightedly as they made their way back down the stairs.

Juliet breathed deeply. It was a great relief to get away from the stifling atmosphere of Mrs Scaife's house and into the fresh spring air.

A thuggish-looking man was loitering on the street corner and Juliet supposed he was one of Mrs Scaife's 'guards'. But then, for all she knew, he could have been one of Perry's men. Whoever he was, she could feel his eyes following them (horrible expression – as if they had detached from his face!) all the way down the street.

'By the way,' Mrs Ambrose said, 'you owe me ninepence. For the *verushka*.'

Dead Letter Drop

RECORD 6 (contd.)

19.50

DOLLY. (contd.) He's sure of them, but how does he know he's sure of them?

GODFREY. Mm. Does he phone?

DOLLY. Yes. And write.

GODFREY. Write?

TRUDE. You could send a postcard.

GODFREY. Is this MONTGOMERY, yes?

DOLLY. Yes, MONTGOMERY. I think he said quite a bit. I asked him if he knew of any of the people who were definitely anti-German and he said there were quite a few Communists. I said did he know who they were and he said, Oh, yes, he knew one or two of them. He didn't tell me at the time. Of course I might persuade him later on. It would be something to go on, wouldn't it?

GODFREY. Yes, yes.

TRUDE. It's a blasted nuisance if you can only see him for half an hour a week.

```
DOLLY. He said he doesn't talk to other people very
    much, not unless he's sure of them.
GODFREY. I don't suppose ... (two words) telephone.
DOLLY. No, it's no good. I'm seeing him on Friday.
    I'm going to meet him at his place of work.
GODFREY. Well, that's very good.


TRUDE and DOLLY prepared to depart and then TRUDE
    said -
```

Juliet yawned extravagantly. The previous evening she had been at the Dorchester where Lew Stone and his band had been playing and it had been well into the early hours before she and Clarissa groped their way home in the blackout. She had drunk rather too much and, as a result, the daily tedium of the typewriter seemed more onerous than usual – she had to listen several times to catch even the gist of what the informants were saying. So when the doorbell rang, she welcomed the interruption.

As a rule, no one but a messenger boy came to Dolphin Square in the mornings, but it was not a boy, it was a man Juliet recognized but couldn't immediately place.

'Ah, the famous Miss Armstrong,' he said when she opened the door to him. (Famous? For what, she wondered?) He removed his hat and entered without being invited in. 'Oliver Alleyne,' he said. Of course. ('He's rather ambitious,' Perry had said.) He was accompanied by a dog, small and cross-looking. With its scowl and its drooping moustache it reminded Juliet of a querulously apoplectic colonel she had met when accompanying Perry to Whitehall the previous week. (*France will fall! Do you understand? Does anyone understand?*)

'I'm afraid Mr Gibbons isn't here,' Juliet said, although the man was already advancing into the hall, the dog trotting obediently behind him.

Entering the living room in a proprietorial manner, Oliver Alleyne said, 'So this is where Perry hides out, is it? Perry's lair.' He seemed amused by the idea. He was very good-looking, a fact which had rather knocked Juliet for six. Would she have let him in if he had been less handsome?

'He isn't here.'

'Yes, you already said that. He's at the Scrubs, I've just seen him there. It was you I wanted to talk to.' The dog lay down and went to sleep as if it knew it was in for a long wait.

'Me?'

He set his hat impertinently on top of Perry's roll-top, next to the bust of Beethoven. Picking up the bust, he said, 'God, this thing weighs a ton. You could kill someone with it. Who's it meant to be?'

'Beethoven, sir.'

'Is that so?' he said dismissively, as if Beethoven were a nobody. He replaced the bust on the roll-top and perched himself casually on a corner of her own desk. 'I was wondering if you had any spare time on your hands?'

'Not really.'

Picking up the sheaf of papers she had just finished typing, he said, 'Dear God, girl, this is dog work of the lowest order.' He had a nice speaking voice, educated but with a slight burr, a hint of old Caledonia. ('Anglo-Scot,' Clarissa told her later. 'His family owns huge swathes of the Highlands but they only go there to kill things. Stags, grouse and so on.')

He began to read out loud as if it were a script and he a rather poor actor. (She felt sure that he wasn't.) '*But then he might have said that to me, you see, he might not say so much to other people.*' Dolly, the real Dolly, had an unfortunate Midlands accent, but Oliver Alleyne read her in the style of Celia Johnson, transforming her into some-thing both ludicrous and oddly affecting.

'*He's sure of them, but how does he know he's sure of them?*

'Godfrey. Mm. *Does he phone?*

'Dolly. *Yes. And write.*

'Godfrey. *Write?*

Juliet glanced at Oliver Alleyne's dog, sleeping beneath Perry's roll-top. It opened one speculative eye and looked back at her. It was feigning sleep, she realized.

'Trude – the Norwegian?'

'Yes, sir.'

'Trude. *You could send a postcard.*' (His imitation of Trude was absurd, more cod Spanish than Scandinavian.) 'Dear God, Miss Armstrong, how can you bear it?'

'You shouldn't really be reading that, you know, sir.' She couldn't suppress a smile. His attitude invited informality, familiarity even. He had a trivial air about him compared to Perry. She supposed she had a trivial soul herself, why else would she find it an attractive quality?

'I'm allowed,' he said. 'I'm the boss.'

'Are you?' she said doubtfully.

'Well, Perry's boss anyway.' Perry had never mentioned this fact. Juliet didn't think of Perry having a boss. It made her see him in a different light.

'I hear "Miss Carter-Jenkins" is doing splendid work,' Oliver Alleyne said. 'Getting close to Mrs Scaife and so on. Little tête-à-têtes.'

Yes, Juliet was a 'great success' with Mrs Scaife, Mrs Ambrose had reported to Perry. She had spent several afternoons now taking tea in Pelham Place with Mrs Scaife and different permutations of the 18b 'widows' – women whose husbands, like Mrs Scaife's Rear Admiral, had had their *habeas corpus* suspended. 'My young companion,' Mrs Scaife called her. 'I wish my own daughter was as attentive,' she laughed. ('Reel her in slowly,' Perry said. 'It's a game of patience.')

'You are perfectly placed to see who comes and goes in that house, find out what everyone is saying,' Perry said. 'Just listen. She'll say something useful eventually. Everyone does.' But really the conversation never stretched much beyond the horror of butter rationing or where to get good staff when they were all joining the armed forces, sprinkled with the usual anti-Semite comments. The Red Book was referred to once or twice and Mrs Scaife gave the distinct impression that it was somewhere in the house, but didn't elaborate.

Perry had supplied Juliet with a tiny secret camera, hidden in a cigarette lighter – in fact the cigarette lighter that Perry had produced on their otter expedition. (Had he secretly photographed her, sitting on that cold tarpaulin?)

'Microfilm,' he said. Conjured up by MI5's 'boffins'. So far, however, Juliet had had little opportunity to use the camera as she spent most of her time corralled in the salmon-pink drawing room.

If she wanted to 'powder her nose' – Mrs Scaife's preferred euphemism for the inevitable result of all the tea-drinking – then she was firmly directed to a downstairs cloakroom, when in fact all the interesting things in Pelham Place were on the upper floors. There had been a small triumph a few days ago when she had managed to photograph some envelopes that were waiting on the hall table for poor little Dodds to convey to the post office.

MI5 believed that the Right Club kept in touch with its contacts in Germany through a third party in the Belgian Embassy, and Perry was keen to see whom Mrs Scaife was corresponding with. He had dispatched Juliet to an obscure department in the GPO at Dollis Hill to learn how to open and reseal envelopes, as well as how to prise open locks on briefcases and trunks and so on. She was eager to put some of these new-found skills into practice.

An envelope addressed to 'Herr William Joyce' ('The fifth column's damn hero,' a disgusted Perry said) lay temptingly on top of the pile, but unfortunately Mrs Scaife's cook had interrupted Juliet's efforts at espionage, clumping up from her kitchen cave with a dinner menu for her mistress's approval.

'Lobster,' she said, rolling her eyes at Juliet and blowing air out of her mouth as if the lobster were a particularly irksome dinner guest that she was going to have to deal with.

Lobster, to Juliet's surprise, wasn't rationed, simply difficult to come by, and she had eaten it in Prunier's with Perry just last week. When he invited her she had hoped for the romance of flickering candlelight and perhaps a second round of more hand-holding (or painful grasping) across the table. The kind of dinner where a man reveals his suppressed passion for you (*Miss Armstrong. I cannot keep my feelings to myself any longer*), instead of which she was subjected to a lecture on their dinner.

'The common European lobster, or *Homarus gammarus*,' Perry said as the unlucky crustacean was placed before them. 'The exo-skeleton is blue in the wild, of course, the red pigment only released when it is boiled – generally alive,' he added, twisting off a claw as if conducting an autopsy. 'Now, pull the legs off and suck out the meat.'

Despite some reluctance, she followed his instructions. After all, it seemed a shame to be boiled alive for nothing.

Post-prandial dalliance took the form of ten pages of dictation over coffee until she was cross-eyed. ('*He was informed that the BBC have been listening in day and night and have heard* – capitals, Miss Armstrong – *NO SUCH BROADCASTS.*') Plenty of unsup-pressed passion, but not for her.

'Yes, actually I'm going to Pelham Place for tea this afternoon,' she said to Oliver Alleyne. The prospect of more tea was tedious, she had drunk enough with Mrs Scaife to sink HMS *Hood*. How was Ian, she wondered? Iris's imaginary fiancé (and by default hers too) was growing in stature every day. A rapid promotion to captain, a broader chest, a fuller head of hair. Charming manners, but under-neath a heart of steel as he stood manfully on the bridge as HMS *Hood* floundered around on the high seas somewhere—

'Miss Armstrong?'

'What is it exactly that you want, sir?'

'You, Miss Armstrong,' Oliver Alleyne said. 'I want you.'

'I am quite busy actually.'

'Of course,' he said. 'And I can hardly compete with the high drama of this work.' He tossed the typed pages back on the desk so that they scattered everywhere. I'm going to have to re-collate all those later, Juliet thought crossly. 'But it will take up hardly any of your time – virtually none, in fact. What do you say?'

'Do I have a choice, sir?'

'Not really.'

'Then the answer's yes, I suppose.'

'Excellent. So – to business. This is to be kept just between the two of us. Do you understand?'

'Yes.'

'It's rather delicate. It concerns our friend Godfrey Toby.'

'Godfrey?'

'Yes. I would like you to keep an eye on him for me.'

Yet another perfectly horrible expression, Juliet thought. 'On Godfrey?' she puzzled.

'Yes. Keep an eye out' (worse!) 'for anything that strikes you as odd.'

'Odd?' Juliet echoed.

'Out of the ordinary, out of character,' he said. 'Even slightly.'

Juliet was surprised. Godfrey was the model of probity.

'Has anything struck you recently?'

'Well . . . he was late a couple of days ago,' she offered.

'Is that unusual?'

'Only because he's never late.' (*You can set your watch by Godfrey.*) 'Hardly grounds for conviction though. I'm late all the time.'

Juliet and Cyril had been in the flat – Cyril nurturing the equipment and Juliet working her way stoically through Godfrey's transcripts from the previous day – when they heard voices raised in concern in the corridor outside. Someone began to knock very loudly and insistently on the neighbouring door, audible even through their soundproofing (which had turned out to be rather flawed).

A worried-looking Cyril emerged from his burrow and said, 'Godfrey's late, miss. He's never late. They're out there waiting for him.'

They crept to their front door and put their ears against it. Juliet could make out Betty's shrewish pitch and Victor's northern grumble. They seemed upset, anxious that Godfrey hadn't turned up – worried, perhaps, that his identity had been uncovered by the Security Services (and therefore, by association, theirs too). They were fractious, sheep without a shepherd. Or rats without a Pied Piper. ('They are very loyal to Godfrey,' Perry had said to her not long ago.)

'If he's taken, then we'll be next,' Victor said.

'We should go,' Betty said. 'I'll telephone him.' There was some muttering about how that would be incriminating if there was anyone listening to Godfrey's calls, and then more assertive knocking next door, and then to Juliet's relief she heard Godfrey's affable voice growing louder as he approached, apologizing for his tardiness, followed by a twittering of (rather resentful) relief from the neighbours. They had been afraid, Juliet thought. She was glad. They should be.

'Did he say why he was late?' Oliver Alleyne asked.

'It was nothing,' Juliet said. 'A delay on the Underground. I don't know why I even mentioned it.'

'But it's exactly the kind of thing I'm interested in!' he said. He smiled at her. Wolfishly, she thought, a cliché from her mother's romances, but apt, nonetheless. It depended on whether or not you found wolves attractive, she supposed. He did have a certain vulpine quality – as if he was about to ravish you – and she wondered what it would be like to be kissed by him. Rather brutal, she imagined.

'Miss Armstrong?'

'Sir?'

'Anything else?'

'No.'

Of course, there had been that rather odd thing last week when she had come across Godfrey in Kensington Gardens. Perry had told her to take the afternoon off – he seemed to want the Dolphin Square flat to himself but didn't volunteer the reason and she didn't ask – so she went into town, looked around the shops and had a pot of tea and a slice of walnut cake in Fuller's in the Strand before going to see *Rebecca* at the Curzon in Mayfair. She decided to walk home through the parks. It was early evening – the magic hour – and Juliet took a detour around Buckingham Palace as she had glimpsed a bed of red tulips there from the bus and she wanted to take a closer look at them. London was in martial drab and any patch of colour was welcome. It wouldn't be long probably before they dug them up and planted cabbages or onions instead. It was doubtful that vegetables would lift the heart in quite the same way. Cyril told her that he had seen sheep grazing in Hyde Park and she thought she must try to find them. She thought of Mrs Scaife's Sèvres. She supposed Hyde Park wouldn't look much like Arcadia. It didn't. No sheep, just the platforms for the ack-ack guns being assembled.

In Kensington Gardens she had spied Godfrey Toby sitting on a bench, although it took her a moment to recognize him outside of his Dolphin Square habitat. (He was 'roaming free', she thought. A rogue elephant.) She presumed he was on his way to the flat, taking the opportunity to enjoy the spring air before having to closet himself with the informants. There was a newspaper – *The Times* – beside him on the bench but he wasn't reading it, instead he was sitting like a contemplative in the cloisters, his hands resting on his knees and his eyes closed. He looked so peaceful in repose that Juliet couldn't bring herself to disturb him. On the other hand, it seemed rather rude to behave as if he wasn't there.

Before she could resolve this dilemma, he stood up unexpectedly and walked away without apparently seeing her. He had left his newspaper on the bench. It looked unread and Juliet supposed that he was in such a reverie that he had forgotten it. If she hurried she could perhaps catch him up (*Mr Toby! Mr Toby!*) and return it to him. Before she could reach his abandoned bench, however, a man came walking quickly along the path. He was large and imposing and wearing a heavy overcoat with an astrakhan collar that made him seem even more large and imposing. He strode past the bench and as he did so swooped up *The Times* and carried it off without breaking his stride.

Although she had nothing against the purloining of discarded newspapers – why should they go to waste, after all? – Juliet nonetheless felt irritated on Godfrey's behalf. The man in the astrakhan-collared coat was moving so quickly that he was almost out of sight now. He was going in the opposite direction to Godfrey so there was no way of reuniting him with his newspaper. Nonetheless Juliet trotted after Godfrey, thinking she would at least say hello now that his meditation was over.

She recognized one of his gloves lying on the path – leather, lined with wool, rather worn – and stooped to pick it up. How much more jetsam was he going to discard in his wake, she wondered? Or maybe he was laying a trail like Hansel and Gretel with their bread-crumbs and hoping to find his way back out of Kensington Gardens (and now, thanks to her, he would not be able to). She examined the glove as if it were a clue to something. This was how a woman was supposed to entice a man into noticing her, wasn't it? (*Oh, miss, I think you have dropped something.*) It seemed unlikely that this was Godfrey's motive.

She picked up her pace and managed to tag the sleeve of his overcoat. He turned, looking really quite alarmed, as if he might be about to be set upon by footpads. He held up his cane – rather menacingly – but then he recognized her and the alarm on his face was replaced by surprise.

'It's only me, Mr Toby,' she said. 'You dropped a glove.'

'Why, thank you, Miss Armstrong,' he said, looking rather abashed at his response. 'I would have been perplexed as to its whereabouts.' He produced its partner from his pocket and, pulling on both gloves, said, 'There, now they can't get lost.' Why hadn't he been wearing his gloves, she wondered? The twilight had brought a chill and it was almost dark now. 'Were you following me?' he enquired pleasantly.

'No, not at all. I was on my way home.'

'Ah. Perhaps I can escort you as far as the Albert Hall?' He offered his arm and Juliet wondered if they looked like mismatched sweethearts as they strolled through the crepuscular park. Or perhaps something more morally questionable. (*You have a bit of fluff, after all, Gibbons. Who would have thought it?*)

They chatted inconsequentially, nothing that she could really recall afterwards, except for something about Holland's neutrality ('It will not help them in the end'), accompanied by the *tap-tap-tap* of his cane on the path. They parted at the Albert Hall. 'Well, that's me,' he said, and she only realized when he had left that she had forgotten to tell him about his newspaper. It was hardly important, she supposed.

And yet. The way the man in the astrakhan-collared coat had pounced so swiftly on Godfrey's *Times*, almost as if he had been waiting for it. Although at the time she had felt sure that Godfrey really *had* simply dropped the glove, perhaps she was wrong, perhaps it was a signal of some kind. And his consternation when she had accosted him, as if he was half expecting to be attacked. Astrakhan was the pelt of an unborn lamb, wasn't it? *From his mother's womb untimely ripped*, Juliet thought, and shuddered at the image.

'Anything?' Oliver Alleyne asked.

'No, sir. He never does anything out of the ordinary.' It was a question of loyalty really, wasn't it? Or trust, perhaps. She trusted Godfrey in a way that – instinctively – she didn't trust Oliver Alleyne. 'Why?' she asked, her curiosity piqued.

'Well, no one is entirely innocent of everything, Miss Armstrong.' An unborn lamb perhaps, Juliet thought. He gave her the full benefit of his rakish smile. He was married, according to Clarissa later, to an actress, 'Quite well known. Georgina Kelloway.' (Perhaps that explained his leanings towards theatrics.) Juliet had seen his wife on stage in a Noel Coward play. She had been rather showy, but then the part had demanded it, she supposed. Innocence had not been on offer.

Oliver Alleyne retrieved his hat from the roll-top and said, 'I'll be off then.' The dog woke up instantly and sat to attention expectantly. 'And, please, as I said, keep this between the two of us, Miss Armstrong. Strictly on the QT. Don't mention it to anyone.'

'Not to Perry?'

'Especially not Perry. Godfrey is Perry's man.'

'I'm Perry's girl,' she pointed out.

'I don't think you're anyone's girl, Miss Armstrong.'

He moved towards the door. The dog remained where it was and Juliet said, 'Sir? Mr Alleyne? You've forgotten your dog.'

He turned to look at the dog and said, 'Oh, it's not mine. I thought you could perhaps do me the favour of looking after it for a short while.'

'Me?' she said, startled.

'Its name is Lily. Apparently it's a miniature Schnauzer.' Rhymes with Mauser, Juliet thought.

The dog, which had been gazing uneasily up at Oliver Alleyne, now turned its attention to Juliet. She hadn't realized that a dog could look doubtful.

'The owner has had to go abroad,' he said.

'For you? For MI5?'

'On the condition that we take care of her dog.'

'A woman?'

'The dog is a kind of . . . ransom, I suppose you could say.' The dog looked inquisitively at him as if it was wondering about the meaning of the word 'ransom'. 'To ensure that his owner returns to these shores. You don't need to know more than that, I assure you.'

'I don't know anything about dogs,' Juliet said.

'Well, now's your chance to learn,' he said cheerfully. 'We'll pay. For the food and so on. We're very grateful. And Miss Armstrong? Do make sure nothing happens to the dog. It's really rather important.'

She saw him to the front door. He gave her the benefit of the rakish smile again. Its effect was beginning to wear rather thin. 'And Miss Armstrong – that other business with our friend? *Semper vigilans*, Miss Armstrong, *semper vigilans*. Now, don't let me keep you from your work.'

War Work

RECORD 7

(contd.)

D. No, I just wondered.

G. It's a bit far away to go, isn't it?

T. Yes, it is really. I haven't been able to think of anyone else who would be interesting.

G. Can you think of anyone who's died (?Could not be sure of this sentence)

T. No. (laughs) Not that they'd be any good, would they? It's a pity that man had died, isn't it?

G. ... (inaudible)

D. What man?

T. ... (?)(laughter)

G. Yes, a great pity that. He would have been a very good man.

T. Yes, quite useful.

G. What was that telephone number?

T. BUNTINGFORD (?)214 BUNTINGFORD (HUNTINGFORD??) is the nearest telephone exchange (three words).

G. And he definitely said -

T. Yes, yes.

Following a directive from above, every effort had to be made to conserve paper, so Juliet now abbreviated names to initials, and typed on both sides of the paper. Less to dispose of if they won the war, she supposed, and less to destroy if they lost. ('Everything will have to be got rid of,' Perry said. 'We shall burn the building down if necessary.')

```
GODFREY goes out to buy sandwiches. TRUDE and DOLLY
conduct a frenzied search for microphones. Shrieks
of laughter. GODFREY returns with sandwiches and
asks them if they have conducted a 'thorough search'.
More laughter. They seem to believe the Gestapo is
recording their conversations (not MI5). They com-
ment on the quality ('good') of the sandwiches.

(Biscuit interval.)

D. I forgot to say - I've got a £5 contribution from
   MRS BRIDGE. For the Gestapo fund.
G. Oh, it leads to all sorts of trouble with book-
   keeping and so on. They don't want funds from
   outside sources. Paperwork, you know.
```

Juliet burst into laughter.

'Miss?'

'Oh, hello, Cyril, I didn't see you come in. They're giving Godfrey money for the "Gestapo fund".'

'What's that?'

'Lord only knows. Something their collective fevered imagination has dreamt up. It was a fiver to boot.'

'We could all go have a good night out on that, miss.'

The very word 'Gestapo' seemed to excite the neighbours. Betty and Dolly in particular were always asking to have a look at Godfrey's 'Gestapo card' – the Gestapo identity card supposedly issued by the 'Berlin *Polizeidirektion*' in '38. MI5 had a very good forgery department, needless to say.

He spoke good German, indeed to Juliet's ear it sounded fluent. He had spent some time there when he was younger, he told Juliet. 'Heidelberg. And the war, of course.' What did he do in the war?

'This and that, Miss Armstrong. This and that.'

Trude would sometimes converse in German with him, although her German wasn't very good. (She liked to think it was, of course.) Betty and Dolly loved it when he spoke German, it reassured them of his legitimacy, and of theirs too. They were servants of the Third Reich and Godfrey was the proof of that.

-18-

RECORD 7 (contd.)

They talked quietly about people but little could be heard consecutively. At about 14.45 they spoke of when VICTOR might be expected. 16.05 TRUDE went out to buy something and returned. More chat. TRUDE returned.

RECORD 8.

16.25

TRUDE and EDITH talk flippantly to GODFREY about what they should do with his body if he died. TRUDE said that it was just as well that he hadn't died, as yet. GODFREY laughed. They both talked jokingly about the disposal of the body.

T. I have a good idea for where you can hide a body. We can put it down a coal hole in the pavement.

(Laughter all together)

```
G. Which coal hole?
T. The Carlton Club
```

(Laughter.)

```
G. And what should I do if you die?
T. Same thing!
E. We could soon fill up the coal holes!
T. With Jews!
```

The doorbell rings. GODFREY goes to answer it.
GODFREY returns.

```
G. Here's VICTOR.
```

'Did you listen to this yesterday, Cyril? The bit where they're talking about how to dispose of a body?'

Cyril laughed. 'The coal hole at the Carlton Club? We'll know where to look if Godfrey disappears.'

'Quite clever, I suppose.'

'You'd want to do it just before they had a big delivery of coal, wouldn't you? And then the body wouldn't be discovered for a long time. Not so good at this time of year, I suppose, with the warmer weather on us now.'

'You've given this a considerable amount of thought, Cyril.'

'I have. I'd be happy to put that Trude down a coal hole. She's a nasty piece of work.'

'She is a bit,' Juliet agreed. 'I wouldn't want to come across her in a dark alleyway.'

The ribbon on the Imperial needed changing. Juliet wondered how much more she could get out of it before the neighbours' words faded into nothing. The march of time would do the same one day. They would all succumb to it, all fade into nothing eventually, wouldn't they?

RECORD 9

GODFREY counts out change.

G. And two threepences make 5/6. How long does it
   take you to get through to Liverpool?
V. Five minutes (25?) sometimes. From a box in St
   James Street Post Office - Whitehall 4127.
G. How much does it cost?
V. About 2/6.

Much rustling of paper, making several minutes of
conversation inaudible.

19.50

Observing that it was raining, GODFREY suggested
that they should go to the Italian restaurant across
the road and he would join them later with VICTOR.

TRUDE and EDITH leave.

'He's quite chummy with them, isn't he?' Cyril said, reading over
Juliet's shoulder.

Who was looking closely over the content of these conversations? Obviously it should be Perry, but he often read Godfrey's own
reports rather than face the tedium of the transcriptions (Juliet
could hardly blame him). Recently she wasn't sure that he was reading anything as he seemed mired in gloom. (*Apologies, Miss
Armstrong, the black dog has got me in its teeth.*) Again, she thought.

'They do go out quite a bit afterwards,' she said to Cyril. There
was the Italian restaurant across the road that Godfrey seemed to
favour, and a Swiss one too that was nearby. And there was a pub
they all liked – the Queen's Arms – although he tended to go there
with the men rather than the women. 'I wouldn't call it "chummy"

exactly,' Juliet said, putting the dustcover on the Imperial. 'I presume it's all part of the job, to make them feel at ease with him, you know?'

'Yes, but we can't record them, can we, miss? Not when they're eating their *spaghetti*.' He said the word derisively. Foreign food had no part in Cyril's vocabulary, being, as he was, an eel pie and mash boy from Rotherhithe.

'No, I suppose not.' She stood up and fetched her coat. 'You're early, aren't you, Cyril?'

'No, miss. I expect you're late. Have you heard the news?'

'Churchill's to be PM? Yes.'

'Where are you going tonight, miss?'

'I'm going to the cinema, Cyril,' Juliet said, peering in the inadequate hall mirror to check that she was putting her hat on straight.

'What to see, miss?'

'I don't know, actually. I'm going with a friend, she's chosen the film. Does this hat look right to you?'

'You look smashing, miss.' He was sweet on her, she knew.

'Yes, but the *hat*?' She frowned at her reflection. She didn't suppose Cyril knew much about women's hats. 'What time is Godfrey due?'

'Six o'clock.' Godfrey's routine had become more complicated recently as he had started seeing the neighbours during the day as well. ('They have so much to say.') He had begun, too, to knock on their front door with his cane, a coded *rat-a-tat, rat-a-tat-TAT* to show he had arrived.

Lily had been following Juliet around hopefully as she got ready to leave.

'Sorry, we're not going for a walk,' she said to the dog, crouching down and giving it a compensatory kiss on the top of its silky head.

'You're coming home with me tonight, Lil,' Cyril said to the dog. 'We'll have fun and games, eh? Silly Lily,' he said, tossing a knitted golliwog that had been made by his 'Gran', a mysteriously powerful matriarch who had raised Cyril in the absence of his rather feckless-sounding parents. Gran knitted feverishly on Lily's behalf – a pixie, a teddy bear, a policeman, and many other woollen toys which the dog had joyfully torn to bits. Lily had proved a welcome addition to their little Dolphin Square club. Despite her rather grumpy appearance, she was a cheerful creature, eager to please and quick to forgive. Cyril came earlier every day so he could rough-house with Lily on the autumn-leaves carpet, and Perry spent a lot of time investigating her canine nature, setting up little behavioural experiments. ('Now, Juliet, I want you to go and stand behind that door and say the word "walk" in a neutral whisper – no intonation – so that I can see how she responds.') Sometimes the little dog looked at Perry with such curiosity that Juliet wondered if perhaps their roles weren't reversed and it was Lily who was making a study of Perry.

Juliet knew a little more about the dog's provenance now, thanks to Perry, as well as something of her erstwhile owner's pedigree. She was 'Hungarian, quite mad,' Perry said. In his opinion all Hungarians were mad – something to do with the collapse of the Austro-Hungarian Empire, but Juliet hadn't really been listening.

Lily's owner, the mad Hungarian, was called Nelly Varga and, according to Perry, had been caught spying for the Germans. 'We "converted" her.'

What did that mean?

'She was given a choice – she could go quietly to the gallows, like the German spies we have previously captured – or she could work for us instead. The threat of the noose can be quite persuasive,' Perry said.

'I expect it can be.'

'And now she's on a mission for us, in France. And we need her to come back, and that –' he said, indicating the dog (the dog cocked its head), 'is what will make sure she does. We promised no harm would come to her. She's obsessed with the dog – it's the only method we have really of controlling her.'

'Apart from the noose.'

The Germans were knocking on Belgium's door, and after Belgium it would be France's turn. It seemed unlikely that Nelly Varga would escape the iron maw that was swallowing Europe. Juliet hoped not – it would be a wrench to have to give the dog back to her.

In the meantime, the dog had been 'converted' too. Blithely unaware of its ransomed status it seemed to have transferred its love wholesale to Juliet and Cyril. Even the monastically untouchable Perry was pulled into its circle of warmth and could often be found sitting on the sofa with Lily on his lap, absent-mindedly stroking her soft ears. 'Helps me think,' he said sheepishly when caught in the act of affection.

'Well, I'm off, Cyril.' She'd given up all hope for the hat, it was never going to look right.

'Goodnight, miss. Enjoy the flicks.'

Yes, it would have been nice to 'enjoy the flicks', she thought. Nice to sit in the warm fug of the Odeon in Leicester Square and watch a film or quietly doze and catch up on some sleep or even daydream about 'Ian', but unfortunately she was on a mission for the Right Club.

Subsequent to her debut in Pelham Place, Juliet had been invited to a meeting in the smoky cramped room above the Russian Tea Room. Most of the attendees were 18b widows. There was naturally a good deal of grousing on this topic. Mrs Ambrose was there, of course, wearing a crocheted beret in an alarming shade of fuchsia. She knitted throughout, occasionally looking up from her stitches and smiling beatifically at the rest of the members.

Mrs Scaife rarely attended meetings, but she had come once or twice with Juliet to the Russian Tea Room and they had eaten food prepared by Anna Wolkoff's mother, who was the cook in the establishment and who appeared like a troglodyte from the basement kitchen with 'goulash' – which, on first hearing, Juliet had mistaken for 'ghoulish'. 'And it was rather,' she reported to Perry. 'I dread to think what animal was in it, it tasted quite zoological.'

There were only two people close to Juliet's age at the Right Club meeting. One was a callow youth who spouted a good deal of polemic and could just as easily have been at a Communist meeting. And a young woman, rather beautiful and haughtily Gallic ('Belgian, actually'), who smoked incessantly and seemed almost overcome by lassitude. Her name, she said, was 'Giselle'. Rhymes with gazelle, Juliet thought. Giselle would rouse herself from her torpor occasionally (she moved like a particularly lazy cat) in order to despise something. In no particular order, she 'loathed' the Duke of Kent (no reason given), the District and Circle line, English bread and Mrs Ambrose's hat (the latter condemned in a stagey whisper in Juliet's ear, 'I 'ate 'er 'at.').

Juliet had been invited to participate in their 'sticky-back' campaign, for which they were paired up as if preparing for a party game. She had been relieved to be given Mrs Ambrose as a partner and thought they would be able to talk openly, but Mrs Ambrose remained stoutly in character as they made their way round the centre of London.

They crept along in the blackout, staying close to walls and railings, avoiding policemen and air-raid wardens. 'Jews,' Mrs Ambrose sniffed, posting a 'This is a Jew's War' leaflet on the door of an airraid warden post. (Which one, Juliet wondered, looking at the apostrophe.) They were 'stickering', pasting their own propaganda (*War destroys workers!*) anywhere that seemed suitable – over government posters, on telephone kiosks, Belisha beacons, Montague

Burtons and Lyons Corner Houses. 'Wherever there are Jews,' Mrs Ambrose said.

Not for the first time, Juliet found herself wondering if Mrs Ambrose really was against the Nazis. She certainly didn't seem to be for the Jews, and she entered into her role so convincingly that Juliet found it quite easy to forget that she was 'one of us' as opposed to 'one of them'. If she'd been on the stage you might have accused her of over-acting the part. ('She has outstanding "tradecraft" skills,' Perry said. 'The mark of a good agent is when you have no idea which side they're on.')

It seemed to Juliet that there were some rather blurred boundaries when it came to beliefs – Perry had once been a member of the British Union of Fascists ('It was useful,' he said. 'Helped me understand them') and Hartley (Hartley, of all people!) had been a member of the Communist Party when he was at Cambridge. 'But everyone was a Communist before the war,' he protested. And Godfrey, of course, had been mixing in Fascist circles for years on behalf of MI5 and seemed some days to be almost fond of his informants.

'Get a move on, dear,' Mrs Ambrose said. 'You're very slow. You've got to paste and *run*.' Mrs Ambrose didn't look as if she could run even if there was a bull behind her.

On another occasion, Juliet had gone out with Giselle, who at least made no pretence of stickering and headed straight for a pub. 'I need a drink,' she said. 'Can I tempt you?'

What did that mean? Were they speaking in code? Was it always the same one? A very poor kind of secrecy if it was. Juliet hesitated. She would have to say it, she supposed. 'That's very kind of you,' she said guardedly. 'I think I will.'

Giselle scowled at her. 'I wasn't offering to pay.'

The pub was crowded and noisy and full of sailors rather a long way from the sea, and the two of them attracted a good many ribald comments, which were shrugged off with impressive hauteur by Giselle.

They managed to squeeze into a corner table from whence Juliet was dispatched to the bar for rum, which she also paid for. It was rather taxing being with Giselle. What was her story, Juliet wondered? ('She was once a mannequin for Worth,' Mrs Ambrose had confided.) They drank the rum, it was too noisy for any conversation and they departed almost as quickly as they had arrived. They were catching different trains and Juliet was dismissed at the top of the escalator without a hint of gratitude.

'Ah, Mam'selle Bouchier,' Perry said later. 'She is rather fond of alcohol, I'm afraid. Other things too, unfortunately.'

'You know her?'

He frowned at Juliet. 'Of course I know her, she's one of us. She's an excellent agent. Didn't she identify herself to you?'

'Sort of. I suppose.' (How many agents did Perry *have* in the Right Club? It seemed like half the membership.)

His frown deepened, considering her incompetence, she supposed. 'Are you sure all this underhand stuff is your forte?' he asked.

'I am,' Juliet said. 'I absolutely am.'

After a week or two of these malicious activities Juliet was given a badge. Anna Wolkoff herself had pinned it. She had fierce eyebrows and seemed mournfully Russian, sighing in the tragic way of a woman whose cherry orchard had been chopped down as she fixed the badge on to Juliet's dress. 'You are one of us now, Iriska,' Anna said. She took a step back in order to admire Juliet and then kissed her on both cheeks.

The badge was red and silver and depicted an eagle destroying a snake, beneath which were the initials P and J.

'Perish Judah,' Mrs Ambrose explained amiably when asked.

'What is that ugly thing on your dress?' Perry asked.

'I've earnt a badge. It's like being in the Girl Guides again. It all seems rather silly.'

'These people are more dangerous than they look,' he said. 'We'll catch them out if we're patient. Softly, softly, catchee monkey.'

What does that make me, Juliet wondered – the bait? What would you bait a monkey with? (*Can I tempt you?*) Bananas, she supposed.

'It's like being Jekyll and Hyde in some ways,' Juliet said.

'Good and evil, dark and light,' Perry mused. 'You can't have one without the other, I suppose.' (Was he describing his own character?) 'Perhaps we are all dualists,' he said.

Juliet was unsure what a dualist was. Not, she supposed, someone who crossed swords at dawn. Someone who was in two minds about things, perhaps.

In the Odeon, the National Anthem started up at the end of the programme and Juliet struggled sleepily to her feet. Giselle, who had been sitting next to her, uncoiled herself languidly from her seat like a rather dreamy cobra. Juliet had just begun to sing 'God save our gracious King –' when she found herself being prodded by Giselle's bony elbow in her side.

Oh, good Lord, Juliet thought, for the Right Club didn't stand and sing for their King, instead they substituted their own version of 'Land of Hope and Glory'. The pair of rather strident Regulation 18b widows whose company they were in had already launched into 'Land of Hope and Jewry' in their reedy church voices. ('All the Jewboys praise thee / as they plunder thee.')

'Sing,' Giselle hissed to her.

'Land of Jewish finance / fooled by Jewish lies,' Juliet sang quietly. It felt like such a travesty, a counterpoint in every possible way – musically and morally – to the National Anthem. The neighbouring members of the audience glanced at them in alarm but seemed too surprised to say anything.

It wasn't the only infraction they committed in cinemas. They cat-called and jeered in the middle of newsreels – 'Jew-lover', 'war-mongers' and so on – and then ran away from the cinema before anything could be done about it.

'They were showing *Gaslight* with Anton Walbrook, he was awfully good,' Juliet reported to Perry later (and dishy, too, but she didn't say that in case he took it as a judgement on his own looks). 'He persuades his wife that she's going mad.'

Perry laughed rather mirthlessly and said, 'And you enjoyed that, did you?'

'Don't you know?' Hartley said. 'His wife went loopy and hanged herself in the wardrobe.' More Rochester than Heathcliff then. 'That was his first wife, of course,' Hartley continued cheerfully. (His *first* wife?) 'Nobody knows what happened to the second one.'

Bluebeard then. There were – happily – no locked rooms in the Dolphin Square flat and Juliet could find no dead wives hanging bloodily on butcher's hooks – or in wardrobes, for that matter. Perhaps they were stored in his 'other place' in Petty France.

'I'm surprised,' Clarissa said. 'Men like Perry don't usually marry.'

-6-

15.05.40

G. When you went with MRS SHUTE?
T. GLADYS? Yes.
G. And got wet through? (both laugh)

(Cigarettes)

18.30 The doorbell rings.

G. Here's BETTY.
T. Did you get the job in the NAAFI?
B. Still waiting to hear.
G. I see.

B. And I still have to finish up where I am so it'll be another week before I could start.

G. At the NAAFI?

B. Yes. (Inaudible)

T. She would get ten years for that letter.

B. She would, wouldn't she?

T. What would you get for receiving it?

(Laughter all round)

G. Has anyone got Welsh blood here?

B. A long way back, but I'm not proud of it.

T. I went to Manchester to see that woman.

G. The German? And she's called BERTHA?

T. BIG BERTHA. (laughter)

B. She takes after her mother. I've seen a photograph.

T. German sort of face?

B. I would say. (laughter) Will she write? SW6 - is that Fulham?

(Biscuit interval)

B. Did I tell you about that Jew that came round? He said he could get me anything in the way of underthings.

G. Yes, yes.

B. They've got everything somewhere.

T. He's not the worst of them. (inaudible) Poisonous (?)

B. Well, a friend of mine knows a Jewess who (inaudible) often for Easter. That's not their holiday!

G. They have Passover.

T. Well, they're soon going to find out, aren't they? Get what's coming to them.

G. Hm?

The nearer the war got to their own shores, the more excitable the informants had grown. The more sure of themselves, too. 'Cocky lot, aren't they?' Cyril said.

Godfrey and Perry had cooked up a scheme to reward them for their loyalty with small iron crosses – lapel badges, several of which were delivered to Juliet one afternoon by a messenger boy.

'Has an admirer sent you something, miss?' Cyril asked, looking at the cardboard box on her desk.

'I don't think it's from an admirer, Cyril,' she said when she opened the box. 'At least, I hope not.'

'War merit second class,' Godfrey chuckled when he came in early (*rat-a-tat, rat-a-tat-TAT*) to pick them up. 'A *Kriegverdienstkreuz*,' he said. 'Shall I spell that for you, Miss Armstrong? For the transcript?'

'Yes, please, Mr Toby.'

'For services to the Third Reich!' Godfrey smiled at her as though they shared a secret, one that went beyond Dolphin Square. (She thought again of their stroll through the twilight in Kensington Gardens, the fallen glove. *Perhaps I can escort you as far as the Albert Hall?*) 'The medals to be worn concealed, of course,' he added. 'They will be told that the German government wants to show appreciation for their work. And if there's an invasion they will be able to identify themselves as friend rather than foe to the Nazis.'

But surely that wasn't a good idea, Juliet puzzled? The Germans would have a cohort of ready-made collaborators waiting for them.

'But *we* will be able to identify them by their medals! Also they have been given addresses to go to if the Germans invade. Muster stations, I suppose you could say, but the minute they turn up there they will be arrested.'

Juliet couldn't remember reading that in any transcript. Perhaps they had talked about it over spaghetti.

'And then what, Mr Toby?' Cyril asked.

'Oh,' Godfrey said casually, 'we'll shoot all the informants the minute the first Nazi sets foot on our soil.'

Who would be the one holding the gun, Juliet wondered? It was difficult to imagine Godfrey putting a blindfold on Betty or Dolly and pushing them up against a wall.

'I would do it,' Cyril said. 'I don't mind. They're traitors, aren't they?'

They had all deliberated several times recently about what they would do in the event of invasion. 'It's imperative we defend the BBC,' Perry said. 'The Germans mustn't get their hands on the radio transmitters.' Juliet imagined herself with the Mauser, heroically fighting to the death outside Broadcasting House on Portland Place. She rather liked this image of herself.

'Miss Armstrong?'

'Yes, sir?'

'Shall we listen to Churchill's speech on the wireless? I have some gin, foraged from War Office.'

'Splendid, sir.' It was the end of the working day and she had planned to go to the Embassy Club with Clarissa, but she supposed she would be failing in her patriotic duty if she didn't listen to their new prime minister, although she would rather have been dancing and forgetting their country's woes. Especially as all he was offering them was a wretched cocktail of blood, toil, tears and sweat. *We have before us an ordeal of the most grievous kind.*

Yet it was stirring stuff and she suddenly felt immensely grown-up and serious, although that might have been due to the gin. 'Can we do it, do you suppose?' she asked Perry.

'God knows,' he said. 'The situation is grave. All we can do is try our best.'

They chinked their glasses and Juliet said, 'To victory,' and Perry said, 'To courage. The watchword is courage, Miss Armstrong,' and they downed their gin.

Masquerade

'A PARTY?'

'A soirée. You will come, dear, won't you?' Mrs Scaife said.

'I'd love to,' Juliet said. 'Is it in Pelham Place?'

Mrs Scaife laughed. 'Goodness me, no. A friend has lent me a room.'

The 'soirée' was to be a gathering of 'like-minded people'. 'Great times are ahead of us, Iris, dear.'

The idea of attending on her own made Juliet rather nervous. She had grown accustomed to the unflappably woolly presence of Mrs Ambrose and even the glorious indifference of Giselle, but now Iris was going to have to go it alone. Her solo debut.

The 'room' turned out to be a thing of grandeur – the ballroom of a splendid house on Pall Mall – and Juliet wondered who Mrs Scaife's friend was that he (or she, possibly) was able to provide such an opulent venue. Massive pillars made from a meaty kind of marble ran in a double colonnade, their distant capitals gilded with acanthus. Glittering mirrors walled the room and reflected the gigantic chandeliers. It was the kind of room where men signed treaties that damned both victor and loser, or where girls in disguise mislaid their glass slippers.

The sticky-back campaign, the hectoring and so on were all

inconsequential, weren't they? A diversion even. The real power of the Right Club lay somewhere else. In Whitehall, in the back rooms of stuffy London clubs, in lustrous rooms like this. The Bettys and the Dollys of this world were the troops, niggling over the weather and bus fares and rationing, but here there were only generals. They would constitute the new world order if the Germans came.

Perry had bought Juliet a new frock for the party. It was a bias-cut satin affair that was rather revealing, a purchase he had encouraged. Indeed, he had accompanied her to Selfridges and the saleswoman had whispered to her in the changing room, 'What a generous chap. You are a lucky girl,' and Juliet had said, 'Well, perhaps *he*'s the lucky one.' I am a gift. An apple waiting to be plucked. A rose. A pearl.

'And I thought this would help,' Perry said, producing a little green leather box. When she opened it there was a pair of diamond earrings nestling inside the white satin interior.

'Oh,' Juliet said.

'Diamonds,' he said, as if she might not know what they were. 'Rather good – or so I'm told. Insured, but try not to lose them. They're to be returned tomorrow.'

'Oh.' Not a gift then. Why not just give me a pumpkin and six white mice and be done with it, Juliet thought.

'A twenty-first-birthday present from your father, if you're asked.'

'I'm only eighteen.'

'Yes, but you seem older.' (Did that make her more or less attractive to him, she wondered?)

'And you said my father was dead,' she reminded him.

'So he is.' She was surprised – Perry never forgot anything. This morning, during elevenses, a cup had slipped out of his hands in the tiny kitchen of Dolphin Square and he had stood for quite some time simply staring at the scattered shards on the kitchen floor. 'I'm not myself,' he had said eventually. He is himself, she thought, it's just that he has two selves, like revolving doors. Dr Jekyll, may I introduce you to Mr Hyde? A dualist.

He had walked away and left her to pick up the pieces.

Now he sighed and visibly gathered himself. 'The earrings are a family heirloom then – your mother's.'

Sitting beneath the fearsomely hot dryer in a hairdresser's in Knightsbridge while a girl gave her a manicure, Juliet felt not so much like Cinderella as a victim being prepared for sacrifice.

'Ah, Iris, dear,' Mrs Scaife said, tacking a course towards her, lace billowing in her wake. 'I'm so glad you could come. What pretty earrings.'

'My mother left them to me when she died.'

Mrs Scaife put her arm around Juliet's shoulders and gave her an encouraging squeeze. 'Poor, dear Iris.'

Mrs Scaife herself was wearing pearls, a three-strand choker in the style of Queen Mary. She always wore something around her neck – a silk scarf or a tippet of some kind. Juliet thought she must be hiding a scar but Mrs Ambrose said flatly, 'Just wrinkles.'

At the far end of the room a professional bar had been set up, incongruously modern in gleaming chrome and glass amongst all the marble, but Mrs Scaife seized a glass of sherry from the tray of a passing waitress. ('Stand up straight, this isn't a Lyons.') She handed the sherry to Juliet. 'Here, dear. Now, there are so many people I want you to meet.' Oh, Lord, Juliet thought. Here we go.

Mrs Scaife pushed the rounded prow of her bountiful bosom through the crowd, clearing a channel, Juliet trailing obediently behind. She was introduced several times as 'our new little storm trooper', and people laughed as if that were a charming description. Perry had told her that she must try to remember the names of everyone she encountered, but there were so many people and their names tumbled over one another, a Lord here, an Honourable there, a judge, member of parliament, a bishop, and . . . Clarissa?

'Lady Clarissa Marchmont. Clarissa, dear, may I introduce you to Iris Carter-Jenkins.'

Clarissa said, 'How d'you do, Iris. Nice to have another young face here, isn't it, Mrs Scaife?' She was wearing a gorgeous dress. ('Schiaparelli. Ancient, of course. I've had nothing new since war was declared. I'll be in rags soon.') 'Tell you what, Iris, why don't you ditch that sherry and we'll see if the barman can make us a couple of cocktails. Can I tempt you?'

'Why didn't you say?' Juliet murmured as they sipped decorously on something indescribably sweet and alcoholic and surveyed the room.

'I didn't know! It was a last-minute thing. Don't worry, I'm not one of your precious Perry's girls,' Clarissa said, laughing.

'He's not mine.' (If only.)

'He thought I'd come in handy, because of Daddy.'

'Daddy? The Duke?'

'If you like. He's over there,' Clarissa said, nodding in the direction of a knot of men in earnest conversation. 'They look like a group of penguins in their evening dress, don't they? A – what's the collective noun?'

'Huddle, I believe.' Penguins were comic creatures, Juliet thought. These men weren't funny. They were in charge of the country, one way or another. Were they even now discussing how they would carve up power if Hitler marched along Whitehall?

'Daddy's ferociously right-wing, completely pro-German,' Clarissa said. 'We met Hitler, you know. In '36, at the Games.' (*We?*) 'So, obviously, I fit the part. You're doing a good job of not looking shocked. Have a fag, why don't you?'

Juliet took a cigarette from the familiar gold-crested packet. 'But you're not . . . you know, are you?'

'One of them? Dear God, no. Of course not. Don't be silly. My sisters are, mind you. And Mummy. And poor Pammy, of course – she *worships* old Adolf, dreams about having his baby. Oh, look out, here comes Monty Rankin, I have to say hello to him. Nice earrings, by the way, I hope you get to keep them.'

Clarissa moved away and Juliet was left feeling rather exposed, and not just because of the flimsy nature of her dress. She threaded her way through the throng, catching snippets of conversation as she went. '*Germans are at the Meuse . . . the French are trying to blow up the bridgeheads . . . their troops are colonials . . . no loyalty . . . Dutch are finished . . . Wilhelmina in a boat on her way over here as we speak.*' They knew so much, it was frightening. Perhaps they knew everything.

Juliet found herself in an anteroom, where there was more drink and also food laid out. The food looked delicious – no sign of rationing here.

Beyond the anteroom was another kind of antechamber – hordes of refugees and evacuees could be housed here without anyone even noticing them. Beyond this room was a staircase, not the grandiose marble affair that climbed its way ostentatiously from the entrance hall, but a more everyday one, still richly carpeted, so not intended for servants. Juliet walked boldly up it ('Always behave as if you belong,' Perry advised) and found herself in what seemed like the true heart of the house. A drawing room, a dining room and a study that was lavish with cupboards and drawers and shelves. Perry had told her to bring the camera that was hidden in the lighter and it was currently lying heavily in her small evening bag. ('See if you can find anything, documents and so on. A copy of the Red Book, perhaps. Who knows.')

She entered a library – wall-to-wall leather-bound volumes and a massive refectory-style table that ran almost the length of the room. It was covered in documents and papers, quite a few of which were in German (there was a good deal of talk about *das Reich* and *der Führer*). Here we go, Juliet thought, taking out the camera, but she hadn't even managed to take one snap when she heard a deep, mellow voice behind her saying, 'Do you need a cigarette to go with that?'

Her heart dropped several floors – was the game up? Was she going to end up floating down the Thames like a log? Or delivered down a coal hole into the everlasting dark?

Courage, she thought, and turned to face the tall, strikingly ugly man who was standing behind her. There was something familiar about him and it took her a few seconds to place him. He was the man in the astrakhan-collared coat! No astrakhan collar tonight as of course he was in white tie, but even so he was recognizable. Juliet could feel her blood draining away. Was this what swooning felt like? Not something transcendent and romantic, but one's heart about to give out from fear.

'Oh, that would be wonderful, I seem to have left mine somewhere,' she managed to say.

'Are you all right?'

'Quite, thank you.'

He produced an enamelled cigarette case. It seemed he really was just offering her a cigarette.

'Thanks.'

He took the lighter off her and sparked it up. To her relief, a steady flame appeared.

'I don't believe we've met,' he said.

'Iris Carter-Jenkins,' she said, but he didn't reciprocate the introduction and instead he said, 'May I escort you downstairs? You seem to be lost.'

'I do rather, don't I?' she laughed breezily. Her heart still hadn't quietened down and she felt rather sick.

He shepherded her back down the same carpeted staircase and

said, 'I shall leave you here, I'm afraid, I have an appointment elsewhere,' and then in a voice so low that she had to lean close to hear
him, he said, 'Do be careful, Miss Armstrong.'

'Great God, what is that you're drinking? It's purple.' A man. One
of the penguins from the huddle.

'I believe it's called an "Aviation",' Juliet said.

'Can I tempt you to another?'

'No,' Juliet said. 'I don't believe I will, thank you.'

As instructed, the morning after Mrs Scaife's soirée, Juliet went to
return the diamond earrings to the jewellers. As fate would have it,
when she entered the shop she encountered, of all people, Mrs
Scaife herself. It seemed an odd coincidence, but then that was the
nature of coincidence, Juliet supposed – it always seemed odd.

Through the window she could see one of Mrs Scaife's personal
thugs standing guard outside the shop. Juliet was pretty sure they followed her whenever she left Mrs Scaife's house so, as instructed by
Perry, she had got into the habit of taking a meandering route away
from Pelham Place. Sometimes she would step on a bus on the Fulham Road and step off again after one stop, or take the Tube at South
Kensington station. And, of course, following Perry's instructions,
when she was in a taxi she was supposed to get out at Victoria and
walk the rest of the way to Dolphin Square. It was rather exciting, as
if she were in a Buchan novel or something by Erskine Childers.

Now she wondered if they had followed her here from Dolphin
Square this morning. They couldn't know what she did there though.
Could they? It would explain why Mrs Scaife happened to be in
exactly the same place at the same time. The thought made her feel
rather panicky. ('It's important not to fall prey to delusions and neuroses,' Perry said. But then he also said, 'Never trust a coincidence.')

Juliet was also finding herself unnerved by Mrs Scaife's fur

129

tippet – a stoat or a weasel – that was wound so tightly round her neck that it appeared to be trying to strangle her. The sharp little face of the animal was frozen in a snarl, fixing Juliet with its beady black glass eyes as if willing her to confess her true self.

'Oh, Iris, dearest, fancy seeing you here! Are you all right? You look quite pale. Have you come to browse? I'm just bringing in some pieces for cleaning.' Juliet had been feeling very much like Juliet, a Juliet who was rather the worse for wear after all the alcohol she had consumed the previous evening at Mrs Scaife's soirée. It took considerable effort to transform herself so abruptly into Iris.

'Yes,' she said. 'Actually I'm looking for a christening bracelet. My sister's baby. I'm to be godmother.' How nice it felt to say 'my sister'. The dearest wish of an only child. I could be a godmother, she thought. I'd be a good one.

'Oh, how charming. You never mentioned you had a sister.' Mrs Scaife turned to address a man behind the counter. 'Can you find a nice selection of christening bracelets for Miss Carter-Jenkins?'

Once the velvet tray of little silver bracelets was arranged to Mrs Scaife's satisfaction she said, 'Well, I would love to stay and help you choose, but I have lunch at the Ritz with Bunny Hepburn beckoning. Cook has taken a week's holiday. Can you believe? I must go. Lovely to see you again so soon, dear. Why don't you come and have coffee with me tomorrow morning?'

'Madam?' the man behind the counter prompted when Mrs Scaife had steered her way out of the shop. 'Can I tempt you with any of these bracelets?'

'No,' Juliet said. 'I'm afraid not. I'm terribly sorry but I have to go, I'm in a bit of a rush.' She was. She hotfooted it round to Pelham Place. Mrs Scaife would be hours at lunch and this was the perfect opportunity to look for the Red Book. All she needed was for poor little Dodds to let her in.

*

'Hello, Dodds.'

'Hello, miss,' Dodds said shyly. The maid peered timidly round the imposing door at her, guarding the threshold. The black paint on the door was so glossy that Juliet could see her face reflected in it. 'Mrs Scaife isn't here, miss.'

'Oh, that's all right. I'm afraid I left something when I was here the other day.'

'I didn't find anything, miss.'

'It was something very small. A ring. I think it must have got lost in the sofa. Can I come in and look for it, Dodds?'

'I'm not allowed to let anyone in when Mrs Scaife isn't here, miss.'

'My mother gave it to me before she died,' Juliet said softly. I could have been a great tragedienne, she thought. Although the mention of her mother caused genuine sorrow. If her mother *had* given her a ring, she would never take it off.

Dodds hesitated, no doubt thinking of her own dead mother. They were comrades in grief. Orphaned girls making their way through the perils of the dark forest. 'Please, Dodds?'

'Well . . .'

'Please?' It was like trying to coax a hesitant woodland creature to eat out of one's hand. Not that Juliet had ever done that. She expected Perry had. 'I'll be in and out in a shake of the lamb's proverbial tail. Honestly.'

Dodds sighed. 'Promise, miss?' The imposing door opened reluctantly.

Juliet rummaged amongst the salmon damask cushions, overseen by a nervous Dodds. It was very off-putting. 'Do you know, Dodds,' Juliet said, 'I am absolutely parched. Do you think you could make me a cup of tea?'

'I shouldn't leave you alone in here, miss. Mrs Scaife would kill me if she knew.'

Poor girl, she had no free will, always having to do as she was told. It was one step above servitude really, wasn't it? She must have another name, surely, Juliet thought. 'What's your name, Dodds?'

'Dodds, miss.'

'No, I mean your first name.'

'Beatrice, miss.'

They were all equals, weren't they? It was just luck that separated them. Juliet's own mother had been in service before she became a dressmaker. Juliet could easily have become 'Armstrong', waiting hand and foot on some pampered poodle of a woman like Mrs Scaife. 'Beatrice?'

'Yes, miss?'

Juliet took her purse out of her bag. It contained five new one-pound notes, collected from the bank that morning for Perry. She held them out to the girl, who stared at them in a kind of fascinated horror. 'Take them,' Juliet urged.

Dodds looked at her askance. 'What for, miss?'

'For nothing.'

'Nothing, miss?'

'Very well, then, how about for taking an inordinately long time to make a pot of tea?'

'I can't, miss.' (*Honourable and upright*, Juliet thought. Miles Merton would have recruited Beatrice Dodds.)

They said that truth could set you free, but Juliet had never set much store by that idea. But now she thought it might be worth a try and so she said, 'Beatrice, my name isn't Iris Carter-Jenkins. It's Juliet. Juliet Armstrong. I work for the government,' she added solemnly. It was true and yet it felt oddly like a lie, as if she were acting the part of being herself. 'You'll be doing your country an enormous service if you help me.' A small pause for effect. 'I believe Mrs Scaife is a traitor.'

Dodds needed no other explanation. Ignoring the money, she

said, 'I'll make you some tea, miss.' She bobbed a little curtsey, directed more towards her King and country than Juliet. With a little smile of proud heroism, she said, 'It may take some time, I'm afraid, miss.'

As soon as Dodds – Beatrice, Juliet reminded herself – had scurried out of the room, Juliet abandoned all pretence of searching the salmon damask and turned her attention to the rest of the room. She began with the most promising – the escritoire – pulling out one drawer after another and combing through the contents of each. She had no idea of the size of the Red Book – it might be as big as a family Bible or as small as a policeman's notebook – but there was no sign of it amongst Mrs Scaife's bountiful stationery, her invitations or her pile of bills and receipts. It appeared Mrs Scaife was a very tardy payer of tradesmen.

An exploration of the drawing room – behind the pictures, beneath the corners of the rugs, even a careful investigation of the cabinet of Sèvres – revealed nothing. In the hallway she found Beatrice still hovering nervously. To Juliet's chagrin, she didn't seem to have made any actual tea. 'Did you find what you were looking for, miss?'

'No. Unfortunately. '

'What *are* you looking for, miss?'

'A book, it's red.'

'The Red Book?'

'Yes!' Why hadn't she thought to ask the girl in the first place? 'Have you seen it?'

'I think so, miss. Mrs Scaife keeps it in the—'

She was interrupted by the unmistakeable sound of the front door opening and Mrs Scaife's voice calling, 'Dodds? Dodds, where are you?' as if history was doomed to repeat itself endlessly (but then it was, wasn't it?).

Juliet and Beatrice stared at each other in horror as Mrs Scaife sailed into the hall downstairs on a raft of complaints. 'The Ritz got my reservation wrong, they claimed that there were no tables free. Well, that was nonsense. Bunny Hepburn was useless, of course . . .' and so on. Oh, Lord, they were in for it now, Juliet thought.

Beatrice was the first to come to her senses. 'Upstairs,' she whispered urgently, indicating the staircase to the second floor. 'Go up. Hide.'

'And I said to the maître d', "My husband is a Rear Admiral, you know."' Mrs Scaife's words floated up the stairs, slightly ahead of her own less buoyant ascent.

As she put her foot on the first tread, Juliet suddenly remembered her handbag, sitting where she had left it in plain sight on the carpet next to the salmon sofa. Not Iris's handbag, but Juliet's. What would Mrs Scaife make of the materialization of a strange handbag in her drawing room?

Mrs Scaife was very observant and the handbag was quite distinctive – red leather with a shoulder strap and a clasp that looked like a buckle – she would surely recognize it as the one that Iris was carrying when she met her in the jeweller's. If she looked inside it she would find it contained not Iris's but Juliet's identity card and ration book. Not to mention her security pass! At least the Mauser wasn't in there, Iris had that, and Juliet always kept the keys to Dolphin Square in her coat pocket for convenience. Nonetheless, it would hardly take a genius to realize that 'Iris' was actually someone called Juliet Armstrong and that she had been sent into the lion's den to spy.

She could hear Mrs Scaife getting nearer. She might as well have been singing *Fee-fi-fo-fum* for the terror she was inducing. 'Dodds, bring me some tea, will you? Where are you?'

Juliet grabbed Beatrice's hand as the girl turned to go (she felt her quivering with fear) and hissed, 'My handbag – in the living room.'

Beatrice grimaced and nodded her understanding, before

whispering urgently, 'Go,' and pushing Juliet up the stairs. The girl looked as if she was going to disintegrate from terror.

It was like a nasty game of hide-and-seek, Juliet thought as she ran up the stairs. She dived into the first room she came to – Mrs Scaife's bedroom, by the look of it – a large and rather gloomy nest, thanks to the thick net curtains that shrouded the French windows. The room smelt of face powder and something faintly medicinal, mixed with the scent of lilies, although there were no flowers in the room.

Juliet could hear the sound of Mrs Scaife's heavy tread on the stairs and her strident tones calling on Dodds. 'Dodds, can you hear me? Has the cat got your tongue?' (What an awful idea, Juliet thought. And how would the cat get it – by accident or by design?) 'Bring the tea up to my bedroom, Dodds. I'm going up to have a little lie-down.'

Oh, for heaven's sake, Juliet thought. What an exasperating woman. What on earth was she going to do now?

'What's this? Been acquiring new gew-gaws, have you?'

'Oh, that,' Juliet said, regarding the little yellow-and-gold coffee cup with its pretty cherubs that Perry was examining on her desk. 'Found it in a junk shop,' she said. 'I think it might be genuine Sèvres. I got it for sixpence. Quite a bargain.'

Spoils of war, Juliet had thought, as the little orphaned cup nestled like a precious egg in her pocket all the way down the Virginia creeper outside Mrs Scaife's bedroom. She was sorry she hadn't been able to manage the saucer as well. Perhaps she could filch it the next time she was there and reunite the pair. Perhaps she could pilfer the whole collection, piece by pretty piece. The coffee pot would be awkward, especially if she had to exit via Mrs Scaife's bedroom window again.

She had managed to escape by fighting her way through the

heavy nets at the French windows, like a fly trying to disentangle itself from a web, and stepping out on to what proved to be a perilously small wrought-iron balcony just in time to hear Mrs Scaife saying, 'Just put the tray down on the ottoman, Dodds.'

The bedroom overlooked the back garden and a tough old Virginia creeper ran past the balcony. It seemed an awfully long way down from the second floor and Juliet wondered what Mrs Scaife would make of it if she found Juliet laying in her garden with a broken neck.

Iris was the plucky sort, she reminded herself as she reached out and grabbed the creeper and then climbed awkwardly over the little balcony. Wiggins, Mrs Scaife's ancient factotum, chose that moment to totter into view, holding a pair of long-handled pruning shears that looked too heavy for him. Juliet held her breath. What would he do if he glanced up and saw her hanging like a monkey? Luckily his eyes remained firmly on the garden. He looked around for a bit and then, as if giving up on the idea of work, he doddered away again. Juliet breathed.

She proceeded to shin gingerly down the creeper to the garden below. They had done rope climbing in the gymnasium in her school, although she had never expected it to be a skill she would need in later life. It seemed to Juliet that between her school and Guides she had received as good a training for the Security Service as anything. It was rather thrilling, this espionage lark, like an adventure in the *Girl's Own*.

'I bumped into Mrs Scaife in town and she invited me back to tea, in Pelham Place,' she reported eagerly to Perry on her return to Dolphin Square. 'And the Red Book is there, according to Mrs Scaife's maid – her name's Beatrice, I think she could be useful to us. I had to escape through an upstairs window,' she added breathlessly.

'Goodness,' Perry said. 'Look what happens when you're let off the leash, Miss Armstrong.' And this, Juliet thought crossly, was when she should be pulled into a strong pair of tweedy arms and her would-be lover would gaze deeply into her eyes and say—

'You look rather dishevelled, Miss Armstrong. Do you need to borrow a comb?'

'I have one in my handbag, thank you, sir.' Or at any rate, Iris did. Juliet didn't like to spoil her moment of heroism by confessing that she had left her own handbag in Pelham Place. Surely she could retrieve it without Perry needing ever to know what a careless idiot she was? He had warned her of a spate of bag-snatching in the vicinity of Victoria station. If the worst came to the worst, she could always blame it on some random robber in the street.

But what of Mrs Scaife – had she already discovered it? Did the handbag have a big sign on it saying, *Open me and find a clue to Iris's real identity*? Let's hope not, she thought. Beatrice Dodds seemed a resourceful sort of girl and it was in her interests, too, to remove all signs of an intruder.

Juliet returned to Pelham Place the following morning, as invited by Mrs Scaife in the jeweller's.

The door was opened by a new girl, tall and pale and rather sickly-looking, as if she'd been raised in the dark, like a mushroom.

'Where's Dodds?' Juliet asked.

'Who?'

'Dodds. Mrs Scaife's maid.'

'I'm Mrs Scaife's maid.'

'But where's Beatrice? Beatrice Dodds?'

'Never heard of her, miss.'

'Iris, is that you?' Mrs Scaife called down from upstairs. 'Do come up, dear.'

Mrs Scaife sent the sunless stalk of a girl to make coffee. She returned, staggering beneath the weight of the tea tray.

'Put it down, Nightingale, before you drop it,' Mrs Scaife said.

'Where's Dodds?' Juliet asked lightly, feigning an indifference that she was not feeling.

'Dodds?' Mrs Scaife said. 'She took off, can you believe, without a by-your-leave. One minute she's here, the next she's gone.'

'She disappeared?'

'Into thin air. She took a piece of the Sèvres though as a souvenir of her time with me – a little coffee cup. It turns out she was a common thief and yet you would have thought butter wouldn't melt in her mouth.'

'What about her belongings – did she take them with her?' Juliet asked. 'Her clothes and . . . so on?'

'No, she left everything behind in her room. Nothing of value. I've had the trouble of clearing it all out.'

Nightingale, in the act of pouring coffee, glanced at Mrs Scaife. It was she, Juliet suspected, who had had the trouble. Poor girl, she thought. She couldn't have looked less like her avian namesake.

Mrs Scaife handed Juliet a cup. 'Do have a scone. Nightingale made them. She has a very light pastry hand. Cook had better watch out when she comes back.'

The tray, Juliet noticed, was set for three, and she asked, 'Is Mrs Ambrose coming?'

'No, a new friend, she is a little late.'

On cue, the doorbell rang and Juliet listened as Nightingale herded someone upstairs. Juliet was curious as to the identity of this new friend as Mrs Scaife usually kept very close to her familiar circle of 18b widows. Juliet almost spilt her coffee when she heard the familiar querulous Scandinavian tones. Trude! Juliet's two worlds colliding unexpectedly right there in the sea of salmon damask. *These people aren't your Bettys and Dollys*, Perry had said about the Right Club, and yet here was Trude, a bridge between the worlds. It suddenly made the informants seem more powerful, more insidious.

'Ah,' Mrs Scaife said to Trude, 'there you are. I was worried that perhaps you couldn't come.'

'I got lost,' Trude said. 'The streets all look the same.' She was fractious, as though Mrs Scaife might be to blame for the topography of SW7. In the flesh she was surprising. Juliet had imagined her to be thin, scrawny even, given the sharp, scratchy character that came across in the recordings, but in the flesh she was quite large and well cushioned. 'Big-boned', as Juliet's mother would say kindly to her 'larger ladies'.

'Well, you're here now,' Mrs Scaife placated. 'Do let me introduce you to Iris Carter-Jenkins, one of our loyal young friends. Iris, this is Miss Trude Hedstrom.'

They shook hands. Trude's hand felt like a limp fillet of wet fish.

In a confidential voice, as though someone might be listening (me, Juliet thought), Mrs Scaife said, 'Miss Hedstrom is doing sterling work. She is the head of a network of German spies, all across the country. They are bringing valuable information to the German government.'

'Oh, how fascinating,' Juliet said. 'Do you report directly to Berlin?'

'To a Gestapo agent here. But I can't talk about it. It's highly secret and extremely dangerous work.'

'Well, good for you,' Juliet said. 'Keep it up.' What self-importance, Juliet thought. Imagine how awful Trude would be if she were given real power, a female *Gauleiter*, throwing her (considerable) weight around.

Juliet couldn't wait to get back to Dolphin Square and tell Perry about Mrs Scaife's visitor, but had to endure a good deal of prattling about the imminence of German victory in Europe and how lovely the Bavarian countryside was at this time of year (Mrs Scaife, like Trude, had spent several summer holidays in Germany). At one point Trude suddenly declared vehemently, 'Let's hope the Germans bomb us the way they bombed Rotterdam.'

'Goodness, why?' Mrs Scaife asked, rather taken aback by the savagery of this outburst.

'Because then the cowards in government will capitulate and make peace with the Third Reich.'

'Do have a scone,' Mrs Scaife said appeasingly.

Who was to say that in a few weeks' time the lovely drawing room of Pelham Place wouldn't be full of *Wehrmacht* officers perching on the salmon damask and helping themselves to Mrs Scaife's baked goods? The Germans had crossed the Meuse. What Churchill had called the 'monstrous tyranny' was about to cover the whole of the continent, a delta of blood on the floodplain of Europe.

'And what do *you* do?' Trude asked, suddenly turning her full, rather frightening attention on Juliet.

'Oh, you know . . . this and that.'

Nightingale saw Juliet to the door. She wasn't quite as fond of curtseying as Dodds had been. She had retrieved Lily for her. The dog was always relegated to the servants' quarters when Juliet visited Pelham Place. Mrs Scaife found animals 'unpredictable'. (As if people were not!)

'Nightingale,' Juliet said, dropping her voice, 'was there a handbag amongst Dodds's things?'

'Yes, miss.'

'Red leather, shoulder strap, clasp that looks like a buckle?'

'No, miss, nothing like that.'

Deception Game

THE BATTLE FOR France was underway. German Panzer divisions were tearing their way through the Ardennes. Amiens was under siege and Arras was surrounded, but in London summer had begun and on a Saturday afternoon it was still a pleasure to take a dog for a walk in a park. Juliet was doing just that in Kensington Gardens.

Lily was easily distracted and had alarmed Juliet by suddenly running off in the – vain – pursuit of a lurcher. Juliet trotted obediently after her and just as she managed to retrieve the dog and wrangle it back on to the lead she spotted the unremarkable yet unmistakeable figure of Godfrey Toby. He was walking slowly yet purposefully near the Round Pond.

She decided to follow him, even if Godfrey was doing nothing more doubtful than taking a saunter in the park. She had been charged with keeping an eye on him, so keep an eye on him she would. Two, even. Four, if you counted the dog.

They trailed him for a long time, past the Albert Hall and the back of the Science Museum, on to Exhibition Road and finally turning left on to Brompton Road. He swung his silver-topped cane or occasionally tapped it on the pavement as if in time to something. At one point Juliet had boldly moved so close to him that she could hear him whistling 'You Are My sunshine', if she wasn't mistaken. She hadn't thought of him as a whistling man. Or even a tuneful one.

If he turned round suddenly and caught her – like a game of statues – she could say she was going to Harrods. She rehearsed an attitude of casual surprise – *Oh hello, Mr Toby, fancy bumping into you!* She hardly needed an excuse, this was her neighbourhood, after all. Perhaps it was Godfrey who was going to Harrods. Perhaps it was the mysterious Mrs Toby's birthday and Godfrey was going to buy her a little spousal token – perfume or embroidered handkerchiefs. *Don't let your imagination run away with you, Miss Armstrong.*

He didn't turn round once, however, and to her surprise, his path swerved abruptly and led him into the Brompton Oratory. Was he a Catholic? If anything, she would have guessed Low Anglican.

Rather warily, Juliet followed him in. There were a few people scattered around the pews, most kneeling in silent prayer.

She quietly pulled the dog into one of the pews at the back. From here she could see Godfrey, hat in hand now, strolling along one of the side aisles in the direction of the altar, more like a flâneur than a man intending worship. *Tap-tap-tap* went his cane on the stone floor.

And then, with only the slightest pause and an admirable sleight of hand, he removed a piece of paper from his overcoat pocket and seemed to tuck it into what Juliet presumed must be a gap between a pilaster and one of the many elaborate memorials on the wall.

He continued his leisurely progress, crossing in front of the chancel to return down the opposite aisle.

Juliet bobbed down hastily and pretended to be at prayer. Lily thought this was a great game and kept pawing at her until Juliet grabbed her round her solid middle and held on to her tightly. She could feel the tremor of excitement in Lily's body. She hardly dared glance in Godfrey's direction in case she caught his eye. (Dreadful idea!) She imagined him suddenly looming over her (*Why, Miss Armstrong, what a surprise, fancy encountering you here, I didn't take you for a churchgoer*), but when she eventually mustered the courage to look up she found that there was no sign of him.

She clambered to her feet and was about to investigate Godfrey's little act of legerdemain when the man in the astrakhan-collared coat made another appearance. Juliet ducked down again; she was beginning to feel almost religious. The man walked briskly up to the memorial and, without any hesitation, removed whatever it was that Godfrey had concealed there, before turning on his heel and making for the exit at the same brisk pace. The astrakhan-collared man left the Oratory as rapidly as he had entered it and if he had seen her he made no sign of it.

Juliet thought about his warning to her at Mrs Scaife's party. *Be careful, Miss Armstrong.* He frightened her in a way that the war didn't.

-11-

RECORD 7.

G. What is the 236 battery? Is it Royal Artillery?
D. I think infantry of some kind. First Infantry
   division maybe.
G. Aren't they in France?
D. Well, I don't know. Maybe a Highland Division.

(Two minutes lost due to a technical hitch.)

DOLLY's dog's frenzied barking makes much of the
conversation inaudible.

G. Does he want a bone (??)
E. The envelopes.
G. Yes, good, the envelopes.
D. Oh, yes, the envelopes, of course. I can't find
   out their telephone numbers. I'll keep trying
   but I have had no success yet. I haven't been

```
there to answer the telephone when they've
called me.
```

'The Nazis are knocking on our door now, miss, aren't they?' Cyril said. A statement that was followed – rather unnervingly – by a *rat-a-tat, rat-a-tat-TAT* on their own front door that made them both jump.

'Godfrey,' Cyril said.

Rat-a-tat, rat-a-tat-TAT again.

'He must want to talk to us,' Cyril said.

'I'll get it,' Juliet said.

It was indeed Godfrey. 'Miss Armstrong,' he said, tipping his hat when she opened the door.

'Why don't you come in, Mr Toby?'

'I won't, if you don't mind. I'll just hover here. Our friends will be arriving any minute – we don't want them to catch us hob-nobbing. You are the enemy, after all, Miss Armstrong.' He smiled at her.

Had he seen her in the Brompton Oratory? Did he know that she had witnessed his strange assignation and odd jiggery-pokery with the piece of paper? It was a difficult topic to drop into a conversation. (*I suspect you might be a double agent, Mr Toby.*) And perhaps it had not been something underhand, but a necessary act of war. He was a spy, after all, and it was Perry who was his taskmaster, not Alleyne.

'A penny for them?' Godfrey said. He was a man who wasn't above a cliché if necessary.

'Sorry, Mr Toby.'

'I find myself without paper and pencil,' he said. 'I wonder if I could borrow some from you? I imagine you are always well supplied.'

'Yes, of course, I'll just get you something.'

'Oh, and some of the invisible ink, if you have it.'

'I do.' She gathered the required items and gave them to Godfrey.

He sighed unexpectedly and said, 'It's rather tiresome, isn't it?'

'The war?'

'All the resentment, I mean,' Godfrey clarified, seeing her blank response. 'These people –' he indicated next door, 'they are so very . . . rancorous, are they not?'

'I suppose,' Juliet said.

'Human nature favours the tribal. Tribalism engenders violence. It was ever thus and so it will ever be.'

Juliet stifled a yawn and was grateful when she heard the lift doors opening. Godfrey gave her a silent salute and disappeared into his flat.

She kept the gap in her own door open long enough to hear Victor's voice growing nearer. 'Mr Toby! I need to tell you –' and Godfrey whispering, 'Shush, walls have ears, Victor. Come inside.'

Juliet closed the door very quietly. 'Do you ever doubt Godfrey?' she asked Cyril.

'Me, miss? No, never. Why, do you?'

'No, of course not. Is that really the time, Cyril?'

'Off to see Mrs S again, are you, miss?'

'For my sins.'

'Anything to tell me, Miss Armstrong?' Oliver Alleyne was leaning casually on the bonnet of a car parked on Chichester Street, at the back entrance of Dolphin Square. Lily moved closer to Juliet and leant against her leg as if she needed the reassurance of her presence.

'About Mr Toby?'

'Anything suspicious?'

'No,' Juliet said. 'Nothing.'

'Sure?'

'Quite sure, sir.'

'Can I give you a lift somewhere, Miss Armstrong? Pelham Place, perhaps?'

'No, thank you, sir. The dog needs a walk, she's been inside all day. Is her owner coming back, do you think?'

'Who knows, Miss Armstrong. Things are in a parlous state over there.'

There had been another cup-dropping incident yesterday.

'Butterfingers,' Perry said by way of explanation, although from where Juliet had been in the next room it had sounded awfully like someone smashing something deliberately. Soon there would be no crockery left in the flat. She had already removed the little Sèvres cup to Kensington, a place of safety.

'I think perhaps we both need a break from all this, Miss Armstrong. A little holiday.'

Holiday! She imagined a weekend in Rye or even a few days in Hampshire. A hotel or a cottage where they would open a bottle of wine by candlelight and sit on a rug in front of a blazing log fire and then he would put his arm around her and say—

'Verulamium? Near St Albans,' he said.

Having learnt from the otters, she packed sandwiches and a Thermos for the trip.

They were disgorged next to an underwhelming ruin beneath a menacing sky and Perry said to the driver, 'Come back for us in three hours.' (Three hours! Juliet thought.)

A Roman villa, he told her. 'A very well-preserved mosaic floor. It covers the hypocaust. *Hypocaustum* from the Ancient Greek – *hypo* meaning "beneath" and *caust* "burnt". Which word do you think we get from that?'

'I have no idea,' she said, caustically. Not that he noticed. Adverbs were too subtle a part of speech for him. Could he not see that she was ripe for the plucking? And not as a rose or a pigeon. She was a gift. A pearl. The apple beckoning on the tree – a fact he seemed blithely unaware of as he expatiated upon the subject of the Roman Watling Street that was somewhere beneath their feet.

It began to rain – a miserable kind of drizzle – and she trudged resentfully round the ruins in his wake until the three hours of purgatory were up and the driver returned, smelling of beer and cigarettes.

So much for a holiday. It did neither of them any good, particularly Perry, it seemed.

'By the way, Garrard's telephoned while you were out,' Perry said on their return. 'They say that they haven't received those earrings back.'

'Oh, I meant to tell you—'

Perry made a dismissive gesture. Apparently the diamonds had been trumped by war. 'We're on the run,' he said. 'Our troops are heading for the coast. It's over. Europe is finished. One's heart breaks, does it not?'

-8-

RECORD 5

15.20

GODFREY enquired about EDITH'S friend MRS TAYLOR'S son who had been called up into the Signals Corps.

E. Told his mother -
G. MRS TAYLOR?
E. Yes. That it was amazing how many pacifists there are in the Army.
G. Yes?
E. (several words inaudible) Do you remember those men who went to work at Rolls-Royce?

```
G. The Belgians.
E. They've got a very poor opinion of the Royal Air
   Force.
```

<u>15.30</u>

```
There is an incoming telephone call.

G. Hello ... hello? (puts receiver down again)
E. Who was that?
G. Nobody. A wrong number.
```

Who was phoning him, Juliet wondered? She heard him say, 'Yes, right, understood,' in a different tone of voice to the one he used with the informants. Juliet wondered if it was the man in the astrakhan-collared coat.

She didn't like Oliver Alleyne, didn't really trust him, but she supposed it was her duty to say something about Godfrey's clandestine meetings. Sometimes she found herself wondering if all was as it seemed. What if there was a greater deception game in play? What if Godfrey really *was* a Gestapo agent? A Gestapo agent pretending to be an MI5 agent pretending to be a Gestapo agent. It made her head hurt to think about it. And how perfectly placed he would be, the puppet-master of a network of sympathizers. The spider at the centre of the web.

She wished she could talk to Perry about it, but Oliver Alleyne had told her not to say anything to anyone. I practise to deceive, she thought. Rhymes with Eve.

After some hesitation she typed a cryptically short note to Alleyne. *I have something to discuss with you.* She would give it to the messenger boy next time he called. On the envelope she wrote, 'To be delivered directly into the hand of O. Alleyne.'

She returned to typing – one of Giselle's reports (although it hardly merited the noun). It was an analphabetic jumble, rather like being given an insight into the chaotic workings of a cat's brain, although there was a rather well-doodled cartoon of a fat man in white tie and tails, an equally fat cigar in his mouth. Beneath it Giselle had scribbled 'La Proie du soir'. La Proie – was that prey? There was no Larousse in Dolphin Square. Juliet supposed it was a portrayal of the Swedish arms dealer Giselle had spent the evening seducing. Successfully, apparently.

It was only when she paused to consider elevenses (although it was only half past ten) that she heard an odd noise coming from Perry's bedroom. There had been no sign of life in the Dolphin Square flat when she arrived this morning so she had presumed Perry was elsewhere. The noise was a kind of snuffling, as if an animal – a large rat or a small dog – was running amok in there. Lily had heard it too and was standing attentively, her head cocked to one side, staring at the closed door.

Juliet got up from her desk and knocked cautiously – although if it was a rat or a dog it seemed unlikely that it would care whether or not she knocked. There was no answer so she opened the door warily, half expecting something to come running out, but nothing did. Lily, less daunted, pushed the door open wider and entered Perry's bedroom. Juliet followed the dog.

Not an animal, but Perry – he had been in there all along! He was kneeling by his bed as if in prayer. He turned to look at her and she could see that his face was soaked with tears. Was he ill? He seemed wounded in some way, although not by anything visible. Lily licked his hand encouragingly but his attitude remained one of despair.

'Can I do something, sir?' she asked.

'You can't help me,' he said bleakly. 'No one can.'

'Are you having a spiritual crisis?' she hazarded – tenderly, as seemed befitting for spiritual crises – but he laughed (rather maniacally). She cast her eye around the room (dreadful phrase) to see if it held any clue to this sudden collapse. But the room rendered up nothing – the neatly made bed (military style), the carefully placed grooming items, the white shirt hanging on the wardrobe door. She couldn't help but stare at the wardrobe. Had it come with the flat, or was it perhaps the one that the mysterious 'first wife' had hanged herself in? That must have been quite a surprise for Perry when he opened the door.

Perry gave a wretched kind of sob and, unable to think of anything else, Juliet made a cup of tea and placed it silently on the carpet next to him, where he remained in supplication. She shut the door quietly and got on with her work. It turned out that discovering a man on his knees, weeping, was a surprisingly effective deterrent to romantic feelings about that man. And the wardrobe, too, of course.

An hour later, Perry emerged and seemed restored to his usual condition of constraint, although he still had a rather haunted, woebegone look about him.

Was it a coincidence that this episode followed a visit yesterday from a pair of Special Branch officers? They had closeted themselves with Perry in the living room, from which Juliet had been summarily banished. 'Perhaps you can do something in the kitchen?' Perry said vaguely. Perhaps I can't, Juliet thought, and still rather cross at having been subjected to Verulamium the previous day she said, 'I'll take the dog for a walk.'

She left the door to the living room slightly open, so she was able to hear one of the Special Branch officers say, 'Mr Gibbons, could you tell us where you were last night?' She envied the dog's hearing. All she could catch was Perry muttering something about the 'War Office'. She clipped on the dog's lead and left. She knew exactly where Perry was last night because she had seen him.

She had been in the Rivoli Bar at the Ritz drinking cocktails with Clarissa and forcefully expressing her feelings about Roman ruins.

'Oh, the Romans,' Clarissa said dismissively, as if they were tiresome family friends.

At the end of the evening, Juliet had spotted Perry exiting the basement bar – 'the Ritz below the Ritz', she'd heard it called. Someone had told her that it was also known as the 'Pink Sink'. Because it was painted pink, presumably, although Clarissa hooted with laughter at this idea. Juliet was surprised, as Perry seemed to do nothing but work and she never thought of him drinking in a bar, especially not a pink one.

'Come on,' Clarissa said, looping her arm through Juliet's and pulling her in the opposite direction from Perry. 'Let's go this way, I don't think he's going to want to see us.'

Why ever not? Glancing over her shoulder she saw a man in naval uniform, a rating, approaching Perry. He was what Perry dismissively called 'the mincing sort'. Once or twice when she had been in a car in the evening with him, he had pointed out the 'fairies' in Piccadilly, 'Touting for trade like common tarts.' She wasn't sure what he meant. She knew about the Piccadilly tarts – but men? She hadn't known such things existed and even now she could only conjecture.

'You can tell them by the way they walk,' Perry had told her. He had sounded disgusted and yet there he was, allowing the rating to lean in and light a cigarette for him. Perry had clasped his hands around those of the rating in order to steady the lighter. It was the gesture of a man with a woman, not a man with a man. The flare of the little flame had illuminated Perry's features, revealing a tortured expression on his face, as if he was being forced to do something he disliked.

But he doesn't smoke, Juliet thought.

Die to Live

GODFREY HAD NO meeting with his informants so Juliet and Perry were alone in Dolphin Square, working diligently late in preparation. 'Ducks in a row, Miss Armstrong,' Perry said, 'ducks in a row.' When they finished they listened to the *Nine o'Clock News*, sitting companionably on the Dolphin Square sofa with a glass of whisky each. Perry said, 'Miss Armstrong?'

'Mm?'

'May I ask you something?'

'Yes, of course.'

He frowned as if he was having difficulty formulating the next sentence and then, without any warning, he dropped like a penitent to his knees on the carpet in front of her and Juliet thought, Oh, no, here we go. Surely he's not going to start praying again? But he didn't. Instead he said, 'Miss Armstrong – would you do me the honour of consenting to be my wife?'

'I'm sorry?'

'Will you marry me?'

'You should stay the night,' Perry said. 'Doesn't that make sense? The blackout and so on.'

Juliet had been so dumbstruck by his proposal that she had said neither 'yes' nor 'no' but had mumbled something that he seemed to take as an acceptance.

'On the sofa?' she queried and he laughed and said he had a perfectly serviceable bed she could share. 'We're engaged now, after all.' He seemed light-headed, as if he had found the solution to something fretful.

'Are we? Engaged?' she said faintly. But I don't want to be married, she thought.

Perry handed her a pair of his pyjamas to wear – pale powder-blue silk with a burgundy piping, rather nice if a bit on the roomy side, and she went into the (freezing cold) bathroom to change into them. When she returned to the austere bedroom she found that Perry was similarly attired, sitting up in bed leafing through what looked like official papers – arrest warrants, by the look of it.

'Ah, Miss Armstrong,' he said, as if he had forgotten about her. He patted the bed as though he was encouraging Lily to jump up and join him. It still wasn't the satin sheets and champagne flutes of her imagination, but it was perhaps as good as it was going to get. She climbed into the chilly bed and lay expectantly. He arched over her and she closed her eyes, but all she received was a dry kiss on her cheek. 'Good night then,' he said and turned off his bedside light. And that was how they slept, modestly side by side, as chaste as effigies on an icy tomb. She was not to be ploughed, but left fallow and parched. The kiss had been an imprimatur that closed rather than opened her.

Juliet lay awake for a long time before the dog scrambled up on to the bed and started licking her face and nuzzling her neck, more affectionate than the man lying fast asleep next to her. Was Perry a tortured Catholic? One who had taken a vow of celibacy that would be broken only on their honeymoon? (Perhaps they would spend it acrimoniously in St Albans.)

The wardrobe loomed forbiddingly in the dark and she thought about the first wife. And what about the second one – what unfortunate fate had befallen her? If she married Perry, she would be his third wife. Perhaps it was like *Goldilocks* and she would be the one who was *just right*. ('You've got to give him credit for trying,' Clarissa said.)

Juliet gazed helplessly at Perry's sleeping profile in the darkness. Was a little passion too much to ask for? A bit of melting and swooning? Perhaps sex was something you had to learn and then stick at until you were good at it, like hockey or the piano. But an initial lesson would be helpful.

She must have fallen into sleep eventually because she was jolted out of it by a loud hammering on the door. Perry clambered out of bed like a scalded cat, almost as if he was expecting trouble. There was barely any light in the sky, so it seemed likely that it was an emergency of one kind or another. Had Paris fallen?

She could hear voices in the hall and then Perry came back, looking bemused but rather relieved, and said, 'You'd better put some clothes on. Your presence is requested.' Not Paris then.

'What is it?' she asked, still groggy from sleep.

'There are some detectives from Scotland Yard here. They seem to think that you're dead.'

'What?'

He handed her his dressing-gown. The dog, which had been sleeping at the foot of the bed, jumped off and escorted her out of the bedroom, its claws pitter-pattering across the cold linoleum.

It growled when it saw the two serious-looking men – one quite tall, the other quite short – who were waiting in the living room. They introduced themselves as detectives from Scotland Yard. Juliet thought of the little Sèvres cup. Surely they weren't here for that? In lieu of his dressing-gown, Perry had pulled on his big tweed overcoat over his pyjamas. He looked faintly ridiculous. I can't possibly marry him, she thought.

'Here she is,' Perry said, uncharacteristically bright. He introduced her: 'My fiancée, Miss Armstrong.' *Fiancée* – oh, Lord, Juliet thought, was that really what she was now?

'There, you see,' Perry said to the detectives, 'Miss Armstrong looks in rather good condition for a corpse. Admittedly,' he laughed, 'she's always rather slow when she's woken up early.'

The short detective ran his eyes over her, taking in the dressing-gown, the dishevelment. He cast her a look of mild contempt. It's not what it looks like, she thought crossly. (If only it was.)

'Perhaps Miss Armstrong could show us some identification,' the tall detective said. He smiled encouragingly at her.

'Darling?' Perry smiled expectantly at her. (Darling, she wondered? When had he ever addressed her as that?) He put his hand in the small of her back. It felt both intimate and cautionary. The presence of the law seemed to be making him unaccountably nervous. She remembered the visit from Special Branch the other day.

'Miss Armstrong?' the short detective prompted.

'I know who I am.' (Do I, she wondered?) 'Isn't that proof enough? And Perry – Mr Gibbons – knows who I am.'

She looked at Perry and he nodded helpfully and said, 'I do.'

'But do you have anything that proves that, beyond the say-so of both of you?'

'Say-so?' Perry said, frowning at them. 'Surely my word is good enough? I'm a senior MI5 officer.'

Both detectives ignored him and again the short one prompted, 'Miss Armstrong?'

'Well,' Juliet said, 'you see, the thing is, my bag was stolen a few days ago – near Victoria station – in a café. I foolishly put it on the ground while I was having a cup of tea and the next thing I knew it had vanished. I don't know if you know this, but there has been rather a spate of bag-snatching in that area, and, of course, it had all that kind of thing in it. Identity documents and so on.' *If you're going to tell a lie, tell a good one.*

'And did you report this theft?' the short detective asked.

'I keep meaning to, but we've been so busy. There's a war on, after all.'

She looked at Perry and made a rueful face. 'Sorry . . . *darling*, I didn't want you to find out. You had warned me to be careful and I knew you'd be cross with me.'

Perry ruffled her curls fondly and said, 'You are a silly thing, I wouldn't be cross with you.'

They were behaving in a way that was so far removed from their real selves that they may as well have been in a play. Not one that would ever garner critical acclaim.

'Can you describe your handbag for us, Miss Armstrong?' the tall detective said. Of the two, he seemed more inclined to be pleasant.

'Red leather, shoulder strap, clasp like a buckle. Have you found it?'

'I'm afraid to say,' the short detective said, 'that we have. It was with a young lady whose body was found yesterday.'

'Body?' Perry said. 'Dead?'

'I'm afraid so, sir.'

'Some kind of accident?'

'Murdered,' the short detective said bluntly.

Beatrice, Juliet thought and gave a little cry of pain, and Perry said, 'Juliet?' in a concerned way that was touching. 'Murdered?' he puzzled to the detective.

'I'm afraid so, sir,' the taller, nicer detective said. 'Would you have any idea who the young lady might be, Miss Armstrong?' Perry's hand on her back became a grip, so she supposed she was to say nothing.

'No,' Juliet whispered. 'I don't, I'm afraid. No idea at all.'

Had Beatrice been trying to return the handbag to her? Had she been murdered because of that? Did one of Mrs Scaife's thugs follow her and kill her? It was too awful to think about.

'So, naturally, Miss Armstrong,' the short one said, taking over the double act, 'we originally presumed the young lady was you as the handbag contained your identity documents.' Juliet thought that she might be about to be sick.

'So you don't know who it is? This person? This young lady?' Perry asked the short detective.

'We don't. Do *you* know who she might be, sir?'

'Of course not. I can only suppose she stole Miss Armstrong's handbag, or a man of her acquaintance did and gave it to her. May I ask how she died?'

'Strangled, with a headscarf,' the short detective said.

Juliet moaned quietly. The dog gave her a worried look.

'And she was found where?' Perry asked. He had a relentlessly forensic nature.

'She was discovered in the coal hole of the Carlton Club.'

'The Carlton Club?' Perry echoed. He exchanged a glance with Juliet. He had obviously read the transcript of Trude's conversation with Godfrey.

'Sir?' the short detective said. 'Does that mean something to you?'

'No, not at all.'

'We think she had been there several days before she was discovered.'

Three days, Juliet thought. Just three days since she last saw Beatrice in Pelham Place.

'Are you all right, Miss Armstrong?' the tall detective asked.

'Yes,' she said quietly. No, she thought. Not at all.

'Obviously Miss Armstrong had nothing to do with this,' Perry said.

'Obviously not, sir.'

*

The detectives, both tall and short, left eventually, but neither of them seemed entirely satisfied.

Perry closed the front door and turned to her. 'What on earth is going on?'

'My handbag wasn't stolen,' she said in a rush. 'I left it in Mrs Scaife's house, but I didn't want to tell you because it was *my* handbag, not Iris's, and I thought I could get it back. And I thought you'd be annoyed because I was so careless – the diamond earrings were in the handbag, I didn't have time to return them before I bumped into Mrs Scaife in Garrard's. The dead girl must be Beatrice Dodds, Mrs Scaife's maid. I thought she'd run off, but now I think perhaps she was trying to return the bag to me and they found out and killed her.'

'Don't upset yourself, Miss Armstrong.' (No longer his *darling*, then.) 'Have a seat, why don't you?

'It was Trude who joked with Godfrey about the coal hole at the Carlton Club,' he continued thoughtfully, 'and we know she's in cahoots with Mrs Scaife. Could it have been Trude who killed Beatrice?'

'It was probably one of Mrs Scaife's thugs – they often follow people when they leave Pelham Place. And Beatrice knew where the Red Book was. Perhaps she had it in her bag – my bag, rather. Perhaps she was trying to bring it to me.'

'We can't know anything for sure. In fact, we can't know for sure it is this maid.'

'Beatrice.'

'We have to be certain. Someone will have to identify her.'

'Mrs Scaife, I suppose,' Juliet said. 'Surely we should be telling the police all this?'

'Good God,' Perry said, 'we don't want the police blundering about in Pelham Place, interfering with the operation. The fewer people who know anything, the better. If it *is* this girl, then she'll have to be given a different identity. For the present anyway. You'll have to go to the mortuary.'

'Me?'

Beatrice Dodds, if it was her, was no more than an insubstantial shape beneath a white sheet in the Westminster Public Mortuary.

The mortuary assistant was reluctant to display the body to Juliet. 'Can't you identify her from her clothes, miss? It's not the sort of thing a young lady should be looking at.'

And yet it was the sort of thing that had happened to a young lady, Juliet thought. She had no idea what clothes Beatrice had worn – apart from her black-and-white maid's dress, which was not, according to the assistant, what she was found in. 'I have to see her face.'

'Are you sure, miss?'

'Yes.' For a moment Juliet felt her nerves quail, but then she thought, No, I must. Courage was the watchword.

'Ready?'

'Yes.'

Beatrice looked as though she had been modelled from clay, rather badly, and the clay had begun to deliquesce slightly. Someone had washed her, but the coal dust was ingrained in her skin and her mousy hair was sooty. Something had already started nibbling at her and Juliet wondered what kind of creatures lived in coal holes waiting for this dreadful food.

It was, however, undeniably Beatrice Dodds. I will not be sick, Juliet thought. I will not dishonour her with revulsion.

'Miss?' the mortuary assistant prompted gently. He replaced the sheet, covering Beatrice's small, tragic face. (*Cover her face; mine eyes dazzle.*)

I did this, Juliet thought, Beatrice would probably be alive if I hadn't asked her for help. And now she's a rotting corpse.

'Miss Wilson?'

'Yes?'

'Is this your sister, Miss Wilson?' the assistant asked softly. He was used to grief, Juliet supposed. Juliet was posing as 'Madge Wilson', although no one at the mortuary had asked her to 'prove' herself. It seemed only too easy to become someone else in a war.

'Yes,' she murmured. 'This is my sister, Ivy. Ivy Wilson.' Juliet had a birth certificate in the name of 'Ivy Wilson', forged by MI5.

'You're sure, miss? You know there was a bit of a mix-up to begin with?'

'How awful,' she murmured. 'No, this is definitely Ivy.' Juliet felt a sob rising in her chest.

'I'm afraid that there are some forms that have to be filled in,' the mortuary assistant said. 'And you know that there'll have to be an inquest? The police might not release your sister's body until their investigations are over.'

'Yes,' she said, 'of course. We need to know what happened. I don't know how Mother is going to bear it.'

The assistant led her next door, to a sparse anteroom where she filled in the forms he brought to her. The room was painted hospital green and the table and chairs were metal. It was a horrible place to bring the bereaved. She finished the forms and signed at the bottom 'Madge Wilson'. A counterfeit person, a fakery, signing away the life of another counterfeit person. Juliet was possibly the only person in the world who cared about Beatrice Dodds. And now the poor girl didn't even have her own name any more, erased from the world as successfully as if she had never existed.

'I'm sorry, but I feel rather faint,' Juliet murmured. 'Do you think I might have a cup of tea? It must be the shock, I suppose. Hot, sweet tea – that's what they say, isn't it?'

'Yes, miss, they do. You stay here, I'll be back in a tick.' He was a nice man – kind, she thought. She did feel a little faint, she hadn't expected the sight of Beatrice to be quite so awful.

What was left of Beatrice's worldly possessions was in a lumpy brown-paper parcel on a table at the side of the room. Someone had written 'Juliet Armstrong' in black ink on the paper and then had crossed it out and written 'Female – unknown'. The whole of a person's life, Juliet thought, fitted into one parcel. She thought of Pelham Place, stuffed to the gills with Mrs Scaife's 'better pieces'. It would take a lot of brown paper to wrap up Mrs Scaife's life.

Juliet picked the parcel up and found it was much heavier and more awkward than she had expected; it could almost have been the burden of Beatrice herself that she was lugging in her arms. She walked out of the room and down the corridor towards the exit. As she turned the corner she heard the voice of the mortuary assistant calling after her, 'Miss Wilson, Miss Wilson!'

Back in Dolphin Square, Juliet laid out newspaper on the carpet of the living room and unpacked the bundle of Beatrice's cheap clothes. Soot and coal dust came cascading off them in filthy showers. Filthiest of all was a headscarf. Was this the murder weapon? The police surely should have held it as evidence? It was silk, Hermès, expensive. The last time Juliet had seen it had been tied around Mrs Scaife's wattle neck. Was it possible that Mrs Scaife and not one of her thugs had killed Beatrice? It seemed unlikely, but Mrs Scaife had the heft and ballast and Beatrice was a tiny slip of a thing. But then what of the Carlton Club coal hole? Did Mrs Scaife bemoan to Trude over the tea and scones about having an unwanted body on her hands and did Trude say, 'Oh, I know what you can do with that!'

The handbag itself was empty – no Red Book. No scrap of paper with 'clue' written in bold letters. No diamond earrings, of course.

'Juliet?' Perry said, appearing in the doorway. 'My God, you're filthy. Are these the poor girl's things?'

'Beatrice. Yes.'

'Is that your handbag? I don't suppose those earrings turned up?'

''Fraid not.'

He shrugged indifferently and said, 'Garrard's have them insured. So – we're using our powers to bypass the usual police procedures. She's been taken to an undertaker's in Ladbroke Grove, she'll be buried in Kensal Green on Friday.'

'She's an orphan,' Juliet said. 'I don't suppose anyone will care too much.'

'I'm sorry,' he said. 'I really am. But, you know, the greater good and so on.'

'A thought has struck me,' Perry said. He reached for her hand across the starchy white tablecloth in Simpson's. He had taken her to dinner to 'cheer her up' after the mortuary. He seemed unmoved by Beatrice's death, as if she were just one more casualty of war. A girl. A nobody. A mouse.

'And, of course, we are celebrating our engagement,' Perry said. He had bought her a ring – a modest sapphire that had already left a circle of black around her finger. He kept reaching for the hand with the ring and holding it aloft as if he wanted everyone to see that she was his fiancée. Better than being a *bit of fluff*, she supposed. But, then again, perhaps not.

The great silver carving trolley approached menacingly. It was arched open by a waiter to reveal a huge joint of beef so raw and bloody that the poor beast's heart might well have still been beating. So much for rationing. Slices were carved and laid on their plates.

'A thought struck you,' she reminded him.

'Yes, thank you. I was thinking that if this was a case of mistaken identity, then whoever killed this girl—'

'Beatrice,' Juliet said wearily.

'Yes, might have thought that they were killing you. She was carrying your handbag, your identity papers. You must be extra careful for the next few days, until these people are safely behind bars.'

It did seem strange, she thought, that for several days 'Juliet Armstrong' had ceased to exist officially. Perhaps she had gone AWOL in order to frolic with cherubs and goats and lambs. In her absence, had Iris been called in to understudy her? Had she made a good job of it? Had Perry noticed the imposter? Did he think that it was—

'Eat up,' Perry said cheerfully. 'We won't be seeing much more of this and you need to put some flesh on your bones.'

Juliet's usually strong stomach quailed and she quietly dropped most of the beef (*flesh*, she thought queasily) into the napkin on her knee.

She stood up and said, 'If you'll excuse me.' She carried her napkin through to the Ladies, and disposed of its meaty contents in a bin. She wondered what the poor attendant would think if she came across it.

Think of it as an adventure, Perry had said right at the beginning of all this. And it had seemed like one. A bit of a lark, something from Buchan or Erskine Childers, she had thought. A *Girl's Own* adventure. The Russian Tea Room, the stickering, the escape down the Virginia creeper. But it wasn't an adventure, was it? Someone had died. Beatrice had died. A sparrow. A mouse. An insignificance to everyone except Juliet.

The Die is Cast

PERRY SEEMED IN good spirits again. Juliet was relieved to see that the cloud that had been threatening him had passed away. It was becoming harder to keep up with his moods.

'We have this American chap in our sights,' he told her. 'He's called Chester Vanderkamp.' He said the name with distaste, he had an aversion to Americans. 'He works at the American Embassy in the cypher department.'

'Cypher?' Juliet said. 'Codes, secret cables and so on?'

'Yes, he sees everything – all the correspondence going in and out of the Embassy. He's fiercely against America joining the war. A tone set by their appeasing Ambassador, of course.' Perry reserved a particular animosity towards Kennedy. 'Admires the Germans. Has it in for the Jews, says they run industry, government, Hollywood, et cetera – the usual diatribe. This chap Vanderkamp codes and decodes some of the most sensitive telegrams and apparently he takes copies of them home with him – he has a flat in Reeves Mews, just round the corner from his Embassy.'

'How do you know all this?' Juliet puzzled.

'Mam'selle Bouchier has been "courting" him for us.'

'Giselle?'

'Our own Mata Hari. She excels at pillow talk. Unfortunately for us, a lot of his correspondence is between Churchill and Roosevelt – how

Roosevelt can support us. If the isolationists and appeasers in America get hold of it they'll have a field day. It'll be the end of Roosevelt. And probably the end of our hopes of getting the Americans into the war. And there's a great deal of other material which would be extremely injurious to our troops in Europe – military secrets and so on.'

'Crikey.'

'Crikey indeed, Miss Armstrong. The bad news is that this Vanderkamp is considering sharing this information not just with America, but with the Germans as well.'

'And yet you seem egregiously cheerful,' Juliet said. He smiled his lovely smile. Kiss me, she thought. Some hope.

'Because Mr Vanderkamp wishes to meet Mrs Scaife. He has been told about her contacts abroad. He is entirely sympathetic to her politics. We can catch them both red-handed and stop those bloody telegrams getting out. And thus we shall kill two birds with one stone.'

'What a horrid image,' Juliet said.

'They will need a go-between,' Perry said.

'Me?'

'You. Exactly.'

'And so,' Mrs Scaife said, stirring sugar lumps thoughtfully into her tea, 'this American . . . Chester Vanderkamp?'

'Yes.'

'He has information he wants to share with us?'

'Yes. Important information. He has copies – decrypts – of a large number of diplomatic telegrams between Roosevelt and Churchill.' ("Undreds of them,' according to Giselle, who also passed on the unnecessary information that "E is boring in bed.') 'Apparently they contain a lot of correspondence about Roosevelt's support for us.'

'And he's willing to share them with us?'

'He's willing to *give* them to us. To *you*, Mrs Scaife. He wants to make sure he places them in your hands personally.'

'Well, we have someone who can get them in a diplomatic bag to Belgium, and then on to the German Embassy in Rome. And the Germans will broadcast them to the world, I expect. And if they don't, then our good friend William Joyce will. The Germans understand propaganda. As do the American isolationists.'

'Two birds with one stone, Mrs Scaife. Two birds with one stone.'

'He can't come here though – I'm being watched. And perhaps he is being watched too.'

'*I'm* not being watched, Mrs Scaife,' Juliet said. 'Why not meet him at my flat. I can be your go-between. More tea? Shall I be mother?'

The wheels were set in motion. The day after tomorrow, the meeting between Mrs Scaife and Chester Vanderkamp was to take place at an MI5 flat in Bloomsbury – a dingy place, a hymn to the horrors of brown varnish and grimy windows – that would masquerade as Juliet's. The flat was wired with microphones and the exchange of the telegrams would be recorded. When the telegrams had changed hands, Juliet would give a signal and the police would arrest both Mrs Scaife and Chester Vanderkamp.

Eleven o'clock the following morning was the time designated for the arrests. Juliet had stayed the night in Dolphin Square again. She had received the same dry goodnight kiss and had lain in the effigy position once again, while Perry slept what seemed an untroubled sleep next to her. She woke early and made tea and drank it looking out of the living-room window at the garden down below. The early-morning sky was pearlescent. The fountain was playing. The magnolia and lilacs were over but the summer annuals were flushing the beds with colour.

'Ah, you're up,' Perry said, making her jump. 'And tea too. Splendid. Are you ready for the endgame?'

Juliet was surprised to see that Mrs Ambrose had accompanied Mrs Scaife to the Bloomsbury flat. 'Mrs Ambrose is such a loyal servant,' Mrs Scaife said.

'Friend, not servant,' Mrs Ambrose amended mildly. 'I wanted to be in at the kill,' she murmured to Juliet as she passed her in the hallway.

'Goodness,' Mrs Scaife said, glancing around with something akin to repulsion. 'Do you really live here, Iris, dear?'

Juliet laughed and said, 'Dreadful, isn't it? Temporary digs though, Mrs Scaife. I'm moving to a flat in Mayfair next week.'

'Oh, that sounds much more suitable. Let me lend you Nightingale to help you with things.'

At this very moment police were raiding Mrs Scaife's house in Pelham Place, looking for evidence to incriminate her. Would Nightingale have anything to say about that, Juliet wondered?

There followed some interminable chit-chat about the German advance and what it would mean for the likes of the Right Club.

'Medals, I expect,' Mrs Scaife said.

'An iron cross?' Mrs Ambrose said, looking rather pleased at the idea. She had her knitting out, her needles click-clacking like an express train.

'Tea?' Juliet offered. 'I'm sure Mr Vanderkamp won't be long.'

Juliet put the kettle on the hob in the mean little scullery and tiptoed back out to the hall to check on Cyril. He had been drafted in and was already installed in the hall cupboard, monitoring the recording equipment.

He gave her the thumbs-up and whispered, 'It's the Black Hole of Calcutta in here.'

'I'll sneak you some tea,' Juliet whispered back.

'Who are you talking to out there, Iris, dear?'

'Just myself,' Juliet called out.

The tea had been poured with the usual fussing over sugar and spoons when the doorbell rang.

'Mr Vanderkamp – do come in,' Juliet said. He was shorter than she had expected, but spry and sporty-looking and, in contrast to the native males of Juliet's acquaintance, he seemed radiant with New World health and energy. She led him through to the living room and there were introductions all round.

'I think we know some of the same people,' Mrs Scaife said, every inch the society hostess.

'I think we do, ma'am,' he said, every inch the guest. The rats were in the trap. They had excellent manners for rats.

There was more business with the teacups, more prattling about imminent Nazi victory. 'It will be a great day when the Germans march down Whitehall and help us restore sanity to this country, won't it, Mr Vanderkamp?' Mrs Scaife said. 'Then we'll throw out all the Jews and foreigners, regain our true sovereignty.'

'Bully for you,' Chester Vanderkamp said.

And then, finally, the telegrams were produced. Vanderkamp opened his briefcase and took out a Manila envelope. He removed the telegrams from the envelope and pushed the tea things aside so that he could spread the papers out on the table. Mrs Scaife leant in to examine them. Juliet feigned indifference, getting up from her chair and wandering over to the window. She had a good view of the street from here. There was no sign of any of Mrs Scaife's thugs. They had been 'dealt' with, presumably. She could see a man standing on the pavement opposite. One of the grey men. He was staring up at the window. Juliet stared back down at him.

'Wonderful,' Mrs Scaife said. 'I can't tell you how useful this will be to our cause.'

'Glad to help,' Vanderkamp said, gathering up the telegrams and stuffing them back into the Manila envelope. Juliet took her hand-kerchief from her sleeve. 'There you are,' Vanderkamp said, handing the envelope to Mrs Scaife. Mrs Scaife took the envelope. Juliet blew her nose. It seemed a rather mundane signal.

'You're not getting a cold, are you?' Mrs Scaife asked solicitously, the envelope clutched now to her grand bosom.

'No,' Juliet said. 'I'm not.'

Where were they, she wondered? They were certainly taking their time. But then there was a tremendous crash as the front door was broken down. Did they have to be quite so melodramatic? If they had rung the bell she would have simply let them in.

'Here we go,' Juliet said to Mrs Scaife, who frowned and said, 'What do you mean, dear?'

A swarm of assorted policemen entered the flat. Mrs Scaife gave a little scream and struggled to her feet and Chester Vanderkamp said, 'What the heck?' Juliet recognized the tall detective from the other morning. He tipped his hat at her.

Vanderkamp was arrested and handcuffed. He stared at Juliet in disbelief. 'You bitch,' he spat at her.

'Now, now,' the tall detective said. 'No need for language like that.'

Mrs Scaife, meanwhile, had dissolved into a puddle of lace on the sofa. 'Iris, dear,' she said feebly, 'I don't understand.'

Before Juliet could say anything Perry appeared, Giselle trailing in his wake. She seemed vague, like someone surprised to find themselves suddenly on stage. Perry said to Mrs Scaife, 'We have you now, madam. We have recorded this meeting and in your house we have found letters to Joyce and other kinds of Fascist low lifes, even a "fan" letter to Herr Hitler, and –' a dramatic pause unchar-acteristic of Perry before he produced '– the Red Book.' It turned out to be more burgundy than red, but Juliet supposed that no one present was about to quibble over the shade. He held the pièce de résistance aloft and turned to Juliet. 'In this lady's house, just as you said, Miss Armstrong.'

Mrs Scaife stared open-mouthed at Juliet. 'Iris, dear, what is this?' She reached for Mrs Ambrose's hand as if she were a lifebuoy and said, 'Mrs Ambrose – Florence – what is going on?' Mrs Ambrose said nothing. Juliet wondered if Mrs Scaife had read her horoscope for the day and what it would have said if she had. *You will have a surprise today.*

Mrs Scaife turned helplessly to Giselle. 'You too?'

'*Oui. Moi aussi,*' she agreed indifferently.

It was rather like a farce, Juliet thought, and wondered who would wander on the stage next. A butler, perhaps, or a bluff brigadier, but Giselle proved to be the final cast member assembled and, indicating Mrs Scaife, Perry said to the nearest policeman, 'Arrest her. Take her to Bow Street.'

'But I've done nothing,' Mrs Scaife protested. She looked suddenly old and helpless. Juliet almost felt sorry for her. Almost.

'There is no action without consequence, madam,' Perry said sternly.

'What about these other ladies?' one of the policeman asked. 'Are we to arrest them too, sir?'

'No,' Perry said. 'They're MI5 agents.'

'All of them, sir?'

'Yes.'

How absurd, Juliet thought. She glimpsed the briefest of smiles on the face of the tall detective and wondered if he felt the same.

'I'll kill you, you little traitor,' Chester Vanderkamp yelled at Juliet as they hauled him away.

'I wouldn't worry,' the tall detective said to Juliet. 'He probably won't.'

And that was that. The end of the operation meant the end of their careers as spies, apparently. Perry took them all to Prunier's for a late lunch; Cyril was included in the party and was overwhelmed into silence by the restaurant and the food and being in the company of Perry's harem of women. 'A bevy of beauties,' the maître d' smarmed as he seated them. Mrs Ambrose gave him a withering look.

Giselle smoked one cigarette after another. She seemed distracted and only picked at the chicken in front of her. Juliet had wondered if they would have lobster again, but the waiter said quietly to Perry that he had a *Poularde au Riz Suprême*. The chickens had 'come up that morning on the milk train from Hampshire', he said, and Juliet laughed because she imagined the station platform of some sleepy halt crowded with chickens fussing and clucking like commuters waiting for the train to arrive.

Perry raised an eyebrow at her. She presumed that as his fiancée she was supposed to behave with dignity. He had not – thank God – announced their engagement to the assembled company, she would not have been able to bear the curious looks. (Was that how prospective brides normally felt? Probably not.) It was as well that he was a man who liked secrets. Her engagement ring had been consigned 'for safekeeping' to one of the multifarious drawers of Perry's roll-top.

'If you're not having that, then I will,' Juliet said, sliding Giselle's plate over.

'You'll get fat,' Giselle said.

'I won't,' Juliet said. The unfathomable hollow inside her would never be filled. 'What will happen to them? Mrs Scaife and Vanderkamp?' she asked Perry.

'I expect they'll be tried in camera in the Magistrate's Court. Mosley's been arrested as well and quite a few of the others. Mrs Scaife will probably be interned in Holloway along with her pals.'

'I rather thought she might hang,' Juliet said. A noose tight around that wrinkled neck instead of a Hermès scarf.

'We don't want to make martyrs. We'll probably have to hand Vanderkamp over to the Americans. I expect they'll pack him off home with a flea in his ear, post him to some God-awful South American country. They'll be furious that we haven't involved them in the operation.'

At the end of the meal, Mrs Ambrose said, 'Well, must be getting on,' as if she were leaving a Women's Institute meeting. 'I'm moving to Eastbourne to live with my niece.'

'I thought she lived in Harpenden?' Juliet said.

'I've got more than one niece,' she said with a little laugh. Before leaving, she presented Juliet with the results of her knitting, a piece so perplexingly shapeless that it was impossible to work out its purpose. It would do for Lily's basket, Juliet supposed.

Giselle roused herself from her dormant state and said she was bidding them all adieu. Not au revoir then?

She was going on active service, Perry explained when Giselle had left.

To fight? To kill people, the enemy, Juliet thought. No wonder she had seemed even more abstracted than usual.

The arrests had, in the end, proved to be a rather disappointing anti-climax. Juliet had hoped for something more than the cold hand of the law. A little violence would not have gone amiss. Perhaps I would like to be 'on active service' too, she thought. To kill the enemy.

'Time and tide wait for no man,' Perry said. 'Or woman, for that matter. Back to work, Miss Armstrong.'

Juliet sighed and said, 'Come along, Cyril. Let's return to the fray.'

Juliet delved into her coat pocket for the key to Dolphin Square. Her hand closed on the little green leather box. She had slipped the diamond earrings in there when she had bumped into Mrs Scaife in Garrard's and couldn't quite bring herself to return them. And, of course, there was all the drama of the arrests and so on. A girl could be forgiven for forgetting.

'All right, miss?' Cyril asked as she turned the key in the door.

'Yes, everything's all right, Cyril.'

The war stretched ahead, unknown, and yet it felt as if all the drama of it was over.

Juliet hung her coat up and removed the cover from her Imperial. She sat down in front of it and flexed her fingers as if she were about to play the piano.

-9-

RECORD 3 (contd.)

18.10

GODFREY and TRUDE present. General discussion about the weather. Some chat about TRUDE's friend MRS SHUTE who has a daughter who is marrying a man in the Army Intelligence corps. TRUDE proposes going to visit MRS SHUTE next week.

G. In Rochester? Yes, and talk to the daughter?

T. Congratulate her! (Laughter)

G. Do you feel you've made good progress? I wondered if (?) had made you lackadaisical?

T. (Surprised) No! (shouts with laughter. Something inaudible, sounds like news(or views)) It's the same sort of stuff they push down your neck at every newsreel.

G. Yes, yes.

'Back to the hum-drum, eh, miss?' Cyril said.

''Fraid so, Cyril.'

How wrong they were. 'Hum-drum' was the very last word that could be used to describe the horror of what happened next.

1950

Technical Hitch

JULIET RETURNED FROM Moretti's, arming herself mentally for the afternoon's recording of *Past Lives*. The bolshy girl on reception was missing – consumed for lunch by the Minotaur in the basement, presumably. In her place Daisy Gibbs was hovering. A beast would think twice about eating her – edible but indigestible, Juliet thought. 'Oh, there you are, Miss Armstrong,' she said. 'I wondered where you were.'

'I was at lunch,' Juliet said. 'I'm not late. Hardly, anyway. Is there a problem? With *Past Lives*?'

'Perhaps.' Daisy smiled. She was both enigmatic and unflappable. It made her hard to read. She would be a gift to the Service. You could never be entirely sure if she was being ironic or merely diffident. Again, a good trait for the Service.

'We've got a late scratch, I'm afraid,' Daisy said. 'We're a woman down,' she added, leading the way to Juliet's office as if she might be unsure of her own way there.

'Jessica Hastie?' Juliet guessed.

'Yes. The Miller's Wife's a non-runner, I fear. She was also playing the Small Girl, who now seems to have leprosy. You changed the script quite a lot, I noticed.'

'I did,' Juliet admitted. 'There was no disease in it. There was nothing *but* disease in the Middle Ages, I expect.'

'Yes, and we seem to be ignoring the Black Death completely,' Daisy said. 'I had been rather looking forward to that. I've made new copies anyway.'

'Where *is* Miss Hastie?'

'I think she imbibed a bit too much at lunch. I corralled her in an empty studio. She was being somewhat disruptive in the Green Room.' Their Green Room was tiny and Juliet could only imagine the panic that a sodden Jessica Hastie could cause in there.

'She's known as a bit of a lush, I'm afraid,' Juliet said. 'I'll go and see her. We'll start on time, don't worry.'

'I won't,' Daisy said. 'It'll be all right.'

Past Lives, as the title might indicate, was a series about the way people lived in the past, although for a moment Juliet had hoped that it would involve reincarnation. The Juniors' collective imagination might be fired by that. They would all want to come back as dogs, of course – the boys anyway. (Juliet visited quite a few classrooms as part of the job.) 'Workaday lives,' Joan Timpson had told her. 'Bringing Everyman to life through the ages. The ordinary man – and woman, of course – and the society they lived in.' There was a subtle – and perhaps not so subtle – emphasis in Schools on citizenship. Juliet wondered if it was to counter the instinct towards Communism.

Most history for schools was of the dramatized kind. Straight facts were inclined to give them 'hard times', Joan Timpson had said, pleased with the allusion. ('I hope I'm no Gradgrind!') The war had made the world weary of facts, Juliet supposed. There had been an awful lot of them.

Past Lives had already galloped its way through the Stone Age, Celts, Romans, Saxons, Vikings and Normans, and now they had arrived at the Middle Ages with today's programme, entitled *Life in an English Medieval Village*. Joan Timpson had promised to return in time for the Tudors ('I shan't miss that for anything.') Where would they stop, Juliet wondered?

'The war,' Joan told her decisively. 'Everything stopped with the war.'

'Well, not everything,' Juliet demurred.

'I believe,' Charles Lofthouse told her later over drinks in the Langham, 'that Mr Timpson met a gruesome death in the Blitz.' He lingered theatrically over the adjective. The loss of his leg in the war had made him surprisingly unsympathetic to the suffering of others.

'Joan seems quite sanguine,' Juliet said.

'It's all a front, darling.'

But then wasn't everything?

Juliet found Jessica Hastie in an empty studio on the top floor. It was rarely used and on several occasions had proved useful for separating an individual from the herd. Jessica Hastie was snoring peacefully, her large head resting heavily on the desk in the control cubicle. It seemed a shame (if not an impossibility) to disturb her and so Juliet turned off the lights and closed the door.

'You can manage the Miller's Wife, can't you?' she asked Daisy.

'I expect so.' She was undauntable.

The series was recorded; none of the programmes went out live, unlike other Schools broadcasts. Recording was more expensive and Juliet wondered if Joan Timpson had some special dispensation. 'Well, you know,' Prendergast said vaguely, 'poor Joan.'

Of course, Joan favoured a barrage of sound effects – the phalanx of armoured men (something that she was particularly keen on) that had clanked around in *Past Lives* since the Ninth Legion disappeared would alone have defeated all but the most robust of Effects assistants. Over the road, they had drama control desks that looked as though they belonged on the bridge of a spaceship from another planet. Nothing so sophisticated for Schools.

The script for the *Village* (another everyday story of country folk, Juliet thought) was by a woman called Morna Treadwell and was atrocious. Juliet, supported by a glass of good Scotch and a pack of Craven 'A', had stayed up half the night rewriting it. Children deserved better than Morna Treadwell's interpretation of the Medieval quotidian. Morna was a friend of the Deputy Director General and seemed to be commissioned quite a lot, even though she couldn't write for love nor money. She never listened to the broadcasts, apparently, but then why would you, unless you were a small child chained to a desk?

The village itself contained a manor, a church, a mill, a village green (with pond) and Serfs galore (quite happy – most unlikely). The Serfs ploughed and planted endlessly and there was a lot of chatter about strip farming and tithes. Nothing much else happened. The Miller's Wife was unpopular because of her stuck-up ways; a good-hearted couple lost a pig. Oh, and a thoroughly annoying Minstrel kept interrupting everyone with his lute and his parable-like ditties. No sign of an actual *plot*, mind you. History should always have a plot, Juliet thought as she slashed and burned Morna Treadwell's deathly words. How else could you make sense of it?

She culled the Minstrel – they could dub in a lute later if really necessary (although when was a lute ever necessary?). She was rather pleased with herself for having added a poignant ending that hinted at the ravages of plague to come, even if they were going to ignore it and skip straight to the Wars of the Roses. A Servant Girl at the manor spied a rat in the pantry and then almost immediately afterwards was bitten by a flea. 'Dratted things,' she said. (Could they say 'dratted' in Schools? Juliet couldn't remember if it was on the banned list. Probably.) 'It's nothing,' the Cook told the Servant

Girl. But it *was* something and it was definitely not going to be all right for an awful lot of people – up to half the world's population, according to history. Even the war hadn't managed that.

'Miss Armstrong? Runners and riders at the starting gate,' Daisy said into the studio microphone. She gave a little salute to Juliet in the control cubicle.

The cast, sans Minstrel, and without counting Daisy, was composed of two actors and an actress. The actress was well over pensionable age and one of the actors, a superannuated rep 'artiste', was a quivering mess – he could barely stand at the microphone. The third member of the cast was a man called Roger Fairbrother, who was war-damaged in some unspecified way and, in Jessica Hastie's absence, took on the role of the Cook as he had a rather light voice. Radio allowed for a degree of slippage in the gender department.

Was this really the best Booking could come up with? The poor and the maimed, the halt and the blind? In this company, Daisy Gibbs's haughty Miller's Wife positively shone. Daisy was also rather convincing as the Small Girl with leprosy, shrieking enthusiastically as she was driven from the village by a Crowd. The Crowd comprised the other three members of the cast, augmented by a passing copy typist who had been sprung on by Daisy and dragged into the studio like prey. Historically, it was a commonplace procedure in Schools to press-gang anyone handy to help out with the acting side of things, not always to the artistic benefit of the programme.

A happy ending was supplied by the return of the good-hearted couple's prodigal pig and, in one of Juliet's more dramatic alterations, the Miller's Wife, instead of merely seeing the error of her imperious ways, met her comeuppance at the hands of the Serfs and was ducked in the village pond. Wildly inaccurate, probably, but the Juniors would enjoy it. They were serfs too, really, weren't they? In thrall to the State in the shape of the education system.

'You were a star,' Juliet congratulated Daisy when the recording was over. 'Perhaps you missed your vocation.'

'Perhaps not,' Daisy said. The girl was impenetrable.

Lester Pelling (rhymes with lemming, Juliet thought) was adding sound effects. His chinagraph pencil was clenched between his teeth as he listened with a look of furious concentration to the disc on the playback turntable, as if divining his future there.

Juliet hesitated, unwilling to disturb Lester as he lifted the stylus and prepared to mark a groove with his pencil. Some sixth sense, however, made him turn round. He took off his headphones and said, 'Oh, hello, miss,' rather sheepishly, as if embarrassed to be seen at work.

'Sorry, didn't mean to interrupt you,' she said.

'That's all right. I was just dropping the pig in. I've done hens and cows.'

'Have you got geese?'

'No.'

'We definitely need geese,' Juliet said. 'They had a lot of geese in the Middle Ages.'

'I haven't got any music either. I didn't know what we needed.'

'Crumhorns and flageolets, I expect. A sackbut or two as well,' Juliet said, pulling these words off an obscure shelf in her memory. Were these real instruments, she wondered, or was she just making them up? They sounded ridiculous. 'A lute, I suppose,' she added reluctantly.

'I'll nip across the road to Effects,' Lester said.

'No, it's all right. I'll go to BH, you carry on here.'

'You know, I'd like to be a Programme Producer, miss,' he suddenly blurted out. 'Like you,' he added shyly.

'Really? It's not all it's cut out to be, you know.' She shouldn't be discouraging. The boy still had his hopes. She thought of Cyril again. He had been a recording engineer, too. Would Godfrey Toby deny knowledge of him as well, if challenged? Cyril, she remembered fondly, had possessed the optimistic character of a terrier dog, relentless even in the face of horror. (*Come on, miss. We can do this.*)

'Miss? Miss Armstrong?'

It seemed suddenly imperative to be positive. Unlike Cyril, Lester had a future of some kind. 'Of course, it's not unknown, Lester, for someone in your job to be promoted,' she said. 'The Corporation can be good like that. You're a boy soldier now, but you could leave as head of the regiment.'

'Really?'

'Why not?'

He grew visibly taller. He grinned widely, showing a set of frighteningly mismatched teeth. *Joy*, Juliet thought. This was what it looked like. She should shout for Prendergast to come and see. She didn't.

'Thanks, miss.'

'Think nothing of it.'

Daisy Gibbs stopped her as she was leaving and handed her an envelope.

'This arrived for you, Miss Armstrong.'

'You can call me Juliet, you know.'

'I know.'

Juliet examined the envelope while the girl in Effects was trying to locate a flageolet. Her name was handwritten on the front – 'Miss J. Armstrong'. Had it been opened? There was no evidence it had and yet she couldn't quite quell her suspicions. Messages that appeared out of the blue were rarely comforting and frequently annoying. When she opened it, with a degree of caution, there was a folded-up piece of notepaper – no heading – with one sentence written on it. Really? she thought. They couldn't even—

'Miss Armstrong? I found the flageolet. I had to go to Music.' The girl from Effects sounded breathless, as if she'd been chasing the flageolet around the building. (It would be a nice name for a gazelle, Juliet thought. Or a superior kind of rabbit.) 'And there was a message for you – not so much a message as a question – from Mr Pelling. He says, "Is it a watermill or a windmill, and can you get the effect?"'

'Well done you on the mill,' Juliet said to Lester. 'I'd forgotten all about it. I decided on wind – they had some nice . . . what's the word? Whooshing. Or swishing – you know, from windmill sails. Pre-war Norfolk, apparently. In Atmosphere. We'll have to make our own ducking stool, it's not something they seem to have much call for in Broadcasting House.'

They always used to do things live in Manchester with two Effects boys and water tanks and wind machines, bird whistles – the boys did authentic (and rather irritating) gulls. No one did seascapes better. Sometimes the boys would stagger out of their little cubicle looking as though they had survived a terrible maritime disaster. That was when she had moved on from Continuity to *Children's Hour*, of course. They were supposed to share programmes with the other regions, but the North was particularly territorial about their *Hour*. It had been more fun than here. *Children's Hour* was designed for entertainment, whereas Schools was endlessly purposeful. Juliet was discovering that it took its toll after a while.

'Do you miss it? The North?' Daisy had asked once, wistful for something she had never known. She was a vicar's daughter from rural Wiltshire. (Of course she was. What else would she be?) 'All those real people?'

'No more real than here,' Juliet had said, unconvinced by her own answer. Her mother was – had been – Scottish (although you couldn't tell by looking), and they had once made the long journey to her homeland. Juliet had been very small and could remember little of this hejira. An oppressive castle and everything smudged in shades of sooty charcoal. She had expected relatives, but she remembered none. Nor, apparently, were there any on her father's side. 'You have his curls,' her mother said. It seemed a poor legacy.

When she had applied for the post of Announcer at the BBC in Manchester they had been keen to discover if she had links with the North of England; it seemed to be some kind of criterion that they needed to fulfil. She doubted that her mother's vague Caledonian roots would go down well – a quite different Region, too far north of the wall – and so she plucked 'Middlesbrough' out of thin air. 'Wonderful,' she heard someone whisper. People always said they wanted the truth, but really they were perfectly content with a facsimile.

Lester Pelling was waiting patiently. For her to go, she supposed. 'I'll let you get on,' she said. 'Do you need any help?'

He did not.

As Juliet was leaving, she suddenly remembered. 'What *was* your father, Lester?'

'Miss?'

'What was your father?'

'A bastard,' he said softly, taking her by surprise. No one swore in Schools, nothing beyond the occasional 'Damn and blast' on account of some technical problem, and yet this was the second obscenity she'd heard in the last half-hour. On her return from Broadcasting House, Charles Lofthouse had caught sight of her and said, 'Well, Fuchs is fucked.' He was trying to shock her, she knew, but she looked at him coolly and said, 'Is he now?'

He had held up the front page of an early edition of the *Evening Standard* for her to read.

'Fourteen years,' he said. 'They should have hanged him, surely?'

'Russia was our ally when he gave them secrets,' Juliet said, scanning the newspaper. 'You can't be a traitor if it's not the enemy.'

'Sophistry,' he snorted. 'And a naïve defence at best. Whose side are you on, Miss Armstrong?' He sneered like a pantomime villain and she suddenly realized how much he disliked her and wondered why she hadn't seen it before.

'It's not about sides,' she said testily, 'it's about the law.'

'If you say so, dearie.' He had limped off and she had had to restrain herself from taking one of the records in her arms and throwing it at him. She'd wondered if you could decapitate someone if you sliced an acetate-covered aluminium disc through the air at just the right angle. Death by flageolet.

'Apart from being a bastard?' she prompted Lester Pelling.

'Sorry, miss. It just came out.'

'Trust me, I've heard worse. In the meeting this morning, you suggested a day in the life of a trawlerman and you said your father was – I'm just curious, that's all. I find unfinished sentences dis—'

'A fishmonger. He was a fishmonger, miss.'

'There you are then.'

'And a bastard,' she heard him murmur as she left the room.

She had just settled back at her desk when a BBC Boy – they were the cadets of the Corporation – delivered another envelope to her desk. 'Juliet Armstrong' was written on it in a sloppy, rather foreign-looking hand. She sighed – was she to be bombarded all day long by messages? This one, however, was of a quite different quality to the one that Daisy had handed to her earlier. Inside the envelope was a single sheet of ruled paper, quite small, torn from a notebook. In the same scrawly hand as her name on the envelope, someone had written, 'You will pay for what you did.'

Juliet leapt up from her desk as if she'd been bitten by a plague-carrying rat, ran out into the corridor after the Boy and said, so sharply that he cowered, 'Who gave you that note?'

'Reception, miss. Do you want to send a reply?' he asked meekly.

'No.'

'Who gave you this?' she demanded of the uppity girl on reception, returned intact, apparently, by the Minotaur. She thrust the envelope in front of her nose.

'Someone,' she said, refusing to be intimidated.

'Can you be more specific?'

'A man. Short.'

'Anything else?' Juliet urged.

'He had a funny eye.'

'And a limp?' Juliet hazarded, remembering the funny little man in Moretti's.

'Yes, he did. He was most peculiar. Friend of yours, is he?'

I am Ariadne, mistress of the maze, Juliet thought. (Was a maze different from a labyrinth? How?) And I am not going to lift a semi-divine finger to save you when it's time for you to be sacrificed to that great half-bull, half-man. Was the bull the top half or the bottom? She couldn't remember. Whichever way round it was, the Minotaur seemed a very priapic kind of myth. They had done the story of Daedalus and his labyrinth on *Children's Hour*, sanitized and abridged somewhat. It had been popular. Icarus, his son, of course had flown too high and fallen. It was the perfect plot. In some ways it was the only plot.

'Passing sentence, Lord Chief Justice Lord Goddard said: "You have betrayed the hospitality and protection given to you by this country with the grossest treachery."' Juliet was reading her own later edition of the *Standard* while she ate supper.

You will pay for what you did. Fuchs was going to pay now. But who wants me to pay, she wondered? And with what? Blood money?

A pound of flesh? And who was demanding recompense? And for what? Her life seemed littered with misdeeds, it was difficult to pinpoint which one someone might wish to bring her to account for. Her mind was still occupied with Godfrey Toby's snub. There was no way in the world that he didn't recognize her. The war had been a tide that had receded and now here it was lapping around her ankles again. She sighed and chastised herself for a sub-standard metaphor.

Was it something to do with the unexpected reappearance of Godfrey? There was a covenant of guilt between them – had he been sent a bill of reckoning too? And could you drive yourself mad with questions?

She cut herself another slice of bread and buttered it thickly. The tin of spaghetti that she'd planned had, thankfully, been abandoned. She'd had to dive into Harrods Food Hall on the way home to buy provisions for the unexpected visitor who was to arrive later. Harrods was on her way home – she rented a flat in one of the more obscure streets of South Kensington still stoically waiting to recover from the war. She had lived here throughout the duration and it seemed disloyal to leave now. Even when she had moved to Manchester to start with the BBC she had kept the flat on, sub-letting it to a matron at St George's who had seemed the essence of propriety but had turned out to be a raging alcoholic, confirming Juliet in her long-held belief that appearances were invariably deceptive.

In Harrods she had bought bread, butter, ham sliced off the bone while she watched, a thick wedge of Cheddar, a half-dozen eggs, a jar of pickled onions and a bunch of grapes. She put it all on Hartley's tab – he had some kind of special agreement that bypassed rationing. She doubted that it was above board. She filed the receipt carefully in her purse. They would complain in Accounts that she'd been to Harrods and not somewhere cheaper, but Hartley wouldn't care.

Juliet ate some of the grapes and then put the kettle on the hob, laid a fire and lit it. Her visitor wasn't due for another hour. She wished, not for the first time, that there was room in the flat for a piano. She was completely rusty, of course. Sometimes she went over to Broadcasting House and practised on a piano in one of the rehearsal rooms. She owned a gramophone, but it wasn't the same thing – it was the opposite, in fact. Listening, not playing – in the same way that reading was the opposite of writing.

She put on Rachmaninov's Third – his own 1939 recording with the Philadelphia Orchestra – and fetched the envelope from her handbag and read again the note that Daisy had given her. 'The flamingo will arrive at 9.00 p.m.' Hardly code, was it? You would think they could do better, use some kind of cypher if they were going to commit to paper. Was it supposed to disguise the message if someone came across it accidentally? Or indeed, on purpose. She thought of Daisy – had she read this? She acted as innocent as a lamb, but that meant nothing, did it?

And who in their right minds would think she was having a flamingo delivered? A parrot, perhaps, or a budgerigar – Harrods pet department would convey either, probably – but a flamingo? Why not just 'parcel' or 'packet'? The note had been written by Hartley, of course, a fact that made her even more irritated by it.

She threw the paper on the fire. He wasn't a flamingo – obviously – he was a Czech being brought out of Vienna, through Berlin, on an RAF transport. A scientist, something to do with metals, not that she really wanted to know. He was being flown to RAF Kidlington and by tomorrow night he would be gone on the way to somewhere else – Harwell or America or somewhere more obscure.

Recently, MI5 had asked Juliet to run an occasional safe house for them. Since she had worked for the Security Service throughout the war, they seemed to think they had some kind of claim on her trustworthiness. It was a dull business, more like babysitting than espionage.

The Rachmaninov finished and Juliet turned the wireless on and promptly fell asleep. When she woke it was to the chimes of Big Ben announcing the *Nine o'Clock News*. Fuchs again. Someone was knocking on the front door of her flat, so gently as to be almost inaudible.

'There *is* a bell,' she said when she opened the door. She had been expecting the usual indistinguishable grey men, but instead it was the RAF – a Squadron Leader and – translating his stripes – a Group Captain. Blimey, Juliet thought.

The Group Captain was craggily handsome and must have been dashing during the war, but he had no interest in the niceties. 'Miss Armstrong? "Vermilion" is the word of today and this is Mr Smith. I believe he is to stay here tonight?'

'Yes. He is,' she said, opening the door wider. The two officers stepped aside to reveal the Czech, small and rather derelict, standing between two RAF policemen. He looked more like a prisoner than a defector. He was wearing an overcoat that was clearly too big for him and clutching a small, battered leather suitcase. He had no hat, Juliet noticed. A man with no hat looked surprisingly vulnerable.

'You'd better come in,' she said to him.

She laid out food for her guest. 'A midnight feast,' she said encouragingly. 'Do eat, Mr Smith.' How ridiculous to address him as that. 'You can tell me your name, you know. Your name,' she repeated more loudly. He seemed to speak hardly any English. Pointing at her herself, she said, 'My name is Juliet.'

'Pavel.'

'Good,' she said brightly. Poor blighter, she thought. She

wondered if he'd actually *wanted* to get out or if he had been 'persuaded' in some way.

He pecked miserably at the food. It seemed to depress him further – he recoiled when he tasted a pickled onion. He didn't want tea and asked if she had beer. She didn't. She offered whisky instead and he drank it quickly with a frown on his face, as if it reminded him of something he didn't want to remember. After the whisky he took a small creased photograph from his wallet and showed it to her. A woman, in her forties perhaps, aged by war.

'Your wife?' she asked. He shrugged an ambivalent response before replacing the photograph in his wallet and commencing to weep in a silent, reticent way that was worse than if he'd been choking out sobs. She patted him on the back. 'It's all right,' she said. 'Or at least it will be. I'm sure.'

He was white with exhaustion. She put a guard around the fire (she supposed it wouldn't do if he burned to death on her watch) and made up a bed for him on the sofa. He slept in his clothes, even his shoes, and was still holding on to the leather suitcase when – almost immediately – he fell asleep. Juliet gently prised the handle of the suitcase out of his hand, tucked in the blanket around him and turned off the light.

Slipping between her own cold sheets, she thought enviously of the fire next door. This morning's early hint of spring had long retreated back into winter. She should have made herself a hot-water bottle. Cold nights like these were when you needed another body next to you, for warmth if nothing else – although not that of the Czech nesting next door. Heaven forfend. Juliet thought of the poor creased woman in the photograph. Dead, she supposed.

It had been a while since Juliet had shared her bed with anyone. There had been a few, but she thought of them as mistakes rather than lovers, and no one steady in her life since she had endured rather than enjoyed a rather tortuous relationship with the second cello of the BBC Northern Orchestra. He was a refugee – Jewish – and had been one of the listeners in Room M at Cockfosters, and it had rather done for him to have to eavesdrop on Nazis all day long. And, of course, he heard a lot about the camps.

It had been part of her job to go on tour with the Northern Orchestra and her memories of the affair mainly consisted of surreptitious sex in the unwelcoming single beds of boarding houses in Satanic mill towns. 'Jerusalem,' she remembered saying to the cellist as they emerged from a station underpass in some godforsaken shoddy hole and surveyed the blackened townscape. She supposed that, being Jewish, 'Jerusalem' meant something different to him.

She had felt that their shared history of listening to the enemy had given them something in common, but really the affair was doomed from the start. They were both still convalescent from the war and it had been a relief to leave him.

Now, though, she missed him. She had perhaps been more fond of him than she knew. And lately she had begun to worry that she was turning into that dreaded creature, a spinster. Perhaps soon the transformation would be complete and she would be an old maid. There were worse fates that could befall a person, she reminded herself. There could be nothing left of you but a creased photograph. Or just a name. And it might not even be your own name.

She clambered out of bed and opened her wardrobe, where she kept a pair of suede ankle boots – stout zippered things lined with sheepskin that had done sterling service in the bad winters after the war. From its snug hideaway in the left boot she removed the Mauser that Perry Gibbons had given her. She kept it loaded, but it made her feel slightly sick to handle it now in the light of Godfrey Toby's resurrection. (*We must finish her off, I'm afraid.*) Juliet placed the little gun on her bedside table. Better safe than sorry.

It was Perry, of course, who had been Godfrey's case officer in the beginning, but Perry left the service in 1940 and she had seen next to nothing of him since. These days he wrote books and gave lectures about Nature. *A Guide to the British Woodland*, for children – she had read that one as an act of friendship, long after they had ceased to be friends, if that was what they had been. He was a regular on *Children's Hour* these days, where he was known as 'Mr Nature'.

She had a wireless beside her bed, a little Philetta that she turned on, lowering the volume so that she wouldn't disturb her guest. Like many others, Juliet was soothed into the night on the airwaves by the shipping forecast. *Viking, North Utsire, South Utsire, Forties, southerly three or four at first in the Utsires, otherwise cyclonic five or six becoming westerly or south-westerly four or five, rain then showers, good.* She was sound asleep before the litany reached Iceland. She dreamt not of seafaring or maritime weather, but of Godfrey Toby. She was walking hand in hand in a park at twilight with him and when she turned to look at him she could see that there was a black hole where his face should be. Despite this drawback he spoke and said, 'We must finish her off, I'm afraid.'

Juliet woke with a start. She sensed something murky was creeping towards her. It was a cruel thing, trying to sprout and find the light of day. It was truth. She wasn't sure that she wanted it. Juliet felt fear for the first time in a long time.

She woke for a second time somewhere in the dark wasteland of the small hours.

Oh, Lord, she thought – Jessica Hastie. Was she still asleep in the studio?

Juliet woke to *Bright and Early* with Marcel Gardner and the Serenade Orchestra on the radio. It seemed an unnecessarily cheerful way to start the day. She got up to make tea and found that Pavel was already awake. Her visitor had removed the bedding from the sofa and made a neat pile of it and now he was sitting, staring at his hands as if he was a condemned man in a cell and it was the day of execution.

'Tea?' she offered brightly. She mimed a cup and saucer. He nodded. A thank-you would be nice, she thought, even in a foreign language.

They breakfasted on last night's supper. He seemed no better for sleep. Pale and restless, he kept pointing at his watch while staring at her questioningly.

'When?' Juliet queried. 'Do you mean when are they coming?'

'Yes. When.'

Juliet suppressed a sigh. They were really rather late, but he would worry more (if that were possible) if he knew this, so she said confidently, 'Soon. Very soon.' There was no telephone. She had recently taken steps to have one installed but there seemed to be a delay of some sort. If she went out and used a phone box it would mean leaving her visitor alone in the flat, and who knew what kind of disaster that might lead to?

'Shall I put some music on?' she asked, holding a record aloft to demonstrate. He shrugged in response, but nonetheless she took Dvořák's Ninth Symphony from its paper sleeve and placed it on the turntable. It seemed appropriate – a fellow countryman writing about a new world – but the music had no effect on him, one way or the other. And perhaps, after all, he preferred his old world.

He commenced pacing around the small flat like a troubled zoo animal, investigating anything he chanced upon, yet without any real curiosity. He ran his finger along the spines of her books, picked up a cushion and scrutinized its cross-stitched urn of flowers (embroidered by Juliet's mother), traced the willow-pattern journey on a breakfast plate. His nerves were horribly stretched. When he picked up her little Sèvres coffee cup and began absent-mindedly transferring it from hand to hand, like a tennis ball, she was forced to intervene. 'Do sit down, why don't you?' she said, gently removing the little cup and putting it on a high shelf as if rescuing it from a child.

Dvořák played. Dvořák finished. Still no sign of them. Something must be up.

'Tea?' she offered. A pot had been made twice this morning already and in answer he simply glared at her. 'Not my fault, mate,' she murmured. There was a loud knock at the door and the pair of them almost jumped out of their respective skins. 'There you go,' Juliet said, 'they're here,' but when she opened the door it was a messenger boy from Curzon Street. He was an inferior species to the BBC Boys.

'There is a bell,' Juliet said.

'Vermilion,' the messenger boy said by way of introduction. 'I've got a message for you.'

'Go on then.'

'You're to bring the flamingo to the Strand Palace Hotel.'

'Now?'

The boy visibly raked his memory. 'Dunno,' he eventually concluded.

'Thanks. You can go,' she said when he showed signs of lingering. 'I'm not tipping you.'

'Fair enough,' he said and skipped down the stairs, whistling as he went.

'Right, we're off,' she said to Pavel. 'Get your things.' Juliet mimed the charade of retrieving a suitcase and overcoat to him. I could get a job on the stage, she thought. I'd be better than some I know. She thought of Jessica Hastie again and felt a twinge of guilt.

Her charge fetched his meagre worldly possessions. The large coat gave him an odd childlike air, as if he'd raided a dressing-up box. He would be cold without a hat, she thought. What had happened to it? Was a man's hat the first thing he lost in a crisis, she wondered? Or the last?

The only thing to do was to hail a cab on the street, so she coaxed him down the stairs as if he were an infant and she was taking him on a pleasant class excursion rather than throwing his fate to the winds.

Juliet made him shelter from view in the doorway of a block of flats at the top of a side street while she went out on to the main road to hunt for a cab. She had to step so far out into the busy Brompton Road that she considered it a marvel that she wasn't mown down by a bus.

Eventually she managed to bring down a taxi outside the Oratory and hustle Pavel into it before saying, as quietly as she could, to the driver, 'The Strand Palace Hotel, please.'

'It's no good whispering, love,' he said. He was a professional Cockney by the sound of it. 'I'm deaf in that ear. The Blitz,' he added, as if he should be given a medal for surviving it. (Yes, definitely a professional.) And they would all have medals if that was simply the case. She patiently repeated the address to him and in response he yelled, 'The Strand Palace Hotel?' so loudly that most of South Kensington must have heard. She could have throttled him.

After casting a quick glance in all directions, Juliet jumped in the cab. They were about to move off when the passenger door on Juliet's side was wrenched open. Pavel screamed like a fox and Juliet thought about the little Mauser and how handy it would be for moments like these (to shoot the taxi driver, if no one else), but then she realized that the person hijacking their cab was Hartley.

'Can we go now?' the taxi driver said. 'Or are there more of you?' He was the truculent sort. Juliet suspected that he wasn't deaf at all.

'Yes,' Juliet snapped. 'We can go.' She had been terrified for a moment. 'For God's sake, Hartley.' She scowled at him. Pavel was

cowering in the corner of the seat, more rabbit than fox. 'You completely spooked him.

'He's a friend,' she said soothingly to Pavel, prodding Hartley in
the chest to demonstrate. 'Friend. Also he's an idiot.'

'Am I a friend?' Hartley asked curiously.

'No. I was trying to make him feel better.'

Juliet and Hartley had long ago abandoned manners with each
other. It was refreshing to behave without respect towards someone.

Hartley reeked of garlic, unpleasant in the small space of a black
cab. He had always possessed some outlandish tastes in food –
gherkins and garlic, stinking cheeses, and once she had gone to his
cell in the Scrubs for something and had found what looked like a
glass jar of tentacles on his desk. ('Squid,' he said happily. 'Came in
on a flight from Lisbon.')

'You're late,' he said.

'I'm not late, you are,' she countered, offering Pavel a mint from a
roll in her pocket in defence against the garlic – but he waved her
away as if she was offering poison to him.

The poor man was ten times cleverer than she and Hartley put
together (twenty times cleverer than Hartley alone) and yet he was
entirely at their disposal.

Hartley, settled now on the jump seat, grinned inanely at Pavel.
'Has he been any trouble?'

'No, of course not. He wouldn't say boo to a goose. I'm late for
work,' she added, the mention of geese reminding her of *Past Times*.
It was due for transmission this afternoon and she hadn't listened to
it yet. Everything was behind because of Joan Timpson's 'small'
operation. She was in Barts but Juliet hadn't been to visit. She
should. She would.

'Vermilion,' she said *sotto voce* to Hartley. She didn't want the cab
driver to blazon it to Trafalgar Square, which they were currently
negotiating in a very laborious manner. 'Can you go a bit quicker?'

she said, but he ignored her. 'Vermilion,' she repeated softly to Hartley.

'Yes. Password for . . .' he nodded in the direction of Pavel. 'What about it?'

'Has it been changed today?'

'Yes.'

'To what?'

He mouthed a word. He looked like a distraught fish. 'Aquamarine,' she decoded eventually. Were they working their way through the colours and now had reached the more abstruse layers of the spectrum? What would be next – caput mortuum, heliotrope? The colours of the day. Last year it had been all sea creatures. Octopus, prawn, dolphin. Fish of the day. She thought of Lester Pelling and his father the fishmonger.

'You should know it,' Hartley said. 'Why don't you know it?'

'Perhaps because I don't actually work for you any more, you know. You're not even paying me, just expenses. And you're obviously incompetent or I *would* know it.' Pavel made a little whimpering noise. 'He doesn't like it when the grown-ups fight,' she said crossly to Hartley. Perhaps she could shoot Hartley too. 'It was just that the messenger boy said "vermilion" this morning.'

'Oh, messenger boys are known to be careless,' Hartley said. 'If not downright stupid.' He was in the middle of trying to direct the driver to the side entrance of the hotel on Exeter Street. The driver seemed reluctant to take instruction and they drove round into Burleigh Street and then out on to the Strand itself before he was finally persuaded that they really did want to go to where they said they did. They had made a full circuit of the building, occasionally against the honking traffic, by the time he finally pulled up outside the door.

Hartley said, 'I'll hop out and check the coast is clear.'

What an ugly hotel. Juliet could see the Savoy from here, on the opposite side of the Strand. So much nicer. It was one of Giselle's haunts during the war. She had been very free with her sexual favours – in order to acquire information, supposedly, although Juliet suspected she would have been free with them anyway. Then the SOE got their hands on her and she was parachuted into France. She was never heard from again, so presumably she was captured and either shot or sent to one of the camps. Juliet sometimes wondered if—

'We go? Please?' Pavel said, interrupting her thoughts.

'No. We don't go. Not yet.'

Ten minutes passed. 'The meter's running, you know,' the driver said.

'I do know that, thank you,' she said tartly.

Fifteen minutes. This was ridiculous. Pavel was getting more and more agitated. He looked like he might be about to bolt. The cab driver adjusted his rear-view mirror to take in Pavel and said, 'Is he all right? He's not going to be sick, is he?'

'No, of course he's not.' He did look rather green though. Juliet made a decision and said, 'Drive on. Take us to Gower Street,' but Hartley chose that moment to reappear. He opened the door of the cab and said to Juliet, 'All clear,' and to Pavel, 'Shall we?' gesturing like a footman for him to step out of the cab.

'I think he's going to take a bit more cajoling than that,' Juliet said.

The indistinguishable grey men had put in an appearance today. They were sitting in the lobby; one was drinking tea, the other was reading *The Times*. They were not very good at pretence. I would have done a much better job, Juliet thought.

She looked around and found that Hartley had disappeared and she'd been left to do this on her own.

When they caught sight of Juliet, the two men stood up, abandoning their props. Oh, here we go, she thought. She put her arm through Pavel's as if they were about to do the Gay Gordons. He was nervous, she could feel a tremor through the thick worsted of his overcoat. They must have seemed an odd couple to anyone watching their hesitant progress. She looked him in the eye and said, 'Courage,' and nodded at him. He nodded back, but she didn't know whether or not he understood. She guided him gently towards the grey men.

'Miss Armstrong,' the tea-drinker said. 'Thank you, we'll take him from here.'

They led him away. He was squashed between them. Poor flamingo, she thought, always destined to be the meat in someone or other's sandwich. Did people eat flamingo? It seemed like an unappetizing bird.

He looked back at her, an expression tantamount to terror on his face. She smiled at him and gave him a little thumbs-up sign, but she couldn't help thinking that perhaps it should have been a thumbs-down. He looked like a man being led to the gallows.

'They're taking him somewhere in Kent,' Hartley said in her ear.

'Don't sneak up on me like that. What's in Kent?'

'Someone's country house. You know – roaring fire, comfortable sofas, after-dinner whisky. Make him feel at ease and then scoop out the contents of his brain.'

'He doesn't like whisky, he prefers beer,' Juliet said.

'I believe, although you didn't hear it from me, that he's on his way to Los Alamos. A present for the Yanks. Good of us, eh?'

'Very. Good of us to acquire the contents of his brain first, too. I don't suppose we're telling the Americans that. I expect they would be rather annoyed.'

'I expect they would. He got out with original blueprints, you know, didn't leave any copies behind. Soviets'll have to start from scratch again with his research. Do you want a drink?' he added hopefully.

'No – yes, all right. Just coffee. I need to talk to you.'

'People always say that,' Hartley said grimly, 'but usually what they need is *not* to talk.'

'Nonetheless,' she said, indicating a little table in the corner away from the hotel's busy footfall.

'Godfrey Toby,' she said, once the waitress had deposited a pot of coffee in front of them. Hartley took out a small hip-flask and added something from it to his cup. He held out the flask and offered it silently to Juliet. She smelt brandy and shook her head. 'Godfrey Toby,' she prompted.

'Who?'

'Don't be stupid, Hartley – I *know* you remember him.'

'Do I?'

'He posed as a Gestapo agent and swept up all the fifth columnists during the war. Perry Gibbons was his handler at first, he set up the operation. I worked with him in Dolphin Square. You're perfectly well aware that I did. His real name was John Hazeldine.'

'Who?'

'John Hazeldine,' Juliet repeated patiently.

'Oh, old Toby Jug, why didn't you say?'

'I wish you wouldn't call him that.'

'Toby Jug?' He looked hurt at her reprimand. 'Term of affection.'

'You hardly knew him.'

'Neither did you.'

I did, she thought. (*Can I get you a cup of tea, Miss Armstrong? Would that help? We've had rather a shock.*)

'He was in Berlin after the war.'

'Berlin?' she said, surprised.

'Or maybe it was Vienna.' Hartley drained his coffee cup. 'Yes, I think it was. There was a lot of mopping up after the war. Godfrey was good at that. The mopping up.' Sighing, he said, 'I was in Vienna, you know. It was a complete hell hole. Mind you, you could buy anything, there was nothing that didn't have a price. You couldn't *trust* anyone though.'

'Can you now?'

He gave her a sideways glance. 'I trust you.' Juliet supposed he was drunk – he was always drunk to one degree or another, even at this time of day.

'I heard he got shipped off to the colonies after the war,' Juliet said. 'Do you think he really was in danger from reprisals?'

'We're all in danger. All the time.'

'Yes, but from reprisals from the war? From his informants.'

Hartley laughed dismissively. 'Storm in a teacup, all that stuff about the fifth column. Bunch of frustrated housewives, most of them. Gibbons was obsessed with them. Anyway you were looking at the wrong people – you should have been looking at the Communists, they were always the real threat. Everyone knows that. Don't they?'

Hartley tipped the hip-flask up and shook the last drops into his mouth. 'I suppose I should report back to the powers-that-be that everything went like clockwork. Thank Christ.'

'How are the powers-that-be?'

'Same as ever – secretive, devious. Everything you would expect from the Service. You know that Oliver Alleyne is Deputy Director General now?'

'I heard. He was always sly.' *He's rather ambitious*, she remembered Perry saying.

'Yes, he's a slippery sod. Did very well out of the war. Merton, of course, has parted ways with the Service – taken up a post at the National Gallery.'

'Really?'

'Don't you keep in touch?'

'Why should we?'

Merton and Alleyne, Juliet thought, like hackneyed comedians or an old-fashioned musical duo – Merton on piano and Alleyne (a counter-tenor, almost certainly) performing Schubert's arrange-ment of 'Who Is Sylvia?' (*Don't let your imagination run away with you, Miss Armstrong.*) Her war (and her peace too, she supposed) had been shaped by the men she knew. Oliver Alleyne, Peregrine Gibbons, Godfrey Toby, Rupert Hartley, Miles Merton. She thought they sounded like characters in a novel by Henry James. One of the later, more opaque ones, perhaps. Who, she wondered, was the most opaque of them all?

Juliet debated whether or not to show Hartley the note. *You will pay for what you did.* He might feel obligated to report it back to someone – Alleyne, perhaps – and she really didn't want that.

'Anyway,' she said, 'I'm not interested in Service gossip.' (Not entirely true.) 'You can get me a cab, Hartley. Some of us have proper jobs to go to.'

'Ah, the good old Corporation,' Hartley said. 'I miss it. Do you think they'd have me back?'

'Probably. They take anyone, to be honest.'

They went outside, to the front entrance this time. Hartley bypassed the doorman and opened the door of a cab that was already parked outside the Strand Palace. 'The BBC, quick as you like,' Hartley said to the driver, and once she was in he slapped the taxi's flank as if sending a horse on its way. It was only when the taxi pulled away from the kerb that Juliet realized it was the same driver as before. She sighed and said irritably, 'You're one of theirs, aren't you? You work for them,' but he just pointed at his ear and said, 'Can't hear a thing, love.'

'The Blitz, I expect,' Juliet said. 'You should get a medal. I'm not paying, by the way. Hartley is.'

She had a sudden image of Pavel's face, the look of fear. And the grey men. They had given her no password, no colour of any shade. What a nonsense it all was.

*

'Gosh, where've you been, Miss Armstrong?' Daisy said. 'I was about to send out the troops to look for you. You didn't have an accident, did you? An appointment you forgot to tell us about? I told everyone that you had to see the optician.'

'You didn't have to lie on my behalf. I simply had some matters I had to attend to.'

'I was worried. You do look a bit off the pace.'

'I'm fine.'

'You should get a telephone, you know. You'd find it useful.'

Juliet frowned. 'How do you know I don't have one already?'

'Well, you would have called if you had, wouldn't you?'

There was no refuting her logic. And yet.

'I need to listen to *Past Lives*, Daisy.'

'The *Medieval Village*? It went out this morning.'

'How did that happen? I haven't listened to it.'

'*Past Lives* always goes out in the morning. Didn't you know that?'

'Apparently not.'

'Mr Lofthouse checked it.'

'Charles?'

'I would have done,' Daisy said, 'only I had to take Miss Hastie home. She was here all night. She had become quite feral by the time she was released. You missed the drama.'

I had my own, Juliet thought.

Juliet ate lunch in the cafeteria. It wasn't Friday and yet it was fish, or at least an attempt at fish. Small irregular shapes that had been crumbed in something offensively orange and then baked in the oven. The fish inside the orange crumb was grey and gelatinous. It made her think again of Lester Pelling and his fishmonger father. Even a bastard, she thought, wouldn't want to sell a fish like this, if fish it was. Over-boiled potatoes and tinned peas completed the assemblage.

Prendergast loomed. He sat down opposite her and gazed at her plate.

'I've eaten better,' Juliet said.

'I've eaten worse,' he said gloomily.

He watched her eat. It was unnerving. She put her cutlery down and said, 'Was there something you wanted to talk to me about?'

'You must finish your lunch.'

'I don't think I can eat any more.'

'Oh, but you normally have such a good appetite.'

Dear God, she thought, was that what she was known for? Although it was true she was an eater – she had eaten her way through grief, she had eaten her way through what had passed for love, she had eaten her way through the war (when she could). She sometimes wondered if there was some emptiness inside that she was trying to fill, but, really, she suspected that she was just hungry a lot. She drew the line at this fish though. 'I have a headache coming on.'

'Oh dear.' His features contorted in sympathy. 'Miss Gibbs said you had to visit the optician. I do hope everything is all right?'

'There's nothing wrong with my eyesight,' Juliet said testily. 'Forgive me,' she relented. 'I've had rather a trying morning.'

'Perhaps I should leave you in peace?' Prendergast gazed at the sugar bowl with an awkward tenderness that she supposed was meant for her.

'No, it's all right.'

'Have you heard of the British Actors' Equity Association?' he asked. 'It appears that Mr Gorman is a member.'

'I don't know anyone by that name.'

'Ralph Gorman? His speciality is the lute. He was hired for something yesterday and was dropped at the last minute.'

'Is it a problem?'

Prendergast looked distraught, but she recognized this as his usual demeanour. 'No, no, no. Just feathers that need soothing. You know how it is. And then there's the little matter of Morna Tread-well. You know who she is?'

'I do.'

'Apparently she happened to listen to the broadcast this morning – one of her scripts. She didn't seem to recognize it.'

'I improved it. It was terrible.'

'Yes, she is rather ghastly, isn't she? But you know she has the ear of the DDG.'

'She can have his eyes and nose as well, she still can't write.'

'Apparently the script – your *improved* script – was quite – how shall I say . . . ?

'Good?' Juliet offered.

'"Sensational",' he countered, treading delicately around the word. 'More ruffled feathers, I fear. They've had quite a few calls coming in to the switchboard over the road at BH, from teachers. Children who were upset and so on. I believe you tackled leprosy.'

One day, she thought, it will all be on television, and it will be so much better. Not a thought to be shared with Prendergast – it would have horrified him, he would never see beyond radio. She had been offered a television production course at Alexandra Palace. She couldn't bring herself to tell him that either.

'It's as well they don't have the Black Death to cope with then, isn't it?' she said, rather sharply.

'I know, I know. And the word "dratted", it's not really, you know . . .' he trailed off into a place of airy vagueness that Juliet had grown used to. He returned to earth eventually. 'Can I tempt you to a pudding?' he asked solicitously. 'It might help your head. There's a very good treacle sponge.'

'No. Thank you. Was there anything else, Mr Prendergast?'

'Well, there's Miss Hastie, of course. You know who *she* is, I suppose? She was locked in a studio all night, apparently.'

'Well, *I* didn't lock her in,' Juliet said. (Or did she? She seemed to remember once locking Hartley in his cell at the Scrubs.) 'I imagine her feathers were excessively ruffled.'

'The woman is *all* feathers,' Prendergast said, a spasm of pain seizing his canine features. 'Quite a catalogue of mishaps,' he added sorrowfully.

'Do you want to fire me?' Juliet asked. 'You can, you know. I really wouldn't mind.'

He clutched his hands to his heart in horror. 'Oh, goodness, Miss Armstrong. Of course not. I wouldn't dream of it. It's sound and fury, nothing more.'

Juliet felt a pang of disappointment. She had been horribly attracted by the idea of simply walking away. A disappearing act. But where would she go? There was always somewhere, she supposed. She hoped.

Returning to her office, Juliet walked past a rehearsal room, and as she did so the door opened, unleashing a blast of 'Bobby Shafto'. The door closed and Bobby Shafto and his golden hair disappeared. Across the road, the purpose-built rehearsal rooms and studios were buried deep in the core of Broadcasting House, wound round protectively with the offices. Sound and its opposite, silence, were everything, but over here the haphazard nature of the building meant that they were forever stumbling across each other's programmes.

Singing Together, Juliet thought. Schools seemed to be fixated on an Old England of sea shanties and ballads and folk songs. And maidens, lots of maidens. 'Early One Morning' and 'Oh, No John, No John, No John, No'. (What an irritating song!) 'Dashing Away with a Smoothing Iron'. Ridiculous. They were reinventing England, or perhaps inventing it. A memory rose up – during the war, driving past Windsor Castle in the early-morning light, Perry Gibbons turning to her and saying, 'This England – is it worth fighting for?' It depended whose side you were on, she supposed.

Fräulein Rosenfeld was trundling along the corridor towards her, hampered somewhat by – amongst other things – the large Langenscheidt dictionary that accompanied her everywhere. She was also juggling a heavy workbook with 'Intermediate German' written on the cover. The hem of her worn tartan pleated skirt had come undone in places and Juliet itched to find a needle and thread and sew it up again. The Fräulein had a particular musty scent – nutmeg and the ancient oak of churches, not entirely unpleasant. She could be relied upon to be always in the building, as if she had no other place to go. Juliet sometimes wondered if she spent the night roosting in a Listening room somewhere instead of going home.

The Intermediate German – inevitably – slipped out of Fräulein Rosenfeld's grip and fell to the ground, pages fluttering, like a heavy dead bird. 'Intermediate German' would be rather a good name for Fräulein Rosenfeld herself, Juliet thought. She retrieved the workbook and replaced it in the Fräulein's arms, where it balanced precariously. I should invite her for a meal, Juliet thought. Pagani's up the road maybe. She would fit in awfully well in Moretti's, but that would hardly be a treat for her.

'What is that?' Fräulein Rosenfeld asked, her old freckled face furrowing inquisitively at the sound of the music that had escaped again from its confines.

'"Bobby Shafto",' Juliet said. 'He's gone to sea with silver buckles on his knees.' This explanation seemed to satisfy Fräulein Rosenfeld, who nodded and trudged on her way. The burden of Europe was on her dowager's hump. It weighed heavily.

'Miss Armstrong, Miss Armstrong.' An urgent whisper halted her progress along the corridor again. Juliet looked around but couldn't see anyone. The door to a small playback room was open and when she peered inside she found Lester Pelling, his face blanched to the colour of thin milk and looking as if he were in the middle of having a heart attack.

'Are you all right, Lester?'

'I thought I'd listen to *Past Lives*.' His earphones were still round his neck. 'It went out this morning.'

'Apparently.'

'And I wasn't here because Miss Gibbs needed a hand with Miss Hastie. She was raging,' he said, looking suddenly fearful at the memory.

'And?' Juliet prompted gently.

'Miss Gibbs said you were at the optician, and so Mr Lofthouse listened instead.'

'I know.'

'Well . . .' He put on a bold face and said, 'I don't like him, miss. Mr Lofthouse. I don't like him.'

'It's all right, Lester, neither do I.'

'And it's not just his leg, his ears aren't all they should be either. You need to listen to it, Miss Armstrong.' He was wringing his hands. Juliet didn't think she'd seen anyone do that since the war. Lester had been a child during the war, of course.

She was beginning to feel alarmed. 'What *is* it exactly, Lester?'

Silently, he handed her a second pair of earphones and put his own back on. Dropping the stylus gently on to the disc, he said, 'About here, I think.'

They listened together.

'Oh, dear God,' Juliet said. 'Play it again.'

They listened again. It was just the same. The voice of Roger Fairbrother – Miller, First Serf and understudy Cook – incanting, in his rather delicate, feminine tones, 'Fuck, fuck, fuckity fuck.'

They took their headphones off and stared fixedly at each other. Anyone walking in on them might have presumed that they had recently been turned to stone at a moment of absolute horror. Pompeii, perhaps.

They came back to life slowly.

'He had some trouble with his lines,' Juliet remembered. 'He did get a bit flustered. He was at Dunkirk, I believe. Prendergast said there were a lot of complaints, but they didn't go much beyond objecting to "dratted",' she puzzled. 'Although they do say that you only hear what you're expecting to hear.' *We believe what we want to believe*, Perry had said to her once.

'I don't expect the Juniors were expecting to hear *that*,' Lester said, gesturing towards the turntable. They both stared at it as if they could see the words still revolving.

'Fuck, fuck, fuckity fuck,' Juliet murmured and Lester flinched – not so much at the word, she suspected (his father was a bastard, after all) but at the consequences of the word. There was an interesting ethical debate to be had about the difference, but now was most certainly not the time. 'You have to admire the rhythm, I suppose,' Juliet said.

'What do you think we should do?' he asked.

'I think we should keep mum.'

'And hang on to it?'

'God, no. The opposite. We need to get rid of it. And then if anyone complains, we'll deny it. Or say we sent it to Recorded Programmes and they lost it. They would never send it to Archive anyway – all our stuff goes straight in the Scrap. Oh, damn and blast, why couldn't we have done it live? We could have just said people were mistaken. Now there's evidence.'

'We have to destroy it.'

'Yes.'

'I'll take it home with me, miss,' he volunteered bravely, as if it were an unexploded bomb he was offering to defuse. 'I'll deal with it.' Juliet heard Cyril's voice in her head at the scene of a different disaster. *Come on, miss. We can do this. You take the head and I'll take the feet.* She felt suddenly sick.

The tea trolley could be heard clattering along the corridor towards them like a siege engine and they fell into a tense silence. They could have been conspirators, Juliet thought, hatching a plot to blow up the BBC, finish off Hitler's work for him. 'No,' she sighed, 'it's my responsibility. I'll see to it. I might go home early, actually. I've got a bit of a headache. Don't worry about it – worse things happen at sea. It'll be all right.'

She left the building, holding the offensive recording in plain sight, as if she were taking it over to Broadcasting House. As she started across the road, the last person she wanted to see at that moment approached from the other side. Charles Lofthouse.

'Juliet,' he said pleasantly as they met each other in the middle of the road. 'Going to BH? No problems, I hope?'

'Why should I have a problem, Charles?' She clutched the record protectively to her chest. A car whizzed by, too close for comfort. One of us is going to get killed, she thought. (Preferably Charles.) 'Must dash, Charles. I'll see you tomorrow.'

'Undoubtedly.' A taxi hooted loudly and swerved to miss Charles, who was limping rather slowly to the other side of the road. The driver shouted an obscenity and Charles waved his hand dismissively at him. His leg was particularly bad today, she noticed. Juliet had briefly dated a pilot during the war. He crash-landed on the coast coming back from a raid and lost a leg. He made light of it, joked about it endlessly from his hospital bed (*Not a leg to stand on, Pull the other one*, and so on), but it ruined him and he gassed himself in his mother's kitchen after he was released from hospital. Juliet was furious with him for killing himself. It was only a leg, after all, she argued with his phantom presence. It wasn't as if he didn't have two. I would have stuck by him, she thought. But perhaps that was easy to say after the fact. After all, she hardly knew him and anyway, apart from her mother, she'd never stuck by anyone else. Sometimes she wondered if she didn't carry a fatal flaw inside her – the crack in the golden bowl, invisible to the naked eye, but impossible to ignore once you knew about it.

She got in the cab that always seemed to be lurking in Riding House Street, although there was no rank there. It was not – thankfully – being driven by this morning's cabbie. She was imagining it, wasn't she – that the cab that nearly mowed Charles Lofthouse down just now was being driven by the driver from this morning? She was starting to see him everywhere. That's how people went mad. She remembered seeing *Gaslight* during the war.

On the other hand, she felt pretty sure that Charles had heard Roger Fairbrother's linguistic lapse and still let the programme go out. It wouldn't be Charles who would get the blame, it would be her, wouldn't it? Devious old bugger, she thought. Juliet had learnt to swear in the North, where words like 'bastard' and 'bugger' were part of the lingua franca. She had done Outside Broadcasts, talking to miners and trawlermen about their lives. Nor did 'fuck' frighten her. She felt a twinge of sympathy for poor Roger Fairbrother. *Fuck, fuck, fuckity fuck.*

Juliet changed her mind about the cab and got out on Great Titchfield Street, to the driver's annoyance, and then caught another on New Cavendish Street. Before stepping into it she cast a quick glance around the street. She had the uneasy feeling that she was being watched. How else would the funny little man from Moretti's (if it was him) know where to deliver that note? *You will pay for what you did.* Must I, Juliet thought? The war had thrown up plenty of unpaid debts – why should she be the one being presented with the bill? Or perhaps someone was playing a trick on her, some kind of game to drive her mad. Gaslighting. But it still left the question of who. And why.

It was only four o'clock, she thought, as the cab pulled away. Plenty of time for more mishaps to add to Prendergast's catalogue.

*

She made a pot of tea and washed down a couple of aspirins – she really did have a headache now. The food from last night was still lying on the little table at the window, looking rather weary now. She used the eggs and cheese to make an omelette. She ate the omelette. Sometimes it was better to go step by simple step. The funny little man who had stared at her in Moretti's yesterday had eaten an omelette, shovelling it in his mouth with a fork as if he had never been taught manners. Or had been starving at some point in his life.

She turned on the wireless, looking for the news and finding the end of *Children's Hour*. Perry Gibbons. Of course it would be him. Life was nothing more than a long chain of coincidences. He was talking about beetles. 'If you look carefully, children, you will find that there are shield bugs everywhere.' Really? Juliet thought, casting a rather apprehensive glance around the room.

Ever since her return from Manchester she had been wondering if she would bump into Perry. Apart from the odd glimpse from a distance, she hadn't seen him since he left the Service during the war. (*I shall be leaving you, I'm afraid, Miss Armstrong.*) Had he left the Service? Or was it just the pretence of leaving? – which in many ways was more effective. It would be the same if people thought you were dead, wouldn't it? You would be left free to live. She was reminded of the Friar in *Much Ado About Nothing*, advising Hero to fake her death. (*Come, lady, die to live.*) Juliet had seen last season's production in Stratford (Anthony Quayle and Diana Wynyard – both very good). It was a happier outcome for Hero than for Juliet's own fictional namesake when she tried the same trick. *O happy dagger.*

Death was an extreme recourse. Perhaps all you needed to do was put about the rumour that you had left for New Zealand or South Africa. Or, in Perry's case, that you had quit MI5 for the Ministry of Information in June 1940 and had never looked back.

There seemed to be some kind of osmotic membrane between the Corporation and the Service, employees moving from one world to the other without hindrance. Hartley had been a producer in Talks before the war and now Perry was a regular contributor to the BBC. Sometimes you had to wonder if MI5 was using the BBC for its own purposes. Or, indeed, if it was the other way round.

Children's Hour ended with its usual sign-off. 'Goodnight children, everywhere.' *Between the darkness and the daylight.* That was the children's hour, according to the Longfellow poem. It was a sprightly, sentimental kind of poem, yet it always brought on an unaccountable fit of melancholy in her. Perhaps it was nostalgia for her days in Manchester, when she had sometimes been the one to say goodnight.

Big Ben struck the hour and the *Six o'Clock News* began. Juliet was prompted to set sentiment aside and went looking for her small domestic toolkit and took out the hammer, more like a toffee hammer, that she used for putting up pictures. Placing the *Medieval Village* on the wooden draining board in the kitchen, she smashed it to pieces. It would never know history. It was not the first time she had destroyed evidence of wrong-doing and she supposed it wouldn't be the last.

She arrived at Barts halfway through visiting time, bearing the remains of the grapes from the Harrods cornucopia, trimmed to look untouched.

'Oh, how kind,' Joan Timpson said. 'These are rather superior. Where did you get them?'

'Harrods,' Juliet admitted.

'You shouldn't have gone to the expense.'

'Don't be silly,' Juliet said. She could hardly say that MI5 had paid for them. 'How are you feeling anyway?'

'Much better, thank you, dear.'

She didn't look better, Juliet thought. She looked awful.

'How about the *Village?*' Joan asked. 'Went the day well?'

Juliet was getting ready for bed when there was a noisy banging on the door. There was a hint of desperation in it. There's a bell, she thought.

She stood behind the door and said, 'Who is it?'

'It's Hartley. Open up.'

She did, but grudgingly. He was wretchedly drunk, which she attributed to the near-empty bottle of rum in his hand. He was catholic in his attitude to alcohol – anything would do.

'Is he here?'

'Is who here?' Juliet puzzled.

'The fucking flamingo – who else?'

'The Czech? Pavel? No, of course not.'

'Are you sure?' There was an urgent note to the question.

'Of course I'm sure. I think I'd notice. You haven't *lost* him, have you?'

'Flown the coop,' he said. 'Never turned up in Kent.'

Juliet thought of the indistinguishable grey men. England wasn't the only country to breed them like that.

'Even *you* couldn't be that careless, Hartley.'

'I wasn't the last one with him,' he said, turning petulant. 'I wasn't running the safe house either. You were.'

She sighed. 'You'd better come in. You're in no fit state to do anything.'

He entered the small living room and dropped heavily on to the sofa. His presence filled the flat in a way that the Czech's hadn't. The difference between presence and absence. Reading and writing. Playing and listening. Living and dying. The world was just an endless dialectic. It was exhausting.

'I was about to make cocoa.'

'Cocoa?' Hartley echoed incredulously.

'Yes, it will do you good.'

But when she came back with the two cups Hartley was asleep, still in a sitting position. She tipped him on to his side and fetched a blanket. She should hire this sofa out, she thought, before turning out the light.

Two nights running she'd had men sleeping on her sofa. One a complete stranger, the other irritatingly familiar. I'll get a reputation, she thought, although in fact no one in the building could have cared less what she got up to. Her neighbours were mostly eccentrics or refugees, which amounted to the same thing in practice.

She locked her bedroom door in case a befuddled Hartley fumbled his way through in the middle of the night, mistaking her room for the bathroom.

Juliet put the little Mauser next to the Philetta radio. It was best to be ready, even if you had no idea what it was you were ready for. And if the worst came to the worst, she could always shoot Hartley, who was snoring like a goods train next door. She had never been sure about Hartley. He had no real centre. It wouldn't bother him to play for the other side.

You will pay for what you did. The war was a clumsily stitched wound and it felt as if it was being opened by something. Or someone. Was it Godfrey Toby? I must find him, she thought. Perhaps I must find them all. I will be the hunter, not the hunted. Diana, not the stag. The arrow, not the bow.

It's all right. But it wasn't, was it? Not really.

Hartley was gone when Juliet woke the next morning. Only the empty rum bottle remained as evidence that he had ever been in her flat.

The fog of sleep was still befuddling Juliet, rendering her mind a jumble of lost flamingos and unnecessary lutes, not to mention strange men with pebble eyes.

You will pay for what you did. Was the man from Moretti's the one demanding payment, or was he just the messenger? Could he be one of Godfrey's fifth columnists? Trude and Dolly were the only ones whose faces she had seen, that she had ever encountered in the flesh. All the informants' files must be buried somewhere deep in the Registry – did they have photographs attached? Godfrey could easily have fooled them into thinking that photographic identity would make it easier for them to be verified by the Nazis if they invaded. *Come along now, Betty, smile for the camera.* I have a little list, Juliet thought. And it's time to work my way through it. Hunter, not hunted, she reminded herself.

Juliet felt almost overwhelmed by the urge to find Godfrey. He would know the answers to her questions. He would know what to do. (*We must finish her off, I'm afraid.*) After all, he was good at 'mopping up'.

Perhaps all the chatter about relocation at the end of the war had been merely a ruse. What if Godfrey Toby was exactly where he had been all along? Hiding in plain sight. In Finchley. Live to die, Godfrey.

Making her way to the Underground, Juliet felt a frisson of fear, an animal instinct that told her she was being followed. When she glanced behind her she could see no one who looked as if they might be dogging her footsteps. That was no comfort, as all it meant was that if someone was following her then they were very good at it.

Taking a detour, she got off the Tube at Regent Street and headed to Oxford Street to get on another line. On the way she entered a Woolworth's through the front entrance and exited through the back, a rather crude feint designed to flush out anyone who might be trailing after her. She was on high alert and when a rather drab-looking woman, marooned in middle age, bumped into her, she was forced to suppress a cry of alarm. The woman was wearing a headscarf patterned with yellow and green parrots and was carrying a battered leatherette shopping bag on her arm. Were yellow and green the two colours that should never be seen – or was that red and green? Juliet's mother had had quite a list of dressmaker's do's and don'ts – no spots with stripes, and so on – which Juliet was hard-pressed to remember. Whichever combination it was, the headscarf was hideous. The woman's leatherette handbag was easily large enough to conceal a weapon. Even in the grip of her own paranoia, Juliet could acknowledge that it was an unlikely guise for an assassin. She feared that she was beginning to tread the wilder shores of her imagination.

Juliet could only imagine the havoc she would cause if she started brandishing her own gun on Oxford Street. And she couldn't shoot every drab housewife – she'd be here all day. She hadn't realized quite how many of them roamed the streets of London during the daytime. Herds of them were heading into John Lewis, where there was a sale on, all in the same uniform of shapeless gabardine coats and dismally out-of-date hats. It was the war, Juliet thought, remembering the photograph of the flamingo's creased wife, it has made refugees of us all.

When the train arrived, she got in and then got out again just as the doors were closing. No one followed her and the platform remained empty, not a drab housewife in sight. I'm being ridiculous, Juliet thought. When the next train arrived, she climbed aboard and took a seat. Glancing out of the window as the train began to pull away from the platform, she caught sight of the man from Moretti's – the unmistakeable pockmarked skin and pebble eyes. He was sitting on a bench in front of a poster for Sanatogen Tonic Wine (for which he was a very poor advert), the large black umbrella like a staff at his side. He gave her a small salute of recognition, but it was difficult to tell if it was a threat or a greeting. Either way, it was horribly unnerving.

And then something even more unnerving occurred. The woman Juliet had bumped into outside Woolworth's – she of the parrot headscarf and leatherette shopping bag – appeared from nowhere and slid on to the bench next to the man from Moretti's. The two of them stared silently at Juliet, like a pair of resentful bookends. Then the train hauled itself into the blackness of the tunnel and they disappeared from sight.

Who *were* they? Some kind of odd husband-and-wife team? What on earth was going on? Juliet hadn't a clue. Rhymes with true, she thought.

Same oak front door, same brass lion's head knocker. Juliet even recognized the hydrangea that was growing next to the gate, although it was still dormant, waiting for spring. Juliet lifted the lion's head and rapped it sharply against the oak. Nothing. She knocked again and was startled when the door flew open abruptly. A rather harried young woman, wearing a frilled apron and with an artful smudge of flour on her cheek – the perfect picture of post-war young womanhood – said, 'Oh, hello. Can I help you?'

'My name's Madge Wilson,' Juliet said. 'I'm looking for the people who used to live here.'

From the depths of the house came an angry squawk and the woman laughed apologetically and said, 'Look, why don't you come in?' (But I'm a complete stranger, Juliet thought. For all you know, I've come to murder you.) Wiping her hands on her apron, the woman said, 'You'll have to excuse my appearance. It's my baking day.'

She led Juliet trustingly down the hall. Over her shoulder she said, 'My name's Philippa – Philippa Horrocks.' The house smelt authentically of wet nappies and sour milk. Juliet thought she might retch.

The door to the living room was open and Juliet caught a glimpse inside. It had been redecorated since she was last here. For a dizzying second she was back in the past, sitting on the cut moquette of Godfrey Toby's sofa. (*Can I get you a cup of tea, Miss Armstrong? Would that help? We've had rather a shock.*) She gave herself a mental shake.

As she entered the kitchen the source of the squawking was revealed – a furious, small boy, besmirched with egg yolk and strapped tightly into a high-chair.

'Timmy,' Philippa Horrocks said, as if he was something to boast about.

'What a sturdy little chap,' Juliet said, shuddering inwardly. She found most children slightly repellent.

'Can I offer you a coffee?' Philippa Horrocks said. No sight or smell of anything in the oven, Juliet noticed. No bowls or spoons or scales anywhere. So much for baking day. ('It's in the details,' Perry said.)

'No, thank you. I'm actually here looking for the Hazeldines. They lived in this house during the war. They were friends of the family and I was trying to get in touch to invite them to my parents' thirtieth wedding anniversary.' *If you're going to tell a lie, tell a good one.*

'Pearl,' Philippa Horrocks said.

'I'm sorry?'

'Pearl. You know, twenty-five is silver – thirty years is pearl.'

'Yes, yes,' Juliet said, and thought, I sound like Godfrey Toby.

'We had our wood last year. Five years.' One of Philippa's eyelids fluttered.

'Congratulations.'

'Hazeldine,' Philippa Horrocks said, making a great show of thinking. 'Are you sure? We bought the house at auction in '46 and the man who had owned it before had lived here for years before that.'

'Was his surname Toby?'

'No. He was called Smith.' Of course he was, Juliet thought. 'Are you sure you won't have a coffee? I'm having one.'

'Oh, go on then, you've twisted my arm. Two sugars, please.'

As well as Timmy there were the twins, Christopher and Valerie, who had started school this year and were already proficient at Book One in the *Janet and John* series. Their father, Philippa's husband, was called Norman and he was an actuary. (What was an actuary, Juliet wondered? It sounded as if it belonged in a zoo, along with a cassowary and a dromedary.) They moved here from Horsham. Philippa was a housewife, but during the war she was in the WAAF – best time of her life! She couldn't decide between snapdragons and begonias for her summer bedding, 'Do you know anything about gardening, Madge?'

'Oh, it's begonias for me. Every time,' Juliet said. Each day, I expect hundreds of people die of boredom, she thought. She finished her coffee – it was Camp from a bottle, boiled up in the pan with Carnation milk. It was truly disgusting. 'Lovely! I'm sorry, but now I really have to get going.'

She was ushered out as politely as she had been ushered in. Timmy, released from his bondage, was held aloft in Philippa Horrocks's arms. His red cheeks looked as shiny and hard as apples. 'Teething,' Philippa laughed. 'So sorry I couldn't help you, Madge. I hope your parents have a wonderful anniversary.'

'Thanks. By the way,' Juliet said, pausing at the gate, next to the hydrangea, 'the flowers on this are going to be pink. Do you know how to make them blue?'

'No,' Philippa Horrocks said, 'I don't,' but Juliet left without letting her in on the secret.

Juliet lingered on the corner of the street, checking occasionally to see if anyone left or entered the house. Nothing. Nobody came or went; the inhabitants of the entire street might as well have been under a sleeping spell.

'Iris! Is that you?' someone said loudly behind her. It was such a shock that Juliet thought she might die right there on the streets of Finchley. 'Iris Carter-Jenkins! Fancy bumping into you here.'

'Mrs Ambrose,' Juliet said. 'It's been a long time.'

'I didn't know Finchley was your stamping ground.'

'I was visiting a friend,' Juliet said. 'I thought you moved to Eastbourne, Mrs Ambrose – or should I call you Mrs Eckersley now?'

'Florence will do.'

Mrs Ambrose was wearing a hat that was covered in feathers. The feathers were a vibrant blue, but Juliet supposed they were from a chicken and had been dyed rather than having been harvested from the unwilling body of a kingfisher or a peacock. Juliet wondered if Mrs Ambrose – with her fondness for home-made hats – had killed and plucked the bird herself. (*The woman is all feathers.*)

Could Mrs Ambrose's appearance out of the blue really be a coincidence? First Godfrey Toby, then Mrs Ambrose. (It was hard to think of her as anyone else.) What had Perry said about coincidences? Oh, yes – never trust one. Who was going to be next to pop out of the box that the past was supposed to be contained in, Juliet wondered? Yet surely Godfrey and Mrs Ambrose had no reason to have ever met during the war? The only thing that connected them was Juliet herself. Her nerves were not soothed by this thought. Quite the opposite, in fact.

'Eastbourne didn't suit me,' Mrs Ambrose said. 'I need a bit of life around me. I've opened a little wool shop just up the road from here, on Ballards Lane – run it with my niece Ellen.' How many nieces did the woman have exactly, Juliet wondered? (And how many of them were real?) 'Are you catching the Tube? Why don't I walk with you?'

Why – to get me away from here? Juliet wondered as Mrs Ambrose hooked her by the elbow and walked her like a prison wardress to the Underground, chatting all the way about merino and mohair, and the virtues of Patons versus Sirdar. Juliet's arm felt quite bruised by the time she reached the station platform. Was Mrs Ambrose still working for the Service? It seemed plausible, there had always been such an ambiguity about her, even her code name seemed to hint at it. 'Eckersley', on the other hand, indicated nothing beyond nieces and wool shops. She had always wondered about Mrs Ambrose's loyalties, of course. *The mark of a good agent is when you have no idea which side they're on.*

The girl on reception at Schools raised a mute eyebrow of disdain when Juliet entered.

'Was anyone looking for me?' Juliet asked.

'Everyone,' the girl said with a subordinate shrug.

'I was out and about doing some research, since you don't ask. For the *Looking At Things* series.'

'What were you looking at?' the girl asked indifferently.

'Finchley.'

The girl glanced at her and frowned. 'Finchley?'

'Yes, Finchley,' Juliet said. 'Terribly interesting.'

'And everything is transient, after all, isn't it?' Juliet mused over a rather disconsolate cup of coffee with Prendergast. It had started as a relatively cheerful discussion about classroom feedback for a series for Seniors called *Can I Introduce You?*, but somehow an assessment of *Can I Introduce You to Sir Thomas More?* had led them into the doldrums. 'People become hopelessly caught up in dogma and doctrine . . .'

'Isms,' Prendergast said, shaking his head dolefully.

'Exactly. Fascism, Communism, capitalism. We lose sight of the ideal that propelled them and yet millions die in defence of – or attack on – those beliefs.' Juliet thought of the fugitive flamingo. Where was he?

'People are dying for capitalism?' Prendergast asked curiously.

'Well, people have always died having their labour exploited for other people's profit. All the way back to the Pharaohs and beyond, I suppose.'

'True, true. Very true.'

'Yet what does it all mean in the long run? And religion is the worst offender, of course. Sorry,' she added, remembering his Methodist 'calling'. (Although how could you forget?)

'Oh, don't worry about me, Miss Armstrong,' he said, raising the papal hand again, this time indicating dispensation. 'What is faith if it cannot rise to a challenge?'

'Doctrine's just a refuge though, isn't it? If we were to admit that essentially nothing has meaning, that we only *attribute* meaning to things, that there is no such thing as absolute truth . . .'

'We would despair,' Prendergast said softly, his bulldog face wilting.

'*L'homme est condamné à être libre,*' Juliet said.

'I'm sorry, my French is a little rusty.'

'Man is condemned to be free.'

'Are we talking existentialism?' Prendergast queried. 'Those French fellows?'

Can I Introduce You to Sartre? Juliet thought. They hadn't done that. Too challenging for the Seniors – for everyone, really. *Huis Clos. No Exit* was how they translated the title. The play had been broadcast on the Third Programme after the war. Alec Guinness and Donald Pleasence. It had been rather good.

'No. Not existentialism, not really. More like common sense,' Juliet said, avoiding the 'ism' of pragmatism to mollify Prendergast.

He put his hand on top of hers, a gesture of kindness. 'We have all walked in the valley of the shadow of death. Do you despair, Miss Armstrong?'

Hardly ever. Occasionally. Quite often. 'No, not at all,' she said. 'And anyway, if everything is pointless, then so is despair, isn't it?'

'It can leave you rather adrift though,' he said. 'Thinking, and so on.'

They fell silent, each considering their own state, driftless or otherwise. Juliet quietly moved the weighty Prendergast paw from her hand and he roused himself and said, 'I thought Socrates was right on the button, as it were.'

They had come full circle, Juliet supposed, back to *Can I Introduce You?* It was a self-explanatory title for a series about figures from history. Somewhat different from *Have You Met?* for Juniors. (*Have You Met a Fireman? Have You Met a Nurse?* And so on.) 'Yes, he went down well,' she agreed.

'Quite the radical in some ways, wasn't he?' Prendergast said. 'The Seniors seemed to respond well to that.'

'They're at an age when they're beginning to think for themselves,' Juliet said.

'Before the "isms" take over.'

'I liked Charles Dickens myself,' Juliet said. 'Michelangelo was "disappointing". The Teachers said that the pamphlet that accompanied it didn't have enough pictures and I suppose that is rather the point. Christopher Wren went down quite well. It had the Great Fire, of course. Disasters are always popular with them.'

'Florence Nightingale?' Prendergast asked.

'Flimsy.'

'Chaucer?'

'Boring. That's the Seniors talking. The Teachers didn't seem to have an opinion on him.'

'Oliver Cromwell?'

'I wrote that one,' Juliet said.

'Did you? Oh, excellent, that was *very* good.'

'You're just saying that.'

'You are droll, Miss Armstrong.'

Was that a compliment or an insult? It hardly mattered either way. She was deflected from considering further by Daisy appearing suddenly at her elbow. You would think the girl moved on silent castors. Her face was a mask of tragedy.

'Is something wrong, Daisy?'

'I'm terribly sorry to interrupt, Miss Armstrong, but I thought I should give you the bad news straight away.'

'What?' Juliet said, a tad impatiently. She was tempered to bad news – she had been through a war, after all. Not so Prendergast, whose hand flew to his mouth in anticipation of some fresh horror.

'It's Miss Timpson,' Daisy said. She took a dramatic pause, previously employed by the Small Girl with leprosy.

'She's dead?' Juliet guessed, robbing Daisy of her moment.

'Dead?' Prendergast echoed, aghast.

'She did look rather poorly. I saw her just last night,' Juliet said.

'Poor Joan,' Prendergast said, shaking his head in disbelief. 'I thought she was having a bunion removed. She's in a better place, I suppose.'

'We must hope so,' Daisy said solemnly. An undertaker would readily employ her.

Bugger, Juliet thought. She was going to have to see *Past Lives* through to the bitter end now. She didn't feel she had the fortitude for all those Tudors, they were so relentlessly busy – all that bedding and beheading. 'I must get on,' she said, abandoning Daisy to Prendergast. Or perhaps the other way round.

Juliet was sorry now that she had given Joan Timpson secondhand grapes, she would have taken her something unsullied had she known it would be her final meal on earth. Discounting members of the medical profession (and perhaps not even them), Juliet was probably the last person Joan had spoken to. 'How lovely,' she had said, picking a grape off the bunch. As last words go, they were pleasant ones.

Juliet returned to the sanctuary of her desk to brood. On Godfrey Toby, on Mrs Ambrose and on the flamingo. Was there some way in which the Czech's disappearance could be linked to Godfrey's reappearance?

The flamingo had flown, but where had he landed? Did flamingos fly? She thought of them as flightless birds, but her knowledge of ornithology hadn't progressed since Perry Gibbons's attempts to educate her.

And there he was! As if by simply thinking his name she had conjured him up out of thin air. He was walking past the open door of her office in the company of Daisy Gibbs. What was he doing over on their side of the road? Was he looking for her?

The ghosts of the past were gathering. Perry, Godfrey, Mrs Ambrose. A congregation of the past. Who would be next? Not Cyril, she hoped.

Neither Daisy nor Perry glanced in at her. Juliet felt slighted yet relieved. It was curious how you could hold two quite opposing feelings at the same time, an unsettling emotional discord. She felt an odd pang at the sight of him. She had been fond of him. She had been his girl. Reader, I didn't marry him, she thought.

A few minutes later Daisy returned along the corridor, sans Perry. She knocked on the door.

'I can see you,' Juliet said crisply. 'You hardly need to knock.'

'I have some correspondence – Teachers – would you like me to answer it?'

'Yes, please, I thought we agreed you would. What's Perry Gibbons doing here?'

'Mr Gibbons? Oh, Mr Prendergast is borrowing him from *Children's Hour*, to do an *Our Observer* for us. Julius Caesar – crossing the Rubicon, *alea iacta est* and all that. The die is cast—'

'I do know Latin, thank you, Daisy.'

Juliet had a sudden unexpected memory – one of Perry's 'expeditions', to St Albans (Verulamium – at first she'd thought it had something to do with worms) one wet afternoon to see a Roman villa. *A very well-preserved mosaic floor*, he'd told her. *It covers the hypocaust.* Hypocaustum *from the Ancient Greek* . . .

She had been vexed with him about something, but now she couldn't remember what.

'Have you met Mr Gibbons?' Daisy asked. Juliet heard capital letters. *Can I Introduce You to Perry Gibbons?* He would have made quite an interesting subject.

'Once or twice.'

'The man's a polymath!'

'Sometimes you can know too much, Daisy.'

'Miss Timpson's funeral is on Monday, by the way. The Department's sending a wreath.' Daisy lingered. Juliet waited. 'We're contributing.'

'How much?' Juliet asked.

'Five shillings each.'

That seemed like a lot, but you weren't supposed to haggle over a funeral wreath, Juliet supposed. She sighed, opened up her purse and counted out two half-crowns into Daisy's waiting palm, as pink and clean as a kitten's paw.

'Do you know what she died of?' Daisy asked, with the air of someone who did.

'No. Do you?'

'Yes,' Daisy said. 'Mr Lofthouse told me.'

'Charles?' Juliet waited but no more was forthcoming. 'Are you going to tell me?' she prompted. Oh, she thought, please don't say she choked on a grape.

'Yes. Tumours. Everywhere.' Rhymes with rumours, Juliet thought. 'She soldiered on.'

'Don't use clichés, Daisy. It's beneath you.'

'You're right.'

'Anyway,' Juliet said, 'I'm popping over the road. To Duplicating.' Their Roneo machine had given up the ghost. 'Oh, Roneo, Roneo, wherefore art thou?' one of the secretaries said (a little too frequently), and Juliet thought crossly, why does everyone misinterpret that line? She had grown, over the years, to feel proprietorial over it.

For some days now, every time they wanted something copying they had to go over to Broadcasting House. Everyone liked the little break it gave them. They could have sent a Boy, of course, but why should they have all the fun?

'I can go to BH for you,' Daisy volunteered. 'I'm sure you've got more important things on your plate.'

'No, really I haven't. I'll go.'

'Oh, let me.'

'No.' Soon Daisy would be wrestling her to the ground to gain possession of the sheaf of papers in her hand. Most of them were blank. She wasn't going to Duplicating. She was going to the Concert Hall to listen in on a recording of the BBC Dance Orchestra. She knew the producer. The tea girl brought them tea, but they eschewed her plain biscuits in favour of the fruit cake that the producer's wife made for him. He was very world-weary, but then so was Juliet. They had kissed once, quite briefly, an act of solidarity rather than lust.

Juliet sensed a heavy atmosphere when she came back from the Concert Hall. 'Did something happen?' she asked Daisy.

'Lester Pelling was sacked,' she said. 'It's a lot to bear when we're still reeling from the news about Miss Timpson.'

'Sacked?'

'Hauled over the coals. Mr Fairbrother – Miller, First Serf and understudy Cook – remember him?'

'I do.'

'Well, apparently he swore during the broadcast.' Daisy dropped her voice to a prim whisper. 'A particularly *bad* word.'

'Fuck?'

Daisy blinked.

'It wasn't Lester's fault,' Juliet said. 'And there's no proof that anyone swore. There's no record. Literally.'

'Well, Lester admitted knowing about it,' Daisy said, giving an offhand, rather judgemental kind of shrug.

'Oh, for heaven's sake.'

'Did you see Lester?' Juliet asked Charles Lofthouse.

'Who?'

'Lester. Lester Pelling. The boy who was sacked.'

'Was he a Boy? I thought he was a Junior Programme Engineer.'

'Yes, he was,' she said patiently.

'He cried,' Charles Lofthouse said. 'Still, someone had to be blamed, I suppose. The boy was our sacrificial lamb.'

'He has a name,' Juliet said. He's called Lester. And he wants to be a producer. And his father's a bastard. And he cried. Juliet felt a knot of pain at the thought. *Huis Clos.* No exit. He's not dead, she reminded herself.

'Prendergast tried to save him, of course,' Charles said. Good old Prendergast, Juliet thought. 'You know what Walpole says.'

No, obviously she didn't know what Walpole had to say on the subject of a Junior Programme Engineer. How vespine you are, she thought. A mean, crippled wasp. She would like to swat him out of existence. Juliet supposed she should feel sorry for him, the leg and so on, but he had survived and others hadn't. Someone she had once been close to had died in the Café de Paris that night and Juliet had witnessed the aftermath of the carnage in the mortuary, so really a leg seemed a small price to pay.

'No, what does Walpole say, Charles?' she said wearily.

'The world is a comedy to those that think, a tragedy to those that feel,' he said, pompous with the knowledge.

Fräulein Rosenfeld shuffled towards them, clutching her Intermediate German like a life raft. 'Is it true, poor Joan is dead?'

'Gone and never to return,' Charles Lofthouse said.

A Boy was hovering. 'Miss Armstrong?'

'Yes.'

'This came for you.' He held out a piece of paper – not even an envelope, she thought – but it was intercepted by Charles. He snatched it off the Boy and read out loud, '*Meet me outside.* Signed *RH.* You do lead a mysterious life,' he said.

'Far from it, I assure you,' Juliet said.

'Let me walk you to the door,' Fräulein Rosenfeld said. She was lonely, Juliet realized, grateful for any scrap of company.

'Perhaps we can get a drink one evening, after work, Fräulein Rosenfeld,' Juliet said.

'Oh, I would like that very much, Miss Armstrong.' Fräulein Rosenfeld beamed at her. 'Wonderful.' How little it takes to make some people happy, Juliet thought. And how much it takes for others.

'Are you leaving early, Miss Armstrong?'

She checked her watch. 'By fifteen minutes, Daisy.'

'Perhaps you have a dental appointment,' Daisy offered.

'Perhaps I don't.'

Hartley was waiting for her on the pavement, a cigarette dangling from his lips, looking insufferably insouciant.

'What do you want?' she asked him.

231

'I thought you might like to go on a flamingo hunt.'

Did people hunt flamingos? It was a bird Juliet had never given any thought to and now it seemed to be perched on every corner. No, not perched – they didn't perch, did they? Too big, probably. And the legs would be too long. You needed short legs for perching or you would be unbalanced, especially if you had a predilection for standing on one leg. Juliet sighed and wondered if one day she would think herself to death. Was that possible? And would it be painful?

'Retrace our friend's steps,' Hartley said as they entered the Strand Palace. Ghosts leave no footprints, Juliet thought, but she was forgetting that Hartley had always seemed to be intimately acquainted with every member of staff in every hotel and restaurant in London – a useful by-product of his insatiable conviviality and corresponding largesse, she supposed. 'There isn't a thing,' he said, 'that you can't find out from an outrageously well-tipped waiter. Threepence on the shilling is my rule of thumb. The *pourboire*, as the Frogs say.'

'I presume we're not the only people looking,' Juliet said.

'Police road blocks. The Watchers are out and Special Branch everywhere. We're monitoring the air fields, train stations, ports. All the usual. Not a sniff so far. They seek him here, they seek him there. They seek the flamingo everywhere. They want to talk to you, by the way. Debrief. I told them you are innocent of all malfeasance.'

'I am.'

'And that's what I told them.'

Hartley began with the doorman. They had not, the two grey men and their flamingo filling, disappeared into thin air, or even into a waiting car, but had walked out of the front entrance and 'Straight across the road, sir,' the doorman informed Hartley, 'and into the Savoy.'

His counterpart at the Savoy tipped his hat and said, 'Mr Hartley, welcome back.'

232

The entire staff of the hotel seemed to be on Hartley's informants' roster, keen-eyed witnesses to the Czech's exfiltration. The doorman remembered 'a queer trio', and in the foyer the concierge pointed the way towards the River Room and said their quarry had been 'frogmarched' towards it down the marble staircase. A willing pageboy ('Funny-looking blokes, your friends') diverted them towards the lifts.

'I used to work as a chambermaid in a hotel,' Juliet said as they made their way through the Savoy. 'Not a grand one like this though.'

'I had my wedding reception here,' Hartley said. Hartley had been briefly, and incongruously, married to a Polish countess. The motives of both bride and bridegroom had been unclear.

'Therein lies the difference between me and you,' Juliet said. 'You've never had to work for the *pourboires*.'

A door in the wall opened, a service door, and Juliet caught a brief glimpse of the world behind the scenes – a warped wall with the paint peeling off and a torn, dirty carpet. The door was quickly snapped shut again.

Their trail of breadcrumbs took them past a cloakroom girl who directed them to the staircase that led them down, past the ballroom, towards the River Entrance, where another doorman hovered, a somewhat lesser variety than his colleagues defending the front barricades. Nonetheless, Hartley's ridiculously generous ten-bob note secured enough information from him to establish that there had been no car waiting at the back of the hotel and that their 'friends' had gone into the Victoria Embankment Gardens. 'Looked like they were on their way somewhere in a hurry,' he said.

How helpful all these witnesses are, Juliet thought. Neatly choreographing the great escape. You would almost think they had been rehearsed.

'So . . .' Hartley said when they were standing in the Gardens, trying to conjure up the events of yesterday.

He was gazing, rather blankly, at the morbidly erotic memorial to Sir Arthur Sullivan. 'Things are seldom what they seem,' he murmured. '*HMS Pinafore*,' he said when Juliet looked enquiringly at him. '"Skim milk masquerades as cream". I'm rather fond of old G and S. My mother—' He became suddenly speechless, staring fixedly into the middle distance like a stage medium communing with the dead.

'What?' Juliet prompted, irritated by this theatrical show, itself worthy of comic opera.

Hartley propelled her out of the Gardens and on to the Embankment. 'What do you see?' he said.

'Big Ben?' she hazarded. 'The Houses of Parliament?' The half-constructed Festival Hall sat squatly on the opposite bank of the Thames. London was to be made of concrete now, it seemed. She thought of the architect in the Belle Meunière the other evening. He was a 'Brutalist', he said, and for a moment she thought he had been referring to his character.

'No, not buildings,' Hartley said. 'The river. They must have spirited him away on a boat from one of the piers on the Embankment. That's why he wasn't caught at a road block. Or at the ports. Out into the estuary, and then probably they transferred him on to another boat. Over to France, or Holland. Or to the Baltic. Long gone. The Russians, I suppose,' he said morosely.

'Well, it's a theory,' Juliet said, 'but not a conclusion.' This was how people disappeared from history, wasn't it? They weren't erased, they were *explained* away. And what if he had fled of his own accord? Perhaps he had decided that he didn't want to belong to any of them.

They were both silent for a while, contemplating the brown water of the Thames. It had seen much over the years.

'Or the Americans,' Juliet said. 'Stealing the lead on us, not trusting us to hand him over. Not entirely without justification.'

'The Yanks?' Hartley mused. 'Oh, I can't imagine that. No proof of that, is there? Although anything can be made to look like proof, of course, if you set your mind to it. Talking of Yanks – shall we have a drink in the American Bar? I believe the sun is below the yardarm.'

'It's nowhere near.'

'Yes, but it is somewhere,' Hartley said. 'Moscow, say.'

'Does Perry still work for the Service?' Juliet asked, once they had settled with their drinks. They had been given the best seats in the bar, the barman deferential towards Hartley as if he carried VIP status.

'Perry?' Hartley said. 'Perry Gibbons? I couldn't possibly say. Although no one ever really *leaves*, do they?'

'I did.'

'Did you? And yet here we are.'

'And all that *Children's Hour* stuff would be a good cover,' Juliet said, ignoring this remark.

'Well, we all have a façade,' Hartley said. 'Don't you?'

After some hesitation, Juliet decided to show Hartley the note. She needed someone to rifle through the Registry and Hartley was the only person she knew who could do that. 'Someone left me a message,' she said.

'*You will pay for what you did*,' Hartley read out loud. He looked at her with interest. 'What *did* you do?'

'Hard to say. Nothing I'm aware of.' (Not true!) 'I think it might be something to do with Godfrey reappearing.'

'The old Toby Jug. Do you owe him something?'

'No, not at all. But I thought perhaps his informants, you know? I wondered if perhaps they had found out about the operation and wanted revenge in some way.'

'You're not still on about fifth columnists, are you?'

'Yes, I am. Can you look in the Registry for me – see if they have addresses for them?'

'Why don't you ask Alleyne? You can ask him about Perry and the old Toby Jug as well, and this nonsense too,' he said, handing the piece of paper back. 'You were Alleyne's girl, weren't you?'

'No. Quite the opposite.'

'Don't look now,' Hartley said when they had left the Savoy and were making their way down the Strand towards Trafalgar Square, 'but I believe there's someone following us.'

'Is it an odd-looking man?' Juliet said. 'Quite short, pockmarked skin, one drooping eye? With an umbrella? Or a woman wearing a headscarf and carrying a shopping bag?'

'No,' Hartley said. 'Nobody like that at all.'

Juliet could hear someone invisible singing 'I Know Where I'm Going' as she walked along the corridor back to her office. A rather pained contralto, rehearsing presumably for *Singing Together*.

'I always think, "Do I?" when I hear that song,' Daisy said, appearing out of thin air abruptly at Juliet's elbow. She would make an excellent magician's assistant.

'Do you what?' Juliet puzzled.

'Know where I'm going.'

'And do you?'

'Of course,' Daisy said. 'The real question is, "Do you know where you've been?"'

'And where have you been?'

'Helping Perry – with *Our Observer*.' (First-name terms now, Juliet noticed. Perry had got himself another girl.) 'We've been rehearsing. *And today, the Ides of March, we are here in the Senate awaiting the arrival of Julius Caesar. Why, here is Brutus, and over there I spy Mark Antony.*'

236

'Gosh, how exciting.'

'You're being sarcastic.'

'I am.'

'Well, I'm enthusiastic anyway,' Daisy said. She followed Juliet back to her office and watched as she pulled on her coat. 'Where *are* you going, by the way, Miss Armstrong?'

'I'm doing some research for *Looking At Things*.'

'Oh, what are you looking at?' Daisy asked, a little too eagerly.

'A wool shop.'

'*Looking At a Wool Shop?*' she said doubtfully.

'Yes.'

'Can I come?'

'No.'

I have a little list, Juliet thought. Of society offenders who might well be underground and who never would be missed. Should Mrs Ambrose be on it? Was Mrs Ambrose telling the truth? Was she really running an innocent wool shop and was it mere coincidence that she had encountered Juliet in Finchley? Or was she part of the conspiracy of the past that was ganging up on her? *The gang's all here.* Juliet had been so unbalanced by Mrs Ambrose's sudden re-appearance this morning that she hadn't thought to ask her if she knew who might have left the note for her. *You will pay for what you did.* She felt fairly sure that she didn't owe Mrs Ambrose anything.

There certainly was a wool shop on Ballards Lane and indeed the sign above the window declared it to be 'Eckersleys'. Juliet spent some time covertly watching it. *Our Observer*, she thought. A woman went in. After a few minutes, the same woman came out. So far, so good.

The bell above the door clanged merrily as Juliet entered, just the way a wool shop's bell ought to greet a customer, although there was no one behind the counter waiting to serve her.

It was definitely a wool shop, Juliet thought, looking around at the honeycomb of wooden shelves that lined the walls and which were packed with bee-shaped balls of 2-, 3-, and 4-ply. She expected it made for rather good soundproofing. It was just the kind of place that Philippa Horrocks, if such a person existed, would come to buy wool to knit little Timmy a Fair Isle pullover.

There were needles in every size and shape. How lethal was a knitting needle, Juliet wondered? There was a till, as big as a church organ, and a counter made of glass that was exactly how Juliet imagined Snow White's coffin to look. No beleaguered girls or poisoned apples, instead its innards were composed of shallow wooden shelves of embroidery threads and buttons and a multitude of haberdashery items.

Juliet opened and closed the door again several times in order to get attention. The bell, no longer merry, trembled violently in protest at this assault.

The place was a thieves' paradise, if you were the kind of thief who sought circular needles and 4-ply worsted. There was actually quite a lot to look at in a wool shop. It might make a surprisingly good Schools programme. You could start with the sheep, shearing and so on. Lambs. Prendergast would like that.

'Shop!' Juliet called. Perhaps there was no one here? Or perhaps Mrs Ambrose was lying dead in the back of the shop? A thick chenille curtain provided a barricade to this mysterious realm and Juliet was just wondering if she should investigate beyond the veil when a tightly permed woman emerged from behind the curtain. She was hampered by a skein of wool that was handcuffing her forearms. Juliet was reminded of Houdini. Laughing giddily and holding out her arms in front of her as if she wanted to be arrested, the woman said, 'Can you?'

'Can I what?'

'Wind it for me.'

Juliet sighed. She supposed, if nothing else, it gave her a handy captive to interrogate. 'Are you Ellen? Ellen Eckersley?' she asked, ravelling up the wool into a ball with long-neglected competence. She had done the same many times for her mother.

'Yes. How did you know?'

'I think I know your aunt – Mrs Eckersley. Florence.'

'Aunt Florrie?'

'Is she here?'

'No, she's out.'

'Where?'

'Oh . . . somewhere,' Ellen Eckersley said hazily.

What a novice, Juliet thought. Not even a dental appointment as an excuse.

The hank of wool was finally transformed into a ball and Ellen Eckersley was free. 'Did you want to buy something?' she asked.

'I'll just take this,' Juliet said, reaching for the nearest ball of wool – a cream Aran yarn that she took from its honeycomb. 'Well, I'd best be off,' she said, once she had paid for the wool. 'Tell Mrs Eckersley I dropped by.'

'Who shall I say was asking for her?'

'Oh,' Juliet said airily. 'Just say someone from her past life.'

Godfrey's old house looked lifeless. Its respectably netted windows gazed blindly back at Juliet. This morning Philippa Horrocks had seemed over-rehearsed and brittle. Perhaps Juliet could give her a tap, see if she would crack. But this time no one came to answer the lion's head knocker.

Instead, a man, quite elderly, came out of the house next door and said, 'Hello, dear, can I help you?' He had a pair of secateurs in his hand and started clipping randomly at a bush.

'I was looking for the woman who lives here – Philippa Horrocks.'

He paused in his clipping. 'I don't think anyone by that name lives there, dear.' This was the kindly old man in this particular tableau, Juliet thought. The harassed young housewife, the rather distracted wool-shop assistant. All present and correct. (*It's important not to fall prey to delusions and neuroses*, Perry said.)

A man with a dog, an innocuous spaniel, walked past and tipped his hat at both her and the kindly old man. There was always a man with a dog, it was a crucial component in the whole.

And my place in the plot, Juliet wondered? Heroic young woman in danger? Or the villain of the piece? She felt deep in her coat pocket and touched the sharp point of a small sock needle, liberated from its glass coffin. You could take someone's eye out with it, she thought.

'That house has been empty for months,' the kindly old man said.

'Did you remember someone called Godfrey Toby living here?'

He shook his head. 'No, sorry, I've never heard that name.'

'How about John Hazeldine?'

'John?' he said, his face brightening. 'Nice chap, John, he used to mow the lawn for me. The Hazeldines moved after the war. I think they might have gone abroad. South Africa, I think.'

'Thank you.'

'It's a pleasure, dear.'

This would have been an almost perfect encounter, plausible in every way, Juliet reflected as she walked away. And yet.

She lingered on the street corner again. The kindly old man's house and its corner garden was hedged with a substantial privet, perfect for a woman to lurk behind and observe Philippa Horrocks flying helter-skelter along the street at the helm of a large pushchair containing Timmy, while two school-age children sprinted behind trying to keep pace. That would be 'Christopher and Valerie' then, Juliet thought. By the time she reached her front gate, Philippa Horrocks was gasping for breath.

The old man, not so very kindly now, was still standing at his gate and said, 'You're late. You missed her.'

'What did you tell her?'

He must have moved along the path, closer to his house, because Juliet caught only a fragment of what was being said, although they were clearly arguing about who said what to whom. They might at least have got their stories straight, Juliet thought. Amateurs everywhere. Straining to hear, Juliet caught the words 'abroad' and 'rid of her'.

He got rid of me, Juliet thought? Or they're *going* to get rid of me? Two tenses with rather different meanings. Or perhaps it was Godfrey Toby who had been got rid of. Or Godfrey who was going to get rid of her. It was as if a complicated game of chess was being played, but Juliet didn't know all the rules or where anyone else was on the board. She was clearly intended to be a pawn in this game. But I am a queen, she thought. Able to move in any direction.

Her route to the Underground took her past the wool shop once more. It was dark inside and a handwritten sign stuck in the window announced 'Closing Down – Everything Must Go'.

Schools was already shut up for the night when Juliet returned but the great ship across the road was sailing bravely on, all lights blazing.

'Is Perry Gibbons still here?' she asked the girl on reception in the cathedral-like foyer of Broadcasting House.

The girl consulted her log book. 'I believe so,' she said, reluctant to give up information. She had a pruny sort of face, as if everyone who came through the door fell short of her standards. Did they breed these supercilious girls in a special hatchery somewhere?

Juliet waited for her to give up more. (*Sometimes saying nothing can be your strongest weapon.*)

The girl surrendered. 'He's still in the *Children's Hour* studio. Is he expecting you?'

'Yes.' Of course he wasn't.

Despite Juliet's protestations that she knew her way, a Boy was

241

summoned to escort her to the third floor. They waited for the lift next to Gill's statue of 'The Sower', broadcasting his seed beneath the great gilded dedication stone to this 'Temple of Arts and Muses'. There had always been a quasi-religious tone to the Corporation. Broadcasting House itself was dedicated to 'Almighty God', as if the deity was looking down benevolently on the transmitters from the clouds. Was that all a front too?

The lift arrived. 'Miss?' the Boy said. 'Which studio?'

There was a red light above the door and so Juliet slipped silently into the viewing booth, high above the studio. The only other person was a woman Juliet had never seen before, who acknowledged her entry with a curt nod.

Below them a company of actors was reading what seemed to be a dramatization of the Knights of the Round Table. Juliet was surprised to see that one of the actors was the shamed Roger Fairbrother. Apparently they didn't know over here about his faux pas – although perhaps they did, because the woman sitting next to Juliet – a battle-hardened type – was watching intently, like a hawk ready to swoop on her prey. Juliet offered the raptorial woman a cigarette and they both sat silently smoking for a while. Finally, children everywhere were bid goodnight and Juliet said to the woman, 'Perry?' and she shrugged and indicated upwards with her cigarette.

Juliet raised a questioning eyebrow (*Sometimes silence*, and so on) and the woman finally spoke. 'Music Library.'

'Thanks.'

Juliet wound her way up the staircase to the fourth floor, although it wasn't quite that straightforward. The layout of Broadcasting House was Byzantine and you often found yourself emerging from a lift or a staircase into an unknown land. Now she found herself outside a Drama studio on the sixth floor with no idea of how she had got there. 'Have you seen Perry Gibbons?' she asked a passing Boy, but it was past six o'clock and all his thoughts were homeward bound.

Another empty staircase led her further upwards. Girls in fairy tales – or girls in labyrinths – should know better, she thought. The air felt dead, yet she thought she could hear something, someone – shoes echoing on the stone steps. *Tap-tap-tap.* A sudden fear seized her and she pushed open a door and hurried out into a corridor. *Death at Broadcasting House*, Juliet thought – it was one of the worst films she had ever seen. Val Gielgud, the Head of Drama, had made and acted in it in 1934. An actor was strangled during a live broadcast. It was a good idea for a plot (she thought of Roger Fairbrother) but hammily executed.

The deserted narrow corridor spiralled endlessly around the central core of studios. Juliet was beginning to wonder if she would meet herself coming in the other direction. *Tap-tap-tap.* Was it shoes? Could it be a cane? A walnut, silver-knob-topped cane? *Tap-tap-tap.* The noise grew louder, more insistent.

Entering another stairwell, Juliet found herself unexpectedly outside the Band Room at the top of the building. *Tap-tap-tap.* Closer now. Something wicked this way comes. *We must finish her off, I'm afraid.*

There was no red light outside the Band Room so she went in and quietly closed the door behind her. The room was soundproofed, so if there was someone after her they wouldn't be able to hear her in here. Of course, no one would hear her scream either. In the grip of outright panic now, she fumbled with the catch on her handbag and had just got an unsteady hand on the small stock of the Mauser when the hefty studio door was pushed open. Slowly, creakily, as if the door, too, was a hammy actor in a cheap murder mystery.

'Miss Armstrong? Juliet? Are you all right?'

Perry! It was unexpectedly and overwhelmingly comforting to see him. Thank goodness she hadn't taken the gun out of her bag. He would have thought her unhinged. She wouldn't want him to think that. Even after all this time, she realized, she valued his estimation of her.

'Juliet,' he said, taking hold of both her hands. 'It's been a long time. I heard you were back in London. It's so lovely to see you.' Blimey, she thought, when did he start touching people? He seemed genuinely delighted to see her – she could feel the warmth in his lovely smile. He had been wounded, broken, and now he seemed healed. 'Did you get lost?'

'A bit,' she admitted.

'I know, the place is a nightmare,' he laughed. 'I get lost on a regular basis. You were looking for me?'

They walked to the lift together, the corridors and stairwells rendered harmless by his presence. And yet. *Tap-tap-tap*. She looked around nervously. Perhaps she *was* unhinged. 'Did you hear that?'

Perry gestured silently towards a man walking slowly along the corridor, the white cane in his hand tapping on the wall. Despite his darkly tinted glasses you could see the opacity of the eyes behind them as he grew near.

'Can I help you?' Perry asked, touching his elbow gently.

'No, thanks, it's all right,' the man said, rather brusquely. He passed them by and went *tap-tap-tapping* on his way.

'Shot down in flames over the Ruhr,' Perry said quietly. 'Poor chap. He's in *Mrs Dale's Diary*.'

Perry took her to Mirabelle and they had *Raie au Beurre Noisette* and a *Tarte aux Pruneaux*. A whole bottle of Burgundy. He was wearing a tailored three-piece grey pinstripe, expensive and very well cut, and was looking rather handsome. He suited middle age. I might have married this man, Juliet thought as they chinked glasses. I would have eaten well, if nothing else, although 'nothing else' would have been the order of the day.

'It's very nice to see you,' he said. 'I looked for you this afternoon across the road. I'm crossing the Rubicon with a rather keen girl of yours.'

'Daisy.'

'Yes, apparently she has sisters called Marigold and Primrose. A bouquet,' he laughed. 'Or perhaps just a spray.' He laughed a lot more, she noticed, now that there wasn't a war on. Or perhaps because he was more comfortable with himself. Juliet thought it might be the other way round for her, on both counts.

'Yes, well,' she said, 'I try not to talk to Daisy too much. It only encourages her. Perry?'

'Yes?'

'I wanted to ask you about something.'

'Oh, what?'

'I saw Godfrey Toby a couple of days ago.' If he says 'Who?', Juliet thought, or 'Oh, good old Toby Jug,' I'll pour the dregs of the Burgundy over his head.

Perry saved himself from this unholy baptism. 'Godfrey Toby? Good Lord, there's a name from the past. How's he doing? I thought he was relocated. The dominions. Or the tropics.'

'The tropics?'

'Or Egypt, perhaps.'

'I heard Vienna,' Juliet said.

Perry shrugged. 'It's all the same, isn't it? It's somewhere else. Not England.'

Juliet took the note from her bag and pushed it across the table. Perry read it silently and looked at her enquiringly. 'This isn't Godfrey's writing.'

'No, of course not. Do you know whose it is?'

'No, sorry.'

'It was handed in at reception, with my name on the envelope. By a man who I think is following me. A woman too, actually.

Working in tandem, I think. I wondered if they might have something to do with Godfrey's informants.'

'The neighbours?' Perry said. He smiled at the word and the memory, as if they had been rendered harmless by the passage of time. 'Surely not. How would they know who you were – or where you are now, for that matter? You were quite anonymous to them. Weren't you?'

'It just seemed a bit of a coincidence,' Juliet said. 'Seeing Godfrey like that and then getting the note. You told me not to trust coincidences.'

'Did I?' he laughed. 'I don't remember. But I'm concerned that you think someone is following you. What did he look like – this man?'

'Quite short, has a limp, pockmarked skin, a drooping eye.'

'Goodness, he sounds like the villain in a film. A touch of the Peter Lorres.' He went to the cinema now, she thought. And knew the names of the actors. How times had changed. What else did he do these days, Juliet wondered?

'And the woman. I wondered about Betty or Edith – I never saw their faces.'

'It seems unlikely. Surely if anyone was going to be made to "pay" by them, it would be Godfrey himself. You were just a typist, after all.' (Well, thanks, she thought.) 'Godfrey was a good chap,' Perry continued thoughtfully. 'Played with a straight bat. As they say. I always liked him.'

'Mm, me too.'

'How is he?'

'I don't know, he wouldn't speak to me.'

'Good Lord, why ever not?'

'I don't know. I thought you might know.'

'Me?' Perry said. 'I haven't seen Godfrey in ten years, not since I left the Service.' They both fell silent at the memory. *I shall be leaving you, I'm afraid, Miss Armstrong.* He spread his hands on the tablecloth as if he might be trying to levitate the table. 'I'm sorry about that time, Juliet,' he said softly. 'You know . . . everything that happened.'

She put her hands on top of his and said, 'It's all right. I understand. I mean, heavens above,' she laughed lightly, 'the BBC would collapse from a staff shortage without its contingent of men like you.'

He winced and, removing his hands from beneath hers, said, 'Men like me?' A frown pinched his features. 'The majority is not always in the right, you know,' he said quietly. 'You just feel as though you are.'

'Well, if it's any consolation, I've never felt myself to be in a majority.' She felt rather cross with him. It wasn't as if she'd been to blame for how it ended.

'Shall we have a whisky?' he asked, and they were friends again.

He was in Holland Park now, he said, so they shared a taxi as far as Kensington.

He opened the cab door for her and said, 'We should do this again,' and kissed her fondly on each cheek. She steadied herself for a moment with her hand on his shoulder and felt sad.

'I can ask around about Godfrey,' he said. 'But I'm not really in touch with anyone any more, you know.'

'You don't still work for the Service then?' she said, trying to sound as if she were making a joke of it.

'Of course not. What makes you think that?' He seemed excessively amused by the idea. 'They don't want "men like me", as you know. Not the ones that get caught anyway. This cabbie's getting impatient. Let's say goodbye. Have a nice weekend,' he said. 'Are you doing anything?'

Goodness, Juliet thought, he's learnt the art of small talk too.

'I'm going to the seaside,' she said.

'How nice. Have a lovely time.'

The air felt different, Juliet thought as she entered her flat, as if someone had disturbed it with their presence, yet all the small precautionary measures that she had made before leaving this morning were still in place – the thread of cotton between the front door and the jamb, the hair laid across a pile of books, the tiny dressmaker's pin that would fall out if her bedside drawer was opened. Nonetheless, she had the distinct feeling that someone had been here. I am unravelling, she thought. Like a ball of wool.

She washed this morning's breakfast pots and made a cup of cocoa. When all else failed, the mundane remained.

Fish, chips, peas, bread and butter and stewed tea, eaten at a table covered in a gingham cloth in a café overlooking the crashing, rattling waves of the English Channel on a blustery, sunny day. A hooligan posse of gulls wheeled noisily overhead, almost as realistic as the Effects boys in Manchester used to be. The air was imbued with the scents of the seaside – sewage, vinegar, candy-floss. This is England, Juliet thought.

She had been telling the truth when she said to Perry that she was going to the seaside. She arrived in Brighton before lunch. It was Saturday and the sudden good weather had brought the crowds out, although it was still bitterly cold if you got caught in the wind nipping off the sea. As the train slipped out of the capital's grimy grasp, Juliet was surprised at how good it felt to elope from London.

So far she had done what everyone else did – strolled along the pier, walked on the pebbled beach, wandered in the Lanes and gawped at the Royal Pavilion. She had been here only once before – in wartime with the RAF pilot who had courted her before lying down with his head in his mother's gas oven because of his missing leg. He had been the nearest Juliet had ever come to the ordinariness of marriage. They had registered in a guest house as husband and wife, like hundreds, if not thousands, before them. Brighton was a sleazy destination but they had been content for two whole days. That was 1943 and by then the war had ground on for so long that they had forgotten what it was like to be at peace, and any snatch at happiness seemed worth it.

'Finished with that?' the waitress asked, grabbing her plate.

'Yes, thank you, it was delicious.' The waitress, a woman in her late forties, wrinkled her nose slightly. Juliet supposed 'delicious' was the kind of word that spoiled middle-class women down from London employed. And it was only fish and chips, after all, but it had been excellent. Juliet was the sole person in the café. It was open all day, but now it was stranded in the afternoon lull.

'More tea?' the waitress asked, hefting an enormous brown enamelled teapot in Juliet's direction. She wasn't local. Her accent carried a nasally estuary twang.

'Yes, please,' Juliet said. The tea was horrendous, thick and sludgy brown like the river she had left behind in London. 'Lovely.'

The waitress lived in one of the many rather seedy terraces that were set back from the sea-front. Her name was Elizabeth Nattress, but she had once been Betty Grieve. Betty, Dolly and Dib, Juliet thought as she sipped her tea. Dolly and Dib. She suppressed a shudder, but she wasn't sure if it was the tea or the memory that had caused it.

Betty Grieve had divorced her husband during the war and a second marriage had changed her identity, but she was still the same woman who had once been given a war merit second class, a *Kriegverdienstkreuz*, by Godfrey Toby for 'services to the Third Reich'.

Hartley had raided the Registry for the current whereabouts of Godfrey's informants, complying with unusual docility. The good thing about Hartley was that he didn't play by the rules. Of course, that was one of the bad things about him, too. Juliet supposed he must be in a lot of trouble with Alleyne over the fugitive flamingo.

It turned out that MI5 *had* kept tabs on Godfrey's informants. Walter had stepped in front of an express through-train at Didcot station two years ago. ('He seemed perfectly normal when he left for work in the morning,' his wife said at the inquest.) Edith had moved to a Christian community on Iona. Victor had been conscripted and died at Tobruk. Everyone else in the wide web of sympathizers seemed accounted for, all of them defeated and subdued now. Juliet had conjectured that the woman in the parrot-patterned headscarf might be Betty Grieve, but now she could see this was a ridiculous idea.

Betty was pouring the tea rather resentfully, so perhaps she had been hoping to put her feet up before the tea-time rush instead of dancing attendance on a lah-di-dah customer.

The man behind the fryer was taking the opportunity of the hiatus in trade to clean up. He was Stanley Nattress, Betty's husband, the man who had taken her away from her past. Both Betty and her husband were wrapped tightly in white overalls, like swaddling. Stanley's overalls were spotted with grease. *Only the best beef dripping used*, a message above the fryer advised.

'It seems busy for this time of year,' Juliet said conversationally.

'Sun brings 'em all down here,' Betty said, as if to follow the sun was evidence of low moral fibre.

'Not like the war, I suppose,' Juliet said. 'You had all those fortifications, that must have put people off.'

'I wouldn't know, I wasn't here during the war, I was in London.'

'Oh, so was I,' Juliet said brightly. 'Not that I agreed with it, you know. The war, and so on. Thank goodness you can say that now without people trying to lock you up for your beliefs.'

Betty slammed the teapot down on the counter and stared

suspiciously at Juliet. 'The war's over,' she said. 'Gone. I never think about those days.' She scowled at Juliet. 'We have to work every hour of the day to make enough money out of this place. And we have our own troubles.'

'Sorry, I didn't mean to imply anything,' Juliet said contritely, although she wasn't, not in the least.

Sensing distress, Stanley came round to the customer side of the counter.

'You all right?' he said to Betty. He put his arm round her. It was rather touching to see a public display of affection from such a big, lumpish man.

'We were just talking about the war,' Juliet said.

'That's all gone now,' he said. He gave Juliet a long look and said, 'Isn't it?' What did he know about his wife, she wondered?

'Yes, of course it is, and thank goodness too,' Juliet said, springing to her feet. 'Now, how much do I owe you for the fish and chips? Oh, and is there a Ladies on the premises?'

Betty snorted at the idea, but Stanley said, 'There's a privy out the back you can use.'

In the back yard a rather sullen girl, thirteen years old – Betty's niece, according to the Registry, orphaned in the Blitz, who lived with the Nattresses – was preparing potatoes. (What handy creatures nieces were.) The girl took a potato from a galvanized bucket at her feet, peeled it and dropped it into another bucket. Her hands were begrimed with dirt and every so often she used her sleeve to wipe snot from her nose. In retrospect, the fish and chips Juliet had eaten seemed less delicious.

A boy, six years old, was sitting on the concrete of the yard, repetitively hitting an old tin lorry with a wooden hammer. Betty was already in her forties when she married Stanley and had this unexpected child. Drool dripped sluggishly from his open mouth. The girl paused in her peeling occasionally to wipe it away with a rag. The boy was called Ralph and it said 'retarded' on Betty's file in the Registry. Ordinariness came at a price.

Betty appeared in the yard, hands on hips, ready for a skirmish. 'Are you still here?' she said to Juliet. She was seething with resentment. 'Why don't you just mind your own sodding business.' The niece stared tight-lipped at the half-peeled potato in her hand.

'I'll do just that, Betty,' Juliet said. 'Mrs Grieve,' she added for good measure, and left through the back door of the yard without even looking to see how Betty reacted to being called by her old name.

I have a little list, Juliet thought as she waited on the station platform for the train back to Victoria. Betty was ticked off the list. She wasn't about to make Juliet pay for anything other than fish and chips.

As she left Victoria station, Juliet became aware of a car sidling up. The passenger-side window rolled down.

'I heard you went to Brighton for a paddle,' Hartley said. 'Want a lift?'

'Not really.' She got in the car.

Hartley's car was a Rover, all wood and leather and comfort. It was a solicitor's car and seemed a sedate choice for Hartley. 'You used to like drawing attention to yourself,' Juliet said.

'We're living in different times. Tracked down your quarry, did you?'

'Yes. She's harmless.'

'Told you so.'

He took a half-empty bottle of wine from where it had been jammed between the seats and offered it to her. 'Château Petit-Village,' he said. 'Nineteen forty-three. Excellent vintage, despite the war. Pierre Auguste at Le Châtelain gets it for me.'

'No, thanks.'

'You're leaving a trail, you know,' Hartley said. 'The powers-that-be may begin to wonder why there's suddenly all this interest in Godfrey's informants.'

'Do you think it matters to them? Surely they don't care any longer?'

'No, but perhaps they care about the old Toby Jug. Sure I can't tempt you to a drink? How about dinner?'

'No. Thanks.'

'Well, then,' Hartley said, 'I'd better take you to hospital.'

'Are you a relative?'

'I'm Miss Hedstrom's god-daughter. She doesn't have any blood relatives.'

'Yes, it's a shame,' the nurse said in Guy's. 'There have been no visitors since she was admitted. Miss Hedstrom's over here, if you'd like to follow me.'

Juliet wouldn't have recognized Trude if she had been left to find her on her own. She had been a force once, a big woman, but now she lay jaundiced and insensible in a hospital bed, deflated and shrunk to an afterthought. She might have been a corpse already it if weren't for the faintest rise and fall in her chest. Juliet pulled up a chair and sat down, not intending to stay to the end of the visiting hour, but the ward matron approached, creaking with starch, and said, 'Do you think you could hang on?'

'Hang on?'

'The end is going to happen very soon. We like to have someone who is known to them when they go. It's what we would all want, isn't it? And poor Miss Hedstrom seems to have no one.' She was already whisking the green curtains around the bed. Oh, Lord, Juliet thought. It seemed churlish to refuse a request to sit at a death-bed vigil, although if it were me, Juliet thought, I should like to slink away like a cat and die on my own in some corner, not in the company of strangers.

Trude had never married and had spent the years since the war renting a room above a dry-cleaning establishment in Hounslow and working in the offices of a bottling plant. It must have seemed banal after so much wartime activity. Surprisingly for someone so intent on forging bonds during the war, Trude had not kept in touch with anyone since the peace. Juliet imagined an embittered exist-ence for her – isolated in her room, living off meagre stove-top meals cooked on a little Baby Belling.

Trude seemed reluctant to die. Juliet sighed and, in the absence of any other amusement, took Joan Timpson's notes for *The Tudors* from her bag. She had brought them to read on the train to Brighton. They had occupied so much history that they couldn't be crammed into one programme. It was a pacy story – Henry Tudor wrenched the crown from the hands of the Yorkists, Henry the Eighth was born, married and divorced from Katherine of Aragon. Anne Boleyn was married and divorced from her head. The Juniors would enjoy an execution. Poor Joan, she had been looking forward to the Tudors.

Juliet had got as far as Anne of Cleves (always a puzzle – what exactly was wrong with the poor woman that she was rejected so peremptorily?) when Trude's breathing suddenly changed, growing hoarse and loud. Was this it? Juliet opened the curtain to look for a nurse, but sleep hung heavily now on the big, dimly lit ward and she could see no night staff.

She returned to her night-watch. Trude seemed distressed; dying had roused her into some kind of fearful consciousness.

This is what we are all reduced to, Juliet thought. Did it matter what one had believed, what one had done? (Yes!) Trude's breath-ing found a new, harsher tone – a guttural kind of growl – as she turned her head from side to side as though trying to escape from something. The jaws of death, perhaps, intent now on devouring her. She had no final words, not even Norwegian ones. Juliet remembered Joan Timpson's 'How lovely.' She wondered what her own last words would be.

It would have taken the hardest heart – harder even than Juliet's – not to feel a little sorry for Trude, but then Juliet thought of Fräulein Rosenfeld, who had lost all her prettier sisters to the camps. She stood up and said, 'Well, this is goodbye, Trude,' and left her to die on her own.

Tick, Juliet thought as she walked down the endless linoleum corridors and out into the cold night air.

When Juliet woke she sensed that something had changed. She could hear a milk float clanking along the street and the noises off of bus engines and car horns and the usual passing footfall, but everything sounded deadened and muffled. Snow, she wondered? But when she looked out of the window, it was to find not snow but an unseasonal fog that had descended in the night. That's all I need, Juliet thought – atmosphere.

'Good morning.' A new girl on reception consulted a notepad. 'Miss Armstrong, is it?' She smiled, toothily pleased with herself for being so efficient. She seemed to have come out of a more pleasant box than her predecessors. A treat for the Minotaur.

'Yes,' Juliet said. 'It is Miss Armstrong.'

Daisy came through the front door, trailing smoky wisps of fog into the building with her.

'Gosh, you're early, Miss Armstrong. Did you have a nice weekend?'

'Went to Brighton,' Juliet said. As if I'm a normal person, she thought.

A Boy entered the building at a businesslike trot and said cheerfully to no one in particular, 'They say it's going to be a real pea-souper later.' The Boys tended to speak in clichés.

Prendergast followed him in. 'Here I am,' he said, rather unnecessarily.

'Where one or two are gathered,' Juliet heard Daisy murmur.

Prendergast was dithering more than usual. 'Everything all right, Mr Prendergast?' Juliet asked him.

'Oh, yes, Miss Armstrong, I'm just a little anxious about *English for the Under-Nines*. I've got Carleton Hobbs in the studio reading *The Pardoner's Tale*.'

'He's very good. You don't need to worry about him, do you?'

'Poor Joan's funeral is at eleven. I may be late.'

Juliet had quite forgotten about Joan Timpson's final journey. 'It's all right,' she soothed, 'I'll look after Mr Hobbs.'

'Goodness, no, Miss Armstrong. You must go to the funeral. Poor Joan was so fond of you.'

Was she? And, even if she was, Juliet's presence or absence could hardly matter to her now. I am too harsh, Juliet thought. She turned to Daisy. 'Daisy – can you take care of *English for the Under-Nines?*'

'Of course I can.' Of course she could.

'We have entrusted our sister Joan to God's mercy . . .'

Joan Timpson was being lowered uncomplainingly into her final resting place. (*Rather heavier than she looks, I'm afraid. Lift on my three – one-two-three!*)

Only a handful of people had followed the coffin for the committal and burial in Kensal Green Cemetery. Fräulein Rosenfeld was one of them. She was dressed in an odd assortment of black garments, as if she had simply raided her wardrobe for everything in that colour and then piled it all on. She looked like a large, rather distressed bat.

'I like funerals,' she told Juliet in the taxi on the way to the church.

'Oh, me too,' Prendergast said. 'You know where you are with a funeral. And such good weather for it. I always think it would be a shame to be buried in sunshine. There are so few good days in England, one wouldn't want to miss one.'

'Earth to earth, ashes to ashes, dust to dust . . .'

The words took on a distorted, dampened timbre in the fog, as if they were coming from under water. Visibility was so poor in Kensal Green that they could barely see each other across the grave. A solitary wreath had decorated the plain coffin and was now waiting patiently to one side for the grave to be filled in. 'From your friends and colleagues in Schools,' the card on it read. It was extraordinarily depressing to think that this was what a life might amount to. Juliet thought of Trude, who had no one to mourn her at all, and now here was poor Joan (welded now to that unsatisfactory epithet in life and death), who had only Schools to regret her passing.

'In the sure and certain hope of the resurrection to eternal life . . .'

The few remaining mourners scattered after their muted 'Amen's and Juliet walked slowly away with Prendergast and Fräulein Rosenfeld.

The funeral seemed to have propelled Prendergast into a state of abject whimsy. 'For there is good news yet to hear and fine things to be seen,' he said, 'before we go to Paradise by way of Kensal Green.' He looked as though he might be about to break into a jig amongst the headstones.

'I'm sorry?' Fräulein Rosenfeld said.

'G. K. Chesterton.'

'I have never heard of him, I am afraid to say.'

'Oh, he's very good. You must let me lend you a copy of something by him.'

They were at a loose end without a funeral tea to go to. Poor Joan didn't seem entirely dead without a glass of sherry and a slice of Dundee cake to send her across the Styx.

'There is a very nice little tea shop up the road from here,' Prendergast said hopefully.

'Or we could go to the pub,' Fräulein Rosenfeld said more sensibly.

'The Windsor Castle it is then!' Prendergast said gaily.

'You go,' Juliet said. 'I'll catch you up. I'd like to stay behind for a little while. My mother's buried here, you see.'

'Oh, goodness,' a stricken Prendergast said, as if her mother was freshly dead. 'I'm so sorry. Of course you must visit her grave.'

'Would you like me to accompany you?' Fräulein Rosenfeld asked, placing a sympathetic hand on her arm. She is a friend to the dead, Juliet thought.

'That's very kind, but I'd like to be on my own, if you don't mind.'

Her mother wasn't here, of course. Strictly speaking she was nowhere, although she had been buried in St Pancras and on her gravestone was the inscription 'At Home with God', which a seventeen-year-old Juliet had chosen in the futile hope that the words might be true – that her mother might be sitting companionably with Him, listening to the wireless in the evenings or perhaps playing rummy. Juliet could still remember her mother's delighted laughter when she laid down a triumphant fan of cards. It seemed unlikely that God played rummy. Poker, perhaps.

The fog hampered Juliet's search for the grave. It was a modest grave in a large cemetery and she was feeling quite frazzled by the time she finally came across it.

The plot was untended, the grave rather neglected. This is what happened when no one knew where you were buried, when they didn't even know you were dead, for that matter. Juliet thought she should come another time and tidy it up, plant some snowdrops perhaps, although she knew she wouldn't. I am consistently remiss, she thought.

The inscription on the tombstone read 'Ivy Wilson. 1922–1940. Beloved sister of Madge.' It was a simple epitaph but it had been wartime and the funeral had taken place in a hurry. I have been too many people, Juliet thought. The spy Iris Carter-Jenkins, a perky, plucky sort of girl. The 'beloved sister' Madge Wilson, who had falsely identified poor Beatrice – the very same Beatrice who was now mouldering in the grave in front of her under a false name. (How strange it had felt to resurrect Madge on her visit to Philippa Horrocks in Finchley! *Beloved sister.*) There had been other identities too, although she never owned up to them in public. And then there was Juliet Armstrong, of course, who some days seemed like the most fictitious of them all, despite being the 'real' Juliet. But then what constituted real? Wasn't everything, even this life itself, just a game of deception?

The grave's a fine and private place, Juliet thought. Not so for Mrs Scaife's little maid. Beatrice was not alone in her bed of cold earth. She had been given no choice but to share it with a complete stranger, not to mention a dog. It was rather crowded in there. Innocence and guilt, the two entwined reluctantly together for eternity. Two ticks for the price of one, Juliet thought. Tick. Tick.

Something flitted across the corner of Juliet's vision, breaking her contemplation. Was she imagining a flash of green and yellow in the fog? She spun round but she could see no one. Hurrying out of the cemetery, she experienced a horrid sense of foreboding at her back. She was half expecting the graves to gape open and the dead to chase her down the Harrow Road.

By the time she had negotiated her way out of the cemetery and found the Windsor Castle, Prendergast and Fräulein Rosenfeld had already left. The man behind the bar had no trouble remembering them. ('Half a pint of stout each in the snug.')

She hailed a taxi to Tottenham Court Road and made her way on foot to Charlotte Street. She did so much doubling back and shooting off down alleys and side streets in an effort to shake off her invisible stalker that she was quite worn out by the time she sat down at one of the grubby tables in Moretti's.

Amidst the usual dilapidated clientele, Juliet ate a rather questionable corned beef sandwich. She couldn't help but think of Mr Moretti's cheese on toast – a *pain perdu* in so many ways, most of them existential now. Trude's death, followed so swiftly by Joan Timpson's funeral, had engendered a kind of malaise in her. Today the dead were everywhere, tumbling out of the box of the past and inhabiting the world of the living. Now it was Mr Moretti's turn, it seemed.

How frightened he must have been when the torpedo hit the *Arandora Star*. There had been a veiled accusation of cowardice against the Italian internees, as if they could have saved themselves if they had tried harder, but they went down in minutes, elbowed out of the way by the German POWs, apparently. (Yet could one really be blamed for the selfish instinct to survive at the cost to others?)

When she heard that the *Arandora Star* had sunk, Juliet had asked Perry to find out if Mr Moretti was on the passenger manifest and he had come back a few days later and said, 'I'm so sorry, Miss Armstrong, it seems that your friend is one of the dead.' She hadn't cried then, but now she felt tears pricking hotly in her eyes. She lit a cigarette to counter them.

'Can I pay, please?' she said briskly to the Armenian, who seemed irritated by the request. *You will pay for what you did.* Perhaps she was going to spend the rest of her life looking over her shoulder, wondering when the bill was going to be presented. The reckoning of the dead.

The script for *The Tudors – Part One* was waiting, rather threateningly, on Juliet's desk when she arrived back in Portland Place.

Not one of Morna Treadwell's, thank goodness. Somewhere along the line in her own past life she must have taken a wrong turning, Juliet thought. Why else would she be sitting here? Giselle came into Juliet's mind. Despite dying at the hands of the Nazis, she had never merited the soubriquet 'poor'. You had to ask yourself, which was better – to have sex with any number of interesting (albeit possibly evil) men (and some women too, apparently), to be glamorously decadent, to ingest excessive amounts of drugs and alcohol and die a horrible but heroic death at a relatively young age, or to end up in Schools Broadcasting at the BBC?

It was a relief when five o'clock came around.

Pelham Place was only a short detour on Juliet's route home. She hadn't been back here since Mrs Scaife was arrested in the summer of 1940 and it felt strange to find herself standing once more on the pavement in front of the imposing portico and magnificent front door. The black paint on the door no longer shone, the white portico no longer gleamed – due to war or neglect, or both.

If anyone wished to exact reparation from Juliet, then surely it would be Mrs Scaife. Juliet had been instrumental in ruining her life, deposing her from her salmon-pink damask throne and packing her off to jail for the duration of the war. Her fall from grace had been the longest and her landing the hardest of all of them. Her conspirator Chester Vanderkamp had served a year in jail in America and now taught Maths in a junior high school in Ohio. The FBI 'looked in' on him occasionally, according to a man Juliet knew in Washington. She had conducted a brief affair with this man shortly before D-Day, when he had been a major in the 82nd Airborne. She hadn't expected him to survive Operation Overlord and was surprised when he resurfaced in government after the war. They had stayed in touch, although distance was a great encouragement to friendship. He was rather useful.

Along with the rest of the Fascist sympathizers, Mrs Scaife had been released at the end of the hostilities and had returned home to Pelham Place with her husband, the Rear Admiral. He died in '47 and there had been an ambivalent obituary in *The Times*; he had, after all, been a hero of the first Battle of Heligoland Bight and his subsequent unpalatable beliefs were – it was hoped – consigned to history.

The fog was thick now. The Boy had been right, it was a 'real pea-souper', trite description though it might be. Fellow pedestrians loomed out of the murk and then were swallowed up again by it. The fog provided the perfect cover for anyone who might be hounding her.

'Can I help you?' A sharp voice interrupted her thoughts. A tight, upper-class kind of accent.

'I'm sorry?'

'Did you want something?' A woman was standing on the doorstep of Mrs Scaife's house, shaking a duster. She was wearing an overall and her greying hair was tied back with a scarf, but her patrician attitude and accent, not to mention her skin, browned and leathered by the sun, indicated that she was not a member of the cleaning class. 'If you just want to stand and stare there's no law against it, but I would rather you didn't. We do get quite a few "vultures" who come to snoop.'

'I'm sorry,' Juliet said. 'I'm not snooping, it's just that I used to know Mrs Scaife. I wondered how she was doing.'

The woman's expression softened and there was a little catch in her voice as she said, 'You knew Mummy?'

Juliet noted the past tense.

'Oh,' the woman said, as if suddenly inspired. 'Are you Nightingale?'

'Well . . .' Juliet said, baffled momentarily.

'Mummy's maid.' (Of course, Nightingale – poor Beatrice Dodds's pasty replacement. How could she forget?) 'Mummy spoke very fondly of you, you know. You were one of the few people who visited her when she went . . . away.'

To jail, Juliet thought. Call a spade a spade. 'She was very good to me,' she said humbly, adding another role to her repertoire.

'Come in for a minute, why don't you? Out of this dreadful weather. I couldn't imagine living in this country again. The house is a terrible mess, I'm afraid. I'm getting it ready to put on the market.'

'Is Mrs Scaife . . . ?'

'Dead? No, not a bit of it. I've had to put her in a nursing home in Maidenhead. She's a bit frail in the head though. Poor Mummy.'

In the hallway, after a slight hesitation, the woman thrust out her hand. 'I'm Minerva Scaife, but everyone calls me Minnie.' She didn't, Juliet noted, ask if Nightingale was called anything else.

Juliet followed 'Minnie' up the stairs, to the lovely drawing room where most things – Mrs Scaife's 'better pieces', Juliet supposed – were shrouded in dust sheets. The salmon damask sofas had already been removed. Most of the paintings had been taken down and stacked against the grand piano. Their pale geometric ghosts remained behind on the walls. The windows were naked, stripped of the hefty curtains that had been thrown into a dusty heap in a corner of the room. The curtain had come down on Mrs Scaife in more than one way, Juliet thought.

No sign of the Sèvres, Juliet was sorry to note. She had rather hoped to reunite her little cup with its saucer, but it seemed they would remain forlornly sundered for eternity.

'I'm selling everything,' Minnie Scaife said. 'House and contents, all going to auction. I live abroad these days – Southern Rhodesia. Fresh start after the war. My fiancé died in Changi and Ivo's dead, of course. My brother,' she added, when Juliet looked blank. 'He was the captain of a Lancaster. KIA over Berlin, the whole crew. But of course you knew that, didn't you?'

'Of course.'

'Mummy never recovered.'

What a strange irony, Juliet thought. Mrs Scaife's son fighting against the very people she had allied herself with. She remembered Mrs Ambrose saying he was 'rather left-leaning'.

'I say, could you give me a hand with the Constable?' Minerva said. 'I want to get it off the wall, but it's a beast.'

Juliet sighed inwardly. Once a maid, always a maid, apparently. But in the role of Nightingale she said, 'Of course, ma'am.' The Constable was filthy and weighed a ton.

'Worth a fortune,' Minerva said. 'I've decided to buy a farm out in Africa. Cattle.'

'Cattle? Good idea,' Juliet said. What would she buy if she had the kind of money that the Constable would bring, she wondered? Not cows, that was for sure. A car, perhaps. A boat or a plane. Something that would carry her away fast.

When they had finished heaving the Constable around the room ('Shall we put it there? No, wait a minute, over there would be better. No, hang on, over here, out of the light'), Mrs Scaife's daughter said, 'Look, why don't I give you a little memento of Mummy? She would like that. Is there anything in particular that you would like?' Juliet wondered what would be said if she bagged the Constable, but Minnie Scaife was already offering, 'A scarf, perhaps? She has some good silk ones.'

'She did. That's awfully kind of you.'

Minnie Scaife hurried away and came back a few minutes later with a headsquare. 'It's silk,' she said. 'Hermès, rather expensive, you know.' It was the usual kind of gaudy jacquard, but at least it wasn't birds, exotic or otherwise. Nor had it been wrapped around anyone's neck to squeeze the life out of them. (*Strangled, with a headscarf.* Poor forgotten Beatrice.) Or at any rate, Juliet hoped that wasn't the case. She unfolded the square, releasing Mrs Scaife's scent – gardenias, Coty face powder and the medicinal odour that she now recognized as some kind of embrocation cream. The cocktail was so strong that Juliet's memory was jerked back to that afternoon in

Pelham Place when she had climbed down the Virginia creeper. The vine was still there – she could see its bare woody branches fringing one of the drawing-room windows. The view beyond was opaque with the fog. The vine would outlast Mrs Scaife.

And Juliet could still conjure up poor Beatrice Dodds's face, frozen in fear as Mrs Scaife had entered the house. *Fee-fi-fo-fum.* Juliet stuffed the headscarf in her handbag and after a few deferential 'thank-you's and 'I shouldn't really, ma'am's said, 'I'd better be off, I have to go back to work. It's not my evening off.'

'Oh, who do you work for now?' Minerva Scaife asked.

Yes, who did poor old Nightingale work for these days, Juliet wondered? Some grumbling old dowager in Eaton Square, no doubt. 'I work in Lord Reith's house,' Juliet said. (The truth!)

'Oh, I don't think I know him. Mind you, I'm quite out of touch these days.'

Tick, Juliet thought as the magnificent front door closed with a decisive *click* behind her. Mrs Scaife would not be seeking recompense any time soon. She threw the scarf in the first dustbin that she came to.

A sickly yellow twilight had enveloped the streets while she had been inside. The fog had a greasy, gaseous feel now and it stifled sound so you couldn't be entirely sure of anything. Juliet could feel it trying to creep into her lungs, into her brain. She picked her way cautiously, knowing there was still a bomb site somewhere around here, strewn with rubble and potholes to trip up the unsuspecting. She thought again of the architect who was rebuilding London. She wished he would get a move on.

Tap-tap-tap. The sinister sound had begun almost as soon as Juliet had left Pelham Place. Perhaps I'm trapped in some awful radio drama, she thought. *Jack the Ripper* or something histrionic by Poe. *The Tell-Tale Heart*, perhaps. *Tap-tap-tap.* She thought she really would go mad if she was followed all the way home by it, so she decided to stop and stand her ground. She turned and steadfastly faced the wall of fog and whatever wretched emanation that was about to make itself manifest.

Tap-tap-tap. A pair of dawdling schoolboys emerged from the miasma. One of them had a wooden ruler in one hand and was percussing the metal railings with it as he walked past them. The boys doffed their caps at Juliet and mumbled, 'Evening, miss.'

'Hurry home now, boys,' she said. 'You don't want to be out in this.'

A few yards further on, she grew aware of another sound approaching from behind her, not the *tap-tap-tap* that was infesting her brain, but a heavy, clomping kind of tread. And then, without the least warning, a kind of shuffling acceleration accompanied by a banshee shriek and then something hard whacked her on the back. The blow was heavy enough to send her flying and she lurched forward, landing awkwardly on all fours on the pavement like a clumsy cat.

It had been a brutal impact with the pavement, a *thwack* that had sent a jolt through every bone in her body, but Juliet scrambled quickly to her feet, braced to defend herself. Her handbag, with the Mauser inside, had been knocked out of her hand and lost somewhere in the fog. The only weapon available to her was a sock needle but her unseen assailants appeared to have fled.

After much searching she managed to find her handbag in the gutter. While doing so, she nearly tripped over a large black umbrella. It was furled and heavy and she wondered if that was what had been used to strike her. The ferrule was a sturdy metal one. *Tap-tap-tap.* It looked sharp enough to penetrate flesh. (*We must finish her off, I'm afraid.*) It looked very like the one that had been in the possession of the man from Moretti's, but really – didn't all umbrellas look alike?

Juliet assessed the damage as she hobbled on. Her knees ached – they were going to be horribly bruised tomorrow – and her palms were grazed and sore. Could it have been a mistake? Could someone have simply knocked into her because of the fog? She had been felled in the blackout once by a man who was running for a bus. And yet.

South Kensington Tube station beckoned through the fog, a halo of comforting light. Normally Juliet could have easily walked from Pelham Place to her flat, but the fogbound street seemed too dangerous.

And then, just as she neared the bottom of the steps leading down into the station—

Bam! Pounced on from behind. More monkey than tiger. Her aggressor must have leapt from three or four steps higher to land on her back. Juliet was knocked flat, but was quickly helped up by several horrified bystanders who thought the fall was an accident. The monkey – the woman in the parrot headscarf, no surprise there somehow – was already on her feet and shouting in a foreign language. Hungarian, if Juliet wasn't mistaken. She recognized it from Moretti's, where quite a few Hungarians took refuge. 'Foreigner,' Juliet heard one of the bystanders mutter.

The woman had the light of madness in her eyes and squared up to Juliet, circling around her as if they were in a boxing ring. 'Lily,' she hissed. 'You killed my Lily.'

Nelly Varga. The mad Hungarian. Alive and well. She had not, after all, gone down on the *Lancastria*. Juliet experienced a twitch of paranoia. Were there other people who weren't dead? (*I think she's definitely dead now, Mr Toby.* What if she wasn't? What if the graves really had opened in Kensal Green Cemetery?)

Surely Nelly Varga hadn't been holding this grudge since the war?

Juliet experienced a sudden fury and yanked Nelly Varga by her coat lapels and shook her as you would a misbehaving doll. She was small, quite light, like straw. Her nose started to bleed and the blood was flung around when Juliet shook her.

The crowd gathered, unwilling to stop the fracas. A policeman arrived and tried to shoo people away. 'Now, now, ladies,' he said. 'What's all this? Fighting over a gentleman, are we?' Oh, for heaven's sake, Juliet thought.

'She killed my Lily,' the woman said to the policeman.

'Someone killed someone?' the policeman asked, more interested now.

'A dog,' Juliet said to the policeman. 'Lily was a dog. And I didn't kill her. And it was *years* ago, for goodness' sake.'

'MI5 promised they would take care of her if I spied for them,' Nelly said to the policeman. 'And they didn't.'

'MI5?' the policeman said, raising a doubtful eyebrow. 'Spying?' He had preferred it when he thought it was murder that was on offer.

'*She* is a spy!' Nelly shouted, pointing a dramatic finger at Juliet. 'You should arrest her.'

'Are you, miss?' the policeman asked mildly.

'Of course I'm not. What a ridiculous idea. I work at the BBC.'

Juliet glimpsed the man from Moretti's with the pebble eyes slide out of the crowd and advance towards them. He took Nelly by the arm and said something to her that seemed conciliatory, but she shook him off angrily. 'My wife,' the man said, rather sheepishly, to the policeman. The policeman sighed at the idea of wives, or Hungarians, or both. The crowd had lost interest by now and had melted away.

'Come along, now,' the policeman said, as if they were children in the playground. 'This won't do.'

'She has to pay for killing my dog,' Nelly persisted. 'She has to pay for what she did.'

'But *how* do you want me to pay?' Juliet asked crossly. 'This is so unreasonable.'

'Perhaps you could just give the lady a few coins,' the policeman suggested, 'and then she might go away.' Juliet very much doubted that. She knew what Nelly wanted. She didn't want blood money, or even a pound of flesh, she wanted Juliet to understand the pain of her loss. But I do, Juliet thought.

'The whole thing is absurd,' Juliet said to the policeman. 'It was ten years ago, the dog would be dead of old age by now anyway.' Oh, how harsh those words sounded. Juliet had loved that little dog with all her heart.

She was relieved when the man with the pebble eyes persuaded a reluctant Nelly to be led away. Over her shoulder she shouted something at Juliet in Hungarian that sounded very much like a curse.

All her paranoia, Juliet thought, all her fears of being watched and followed, her suspicions about the 'neighbours', not to mention her confusion over Godfrey's reappearance in her life, were all baseless. How ridiculous it seemed that of all the people who might want to harm her, it would turn out to be a deranged and vengeful Nelly Varga – a woman Juliet had never even met. And for the one crime that I am entirely innocent of, she thought. *No one is entirely innocent*, Alleyne had said to her.

I should have been more careful, she thought. It would be the epitaph on her grave, wouldn't it? Not *Beloved Sister*, not *At Home with God*, but *She Should Have Been More Careful*.

The defences to her flat were still in place. The strand of the Eckersleys' Aran wool (handy, it turned out) that she had put between the lintel and the front door was still there, but the flat itself remained in darkness when Juliet switched on the light.

Had she forgotten to fill the meter? Surely she had fed several shillings into its greedy mouth only yesterday? She waited a few seconds for her night vision to fire up – a trick from the blackout – and then picked her way across the room to the meter. One meagre shilling was eventually mined from the bottom of her bag. 'Let there be light,' Juliet murmured, but although there was a promising clicking and whirring noise from the meter, light there was none.

A small shift in the air. The faintest rustle – a bird settling in a nest. Breathing. A sigh. She could just make out the silhouette of someone sitting at the table.

Stealthily, Juliet retrieved the Mauser from her bag and advanced cautiously towards the figure. It seemed impossible. And yet.

The person who had the greatest claim on her soul. A sudden terror made her heart spasm.

'Dolly?' she whispered. 'Is that you?'

1940

Here's Dolly

RECORD 3

20.15

VICTOR produces a map. Tremendous noise of map
being unfolded.

V. About five miles east of Basingstoke. Nothing
comes through there. War Office order.
G. (several words inaudible) I see.
V. Bloody nuisance.
G. I must thank you for the map and the diagrams of
Farnborough.
V. I put it in that note. I think notes are
helpful.
G. Yes, yes.
V. And these are anti-aircraft placements (evidently
pointing)
G. Very helpful. Thank you.
V. (more crackling) You see ... (rustling) over there.
G. Yes. What's this that's marked?
V. The power station. And these are factories in
between.
G. I would like it if you could have it more detailed.

V. Their maps will be out of date now (inaudible)
   before the War. Factories or hangars. They're
   assembling them -
G. In the factories?
V. Yes, and then parking them on this old aerodrome
   over here.
G. Fighter planes?
V. And some bombers. Wellingtons, I think. Ferry
   pilots come by to pick them up.

'Does this seem boring, miss? After all your excitement with Mrs S?'

'To be honest, I prefer this, Cyril.'

'But you did a good thing, putting them away, didn't you?'

'Yes. Definitely.'

'Where've you got up to?'

'Oh, hardly anywhere. Victor and his endless maps. I've got masses to catch up on.'

It was two days since Mrs Scaife and Chester Vanderkamp had been arrested in the Bloomsbury flat. Juliet had been called to give evidence in camera, as had Giselle and Mrs Ambrose, but she had barely seen Perry in all this time. 'Mrs Peregrine Gibbons' she had entertained herself by writing in her notebook while she waited outside the courtroom. It didn't matter how many times she practised the signature, it didn't feel as though it could ever belong to her. She was Juliet Armstrong, that was all there was to it. The modest sapphire remained in a drawer in the roll-top desk where it had been placed while Iris made her final appearance in the Bloomsbury flat. Perry seemed to have forgotten all about it and Juliet was trying hard to do the same.

There was a soporific atmosphere in Dolphin Square. It was a warm afternoon and the air was stifling inside the flat. The stone paths in the garden were shimmering with heat and the flowers in the beds, so fresh a few days ago, were wilting now in the hot glare of the sun. Lily was asleep beneath her desk and Juliet wished she could curl up next to her on the floor and have a nap as well. How could people be at war in such weather?

'Mr Gibbons coming in?' Cyril asked.

'No, he said he wouldn't be back until tomorrow. He's closeted some-where in the country with Hollis and White, some big pow-wow about the Cabinet crisis – what to do if Halifax gets his way.' At Dunkirk the beach was filling up with troops. Three hundred and sixty thousand of them, all needing to come home. The map of Europe was on fire, but in Parliament Lord Halifax was fighting for a peace settlement with Hitler. ('It makes me despair,' Perry said. 'The rank foolishness of it.') Europe was already lost, next it would be Britain. ('We stand alone,' Perry said, as if quoting for the future.)

'Hitler'll march straight in, miss,' Cyril said. 'He won't keep to any treaty.'

'Yes, I know, it's awful. We have to soldier on, I suppose. Who's coming today?'

Cyril consulted the weekly chart drawn up by Godfrey. 'Dolly at four o'clock, followed by Trude and Betty at five.'

A coven of witches, Juliet thought. They would be anxious about the vote, knowing that a peace deal with Hitler wouldn't be worth the paper it was written on. The path would be cleared for them and their ilk. Perhaps it would be best to turn the Mauser on oneself if the Nazis marched up the Mall. Juliet could almost see the parade – the tanks, the chorus lines of goose-stepping soldiers, the spectacular fly-pasts, the fifth columnists cheering them from the pavements. How smugly triumphant Trude and her pals were going to be.

'I'll put the kettle on,' Cyril said. 'We're late with our tea.'

'Thanks, Cyril.'

*

Afterwards – and there was a long afterwards – Juliet could never be sure how it happened. Perhaps they had grown careless, at ease with the routine of their work, their vigilance blunted by the commonplace. Or perhaps it was the heat that made them drowsily inattentive. Perhaps the clock was fast, although Juliet checked it later and there was nothing wrong with it. Perhaps it was Dolly's watch that was out of step with time. However it happened, the fact was that they were caught completely off-guard.

Juliet had taken her tea through to drink it in Cyril's room, where he was busy taking something apart and putting it back together again (his favourite occupation). 'Biscuit interval?' she said. They both laughed – it had become one of their shared jokes.

They ate the last three biscuits – one each and one for Lily, who had woken up. They chatted about Cyril's sister, who was trying to arrange a special licence so that she could get married before her fiancé was shipped off to an Army training camp. Cyril was wondering if Perry might be able to help in some way when Lily suddenly began to growl. It was not her usual growl, which was little more than a playful grumble – a protest when they played tug of war with one of her knitted toys. This was an angry, frightened rumble deep in her throat, a trace of the ancestral wolf.

She was staring fixedly at the door to the living room and Juliet left her tea to find out what was upsetting the little dog so.

An intruder! Dib – Dolly's decrepit poodle.

'Dib?' Juliet puzzled to the dog. He acknowledged his name with a dismissive twitch of an ear. 'What are you doing here?'

'How do you know my dog's name?'

Dolly!

'Bloody hell,' Juliet heard Cyril murmur behind her. 'We're for it now.'

Dolly was standing on the threshold of the living room. Juliet could see that the front door was ajar – it must have come unlatched somehow, and Dib had come in to investigate and Dolly had pursued him in order to retrieve him.

Dolly entered the living room cautiously, a wild animal stepping into a clearing. She gazed around the room in bewilderment.

Juliet found herself seeing the flat through Dolly's eyes – the filing cabinet, the big Imperial typewriter and the two desks, all the paraphernalia that constituted an office. Other people in Dolphin Square worked in their flats – including Godfrey himself – so in itself it wasn't peculiar, was it? On the other hand, other people didn't have a room that was full of what was – quite clearly – recording equipment. Nor did they have playback machines and headphones, and, most incriminating of all, files lying around announcing themselves to belong to 'MI5' or folders that had 'Top Secret' stencilled across them in large red capitals.

Dolly regarded all of this in dumbstruck silence. Juliet could almost see the wheels of her brain turning.

'Dolly,' Juliet said in a conciliatory voice, desperately trying to think of a reasonable explanation, but all she managed to come up with was a feeble, 'You're early.'

Dolly frowned. 'Early? *Early?* You know what *time* I'm due?'

All the cogs finally ratcheted into place. Dolly glared viciously at Cyril, who had taken up a rather pugilistic stance in front of Perry's roll-top. 'You're MI5,' Dolly said, her voice coloured with disgust. 'You've been listening to everything we say.'

She advanced into the room and started pulling papers from a stack on Juliet's desk. She read out loud from the top one. '*Record Three. 19.38. Party reassembled. Godfrey, Trude and Dolly. D. I wanted to show you what I think is the most important thing about it. You have to go through Staines, on the Great West Road. D. –* that's me, isn't it? I remember this conversation from a couple of days ago.' Dolly shook her head in disbelief.

She commenced reading the transcript again. '*T. There's a*

reservoir, surrounded by woods. D. A lot of soldiers there. G. Soldiers? Yes.' Dear God, Juliet thought, was she going to read the whole thing? She seemed hypnotized by it.

'All right, that's enough, Dolly.'

'Don't call me by name as if you know me.'

Oh, I do know you, Juliet thought.

With a violent sweep of her hand Dolly knocked everything off Juliet's desk and roared, 'You bloody, bloody bastards! Everything we talk about with Godfrey – you've listened to it all!' Dib started snarling and growling in much the same apoplectic vein as his mistress. One of the sheets of paper that Dolly had displaced caught Juliet's eye as it floated as quietly as a drifting leaf to the ground. The words jumped incriminatingly off the page. *'Report of Godfrey Toby, 22nd May 1940. I met with the informant Victor alone at 7.00 p.m. Victor wished to discuss a new make of aeroplane engine he had heard about. I asked him if he was able to obtain specifics . . .'* Oh, please don't look down, Dolly, Juliet prayed. Don't find out the truth about Godfrey, because then the game will really be up.

Her prayers seemed answered, for the moment anyway. 'Godfrey!' Dolly said in a choked whisper, more to herself than Juliet. 'He introduced you to me, didn't he?' She jabbed a finger in Juliet's direction. 'You had him fooled into thinking you were just a neighbour. He's due any minute. I have to warn him about you. He's in terrible danger.'

'Do calm down, Dolly,' Juliet urged. 'Why don't we talk about this over a cup of tea?'

'A cup of tea? A cup of *tea*?'

'Well, perhaps not,' Juliet said. Obviously it was an absurd idea, but what on earth were they going to do with her? The front door was still open and half of Nelson House must be hearing the brouhaha Dolly and Dib were making. Juliet tried to gesture silently to Cyril to close the door, but he seemed transfixed by the sight of Dolly.

It was too late anyway, as at that moment Godfrey gave his familiar *rat-a-tat, rat-a-tat-TAT* on the open front door and came into the flat, saying, rather anxiously, 'Is everything all right in here, Miss Armstrong? There seems to be quite a commotion.'

'Here's Dolly,' Juliet said to him, with a kind of mad enthusiasm. She felt herself teetering on the edge of hysteria.

'Yes, yes. I see,' he murmured, more to himself than Juliet.

'They've been spying on us!' Dolly shouted at Godfrey. 'Run, Godfrey, you make a run for it. Quickly!' Dolly drew herself up, heroic sacrifice etched on her face now, ready to fight on behalf of the German High Command in the shape of Godfrey Toby, with her bare fists if necessary.

Godfrey still had his cover, he might be able to explain to the members of the group that he had talked his way out of trouble. MI5 were always bringing fifth columnists in, questioning them and then letting them go. Trude herself had boasted to Godfrey that 'one of the head ones' had interrogated her 'very pleasantly' before realizing what a superior kind of person she was. 'Ran rings round him,' she said. Was that Miles Merton, Juliet wondered? No one could fool Merton, certainly not Trude. *I just needed to ask the right questions.*

And perhaps they could remove Dolly from the entire equation – throw her into prison and spin some tale to the others about her having gone away. All was not yet lost.

Juliet supposed these tactics were running through Godfrey's mind too, hence his indecision, but, in the lapse, Dolly's eye was unluckily caught by Godfrey's report, staring condemnatorily up at her from the floor.

She stooped to pick it up and read, '*Edith arrived shortly after Victor left. The usual chatter from Edith about the shipping lanes. She is not a very intelligent woman and it is difficult to say whether she understands what she is seeing. Dolly reported that she had a new girl, Nora, very keen to volunteer.*' She stopped reading and stared wordlessly at Godfrey. Juliet supposed the disparity between what Dolly had believed and the truth of the situation was stunning. 'Godfrey,' she murmured to him, a woman betrayed. There were tears in her eyes, as though she had been scorned by a lover. 'You're one of them,' she said to him, her voice trembling.

'I'm afraid I am, Dolly,' Godfrey said. He sounded regretful.

The spell was broken. Boiling with rage and frustration, Dolly launched herself into a scream, a full-blooded, top-of-her-register sound that could have shattered an entire cabinet of Sèvres. Dib took his own stand and commenced barking, loudly and monotonously. You could have tortured someone to distraction with the noise being created between the two of them.

Cyril, too, came back to life and hurried to the front door and slammed it shut. Dolly was rabid now, hissing and spitting like a wildcat. Oh, Lord, Juliet thought, Trude and Betty would be here any moment. It would become a brawl. The whole operation was about to go down the drain in the most inflammatory manner possible.

Dolly finally found her voice. 'You traitor, you bloody traitor, Godfrey – is that even your real name? You wait until I tell them what you've done!'

'You won't be telling anyone, I'm afraid, Dolly,' Godfrey said – quite calmly. You had to admire his sangfroid, Juliet thought. His nerves were steady, unlike her own.

'Who's going to stop me?' Dolly said.

'Well, I am,' Godfrey said reasonably. 'As an agent of the British government, I have the power to arrest you.

'Cyril,' Godfrey said, turning to Cyril, 'do you think you could find some wire or some such to tie Miss Roberts's hands?' Cyril went and rummaged obediently in his cupboard and came back holding a length of electrical flex aloft.

Unfortunately, Dolly had somehow manoeuvred herself near to Perry's roll-top and made an unexpected lunge for the only weapon available to her – the little bust of Beethoven. She clearly wasn't expecting it to be quite so heavy and only just managed not to drop it, so that for a moment it hung down heavily in her hand, but then she found momentum, swinging it upwards in an arc just as Godfrey sprang forward to restrain her. He was caught on one shoulder by the bust and sent spinning off-kilter. His legs went from beneath him and he landed heavily on his other shoulder on the floor.

He was already clambering dazedly to his knees, but Dolly was clutching the bust by the base, raising it high, like a trophy, above his head, shouting at Cyril and Juliet, 'Don't come near me! I'll smash his head with it, I promise I will!' Juliet stared in horror at this tableau and then did the only thing she could think of. She shot Dolly.

The noise of the little Mauser was overwhelming in the small space of the flat and it shocked everyone into silence for a moment. Dolly dropped to the ground like a wounded deer, clutching her side. Juliet put the gun on her desk and hurried to Godfrey, ignoring Dolly's howls of pain. Cyril helped Juliet get Godfrey to the sofa, although he kept saying, 'I'm all right, I really am. Just a little winded. You must attend to Dolly.'

'She's not dead, Mr Toby,' Cyril said.

'Of course she's not,' Juliet said. 'I just wanted to wing her, not *kill* her. We don't want a corpse on our hands.'

Dolly started crawling across the floor on her hands and knees, trailing blood like a snail. Her goal seemed to be to reach the front door. Dib was bouncing up and down by her side in a fit of barking that would have woken the dead. I should have shot the bloody dog as well, Juliet thought.

'The others will be here soon,' Godfrey said to Cyril. Did Cyril interpret this as some kind of order? (Perhaps it was.) He reached for the Mauser on the desk and shot Dolly again.

'Oh, dear God, Cyril!' Juliet cried. 'You didn't have to do that.'

'Yes, he did, Miss Armstrong,' Godfrey said. He sighed deeply and tipped his head back wearily on the sofa as though he were going to go to sleep.

'She's still not dead,' Cyril said. He looked awful, all the colour gone from his skin, and the hand that was still holding the gun was shaking violently. Juliet removed it from his slippery grasp. Cyril had never shot a gun before, of course, and had aimed wildly at Dolly, succeeding in only wounding her in the arm. It wasn't enough to stop her progress and somehow she kept moving, although now she was dragging herself in circles, mewling like a sick cat. Finally she stopped and slumped against the wall, still whimpering and moaning. She was made of steel. It was like dealing with Rasputin, not a middle-aged woman from Wolverhampton.

How had the situation got so out of hand so quickly? It was literally a handful of heartbeats since Dolly had understood the full extent of the trick that had been played on her and now Godfrey was struggling to get up from the sofa, saying, 'We must finish her off, I'm afraid.' As if she were an animal and it was an act of kindness.

Juliet felt queasy. She didn't know if she could do the deed. It felt like something you would do in the abattoir, not the heat of battle. Before she had to make that decision, Godfrey did something that she could never have anticipated. Still rather unsteady on his feet, he bent down and picked up the walking-stick that had fallen to the floor in the course of his combat with Dolly.

He fiddled with the silver knob on the top of it, releasing some kind of catch that allowed him to withdraw the sword-stick that, unbeknownst to them, had been hiding quietly inside its walnut casing all this time. And then he pierced Dolly through the heart with it.

After what seemed an eternity of silence, even Dib shocked into muteness, Cyril said, 'I think she's completely dead now, Mr Toby.'

'I think she is, Cyril,' Godfrey agreed.

-18-

D. I was very careful about what I said about the war.
It was just - 'Well, we seem to be going on with
it, don't we?' and she definitely wasn't keen.
G. On the war?
D. Yes, the war.
G. And she wasn't keen on it?
D. Exactly.
G. I see.
T. You should write
G. Yes, yes.

There was some desultory talk, of which little could
be gathered. DIB barks, making what follows difficult to catch.

T. 'And then what about the hare (?) hair (?) don't
like him (a bloke like him?) can't always (four
words)

Several words inaudible thanks to DIB. They seem to
be discussing the invisible ink.

D. Well, it comes out all right, you know but - well,
I don't like to ... (4 words) run one word into
another. (Inaudible) It was bat (? 'cat' or 'rat'?)

Or hat, fat, sat, mat or pat, and that was just the monosyllables. It wasn't the dog barking that was the problem, the dog wasn't even there. The problem was Juliet's lack of attention. But then how could she be attentive, given all that had happened?

'Miss Armstrong?' Oliver Alleyne was slouched against the door frame, self-consciously louche. 'Did I startle you?'

'Not at all, sir.' He had. Horribly.

'And is everything all right here, Miss Armstrong?'

'Absolutely, sir.'

'How are your neighbours?'

'Oh, you know, sir, same as ever.'

'No problems?'

'No, sir. None.'

She could see a flick of blood on the skirting board behind him. In fact, if she looked she could see little freckles and splashes of blood everywhere. She would have to clean again. And again. *Out, damned spot.* Cleaning up the carnage left behind by Dolly's death had been a terrible task, not one that Juliet wished to dwell on.

After they had ascertained that Dolly was dead – or 'completely dead' as Cyril put it, Godfrey said, 'We must carry on as normal, Miss Armstrong.' The three of them stared helplessly at Dolly's body sprawled on the floor. Her skirt had ridden up, exposing her stocking tops and the pale blancmange of the thighs above. It seemed more indecent somehow than the death itself. Juliet tugged her skirt back down.

'As normal?' she said to Godfrey. Surely there was to be no more normal after this?

'As if nothing untoward has happened. I shall take the meeting as usual. We can save this operation if we keep our heads. Do you think you could find me a clean shirt – one of Mr Gibbons's?'

The good white twill was a terrible fit, Godfrey had to cram himself into it, but by the time his jacket had been sponged of blood and he had tightened his tie and stood up straight, he could pass. He rubbed his shoulder and smiled as he said ruefully, 'I think I shall have a bruise tomorrow to show for all this. Now I must get next door before Trude and Betty arrive.'

'But what about . . .' Cyril said, gesturing helplessly towards Dolly on the floor.

'I'll be as quick as I can – I'll curtail the meeting, tell them that I have to radio Germany. Then we'll deal with this . . . problem. But for now we must to our stations. Cyril – you need to record this meeting. And Miss Armstrong, perhaps you could start cleaning up a little?' Why was it that the females of the species were always the ones left to tidy up, she wondered? I expect Jesus came out of the tomb, Juliet thought, and said to his mother, 'Can you tidy it up a bit back there?'

Godfrey was true to his word. Trude and Betty were dismissed within the hour and he returned to them. Juliet had never thought about it before – hadn't needed to – but Godfrey was a natural leader, a general, and they were his troops, who implicitly believed in his command.

Under his instruction, they removed the candlewick cover from Perry's bed. 'Now lay her on it.' Juliet hesitated, but Cyril – a loyal foot soldier – said, 'Come on, miss. We can do this. You take the head and I'll take the feet. Mr Toby shouldn't lift her, not with his shoulder.' But Godfrey insisted, although he winced with pain when they heaved Dolly's body on to the bedspread. The small towel-shrouded bundle was tucked in beside her and the two were wrapped up together like a parcel.

When she looked back to this day, Juliet generally omitted Dib from the narrative that she related to herself. It had seemed the most unpalatable element in the whole story.

After the business with the sword-stick, Dolly's dog had gone into a frenzy of snarling and snapping, quite ready to tear them all into pieces. He was a small dog, no bigger than Lily, but he seemed quite dangerous.

'Can you distract him, Cyril?' Godfrey said, and Cyril threw one of his grandmother's knitted teddy bears towards Dib. It was ripped to pieces in seconds, but it gave Godfrey the opportunity to sneak up behind the dog and catch him by the back of his collar. The dog yelped when Godfrey picked him up and held him at arm's length, his small legs paddling uselessly in the air as he hung there, his eyes bulging with surprise. Godfrey carried him to the bathroom, where he paused at the door and said to them, 'Don't come in here.'

There was a good deal of squealing and splashing behind the closed door and then Godfrey emerged with something wrapped in a towel. Later they found Lily cringing and cowering beneath Perry's bed. It was several days before she entirely trusted them again.

Heavy-duty string that they found in Perry's roll-top was utilized to make the parcel neater. The result was a kind of candlewick mummy. They shifted the desks to free the rug that sat in the middle of the room and lifted Dolly and her faithful companion on to it. 'Rather heavier than she looks, I'm afraid,' Godfrey said. 'Lift on my three – one-two-three!'

'Double-wrapped,' Cyril said as Dolly was rolled in the rug. Cleopatra, Juliet thought. Or a sausage roll. 'No dignity in death, I'm afraid, Miss Armstrong,' Godfrey murmured.

They were all running with sweat by the time they had finished. Cyril had several smears of blood on his face, Juliet noticed. She took out her handkerchief and licked it and said, 'Come here, Cyril,' and wiped the blood away.

'Now what, Mr Toby?' Cyril said. 'What are we going to do with her?'

'Trude's coal hole, perhaps?' Godfrey suggested.

'Wrong time of year,' Juliet replied, thinking how quickly poor Beatrice had been discovered. Cyril nodded wisely. They were all three silent, contemplating the logistics of disposing of a corpse, but then Juliet said, 'Why don't we just give her a funeral and bury her in a cemetery?'

*

Hartley's department was phoned. They were used to requests for transport at all hours. 'Mr Gibbons requires a car, please,' Juliet said, 'Pick-up is at Dolphin Square. I'll tell the driver the destination when he arrives.'

A car was duly provided. Juliet went down and waited at the Chichester Street entrance. It was well after midnight when she saw its visored headlights approaching, slits of light in what was a very dark, moonless night.

When the driver got out, Juliet handed him a generous five pounds (provided by Godfrey), a sum large enough to stifle anyone's curiosity, and said, 'Mr Gibbons is on a highly secret mission, he's going to drive himself.' The driver was used to the eccentricities of MI5 and when she said, 'Will you be able to get home all right?' he pocketed the fiver and, laughing, said, 'I expect so, miss.'

They dragged the rug to the lift, too focused on the task in hand to be feeling very much of anything. There was an alarming moment as they were pulling the rug out of the lift on the ground floor when they encountered an elderly resident waiting to get in it. Juliet said a cheery, 'Good evening, there, we're just taking this rug to Cyril here's sister as a wedding present.' (*If you're going to tell a lie*, and so on.) Cyril burst into a fit of rather manic laughing. The woman stepped in the lift, keen to escape them. She probably thought that the three mismatched people were drunk.

'Sorry,' Cyril apologized to Godfrey, 'it's just it's all a bit much. And Miss Armstrong's so good at lying, she caught me off-guard.'

Godfrey patted him on the shoulder and said, 'Not to worry, my boy.'

The rug-bound Dolly was propped up in the front seat of the car. It was the only way – and they tried several – that she would fit. Cyril and Juliet sat in the back with Lily between them. She had sniffed nervously at the rug and then would have nothing more to do with it. A dog would know the smell of death, Juliet supposed.

Godfrey knew how to drive, which was lucky, as neither Cyril nor Juliet did. He started the engine and said, 'Right then.'

Every time they went round a corner, Dolly listed slightly as if she might still be alive inside the rug. Again, as in Bloomsbury, Juliet had the feeling that she was taking part in a farce, although not one that was particularly funny – not funny at all, in fact. 'Where are we going again?' Cyril asked, holding the rug steady as they rounded the corner at a fast clip into Park Lane. Godfrey was a surprisingly adventurous driver.

'Ladbroke Grove,' Juliet said.

Godfrey had made a phone call to someone. Juliet didn't know who and wondered if it was the man with the astrakhan collar. Whoever it was, they had considerable clout, for two men in siren suits were waiting for them when they arrived at the undertaker's parlour in Ladbroke Grove, and the undertaker himself let them in to his mortuary. The men in siren suits carried Dolly inside with all the usual admonitions of removal men – 'Careful, old Sam', 'Watch that end, Roy', and so on. None of them asked any questions or seemed the least surprised at the delivery and it made Juliet question what the men in the siren suits (and the undertaker too, come to that) did the rest of the time. Was this their job – the discreet disposal of murdered bodies?

Juliet did not want to see poor Beatrice's coffin being opened or Dolly's body being placed inside, but she remained, nonetheless, mutely observant. There was something utterly grotesque about the whole enterprise, even though it had been her own idea. Dib was placed in last and Godfrey said, 'One is reminded of Egyptian pharaohs going into the next life with their grave goods. Mummified cats, and so on.'

They watched until the lid was placed on the coffin and the final nail was hammered. The funeral was to take place the following morning.

'No one will know anything is untoward,' Godfrey said. But we shall, Juliet thought.

They drove Cyril home, all the way to Rotherhithe in the blackout, quite a feat on Godfrey's part. It was after three in the morning by the time they deposited him outside his grandmother's house. He took the comfort of Lily with him. Once they had seen him safely inside, Godfrey said, 'Would you come back to my house in Finchley, Miss Armstrong? I think we should make sure that we are singing from the same hymn sheet, as it were.'

'You mean get our stories straight?'

'Exactly.'

The sky was light with a splendid dawn by the time they parked outside Godfrey's house in Finchley. A new day, but really it was still the old day for both of them.

There was a big hydrangea bush by the gate, not yet in full bloom. 'If it's left to its own devices the flowers will be pink,' Godfrey said – quite conversationally, as if they hadn't just butchered a woman in cold blood. 'The trick to making sure the blooms are blue is to add a few pennies to the soil. Grass clippings and coffee grounds help too,' he added. 'They like an acid soil.'

'Oh,' Juliet said. Was he really giving her gardening tips? But then this was what carrying on as normal meant, wasn't it?

There was a brass knocker in the shape of a lion's head on the front door. The front door was oak. So much solid respectability!

When Godfrey unlocked the door Juliet could smell Mansion House polish and Brasso. 'Ah, the woman who does for us has been in,' Godfrey said, stepping over the threshold and sniffing the air like a delicate dog. He hung Juliet's coat in a cupboard in the hall. His wife – 'Annabelle' – was away, he said, visiting her mother. Annabelle! How intimate it seemed to know her name. Juliet imagined pearls, good shoes, trips up to London to 'the shops', followed by lunch in Bourne and Hollingsworth's restaurant.

'Come through to the drawing room,' Godfrey said, and Juliet followed him obediently. 'Do have a seat,' he said, indicating an immense sofa – no salmon damask here but rather sensible cut moquette. The sofa was the size of a boat. I am adrift, she thought. In Finchley. 'Can I get you a cup of tea, Miss Armstrong? Would that help? We've had rather a shock.'

'Thank you, yes.'

'Do you perhaps need to use the . . .' a slight hesitation, 'facilities, Miss Armstrong?'

'No, no thank you, Mr Godfrey.'

'You have a . . .' he indicated her hands. There was still blood on them, turned rusty now. Her cuticles were encrusted with it. 'First room on the left at the top of the stairs. I'm afraid we have no downstairs cloakroom.'

In the chilly bathroom the towels were freshly laundered and folded and the hand soap was scented with freesia. Both things seemed to verify the existence of Annabelle. As did the pink satin quilted eiderdown on the bed and the reading lamps with flowered parchment shades that she glimpsed through an open bedroom door. When Juliet washed her hands with the freesia soap the water ran pink with Dolly's blood.

Coming downstairs, Juliet could hear Godfrey still moving around in the kitchen. He sounded surprisingly at home in Annabelle's domain.

There were no photographs on display in the drawing room and only a couple of innocuous watercolours on the wall. Several ashtrays, a large lighter, a wooden match-holder. A Murphy radio. *The Times* was spread out on a coffee table. Godfrey must have sat here the previous morning, reading about Dunkirk, smoking his harsh-smelling cigarettes. There was a crushed one in an ashtray next to the newspaper. The woman-who-did did not do very well, Juliet thought.

Finally he returned, carrying a tray. He poured tea into their cups and handed her one. 'Two sugars, that's right, isn't it, Miss Armstrong?'

They drank their tea in silence.

After a long time, just when Juliet feared she might nod off to sleep, Godfrey roused himself and said, 'I think we should keep her around for a while – before we write her out of the story.'

'Dolly? Yes,' Juliet said. 'Good idea.'

She stayed for what little remained of the night in Finchley, on Godfrey Toby's living-room sofa, having politely declined his offer of the spare room. It would have felt outlandish to have gone to bed in the room next to his, to imagine him on the other side of the wall in his pyjamas beneath the pink silk eiderdown. He, too, seemed relieved when she opted instead for the cut moquette.

A couple of hours later, she woke to find Godfrey (fully dressed, thank goodness) standing next to the sofa with another cup and saucer in his hand, like a patient butler. 'Tea, Miss Armstrong?' he said, placing the cup and saucer carefully on the coffee table as if afraid of waking someone elsewhere in the house, although he had assured her last night that there was no one else at home.

'Two sugars,' he smiled, confident now of her saccharine habits. He returned to the kitchen, where she could hear him whistling something that sounded very much like 'Thanks For The Memory'. Perhaps not the most appropriate of songs for the morning after a murder. He returned with a plate of toast and said cheerfully, 'Real butter. Annabelle's sister lives in the country. I'm afraid we finished the last of the marmalade several weeks ago.'

Afterwards he walked her to the Tube station, from where she caught the Northern line to King's Cross, then the Metropolitan line to Baker Street, and finally the Bakerloo line. She fell asleep on the third leg of the journey and would have stayed asleep if a man hadn't woken her at Queen's Park and said, 'Excuse me, miss – I was worried you might miss your stop.' He was avuncular, in big workman's boots and with oily hands. 'Coming off a night shift,' he said, chatty from a long night's boredom, it seemed. 'On your way to work?' he asked when they alighted together from the train at Kensal Green.

'No, to a funeral,' she said, although this didn't seem to shake him off and she began to suspect him of having designs on her, but at the gates to the cemetery he doffed his hat respectfully and said, 'Nice talking to you, miss,' and carried placidly on his way.

She had intended to be here anyway for Beatrice, to testify, albeit silently, to her life, and death, but now she could make sure that the little maid's unholy companions could piggy-back into the afterlife without raising any suspicions.

MI5 had paid for Beatrice's funeral, although it was a skimpy kind of affair, not much better than a pauper's, and the only people in attendance were Juliet and, somewhat to her horror, the tall detective. 'Miss Armstrong,' he said, tipping his hat. 'You do get about for someone who's dead. I'm surprised to see you here.'

'I felt an odd connection – you know, the way that we were confused with each other.'

'I see our girl has a name now.'

'Yes, Ivy. Ivy Wilson.'

'Identified by her sister, I believe. And yet her sister's not here. That's odd, don't you think?'

'Yes. Perhaps.'

'Difficult to be in two places at once, I suppose,' he said. What did he mean by that? Juliet gave him a sharp look, but he was gazing guilelessly at the sky.

Despite the buttered toast in Finchley (which had been delicious), Juliet felt light-headed from lack of sleep by the time she was standing at the edge of Beatrice's overcrowded grave. Beatrice and Dolly and Dib, a cargo large enough to sink the ferryman's boat, she thought.

'Are you all right?' the tall detective asked her as they walked away after the briefest of committals. 'You look rather pale, Miss Armstrong. I was afraid you were going to fall in the grave for a moment there.'

'Oh, no, really, I'm quite well,' she assured him. She grasped at the nearest excuse she could think of. 'My fiancé, Ian, you know, he's in the Navy. On HMS *Hood*. I worry about him.' Wrong! She had got herself mixed up with Iris. It had been bound to happen eventually, she supposed. Did it matter? Did anything matter any more?

It was a beautiful morning though. As they walked away from the graveside, a blossom tree in the cemetery shook its petals free all over Juliet's hair and the tall policeman brushed them off gently and said, 'Like a bride,' and Juliet blushed, despite the unfortunate circumstances. But then that was life, wasn't it? – flowers amongst the graves. 'In the midst of life we are in death.' And so on.

She was back in Dolphin Square just before lunchtime. The flat was empty. It was three days now since anyone had seen Perry, and Juliet wondered if she should be worried. He was probably tied up one way or another with the evacuation. She wondered what she was going to tell him about the missing shirt and bedspread. The shirt would be easy – lost by the laundry – but the candlewick's absence might be harder to explain away. Wouldn't it be better, she had said to Godfrey last night in Finchley, if they just came clean? Dolly had attacked them, they had rallied to each other in self-defence and unfortunately she had died. 'We still have the rule of law, don't we? Isn't that the difference between us and the enemy?' An inquest in camera and they would all be vindicated. She supposed it wasn't as straightforward as that, nothing ever was. Godfrey laughed unexpectedly and said, 'But imagine the paperwork, Miss Armstrong.'

It was the operation he was protecting, of course. She wondered if in later years, looking back, it would appear to be so crucial that it had necessitated a human sacrifice.

Alleyne remained, seemingly intent on conversation. 'And our friend Godfrey?' he said. 'How is he?'

'Nothing to report there, sir.'

'And yet a messenger boy handed me a note saying you had something you wanted to "discuss" with me.'

Oh, good Lord, Juliet thought. She had forgotten about the note, forgotten that she had planned to expose Godfrey's trysts with the man in the astrakhan collar. She wasn't about to do so now. They were too complicit in horror – mired in gore – to ever betray each other for lesser sins.

'Tea, sir,' she said.

'Tea?'

'Tea. The quality of the tea we're being given is shocking.'

'I might remind you that there's a war on, Miss Armstrong.'

'So everyone keeps telling me, but an operation runs on tea.'

'I'll see what I can do. Quid pro quo and so on. Try not to waste my time again, Miss Armstrong.'

'Sorry, sir.'

'By the way, you might like to know that the Cabinet crisis is over. Halifax has been finessed by Churchill. We shall not be making peace. Instead we are to continue our battle for freedom.' He made it sound quixotic, amusing even.

'Yes, sir, I know. What about our troops?'

'We're still making a tremendous effort to get them out of France.'

'There are so many of them.'

'There are.' He shrugged. She didn't like the shrug.

'And Nelly Varga, sir?'

'Who?'

'Lily's owner. The dog,' she said, indicating Lily beneath her desk. He looked at the dog blankly for a second and then said, 'Oh, that. No, nothing.' It had been very important and now it wasn't, but that was war, Juliet supposed.

Alleyne glanced around the room – he was a study in how to be casual – and said, 'Is there something missing? Didn't there used to be a rug here?'

'Yes, sir. It's gone to be cleaned. I spilt ink on it.' The men in siren suits had disposed of the rug for them, along with the bloodied candlewick bedspread.

Beethoven had been subdued and was back in his accustomed place on the roll-top. Alleyne patted his flowing locks and said, 'Is this taken from the life, do you suppose? Or death?'

'I have no idea, sir.'

'Well, I must be off.' He paused at the door, an artifice he had that was particularly irritating. 'I hear you were at a funeral this morning.'

'Yes. Beatrice Dodds, Mrs Scaife's maid. She was buried under a false name. Ivy Wilson. I pretended to be her sister.'

'Mm,' Alleyne said, not even bothering to feign interest in what she was saying.

'I don't suppose anyone's been apprehended – for her murder, sir?'

'No, and I doubt they ever will. It was a small part of something much larger. We are at war.'

'Yes, sir. You said that.'

'Well,' Alleyne said. 'Keep me informed.'

'About?'

'Everything, Miss Armstrong. Everything.'

*

'Miss?'

'Cyril. Hello.'

'Who was that I crossed on the stairs, miss?'

'Oliver Alleyne. Perry's boss.'

'Mr Gibbons's *boss*, miss? I think of *him* as the boss.'

'I suspect there are many ranks above Mr Gibbons, Cyril. MI5 is like the hierarchy of angels. I doubt we would ever meet the ones at the top – cherubim and seraphim and so on.'

'Yes, but does Mr Alleyne suspect something, miss? About . . . you know.'

'No, I don't think so. We mustn't worry.'

She returned to the transcript with an even heavier heart than before.

```
(contd.) Voices died away. Technical hitch, two
minutes unaccounted for.

G. (Several words inaudible) What was it - something
   about Jew hatred?
D. The buses are full of them. I think she was in
   Golders Green, which is where they congregate
   (three or four words inaudible). En masse (?
   three words inaudible due to DIB). This woman I
   know told me that she'd been on a bus and there
   was this Jew on the platform talking to someone
   on the pavement and he was taking up all the room
   and this big girl got on, the hefty sort, and she
   pushed him off!

(Laughter)

G. Off the bus?

(Biscuit interval)
```

It was all a counterfeit, of course. Dolly's words had actually been spoken by Betty. It was the minutes from the meeting that had taken place directly after the Grand Guignol of Dolly's murder. Betty had simply been erased from this particular record and Dolly substituted in her place. Juliet had put Dib in for authenticity. (*It's in the details.*) In this new afterlife, Juliet had also afforded him capital letters.

Perhaps it could serve as an alibi. *But how could we possibly have murdered Dolly Roberts when she was alive and well that evening, talking about Jews and invisible ink?* She should destroy the recording so that only the written transcript remained, in case anyone listened and questioned why Dolly had suddenly taken on an Essex accent. But then the only person who ever listened to the recordings was Juliet. Still, it would do no harm to eradicate the evidence.

Juliet suggested to Cyril that they ate lunch in the restaurant downstairs. They were both listless in the aftermath of so much drama. 'And they have that mutton pie you like today,' she said to him. 'Although I don't know how they can call it mutton. It's not a meat that's ever seen a sheep.'

It was after two by the time they returned to the flat. Victor was due at five. 'We really are carrying on as normal then?' Cyril said.

'What else can we do?'

They had just got settled again – Juliet to the transcript, while Cyril had volunteered to scrutinize the flat for any remaining blood – when there was a knock on the door, a loud businesslike knock. Juliet opened it to be confronted by two Special Branch officers, the same ones who had come to see Perry a few days ago. Two uniformed constables stood behind them. One of the detectives had an official-looking piece of paper in his hand. Juliet recognized it as a warrant. The game was up. They knew about Dolly and they were here to arrest them. Juliet's legs started to tremble, so much so that she feared they might give way.

'We're looking for Mr Gibbons,' one of the detectives said.

'Perry?' Juliet croaked.

'Peregrine Gibbons, yes.'

They were here for Perry, not her and Cyril. 'I don't know where he is.' She was so relieved she happily gave up Perry. 'He could be anywhere – Whitehall, the Scrubs. He has a place in Petty France. I'll give you the address.'

They left, unsatisfied. Cyril said, 'I thought I was going to be sick. I thought they'd come for us. Why do you think they wanted Mr Gibbons? They seemed serious.'

'They had an arrest warrant.'

'Bloody hell, miss. For Mr Gibbons? Why? Do you think he was caught up in the Right Club thing? Do you think he's one of them?'

'I honestly don't know, Cyril.'

There was more knocking at the door and Juliet thought that her nerves couldn't take any more, but then she realized it was the familiar *rat-a-tat*, *rat-a-tat-TAT* of Godfrey.

'I'm hovering,' he said when Juliet opened the door. 'Victor is due.'

'I know.'

'I was just checking that you and Cyril were all right.'

'Yes, Mr Toby. We are.' What other answer was there? Really?

'Has something happened to Perry?' Juliet asked Hartley.

'Happened?'

'I haven't seen him for days. I thought it was something to do with Operation Dynamo, but Special Branch were looking for him. I think they had an arrest warrant. You've got friends in Special Branch, haven't you?'

'I've got friends everywhere,' he said glumly. 'You don't know, do you? No, of course you don't. You're very naïve about some things. He was arrested for cottaging.' Cottaging? What on earth was that?

It sounded rather charming. Juliet could easily imagine Perry, with his liking for expeditions, visiting cottages, cataloguing and assessing their virtues – thatching, timber framing, the arch of roses around the door, the scarlet flowers on the runner beans in the gardens, the—

'It's nothing like that,' Hartley said.

'Then what?'

'"Importuning men for immoral purposes", that's the charge. Going into public lavatories and – you know . . . Do I have to spell it out?'

He did.

Hartley said, 'He's in disgrace with the powers-that-be, although, of course, half of them are inverts or deviants, one way or another. I, personally, don't give a fig about who does what to whom. And everyone knew.'

'Everyone but me.'

'Did you know?' she asked Clarissa.

'Oh, sweetie, everyone knows Perry Gibbons is a fairy. I thought you understood. Half the men I know are. They can be such good fun – well, perhaps not Perry, but you know. And it's just that Perry – in his position it makes him vulnerable. Blackmail and so on. The trick is not to get caught, of course. And he did.'

He came to Dolphin Square to say goodbye. 'I shall be leaving you, I'm afraid, Miss Armstrong,' he said. She was on her own in the flat, but neither of them spoke about his 'disgrace'. Juliet was in no mood to forgive him – he had used her as his disguise, the accessory on his arm. She was still in shock from Dolly's death and she supposed it made her unsympathetic to him, although really it should have made her more sympathetic. It wasn't as if she herself was innocent of harm.

He wasn't going to jail, or to trial – the charges against him were discreetly dropped. He knew a lot of people and they all had secrets and he knew them. He was going to the Ministry of Information. 'Banished,' he said, 'to the outer circle of hell.'

Nominally, Oliver Alleyne became Godfrey's case officer, but they rarely saw him and they continued to work without any real oversight. Alleyne had lost interest in the fifth column, and in Godfrey's doings, too. He had bigger fish to fry.

Two weeks after Dunkirk, Alleyne sent a messenger boy with a note. Nelly Varga had managed to board one of the ships taking part in Operation Ariel that was evacuating the troops and a number of civilians left behind further south. Nelly had died along with thousands of others when the *Lancastria* was attacked off Saint-Nazaire. 'So the damned dog is yours,' he wrote, 'unless you want me to get rid of it.'

They carried on. The informants came to Dolphin Square. Godfrey talked to them. Cyril recorded them. Juliet transcribed their conversations. She wondered if anyone read the transcriptions any more. Godfrey told those informants who knew her that Dolly had moved to Ireland, but she lingered on, ghost-like, in the transcripts, because somehow or other Juliet couldn't let her go and continued to invent words for her, inaudible and otherwise. Dib continued to bark in his spectral existence. Godfrey, too, kept Dolly alive, mentioning her in his reports. Cyril pencilled her in to the weekly timetable. She went to Coventry after the bombing and reported morale was 'very low'. She recruited several 'people' and drew many maps which were of little use. A façade. Fiction and fact became one. There was really very little difference between Dolly being alive and Dolly being dead. Except for Dolly, of course.

*

300

The horror was not over, it was all yet to come. Time passes quickly during a war. On the heels of Dunkirk, the Battle of Britain took place above the summer fields of Kent and within weeks the Blitz had begun.

The Russian Tea Room, Mrs Ambrose, Mrs Scaife, even Beatrice and Dolly, all fast faded into memory, overcome by greater events. Survival trumped memory. There was a greater slaughter than Dolly's to deal with.

Iris, too, was largely forgotten, although Juliet spared a thought for her alter ego's fiancé, Ian, when the battlecruiser HMS *Hood* was attacked in the May of '41. Nearly fifteen hundred men died when the ship sank. Only three survived; Ian wasn't one of them. Nonetheless, Juliet felt sure he had been heroic.

MI5 was bombed out of the Scrubs and most of the girls in clerical moved to Blenheim Palace, but Operation Godfrey remained in Dolphin Square. They all three suspected they had been overlooked, forgotten about, even. In Dolphin Square they had their own shelters and ARP and first-aid post. There was an admirable self-sufficiency about the place. It was bombed many times. Juliet had been on fire-watching duties during the first raid on Pimlico in the September of 1940, which was lucky as one of the shelters took a direct hit and many people were buried. It was the closest she ever came to a bomb. It was a terrifying thing.

Clarissa died in the Café de Paris bomb. Miss Dicker came to Dolphin Square to tell Juliet personally. 'I'm so sorry – she was a friend of yours, wasn't she, Miss Armstrong? Will you identify her for us?' And so Juliet returned to the Westminster Public Mortuary where she had identified Beatrice's body. It had been so quiet then and now it was bloodily over-run.

'You're lucky, she's in one piece,' an assistant carelessly said as he pulled back the sheet. 'There've been limbs and heads everywhere in here.'

When no one was looking, Juliet removed the pearls from Clarissa's perfect swan neck, and when she got home she washed the blood off them and placed them round her own neck. They sat quite high – an executioner could have used them as a guideline for slicing her head off. She felt no remorse. She was sure it was a gift that would have been given gladly.

Cyril and his redoubtable Gran survived the awful days of the Blitz in the East End but were killed in March '45 – cruelly near the end of the war – by the V2 rocket attack on Smithfield's. His Gran had asked him to go with her, she'd heard they had a fresh supply of rabbits. The Dolphin Square operation had been wound up by then, of course, in November 1944. Godfrey was moved to Paris to interview captured German officers. Someone said he was at Nuremberg; after that he seemed to disappear. Juliet herself was reassigned. Miles Merton claimed her for his secretary and she worked for him for the rest of the war, and then, like so many others, she was summarily dismissed from the Service. She found refuge in Manchester and the BBC.

Giselle was never heard from again. Once, years later, Juliet thought she saw her walking on the Via Veneto. She was very smartly dressed, in the company of two children, but Juliet didn't follow her because it seemed so unlikely, and anyway she didn't want to be disappointed by the truth.

Lily ran away during the Blitz, terrified by the noise. Juliet had been in Hyde Park with her when the sirens had sounded, unexpectedly early. They had been swiftly followed by the horrid noise of the ack-ack guns, something that always terrified the poor dog. She had been off the lead and before Juliet could stop her she had bolted and disappeared.

Cyril and Juliet spent a good deal of time imagining the life she had run away to – a big house in Sussex, lots of meaty butcher's bones, children to play games with. They refused to believe her little body was crushed by rubble somewhere or that she was wandering the streets, lost and frightened. After Cyril died, Juliet had to continue the game of make-believe on her own, only now Lily and Cyril were reunited, playing throw and fetch in a perfect green field before walking home, tired but happy, to a huge supper cooked by Gran. *Don't let your imagination run away with you, Miss Armstrong.* But why would you not when the reality was so awful?

And that was that. Juliet's war.

The tall detective had turned up at her door one evening a week or two after she had encountered him in Kensal Green Cemetery. She hadn't given him her address, but she supposed it was in the nature of his job to know things.

'Miss Armstrong?' he said. 'I thought you might like to have a drink.'

She presumed he meant for them to go out to a pub, but he produced a large bottle of beer and said, 'We'd have it here, I thought.'

'Oh,' she said.

'So shall I come in?' the tall detective prompted. ('I'm not that tall, by the way,' he said. 'Six foot one, actually.') He had a name, too – Harry, a good patriotic name. 'Cry God for Harry, England, and Saint George,' she said, and he laughed and said, 'Once more into the breach, Miss Armstrong?' and she thought, Thank goodness he has some Shakespeare.

Then the tall detective – or Harry, as she supposed she must learn to call him – pulled her into his strong detective arms and in a surprisingly short time he was stripping off his clothes, in the eager fashion of a swimmer about to plunge into the sea, before going about the deed as if it were a sport. He demystified the sex act, giving her a thoroughly English translation of the *éducation sexuelle*. It turned out that it was indeed a pursuit like hockey or the piano, and that if you practised enough you could become surprisingly proficient.

Of course, it only lasted a few weeks. He volunteered for the Army, and although she received a couple of letters from him the feelings between them petered out. After the fall of France, the Free French had moved in to Dolphin Square and made it their HQ, and by the time she received her final missive from the tall detective, Juliet was having an affair with one of the French officers billeted on their doorstep.

'Ooh la la, miss,' Cyril said.

1950

Regnum Defende

JULIET HAD SPENT a stultifying morning reading teachers' reports on *Tracing History Backwards*. (How else could you, Juliet wondered, unless you were a Cassandra?) It was another of Joan Timpson's series that had fallen into her lap. She was relieved when Fräulein Rosenfeld, her Langenscheidt clasped to her chest like a breastplate, scuttled into Juliet's office and said that she was 'looking for Bernard'.

'Bernard?' Juliet puzzled politely.

'Mr Prendergast.'

Juliet never thought of Prendergast having a first name. 'No, I haven't seen him at all today,' she said. 'Can I help, or did you want him for something particular?'

'Oh, nothing in particular,' Fräulein Rosenfeld said, blushing. Crikey, Juliet thought – Fräulein Rosenfeld and Prendergast. Who'd have thought it?

Juliet walked to the National Gallery and ate her lunchtime sandwich sitting on the steps, while half-heartedly attempting the crossword in *The Times*. The sandwich contained a depressing fish-paste filling that would probably have horrified Elizabeth David – quite rightly, too. The Gallery's steps provided a good vantage point for keeping a weather-eye out for mad Hungarians.

Still, the fog had lifted overnight and now Juliet could see the beginning of buds on the trees, and, even above the noise of London traffic, she could hear that the birds were singing their tiny hearts out, getting ready for spring. They are all feathers, she thought.

She checked her watch and then folded up her newspaper, fed her crusts to the Trafalgar Square pigeons and went inside the building.

Proceeding through the hushed galleries, she remained unmoved by the walls of religious suffering, the bleeding wounds and the eyes raised in beseeching agony. Implacable eighteenth-century England with its horses and dogs and fashionable costumes passed her by too, as did all the pretty French aristocrats blithely unaware of the Terror coming their way. Juliet walked determinedly past them all. She had a different goal.

The Night Watch. There was a seat in front of the painting, allowing Juliet to meditate on what seemed to her to be an exercise in gloom – although perhaps the painting, like everything else after the war, simply needed cleaning.

'Tenebrism,' Merton said, sitting down next to her and gazing at the painting. They could have been worshippers in church who merely happened to be occupying the same pew. Rembrandt was to neither of their tastes. Miles Merton was an admirer of Titian; Juliet had remained faithful to her cool Dutch interiors.

'Tenebrism?' Juliet said. 'Darkness?'

'Dark *and* light. You can't have one without the other.' Jekyll and Hyde, she thought. 'Chiaroscuro if you like,' he said. 'The *Tenebrosi* were interested in the contrast. Caravaggio and so on. Rembrandt, of course, was a master of it. I chose to meet you here because you once told me that you admired Rembrandt in particular.'

'I lied.'

'I know.'

'And anyway,' Juliet said, unable to suppress her irritation with Merton, 'this isn't a Rembrandt, it's a copy by Gerrit Lundens. "*The Company of Captain Frans Banning Cocq*, after Rembrandt". It says so.'

'Exactly. I thought there was a rather delightful irony in that. The original's in the Rijksmuseum, of course. It is massive – much bigger than the Lundens copy. Did you know that early on in its life, Rembrandt's painting was cut down to fit a particular spot in the Town Hall in Amsterdam? Bureaucratic vandalism in the service of interior decoration. Wonderful!' he murmured, seemingly amused by the idea.

Juliet placed her copy of *The Times* between them, on the seat. She preferred to have some space between herself and Merton nowadays.

'But perhaps what you *don't* know,' he continued, 'is that in another even more delicious layer of irony, Lundens's copy was painted before the original was pruned by the good burghers of Amsterdam. And so now it is our only evidence of *The Night Watch* as it was actually painted – as Rembrandt intended. The counterfeit, although no deception was intended by Lundens, is in some ways truer than the real *Night Watch*.'

'What is it you're trying to say exactly?'

He laughed. 'Nothing really. And yet so much.' They continued to regard the painting in silence.

'You took rather a long time,' Merton said eventually. 'I was beginning to think you had run off.'

'I've had a few problems.' She took the note out of her handbag and passed it to him.

'*You will pay for what you did.*' He frowned.

'I'm being followed.'

Merton twitched apprehensively but didn't look around. 'Here?' he asked quietly.

'I thought it was something sinister, but it turns out it's simply the dead returned to life.'

'The dead?'

'Nelly Varga.'

'Oh, *her*,' he said. He sounded relieved. 'God, I remember her. One of our first double agents. Insane woman. She made such a fuss over her dog.'

'I was told she went down on the *Lancastria*.'

'Yes, we thought she had. But it was chaos in Saint-Nazaire. Utter chaos. No proper ship's manifest, obviously. She made her way back here some time after the war.'

'With a man?'

'Her husband. Her new lap-dog, I believe. Acquired him in a refugee camp in Egypt.'

'She wants to kill me.'

'Any reason in particular?'

'I was the one who was charged with looking after her dog.'

'Oh, really? I didn't know that.'

'The dog died on my watch.'

'But that's ancient history, surely?' Merton said.

'Not to Nelly Varga. I rather admire her tenacity. Or the tenacity of her love.'

'How did she know it was you? How did she *find* you?'

'I've got no idea,' Juliet said. 'Perhaps someone told her.'

'Now who would do that?'

She sighed. 'Sometimes, you know, I think my soul has been confiscated.'

'Oh, Juliet,' Merton laughed, 'how abstruse you are become. Are you grappling with your conscience?'

'Every day.' She stared bleakly at the painting before rousing herself and saying, 'I should get back. Henry the Eighth is waiting for me in Portland Place.'

'Yes,' Merton said. 'I myself have an Uccello I need to renew my acquaintance with. I'll be in touch.'

'No!' she muttered. 'Don't be. It's over. You said so.'

'I lied.'

'I'm not doing this any more. You *said* if I did this one last thing I would be free of it all.' She could hear herself sounding rather petulant, like a child.

'Oh, my dear Juliet,' he laughed. 'One is never free. It's never *finished.*'

Juliet left *The Times* on the seat when she departed. Miles Merton stayed where he was, as if lost in profound admiration of *The Night Watch.* After a few minutes, he picked up the newspaper and walked away.

She had cast herself as the hunter, as Diana, but it turned out she was the stag, after all, and the hounds were closing in. I should have been more careful, she thought.

In a moment of heightened madness last night, she had thought that it was Dolly who was stalking her, but she had rapidly come to her senses.

'Who *are* you?' she asked the shadowy figure sitting in the dark of her flat. 'What do you want from me?' She held the Mauser steady. 'I'm quite prepared to shoot you, you know.'

And then, as if turned on by an unseen hand, the electricity came magically back to life and Juliet could see who her uninvited visitor was.

'You?' she puzzled.

'I'm afraid so, Miss Armstrong. Do put that gun down. You might hurt someone with it.'

'We've had our eye on you for a long time,' the man in the astrakhan-collared coat said.

When the electricity came back on in her flat, she discovered him sitting at the table with a bottle of whisky (her own, she noted) and two glasses. His was half empty and she wondered how long he had been there in the dark. Had the darkness been for dramatic effect? There was undoubtedly a theatrical flair about him.

He wasn't wearing the coat with the astrakhan collar. Unlike Godfrey, he had bought a new coat since the war. He poured her a whisky and said, 'Do sit down, Miss Armstrong.'

'Do you have a name?' Juliet asked.

He laughed. 'Not really. Not one you would know.'

'Any name will do,' Juliet said. 'It hardly matters, does it? A name is just a point of reference. *Mr Green ate his dinner. Miss White liked the hat.* Otherwise it would just be someone or anyone.'

'Or no one.' He relented. 'My name is Mr Fisher.' She supposed he was lying. The fisher of men, she thought. The fisher of girls.

'Do you want something, Mr "Fisher", or did you just come here to give me a fright? Because really I've had enough of those for one day. Who *are* you? You don't seem like MI5.' (But if not, then what?)

'Nothing is as simple as it looks, Miss Armstrong. Surely you, of all people, know that. There can be many layers to a thing. Like the spectrum of light. I exist, you might say, in one of the invisible layers. Think of me in the infra-red.'

'Oh, how enigmatic you are,' she said crossly. She took the second glass of whisky he had poured and downed it in one unpleasant gulp. It made her feel worse rather than better. She thought of the Borgias and their poisons. 'What do you want exactly?'

'I thought you would like to know,' Fisher said, 'that the flamingo turned up in Halifax.'

'Halifax?' Why on earth, she wondered, would the Czech land up in a West Riding wool town?

'Not that Halifax. Halifax, Nova Scotia. In transit. The Americans had him, flew him out from Lakenheath, but they had to stop to refuel. He's tucked away in Los Alamos now. They obviously didn't trust us to hand him over intact.'

'It was nothing to do with me,' Juliet said. 'He was "intact", as you put it, when I had him. And anyway, aren't we on the same side as the Americans?'

'Hm. Some might say that.' He offered her a cigarette, which, after a moment's hesitation, she took. 'Don't worry,' he said, smiling thinly at her as he lit the cigarette. 'It isn't laced with cyanide.' He lit one for himself and said, 'Apparently, our friend the Czech, as well as what was in his head, brought out some valuable documents. Diagrams, formulae and so on. Originals, apparently. We believe, however, that someone made copies after he landed in England.'

'Copies?'

'On microfilm. I imagine a scenario where the poor man is exhausted after his journey to our shores. In an MI5 safe house – a warm fire, something to eat, something pleasant from Harrods Food Hall perhaps, followed by a drink – a whisky, maybe –' he tapped the rim of the glass in front of him. 'And then when he's fast asleep, someone – Mr Green or Miss White, a name is just a reference – took the papers from his suitcase – perhaps someone who had once been taught how to pick locks – and then Mr Green or Miss White photographed them. And afterwards replaced them in the suitcase and locked it again. What do you think? Plausible?'

Life had progressed at such a pace in the previous week that the flamingo's arrival on her doorstep seemed like something from a dream now. A small man without a hat, a pawn. They were all pawns, of course, in someone else's great game. She had thought herself to be a queen, not a pawn. How foolish to think such a thing was possible, when the Mertons and Fishers of this murky world were in charge of the board.

'And then Miss White – I imagine it to be a woman, somehow – intended to pass this microfilm to her masters so that all that valuable information would not, after all, be lost to them. I suppose it was a kindness on the part of Miss White not to tell her masters where the poor man was. Allowing him to escape to the West. To be free. I suppose that you photographed what was in the Czech's suitcase because you think that the Soviets should be our friends, that we would not have won the war without them and why should they now be denied the same scientific know-how as us? Fuchs's argument, is it not? Is that why you retrieved the documents for the Soviets? Tell me, Miss Armstrong – the purges, the show trials, the forced labour camps – they don't worry you? Somehow I can't see you working in a rural cooperative or a factory.'

'I don't want to live in Russia.'

'That's your problem, you see, you and Merton and his ilk. You're *intellectual* Communists, but you don't actually want to live beneath its iron thumb.'

'It's called idealism, I suppose.'

'No, it's called betrayal, Miss Armstrong, and I expect it's exactly the same argument that Godfrey's informants used. How tediously naïve you are.'

'As it so happens, I don't believe any more.'

'And yet you are about to hand these documents back to them. To Merton. He's been your handler a long time, hasn't he? I wonder how much loyalty you carry for him?'

'Surprisingly little.'

The die had been cast long ago. Merton already had an introduction to her when she turned up for her interview with him at the beginning of the war. Her headmistress at the good girls' school – an unlikely scout – had recommended her to him as 'the kind of girl he was looking for'. He had usurped Miss Dicker for the afternoon so that he could ask the right questions. Juliet had been easy to recruit. She had believed in fairness and equality, in justice and truth. She believed that England could be a better country. She was the apple ripe for plucking and she had also been Eve willing to eat the apple. The endless dialectic between innocence and experience.

She had walked away from him at the end of the war, but he had reclaimed her when she returned from Manchester, as had MI5, of course. ('Just the occasional safe house, Miss Armstrong.')

One more job, Merton said, that was all, and she would be free of him, of the Soviets. Free to go on her way and get on with her life. And, like an utter fool, she had believed him. She would never escape from any of them, would she? She would never be *finished*.

Fisher drained his glass of whisky, stubbed out his cigarette and said, 'Do you wish you had shot me when you had the chance just now? Like you did Dolly Roberts?' (Was there anything he didn't know?) 'Godfrey got himself into quite a pickle over that,' he laughed. 'He was strangely fond of you, protective even. A lot of people were. I suppose that was how you got away with it. Alleyne, of course . . .' He trailed off and made a dismissive gesture with his hand as if batting the idea of Alleyne away.

'Alleyne was suspicious of Godfrey,' Juliet said. 'He asked me to report back to him. I followed him and I saw you both at the Brompton Oratory.'

'Yes, you were rather obvious. You had a dog, I seem to remember. There's always a dog, isn't there?' he mused, and then, 'Ah,' he said, as if a missing piece of a puzzle had finally been found. 'That was Nelly Varga's dog.'

'Why was Alleyne suspicious of you?'

'I rather think that question should be turned on its head, don't you? Who spies on the spies, Miss Armstrong?'

'You? *You* were suspicious of *Alleyne*?'

'I'm suspicious of everyone, Miss Armstrong. It's my job.'

'What of Mrs Ambrose – is she working for you?'

Fisher clapped his hands as if to signal the end of the entertainment and said, 'Come now, quite enough of exposition and explanation. We're not approaching the end of a novel, Miss Armstrong.'

But what of Godfrey, she persisted. Did he, too, exist in the spectrum of invisible light?

'What of him? We recalled him to these shores for a mole hunt, although I prefer the word "traitor". There are many questionable elements in the Service, as I'm sure you're aware. We suspected that the flamingo might flush one out of its tunnel, if you'll excuse the contorted image. And we were right, weren't we? You are our little mole, Miss Armstrong. Our blind little mole.'

Mopping up, Hartley had said. Godfrey was good at mopping up. She had been looking for Godfrey, but all this time he had been looking for her.

She had an arrangement with Fisher. She would not be arrested and tried for treason ('and possibly hanged') if she would hand false information to Merton.

'We're prepared to save your neck, Miss Armstrong. But at a price, of course.'

'You want me to be a double agent?' she said wearily. 'You want me to carry on working with Merton and at the same time work for you?' The worst of all worlds. A servant with two masters. A mouse being toyed with by two cats.

'I'm afraid it's the only way out of this mess for you. I am the bearer of consequences, Miss Armstrong.'

The copy of *The Times* that she was to leave for Merton in the National Gallery would have the microfilm concealed within its pages as previously arranged between them, but the film would not be of the documents she had taken from the Czech's battered suitcase and photographed as he slept on her sofa. Instead it would contain false information – 'Basically gobbledegook,' Fisher said, 'but it will take the Russians a while before they realize. Hopefully they'll blow themselves up a few times before it dawns on them.

And after that, of course . . .' He raised his arms wide as if to indicate an infinite future for her of feeding false information, of double-dealing.

'Well, I must be off,' he said. 'I've kept you long enough.'

'I expect you can find your own way out,' Juliet said, 'seeing as you found your own way in.'

He paused in the doorway and gave her a long look. 'You're my girl now, Miss Armstrong. Don't forget it.'

This, after all then, was the true bill, Juliet thought as she heard the front door close behind him. And she would be paying it for ever. No exit, she thought.

'I believed,' Juliet said sadly, although there was no one to hear her. 'I believed in something better. In something more noble.' And that, for once, was the truth. And now she no longer believed and that was another truth. But what did it matter? Really?

Juliet went straight from her rendezvous with Merton in the National Gallery to Portland Place. The girl on reception waved an envelope at her and said, 'Oh, Miss Armstrong, someone left a message for you,' but Juliet walked past her as if she wasn't there. She had had quite enough of messages. She made her way to Prendergast's office and knocked on his door. He was alone, sitting at his desk, but the nutmeggy, old-church smell of Fräulein Rosenfeld still perfumed the air as if she had just left the room.

'I've written something,' Juliet said. 'It's a letter of recommendation for Lester Pelling. "To Whom It May Concern – Mr Pelling is an excellent employee . . ." – that kind of thing.' She handed him the letter. 'I've signed it and I wondered if you would care to as well.' She could easily have forged Prendergast's signature, of course – she had a talent for signatures that weren't her own – but she thought it would be better luck not to be underhand. Lester was a robustly honest sort of boy who had been brought down by her own neglect

317

of duty. *She should have been more careful.* She wanted to do right by at least one person in her life.

'Oh, with pleasure,' Prendergast said enthusiastically, signing his name with an inky flourish. 'How thoughtful of you. I really should have written a testimonial myself without being prompted. He was a good boy.'

'He was. He is.'

Juliet hesitated at the door on the way out. She would have liked to say something to Prendergast, something about idealism, perhaps, but he might have objected to the 'ism'. Or perhaps it would be better to urge him to marry Fräulein Rosenfeld. She imagined a future for them, attending other people's funerals and reading G. K. Chesterton to each other. Instead she said simply, 'Well, I must get on. Poor Joan's *Past Lives* and so on.'

She put Lester's reference in an envelope and gave it to a secretary. 'Find Lester Pelling's address and get this sent over to the post room, will you?' Before handing it over, she scribbled on the back of the envelope, 'Good luck, Lester, from Juliet Armstrong.'

She encountered Daisy in the corridor. 'Miss Armstrong?' Daisy sang out. 'Where are you going?'

'Optician, Daisy. You know – the headaches.'

'Miss Armstrong, come back!' There was a new note in Daisy's voice, something authoritarian that was unbefitting a vicar's daughter. She took up a wicket-keeping stance to hinder Juliet's progress towards reception.

So she does work for the Service, Juliet thought. 'Oh, for heaven's sake, Daisy, you'll have to do better than that,' she said and pushed her out of the way.

She could hear the girl on reception's voice growing fainter behind her as she made for the front door. 'Miss Armstrong, Miss Armstrong!'

*

318

Juliet had an escape plan. An exit. First thing this morning she had deposited a suitcase at the Left Luggage office in Victoria. Apart from clothes, the suitcase contained a few things of sentimental value – some embroidered pieces of her mother's, a photograph of Juliet with Lily and Cyril that Perry had taken, the little coffee cup with its promise of Arcadia.

Now she was lying in wait in the tea room at Victoria, from where she intended to take the night train to the Gare du Nord. She had bought a first-class ticket so that she wouldn't have to get on and off the train at Dover and risk attracting the attention of either the Security Services or Merton's people. From France she would make her way to somewhere neutral – Switzerland was the obvious choice – somewhere where no one could own her, where there were no sides but her own.

She planned to board the train at the last minute. The last minute came and she made her way to the boat-train platform where people were still milling around enjoying the general sense of anticipation that surrounds a continental departure. The engine had got up a tremendous head of steam and the guard was chivvying the porters to get the last of the luggage on board.

There were two of them. Burly types in ill-fitting suits advancing purposefully towards her along the platform even as the guard began to slam shut the first of the train doors. 'We're here to escort you,' one of them said as they grabbed an arm each. Oh, Lord, I'm the flamingo now, she thought.

'Escort me where?' she said as they frogmarched her away from the train. She had no idea who they worked for, but it hardly mattered. They could be taking her to Moscow or to a country house in Kent. Or, of course, they could be taking her to a quiet end somewhere.

At that moment the engine let off steam with a sudden ear-piercingly shrill whistle and at the same time Juliet's saviour appeared out of nowhere and ambushed them. Nelly Varga. Nelly

Varga raining blows on Juliet and her guard dogs indiscriminately. The men were momentarily confounded by the barrage from a small, deranged woman yelling in an impenetrable language. As they grappled with Nelly, Juliet seized her chance.

She was the deer. She was the arrow. She was the queen. She was the contradiction. She was the synthesis. Juliet ran.

She had got as far as Vauxhall Bridge when a car roared up and slammed its brakes on beside her. The passenger-side door opened and Perry said, 'Get in.'

'I couldn't let them get you,' he said. 'They're wolves, all of them.'

'Are you a wolf?'

'A lone one.' He laughed.

He drove her, not to Dover, but all the way to Lowestoft. It was dark by the time they arrived and they ate fried fish and drank beer in a trawlermen's pub near the harbour.

'How did you know where I'd be?' she asked.

'Oh, a little bird told me.' He offered her a cigarette and she said, 'You *do* smoke then.'

'I've missed you, Miss Armstrong.'

'I've missed you too, Mr Gibbons.'

There was a sweetness between them now that seemed unbearably poignant. 'This too shall pass,' he said and lit her cigarette for her.

A passage was arranged and paid for, on a trawler. The men agreed to take her across to Holland at dawn. 'I expect that would be a good place to hawk those diamond earrings,' Perry said. I assumed I had so many secrets, Juliet thought, and yet everyone seems to have known them.

'I'm little better than a common thief, I'm afraid.'

'Not common. Most uncommon, in fact.'

'Will you get into trouble? If they find out you helped me?'

'They won't find out.' She supposed there was something beyond even the infra-red. Layer after layer of secrets.

'Whose side are you on, Perry?'

'Yours, Miss Armstrong. You're my girl, after all.'

It was a nice lie and she thanked him silently for it. He always had such good manners. She expected it wasn't a matter of sides at all, it was probably much more complicated than that.

They spent the night in a guest house, asleep in their outdoor clothes on top of the covers. Effigies, one last time.

When the cold dawn broke, Perry accompanied her down to the harbour. He handed her an envelope with banknotes inside ('To tide you over') and then kissed her on both cheeks and said, 'Courage, Miss Armstrong, that's the watchword,' and she climbed aboard the trawler. It stank of fish and oil and the men were unsure how to treat her so they largely ignored her.

She would be away for thirty years, and when she returned it would be to a different country from the one that she had left. Her life in those years away would be interesting, but not excessively so. She would be happy, but not excessively so. That was how it should be. The long peace after the war.

She would be living in Ravello when they came for her. A knock on the door one day and two grey men standing on her doorstep, one of them saying, 'Miss Armstrong? Miss Juliet Armstrong? We've come to take you home.' She had just planted a lemon tree and felt disappointed that she would never see it bear fruit.

Tidying up loose ends, they said. She would be interviewed count-less times. They needed her testament to bring down Merton and 'to close the book on things'. He had remained protected in some mys-terious way. He was a knight of the realm, an Establishment figure, but finally the rumours grew too strong to be ignored. He had flown high, he had fallen. It was the only plot.

She would not be named, although afterwards they wouldn't let her leave. 'We'd like to keep an eye on you, Miss Armstrong,' they said. She didn't mind so very much. Matteo was free to visit her, although the girl who made him unhappy did her best to prevent him.

Oliver Alleyne had already been uncovered by then, in 1954. It took everyone by surprise, even Juliet. He was nimble and managed to get out, pursued by headlines and a manhunt across the continent. He was followed by two others, a diplomat from the Embassy in Washington and a man in a critical position in the Foreign Office. Alleyne resurfaced very publicly in Moscow a year later.

There were persistent rumours about 'a fifth man'. Many believed it was Hartley, although Juliet never thought it likely. A vague shadow of suspicion would always hang over him and, although nothing against him was ever proved, it blighted his progress.

Perry continued in his career in broadcasting. He died in somewhat mysterious circumstances in 1961. Godfrey Toby had long since stepped back into the shadows by then. Someone said that he moved to America. Or it might have been Canada.

The trawler sailed from the port into a smoky, misty kind of dawn that contained a promise of good weather later. *Humber, Thames, northerly, backing south-westerly four to five later, fair to good.* She was crossing the Rubicon. Juliet was glad not to be leaving from Dover. To see those white cliffs receding would have been too sentimental, too much of a metaphor for something she no longer entirely understood. This England, is it worth fighting for? Yes, she thought. What other answer was there? Really?

The trawler approached the mouth of the harbour, preparing to abandon its sheltering arms. Moles, Juliet thought, wasn't that what they were called? A final gift of irony from her country. And there, standing on one of them, appearing slowly out of the morning mist, clearer and clearer as they drew near, was the unmistakeable figure of Godfrey Toby.

Was Godfrey the 'little bird' who had told Perry where to find her? Had Godfrey saved her? Or had he betrayed her? Was Godfrey 'one of us' or one of them? Both? Neither? There would never be an end to the questions, she realized. The Great Enigma. What had Hartley said all those years ago? *Toby is a master of obfuscation. It's easy to get lost in his fog.*

Godfrey raised his hat to her. She raised her hand in silent reply. He lifted his cane in acknowledgement. Prospero's staff, Juliet thought. Godfrey, the Magus. The Master of Ceremonies.

As if at a sign, the mist closed around him once more and he disappeared.

1981

The Invisible Light

'THIS ENGLAND,' SHE murmured.

'Miss Armstrong? Can you hear me?'

She was fading fast now. Her life a memory. She wished she could see her son one last time. Remind him to live his life well, tell him that she loved him. Tell him that nothing mattered and that that was a freedom, not a burden.

She was alone. No longer on Wigmore Street, but beginning her first steps down the long dark tunnel.

'Miss Armstrong?'

A voice in her head – it might have been her own voice – said, *Goodnight children, everywhere*. She was unexpectedly soothed by it.

'Miss Armstrong? What did she say?'

'I think she said "It's all right".'

'Miss Armstrong? Miss Armstrong?'

Author's Note

Roughly speaking, for everything that could be considered an historical fact in this book, I made something up – and I'd like to think that a lot of the time readers won't be able to tell the difference. I'm only stating this to prevent people claiming that I got something wrong. I got a lot of it wrong, on purpose. After many conversations with myself, I went ahead and invented whatever I felt like – the novelist's prerogative, I suppose. If I had to describe the process, I would say that it felt like a wrenching apart of history followed by an imaginative reconstruction. (And yes, I did get a little obsessed – unhelpfully – about the nature of historical fiction.)

That isn't to say *Transcription*'s origins aren't rooted in reality – it was one of the periodic releases by MI5 to the National Archives that fired my imagination to begin with. The documents that caught my eye (apologies to Juliet) concerned a WW2 agent known as 'Jack King' (and almost always simply referred to as 'Jack' in these documents). Jack's identity, after years of speculation, was finally revealed to be Eric Roberts, a seemingly 'ordinary' bank clerk who lived with his family in Epsom.

There is a letter in the file from the Westminster Bank querying why ('why on earth', one feels) the Security Services were interested in their apparently rather insignificant employee – 'What are the particular and especial qualifications of Mr Roberts – which we have not been able to perceive – for some particular work of national importance.' (I love this letter.)

Roberts had in fact been working for MI5 for some time, infiltrating Fascist circles, and his CV hints at someone far from ordinary – his proficiency in judo, for example (he was a member of the Anglo-Japanese Judo Society), and the languages under his belt – Spanish, French, and 'slight' Portuguese, Italian and German.

The new operation for which he had been recruited (his handler was Victor Rothschild) was one dedicated to monitoring the fifth column and any subterfuge they might be planning. Roberts posed as a Gestapo agent and, in a flat off the Edgware Road, he met with a number of British Fascists who reported back to him on Nazi sympathizers. Some, like Marita Perigoe, were paid for their services, but most served the Third Reich from a point of principle. Except, of course, they weren't serving the Third Reich, as all the information they brought to 'Jack' was siphoned off to the Security Services. Virtually every fifth columnist in Britain was neutralized by the operation and important information (amidst an awful lot of dross) was prevented from reaching Germany – although, it has to be said, in the final analysis the fifth column turned out to be relatively unimportant in the greater picture.

There are transcripts of Jack King's meetings – hundreds of pages – that make for fascinating reading. Although I began with 'Jack', it was the transcriptions that began to take over my imagination. There is no record in the public domain of who typed them – it seems to be mainly one person (a 'girl', obviously) – and as I spent a period of my life as an audio typist I felt an odd affinity with this anonymous typist, especially when, on the odd occasion, her own personality breaks suddenly through.

At the time of the National Archives release I was reading Joan Miller's short memoir (I suspect she is not the most reliable of narrators). Joan Miller was one of Maxwell Knight's female agents who infiltrated the Right Club – more fifth columnists – and I thought it would be interesting to conflate fictionally the 'Jack case' with the operation being run by Maxwell Knight from his flat in Dolphin Square, where Joan Miller worked with him. (She also lived with him, in a somewhat unsatisfactory manner.) Joan Miller is not Juliet Armstrong, but they have certainly shared some of the same experiences.

Eric Roberts, Maxwell Knight, Joan Miller, 'Mrs Amos' (Marjorie Mackie), Helene de Munck, Captain and Mrs Ramsey, Anna Wolkoff, Tylor Kent, were the ghostly inspirations that set me off on this particular fictional path, but they are shades and shadows behind the characters and events in this book. (Although Anna Wolkoff appears fleetingly, and the real Miss Dicker – the 'Lady Superintendent' of the female staff – makes an appearance.) The spectres of the Cambridge spies stalk these halls too, and some of Perry's outbursts are based on entries in Guy Liddell's diaries. Nelly Varga and Lily are a tiny nod in the direction of double agent Nathalie 'Lily' Sergueiew, code name 'Treasure', and her dog, variously called Frisson or Babs (I much prefer Babs), who died, to Treasure's fury, while in the hands of MI5. Sergueiew, like so many at the time, led a fascinating life.

The same happened with the BBC, although here I have been considerably freer with invention in the services of the novel and I apologize to those earnest pioneers in Schools. Some – many – of the programmes mentioned are real, but a handful are invented. Much of their content is based on my own childhood memories of listening to them. I hadn't intended to have the BBC in the novel at all, least of all Schools Broadcasting, but I had just read Penelope Fitzgerald's gem of a novel *Human Voices*, as well as returning again to Rosemary Horstmann's memoir, and somehow the 'two great monoliths' seemed to belong shoulder to shoulder on the same pages. Rosemary was a friend in later years of my mother, and I have plundered her life – benignly, I should add. After the war Rosemary joined the BBC in Manchester, first as an announcer, then as a producer on *Children's Hour*, before moving to London and joining Schools Broadcasting in 1950. Her story is full of little nuggets that must surely be otherwise forgotten. (Juliet's nosebleed was actually that of pianist Harriet Cohen.) Rosemary moved over to television in the early Fifties and attended a production course at Alexandra Palace. (One of her fellow trainees was a young David Attenborough.) What surprised me when writing this book was not how much had been remembered and documented, but how much had been lost and forgotten, and my job, as I see it – others might not – is to plug the gaps.

Try as I might, MI5 would not speak to me about the technicalities of the transcription service during the war (and it is good that our secret services wish to remain secret), so I 'borrowed' the recording equipment from that used by the listeners in the M Room at Trent Park, albeit theirs was on a larger scale (a detailed inventory is held in the National Archives).

The transcriptions themselves, apart from the odd direct quotation, are my fabrications, but they mirrored the real ones very closely as far as subject matter, patterns of speech and so on are concerned. The biscuit intervals and social chat and technical hitches, even the iron crosses, are authentic, as are the endless 'inaudible's. Trude's suggestion that a dead body could be concealed in a coal hole was Marita Perigoe's, although she did not specify the Carlton Club. (The Carlton Club was destroyed during the Blitz, so it might have been rather a good idea.) Many of the technicalities of BBC recording are also based on Rosemary's memories as well as *The History of School Broadcasting* and are not necessarily entirely accurate or contemporaneous (but near enough). I am fiction's apologist.

I rather thought that with *Human Voices* Penelope Fitzgerald had cornered the market, as it were, in novels about the BBC during wartime (how could anything be better?), but then Roger Hudson introduced me to George Beardmore's wonderful memoir, *Civilians at War*, and between that and Maurice Gorham's *Sound and Fury* I realized there was so much more material to be mined. (I particularly loved George Beardmore's story of sitting outside the Control Room of the BBC with a loaded shotgun across his knee, ready to defend the engineering equipment to the death.) Too late for me, sadly, but I do recommend the Beardmore to anyone wanting to read something accessible and articulate about daily life in wartime London. (I have appended an abridged bibliography for anyone interested in the material that provided some of my sources and inspirations.)

Finally, one more apology – to the manager at the Dolphin Square apartments who showed me round under the illusion that I was interested in renting one. I expect my enthusiasm at the sight of an original fireplace might have given me away.

Sources

Andrews, Christopher, *The Defence of the Realm: The Authorized History of MI5* (Penguin, 2009)

Fry, Helen, *The M Room: Secret Listeners Who Bugged the Nazis in WW2* (Marranos Press, 2012)

Pugh, Martin, *Hurrah for the Blackshirts!* (Jonathan Cape, 2005)

Quinlan, Kevin, *The Secret War between the Wars* (Boydell Press, 2014)

Saikia, Robin (ed.), *The Red Book* (Foxley Books, 2010)

West, Nigel, *MI5* (Stein and Day, 1982)

Carter, Miranda, *Anthony Blunt: His Lives* (Macmillan, 2001)

Masters, Anthony, *The Man Who Was M: The Life of Maxwell Night* (Basil Blackwell, 1984)

Miller, Joan, *One Girl's War* (Brandon, 1986; originally published 1945)

Rose, Kenneth, *Elusive Rothschild* (Weidenfeld and Nicolson, 2003)

West, Nigel (ed.), *The Guy Liddell Diaries, Vol. 1: 1939–1942* (Routledge, 2005)

Lambert, Sam (ed.), *London Night and Day* (Old House, 2014; originally published 1951 by the Architectural Press)

Panter-Downes, Mollie (ed. William Shawn), *London War Notes, 1939–1945* (Farrar, Straus and Giroux, 1971)

Sweet, Matthew, *The West End Front* (Faber and Faber, 2011)

Bathgate, Gordon, *Voices from the Ether: The History of Radio* (Girdleness Publishing, 2012)

Briggs, Asa, *The Golden Age of Wireless: The History of Broadcasting in the United Kingdom, Vol. 1* (OUP, 1995)

Compton, Nic, *The Shipping Forecast* (BBC Books, 2016)

Higgins, Charlotte, *The New Noise: The Extraordinary Birth and Troubled Life of the BBC* (Guardian Books, 2015)

Hines, Mark, *The Story of Broadcasting House* (Merrell, 2008)

Murphy, Kate, *Behind the Wireless: A History of Early Women at the BBC* (Palgrave, 2016)

Palmer, Richard, *School Broadcasting in Britain* (BBC, 1947)

Fitzgerald, Penelope, *Human Voices* (Flamingo, 1997; originally published 1980)

Gorham, Maurice, *Sound and Fury: Twenty-One Years in the BBC* (Percival Marshall, 1948)

Horstmann, Rosemary, *Half a Life-Story: 1920–1960* (Country Books, 2000)

Shapley, Olive, *Broadcasting a Life* (Scarlet Press, 1996)

Beardmore, George, *Civilians at War* (OUP, 1986)

de Courcy, Anne, *Debs at War* (Weidenfeld and Nicolson, 2005)

From the National Archives

KV-2-3874 (The transcriptions of Jack King's conversations with his fifth-columnist informers)

KV-4-227-1 (History of the MS, the Jack King operation)

WO-208-3457, 001-040 (Inventory of the recording equipment used in the M Room)

KV-2-3800 (The Marita Perigoe case)

KV-2-84, 1-4 (The Anna Wolkoff case)

SOURCES

DVDs

Death at Broadcasting House (Studiocanal)

BBC: *The Voice of Britain, Addressing the Nation* (GPO Film Unit Collection Vol. 1, BFI, 2008)

Acknowledgements

Lt Col M. Keech, BEM, Royal Signals (retd)
David Mattock – for some Home Counties geography
Sam Hallas and the 'cognoscenti' of the Telecoms Heritage Group –
    for their help with telephone area codes of the 1940s
Simon Rook, Archive Manager, BBC

And my agent Peter Straus, my editor Marianne Velmans, Alison
Barrow, and everyone at Transworld who makes my pages into a
book.

Kate Atkinson won the Whitbread (now Costa) Book of the Year Prize with her first novel, *Behind the Scenes at the Museum*. Her four bestselling novels featuring former detective Jackson Brodie became the BBC television series *Case Histories*, starring Jason Isaacs. Her 2013 novel *Life After Life* won the South Bank Sky Arts Literature Prize, was shortlisted for the Women's Prize, and voted Book of the Year for the independent booksellers associations on both sides of the Atlantic. It also won the Costa Novel Award, as did her subsequent novel *A God in Ruins* (2015). *Transcription* is her latest novel.

Ten things I have learnt about writing
by Kate Atkinson

(1) *Read everything that's ever been written.*
Really.

(2) *Forget everything that's ever been written.*
Really. You'll have unconsciously absorbed what's important.
We really do stand on the shoulders of giants and unless we
understand what constitutes good writing (and also bad writing,
of course) then how can we judge our own writing? If we have
read everything (well, OK, not *everything*, just the really good
stuff) then we'll grow to understand what is meant by a writer's
'voice' – that pesky thing that creative-writing tutors are always
urging you to 'find'.

(3) *Your voice. Yes, find it.*
Don't ask me how. It's a discovery that's as mysterious as it
sounds, but at some point you will suddenly realize that you are
channelling an authentic part of you. And that's it. Magic.

(4) *Throw away as much as possible.*
That might often be the very idea that you started with, or what
you consider to be your best shiniest most beautiful sentence. If it
doesn't work in the context of what you're writing then get rid of
it. Learn to be your best critic (by reading everything that's ever
been written). Be ruthless.

(5) *Keep as much as possible.*

Don't *actually* throw it away. Whatever I'm writing, I keep a file going alongside – usually I name it 'holding' – and I put in it all the good juicy things that I had to excise because they didn't work. Believe me, no bit of good writing ever goes in a writer's trash bin. It will get used somehow, somewhere, even if it's years in the future.

(6) *Understand why you're writing.*

Writing rarely works if you sit down and say to yourself, 'What shall I write?' There has to be some initial spasm in your brain (or inspiration, as some people like to call it) that says, 'That would make a great story/novel/play/whatever and I really want to write that.' That moment doesn't last, after that it's just a hard slog, but every so often you can revisit that moment and remember why you're writing the story/novel/play/whatever. It helps.

(7) *Understand what you're writing.*

Think about it beforehand. Not necessarily consciously, but when you're doing the laundry, going for a walk, having a bath – all good times for mindless thinking And let it lurk in the back of your mind, no matter if you're not even aware it's there. Once the seed is there it will germinate. I think about the next novel for about three years on average. The whole time I'm writing one I have another couple backing up like trains waiting for a platform.

(8) *Remember – you're making an artefact.*

That moment of inspiration might kick-start something, but you are making an object in just the same way that a painter or a sculptor or a musician is making something that's outside of themselves. A 'thing', if you will. You need to keep structure at the forefront of your mind, move the pieces around, find a better word, a better sentence. Weave it, *make* it, don't for a minute think that writing is just something that flows out from mind to paper with nothing in between. And rewrite all the time. *All* the time. I start every writing day by reading everything I've already written – sometimes yesterday's work, sometimes the whole novel (yes, the whole novel) – and I rejig and improve and polish. You might be making something, but remember it's not artificial as such, it's coming from that place inside, the one where you found your voice. It gives you the ability to make external order out of internal chaos and I guess that's a definition of creation.

⑨ *Start small. Practise. Learn.*

I began many, many years ago with biographically-influenced fragments (how I was feeling, in other words), and once I'd sluiced out all that dross (because it's personal, it's not fiction, and anyway no one else is interested) then I was free to start making things up. And stories, stories are a wonderful way to learn to write, they teach you everything – character, structure, plot – in a manageable way. I learnt everything I know from writing stories for women's magazines and am still proud of the way I could turn a romantic story on a sixpence (and, yes, with my own voice).

⑩ *Get a title.*

I can't write without one. It means you don't have a blank page. And somewhere at the back of your brain when you're doing all that endless thinking in the bath or on a walk, etcetera, ideas begin to congregate around that title and pretty soon (or, more realistically, in two or three years), *voilà* – a novel.

LONDON.

Dolphin Square
and vicinity, 1940